To Robert,

The Irish Within Us

C. A. Logan (signature)

C. A. LOGAN

D1518679

 FriesenPress

One Printers Way
Altona, MB R0G 0B0
Canada

www.friesenpress.com

Copyright © 2023 by C. A. Logan
First Edition — 2023

All rights reserved.

Author's photograph by Karen Fitzpatrick
Illustration by Afton Jane

This is a work of fiction. Any names or characters,
businesses or places, events or incidents, are fictitious.
Any resemblance to actual persons, living or dead, or
actual events is purely coincidental.

No part of this publication may be reproduced in
any form, or by any means, electronic or mechanical,
including photocopying, recording, or any information
browsing, storage, or retrieval system, without
permission in writing from FriesenPress.

ISBN
978-1-03-916901-2 (Hardcover)
978-1-03-916900-5 (Paperback)
978-1-03-916902-9 (eBook)

1. Fiction, Fantasy, Humorous

Distributed to the trade by The Ingram Book Company

For my father

Acknowledgements

This is my first novel, written during the 2020 pandemic lockdown as a substitute for a planned genealogy research trip to Antrim. I let my imagination take me where the travel restrictions would not allow. Therefore, the fantasy is rooted in my family's history but with extravagant twisting and additions—a valentine to the island of Ireland. In case you are confused—none of this is real.

I thank Dan Hill for his encouragement, sharp red pencil, and meticulous scrutiny of the early drafts, and also Lisle Christie and James Hill who provided answers to my insane queries about land titles, alcoholic beverages, and Dungeons and Dragons.

I am grateful to the Ulster Historical Foundation for their resources, the Ottawa Irish Arts regarding Irish Gaelic names, and my group at Ottawa Writers' Workshops: Nicole McKerracher, Margaret Woodford, our fearless leader David Allan Hamilton, and especially Jo-Anne Stead for critical feedback. My inspiration comes from many storytellers and local historians over the years.

Special appreciation is due Annjane Stevenson Milgrew, who let me ride shotgun in 2022 so we could pursue fairies and ancestors through every village, churchyard, and beach across Antrim, and Karen Fitzpatrick for the author's photo.

Finally, a big thank you to Keith Cole for attending Irish online events with me, and for his advice, humour, and "above the rest," for being his fabulous self.

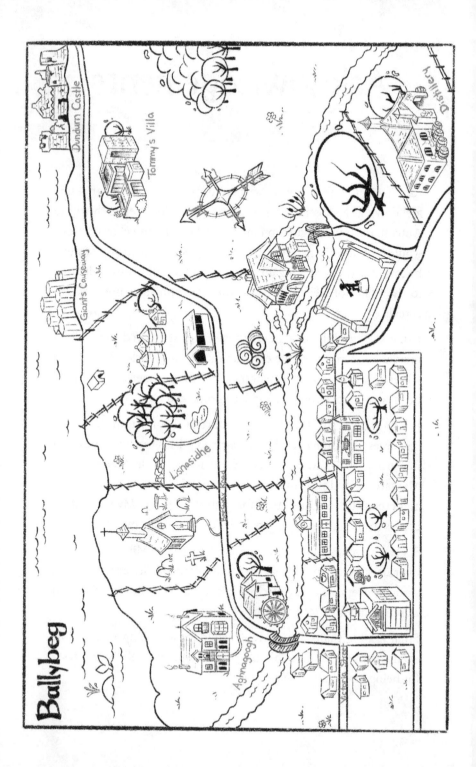

Prologue

The morning fog filled the clearing in Rosheen Wood. Robert McKinney stepped out of the old stone cottage. The mist danced through the trees and the thorns that stood guard around his home. It was midsummer. Hazy shapes peeked from behind the oak and the ash, pretending to be friend, or perhaps foe, but Robert was not fooled. I saw more than he: the fairies laughing in the flowers and the red squirrels hiding in the brambles. Robert lifted his head to study the clear sky above him. The full moon lingered over the western horizon like an actor refusing to take her exit.

Greta closed the door softly behind her and followed her husband across the fields of Lisnasidhe to Beeswax Road. She was careful to step over the fairy path that ran across the fields. Robert wore his best cap and his toughest shoes. He carried a small leather bag. Greta was not dressed to travel. It was time to start the milking. She pulled her shawl tighter against the chill.

Neither of them spoke. They exchanged glances, resigned to parting. At the edge of the road, beside a small pond, she impulsively leapt into his arms for one more kiss. He gathered her up, embraced her, and then carefully placed her back on the family's land. He took to the road. She stared into the pond. Her reflection in the water seemed softer, somehow younger than how she felt.

When the humans stayed within my boundaries, I could protect them. Now, I could only watch Robert McKinney as far as Stranocum but not beyond. Well, even I have my limits. Grounded, one might call it. I have not the fairies' gift of magic. My existence is my strength.

So that morning, which is so very long ago to you, but no time at all to me, I drew energy from my trees, from my streams, and from the misty air to enfold all my lifeforce around Robert McKinney. With each step he took, I transferred another little burst of my strength to him. It travelled through the soles of his feet and along sinews and muscles to settle in his heart.

The nip in the air gave no hint of the midday heat that would make him sweat on the long walk to Belfast. I knew it would not bother him. He preferred the heat to rain. My sleeping village did not awaken as he left. Robert McKinney did not look back. If he kept up the pace, he would pass through the dark hedges early and reach Ballymena by noon. With any luck, he would arrive at the boarding house on the River Lagan for a few hours' sleep before he started his shift in the shipyard.

One

Kara Gordon stepped out into the road. A car horn screeched. *Damn,* she thought, jumping back. *It's right, then left.* There was no sign of the bus that would take her from Belfast up the coastal route to Ballybeg. The guide had told her to wait near the big, blue fish sculpture. She stared across the River Lagan at the old Harland and Wolff shipyard. Her great-grandfather Robert McKinney had worked there in the 1890s. It was now a museum.

Perhaps I should be in a museum. Kara's thoughts travelled back to her retirement party in Ottawa a few weeks previous and to the director raising her glass. "A toast to the best human calculator the department has ever known!" That had made Kara wince. Had thirty years analysing strategic plans and budget projections for the Culture Department turned her into nothing more than a calculating machine?

Her colleague Cindy had crept up behind her. "No one will ever have the passion for the clients that you have, Kara. You're the last of your kind." *Oh c'mon,* Kara had thought, *why work in the Arts Office if you don't care about the arts?* She imagined that one day, in a desolate corner of the Canadian History Museum, there would sit a dusty display case exhibiting Kara's stuffed cadaver, a pencil nestled above its left ear, a line of paper clips adorning its jacket lapel, several rolled-up theatre programs filling its right pocket, and a forgotten lunch peeking out of its left. The figure leaned forward with a look of righteous indignation, one hand squeezing a calculator, while the other brandished a ministerial briefing note at an invisible opponent. Is that what she had become?

A tour guide would drawl, "Behold children, the early twenty-first century cultural bureaucrat. Try to imagine a time when cabinet ministers were advised of the arts organizations' actual needs by workers instead of by computer algorithms. How quaint!" The children would giggle.

She missed her younger self: the one interested in music, literature, history, genealogy, and hiking the country paths. Retirement was her escape. She wanted to travel but had been uncertain where to start. *Did the bureaucratic life flatten me so much?*

Luckily, Kara's little genealogy blog had led to a strange telephone call inviting her to a conference in Belfast. The conference organizer's voice had seemed distant, despite the line being very good and her words reverberating like little glass bells in a gentle breeze. Kara had accepted the invitation, deciding to start her adventures in Ireland. Despite her research, she had never visited, although her grandfather had grown up there.

At the conference, other people had told stories of their visits to old family towns and villages, reawakening old memories. Her grandfather's Antrim accent flooded back into her head. She remembered his bedtime stories of the legends of Finn McCool and the Salmon of Knowledge and of Tir na Nóg and fairy trickery. Everything she heard had revitalized her inquisitive nature. She had traded notes with a number of professional Irish researchers. Her own slightly cheeky presentation, "Ancient Tree Worship and the DNA Infestation," had clearly been included for comic relief but was well-received, nonetheless. Kara had searched throughout the conference for the organizer that had called with the invitation, but she never found the woman. No one else had been able to identify her either.

Kara's grandfather, William Sweeney McKinney, had been born on the family farm, Lisnasidhe, in Ballybeg, on the edge of the Giant's Causeway. He had told Kara that "Lisnasidhe" meant "fort of the fairies," and that it was an ancient place. His fairy stories had been far darker and more complex than anything North Americans knew. He'd shared pictures of Ballybeg and songs his own grandmother had taught him. He'd hinted at gossip about the neighbours and the villagers. Young Kara had fallen asleep each night imagining Ballybeg as a magical land surrounded by glittering seas. Then he was gone and the stories with him.

Kara had grown up proudly and apologetically Canadian, "The world needs more Canada!" becoming her battle cry. Progressive and ready to set the world aright, she'd put away her fantasies. Her family tree research had been diligent and academic but not a lived experience. At the conference, she'd heard the stories of those who had followed the paths back to the farms and villages of their ancestors. Now Kara had the opportunity to do the same—to see where her grandfather had grown up. By the end of the week, while others went to the Titanic exhibits, Kara had discovered the bus that would take her to Ballybeg.

Kara turned away from the fish and the river and examined her reflection in the window of a parked car. An old leather satchel hung from her shoulder. She held a coffee in her hand, still too hot to drink. A large carpetbag sat at her feet. No makeup. Perhaps she should—no, never mind, not worth it. Her big, red frame glasses hid her hazel eyes anyway. Her long grey hair fell back from her face with no discernable style. She had dug out her old bohemian clothing, and all her suits had gone to the Sally Ann. High-top sneakers had replaced the patent leather pumps. She wore loose, brightly coloured jackets in velvet, silk, or cotton, with a base wardrobe of black cotton jersey. Shirts, pants, dresses, or wide flared skirts, whether buttoned, zipped, or laced, everything was black jersey. That was as far as wardrobe planning went. Easy to pack.

A blue bus pulled up and released a hydraulic hiss as the door opened. Kara stepped onto the bus. The interior was roomy and mostly empty. She shoved her carpetbag up onto the rack, her satchel on the seat beside her, and plunked down in the cushy bright-blue seat. She pulled her laptop from her satchel. Balancing the laptop on her knee, she reclined the seat back a smidge, relaxed, and sipped her coffee while Belfast bustled outside the windows. The engine roared and then settled to a mechanical purring as the bus started to pull away from the curb.

She scoured a website for lists of tenants and townlands surrounding Ballybeg through the early 1830s to confirm the correct people on her tree by comparing the tenants on the same farm from one decade to the next. The records also indicated neighbours and often siblings or cousins living nearby. That knowledge would help her to confirm distant cousins if the question arose.

The bus paused at the next stop. Kara was deep into her records. As the bus started up again, a woman's voice interrupted Kara's peace: "Going to move your satchel?"

Kara looked up with a start. Although the bus was only half full, a woman in her seventies stood in the aisle, pointing down at the leather satchel. Kara automatically acquiesced, putting the satchel at her feet. "Sorry."

The interloper threw herself down on the now-empty seat. "You're not going to Ballybeg?" she asked in a familiar accent that Kara had no trouble understanding because of her grandfather.

Kara panicked. "Gosh. I hope so. Is this not the right bus?"

"No, no, calm yourself. You're on the right bus, so you are." She examined Kara down to her red sneakers. "It was just by way of a wee ice breaker."

She smiled. "Hello. I'm Kara."

"Mary Anderson. I have a farm just north of the village called Knocknageragh—Sheep's Hill. Appropriate since I have sheep mostly. But bees too. Do you have a last name?"

"Gordon."

"And you are from…?"

"Canada. Toronto. Toronto, Canada. Toronto, Ontario, Canada."

"That's grand. I don't need your postcode."

Oh, she is the funny type. Mary Anderson had a pleasant face. Kara could tell by her complexion that she spent a lot of time outdoors. She had a small, wiry frame and a vertical shock of short grey hair and wore serious boots and khakis. Cool, practical, and no nonsense with a sense of humour. Or, as they say in Ireland, good *craic*.

Mary pulled a thermos from her rucksack and offered a toast, miming a clink with Kara's paper coffee cup. "Do you have any family?"

"An ex-husband," Kara said. "I guess that doesn't count. I had a dog, but she died last year. She was only seventeen in human years. A hundred and nineteen in dog years or 121.33 if you count the months—" She raised her hand, interrupting herself. "Wait! Does that include the leap years? So that would be 2000, 2004—"

Mary stretched back in her seat and interjected. "Well, my family has raised sheep on Knocknageragh since the 1600s. I travelled about when I was young, but there's nothing better than home. New Zealand came close, but for some reason, I still wanted to come home. There's something about the land that draws you back. What's your opinion of Ballybeg?"

"I don't have one," Kara shot back. This was a bit of a lie. Her imagination ran all over the hills, the valleys, and the village. "I've never visited Ballybeg. My grandfather was born there. William Sweeney McKinney. He was born in 1892."

"Ah! McKinney! Brave number of McKinneys and Sweeneys too." Mary looked over at the archives page on Kara's laptop. "Who else have you got in your wee computer?"

Nosy. Kara quietly closed the laptop and carefully placed it on top of the satchel on the floor. But she offered up a few more names. "McKays? Gillans?"

"Aye, all the usual suspects then. You must belong, right enough."

"That's what I figured. I'm clear on my great-grandparents, but I'm still researching back to 1800."

"When did William Sweeney McKinney leave Ballybeg?"

"The family moved to Scotland in 1898. But he came back each summer to help his grandparents with the cows."

"They raised cows?"

"Yes. At Lisnasidhe up Beeswax Road."

"And these grandparents were McKinneys?"

"No. His mothers' parents. The Sweeneys."

"I know the ones."

This surprised Kara. "You do? How? You're not much older than me."

"In Ballybeg, we remember things. My grandmother would have gone to school with them. Our farm, Knocknageragh, is next to Lisnasidhe, the old Sweeney farm."

Kara wanted to hug Mary and felt that perhaps she had been too cautious about the laptop. Of course, it might be rude if she tried to hug her. But her eyes felt moist.

Mary studied Kara's face. "I can see a resemblance."

"Really! I don't believe you."

"Not a word of a lie. You've never been to Ballybeg?"

"Not yet."

"You took your time."

Kara shrugged. "I was busy. We were pushing Canada forward into the future."

Mary smirked. "I see where you're going with that. But we're getting on. We have Wi-Fi, internet entrepreneurs, art galleries, Thai restaurants, Gaelic lessons." She raised a finger. "We're having our first Pride Parade this year."

Kara blushed. She hadn't meant to sound condescending. She tried to explain. "I hadn't thought Ballybeg was unchanged since 1898 but"—Mary laughed—"my grandfather told me about Finn McCool, about fairies and leprechauns, the fairy changelings, and those little ones that clean the house, although sometimes they also mess things up."

"The brownies," Mary offered.

"Yes. I was ten when Granda died, but well, he's still here." She pointed to her head.

The deep grey clouds hovered, but the rain held back. The coastal road north rolled along the rocky west coast of the Irish Sea. Fierce winds brought waves lashing along the shore. Sea spray hit the windows of the bus hard enough to make a tapping sound. Mary glanced out toward the sea with a fond look. "Sometimes she's blue and calm, sometimes grey and angry. But some nights, when the wind is still and the moon is out, she is bright silver, and oh so beautiful. It is just her moods."

The road was narrow and winding. The bus squeezed between the water on the one side and high rock faces, or the stone walls of villages, on the other, but gradually rose up in altitude with the cliff edge, leaving the sea and the beaches below. The driver handled the bus like a Grand Prix racer. They passed small harbours with boats for fishing and for tourists and the occasional sand beach populated by cows.

The road broke away from the coast and turned inland. Villages rushed past. Green pastures rolled in sharp turns and inclines around lush woods or jagged crags. Cows. Sheep. Goats. Sheep. Llama? Buildings dotted the landscape: barns, stables, a variety of sheds, converted mills, and churches. Then, just as the bus took a curve in the road and plunged into the valley, a village threw itself up on all sides as the bus entered the heart of Ballybeg. It seemed quaint.

The bus stopped in the courtyard of the Ballybeg Inn. Kara stood and moved out to the aisle to pull down her carpetbag.

"You're not staying at the inn?" Mary asked, her eyes narrowing.

"Yes. I reserved two nights."

"Watch out for McKay. He's an awful weasel." Mary stretched over the two seats.

Kara laughed. "What do you mean? Which McKay?"

Mary gave a cheery wave. "Ta-ta for now. The market is on Saturdays. The whole village will be there."

"I'm afraid I won't be here that long."

"Still, I will send a wee jar of honey to the inn for you to try."

Kara walked backwards to the front of the bus, trying to get a sign from Mary as to what she meant, but the farmer slid down out of sight in her seat.

Kara emerged from the bus. The Ballybeg Inn sat on an island in the river with a bridge that connected it on one side to Victoria Street. Trees lined the riverbanks and clustered on the island. She took a deep breath of the clean, sweet air. Her first moments in Ballybeg. Birds chirped. The sky seemed less grey. Perhaps it wouldn't rain today. She dropped her bags in the courtyard and wandered onto the old stone bridge, stopping at the midpoint, where a small plaque stated, "First built in 1209." The ancient river rushed below her and leapt over rocks, whispering, *"As always as always as always,"* and hurried on to the sea. Anglers dotted the riverbank, out for salmon. Further down the other bank sat a well-preserved old mill.

The bridge opened onto Memorial Square: a broad public space with a war memorial at its centre and the riverbank on its northern edge. There were no large office buildings or big box stores in sight, but the trees looked hundreds of years old, their branches shading everything. One gigantic oak tree in particular dominated an entire block on the east side of the village. Bushes and wildflowers encircled the trees and crept down an incline to the river that dropped from the east side of the inn. In every direction, solid, respectable, two-storey buildings lined the streets—mostly shops and cafes with modest signage. The building exteriors were uniform in style with the same roof angles and the same windows. The finishes were painted white or speckled with grey or beige pebbles.

Kara saw a pub called the Standing Stone a little further up the street. It was plain-fronted with modest windows—a real Irish pub—so different from the pubs with etched glass and polished brass façades found in every Toronto neighbourhood, all of them called, ironically, Finn McCool's.

A group of boys on their bicycles slowed down to take a good look at Kara before charging up the street. A couple wandered on the riverbank below. It was all calm and welcoming. There was a harmony between nature and humans here that she loved immediately.

The bus silently trundled up the street, passed the pub and the boys, and turned out of sight. The village was crying out to be explored. Kara started at Memorial Square. The war memorial resembled that of any town or village in Canada: a poignant reminder of the many youths lost to war. A few benches dotted the square.

As Kara passed the Standing Stone pub, its door flew open violently. She jumped instinctively back into the shadow of a doorway on the opposite side of the street. Pub chatter spilled out followed by three bodies: the first body hitting the pavement and staying there, snickering—*Drunk*—the second bouncing off the first one and landing flat against the wall of the pub like a poster—*Somewhat drunk—or is he shaking with fear?* The third one appeared, steady on his feet and stretching out his arms in an attempt to catch the first two before they fell. This one seemed sober and self-controlled. Having clearly failed, he waited to survey the damage. His gaze alternated between the wall and the pavement. Upon reflection, he extended his right hand in a warning to the second man, the wallflower, while with his left, he hoisted the other up off the pavement. "Get up, Frank! You're lit!"

Frank gripped the offered hand and was dragged to his feet, whinging all the way up. "Michael! Michael Garrett! Michael! Listen, man! I'm not trying to start a fight!"

The wallflower started to raise a fist. Michael cautioned him against it. "I see you, Dennis!"

Dennis hugged the wall. "I'm just defending our beloved Ballybeg from—"

"Quiet, Dennis! I'm just after hearing your speech in there. I've got this!"

Michael turned back to Frank. "You never are trying to start a fight, Frank. They just come to you, miraculously." Michael tested Frank's balance and then let go.

Frank remained upright. He brushed his jacket with his hands and pushed his thinning hair off his forehead. He slurred, "It'd be a grand thing if your man there, Mr. Laurel, and his company invested! Think of the money rolling in!"

Dennis took a micro-step away from the wall. "You're having us on! They tried it before! The bother they caused? Foreign developers? Like up the road ten years ago? If there's even a whiff of a new big-scale development, we'll be overrun with chancers!"

Frank spat. "Chancers like your cousin, Dennis?"

"Right, quiet, the two of you!" hissed Michael.

Frank's remark prompted Dennis to attempt another swing at Frank. Michael raise his right arm, blocking Dennis' attack, while holding Frank back with his left. "Enough! We're done!"

Dennis drew himself up and stood at attention. "Yes, sir." He saluted and marched down the street.

Frank steadied himself on Michael then started off in the other direction. He progressed no more than three feet before falling down again. Michael picked him up and slung the man's arm over his shoulders to support him. Kara watched the retreating figures proceed up the street until they faded into the shadow of large trees.

The two fighters, Dennis and Frank, looked a bit rough to Kara, but the one they called Michael Garrett seemed more educated.

And tall and dark and handsome—as well as young enough to be her son. Why were they arguing about developers? Foreign ones. Quite a mystery. Ballybeg was more interesting than she'd imagined. She turned back to the Ballybeg Inn, picking up her bags in the courtyard and entering the elegant foyer of the inn, where she rang the desk bell.

While we wait for the desk bell to ring out, come closer and I will tell you a little of my story. It's not a word of a lie that the inn is a pretty sight now on its island at the bend of the river, but the spot has a complicated past. When I was young, I grew gorse bushes here that fed the sheep and gave pollen to the bees. There was gorse ale for the people too. There were hazel, holly, and rowan trees. At sunrise, the humans gathered for festivals. They danced. They sang. They drank. They recited verse. They fell in love. In amongst the festive crowds, the fairy folk freely intermingled with the humans, exchanging deceptions and pranks in friendly competitions. Great craic! Everyone laughed!

In what proved to be a blinding mistake, a gang of zealous druids rose up and rejected the fairy folk. They replaced the festivals with human sacrifices to the River God. The salmon choked on blood. Such shenanigans displeased the River God so much that he called to Lord Vishnu, Thor, and Jupiter, and together, they hatched a plan. On a Thursday afternoon, at a hair past a freckle, the zealots' grandmothers arrived and dragged each one home to spend their days weaving little straw figures. Weaving straw men is a very dreary task to a young druid; by contrast, old men prefer it.

Then I was overrun with patricians, and the druids disappeared. They cleared the island. They erected the building—the one that is there now—as a small abbey and engaged in self-torture for a long time. It was not all misery; they made some very fine music and wine that I enjoyed enormously. It all changed again one evening when a battalion of puritans with vinegar for blood marched in, and the abbey became a garrison. Now the patricians were driven into the wilderness. I missed their song and drink. These new saviours had nothing to offer but shame. Nettle, thistle, and elder grew all around the building and surround it still.

Abandoned in the gloaming, decrepit and cursed, the building bowed under the weight of its own roof. The soil was just as sick, and I could grow nothing good on it. A local farmer, whose faith extended to nothing but coin, bought it all for a pig farm. Squeals rang throughout the village day and night. Then, just as quickly, the little island lay abandoned again. The instruments of slaughter lay rusting under old straw for many years. Truth be told, it was an awful mess when James McKay bought it for the price of a chicken and remade it into the Ballybeg Inn. At least he has done a grand job of making the old, cursed place attractive.

The wee bell on the front desk has a clear pure tone.

The inn's brochure lay open on the reception desk. "This sixteenth century coaching inn, one of the oldest in Ireland, is walking distance to local attractions such as Dundurn Castle, the Giant's Causeway, and the Ballybeg Whiskey Distillery. The inn is the ideal location for dining, celebrating, or holding conferences and offers four-star accommodation with thirty-two rooms and suites, each with their own unique charm and character." The charm and character thrilled Kara. The authentic atmosphere enthralled her. She examined the jumble of antiques and old paintings, the darkened corners, and the little hidden rooms. *How could she be enchanted so quickly?* What was it that captured her soul? Kara could not deny that she felt almost giddy just standing there, taking it in.

She accepted her keys with polite thanks and wandered into the dining room. It was a page right out of *Victoria Magazine*, with a coffered ceiling, painted panelling, and chintzy wallpaper. The silk-draped French doors, well spaced and identical, opened out to the front courtyard. The courtyard was simple with bistro tables and whiskey barrels dotted across grey flagstones. Beyond this, Memorial Square could be seen on the other side of the river.

Across the lobby opposite stood the Ye Olde Coach House bar. This room evoked an old coaching inn, dark and smoky with exposed walls of hand-cut stone and oak ceiling beams. Pairs of overstuffed chairs sat smugly under well-polished but unrecognizable farm implements that hung on the walls. Some chairs jealously surrounded their own small fireplace. This room wrapped around the east side of the inn and eventually led out to a set of modern glass doors and a back garden of ancient trees.

It was very quiet. It was too early for dinner, so Kara went up to her room, a cozy miniature of the chintzy dining room. The window overlooked the back garden and the north side of the river. The bed looked comfortable, and she lay down just to try it out. There was so much new information to absorb. Her eyelids felt heavy. In minutes, she fell asleep and found herself wandering …

> … *through the dark, stony ruins of Dundurn Castle on the edge of the silvery sea. On the ramparts, she found a small table with white linen and gold cutlery. She sat down. A waiter presented a plate of "barbequed salmon on a reduction of hazelnut puree with Ballybeg Whiskey." With each exquisite mouthful, her understanding of her surroundings grew. She looked beyond the ramparts to the Giant's Causeway on the coast and saw the endless line of hexagon stone structures. In a line atop each stone stood*

living figures, one generation after another reaching back, aligned like chess pieces. They faced a dragon arising from the water. Some chanted, "Heigh ho, dragon go!" Some brandished protest signs. The Earl of Ballybeg tried to dismiss the protestors. They ignored him. He approached Kara to offer her a gold coronet. She told him to take a running jump.

Behind the dragon, the legendary warrior Fionn mac Cumhaill, or Finn McCool, appeared from the sea. He was the giant who had built the Giant's Causeway as stepping stones to Scotland. The Scottish giant Benandonner materialized behind Fionn, but instead of the two giants fighting each other, they turned on the dragon and drove it back under the waves. The people cheered. Fionn reached out and lifted Kara with his massive hands, placing her on her own stone in line with her ancestors. Benandonner disappeared, and Finn McCool retreated into his cave to continue his long sleep until he was needed again to save Ireland.

The clock struck eight as Kara awoke in her little room at the Ballybeg Inn. She rushed downstairs, fearing she'd missed dinner altogether. The server assured her otherwise. A few guests lingered at their tables. The evening was warm, so Kara sat next to an open window.

A thin, pale man with wire glasses and an industrious attitude passed by her table much too frequently, ignoring the other guests. He asked if it was her first trip to Ireland. He informed her that the salmon was fresh, pulled from the river below just that morning. He enquired on her first impressions of the village. He returned with a local tour brochure. He wondered if she wanted to see Dundurn Castle. The Giant's Causeway? Had she toured the distillery yet? Perhaps she was more interested in churches?

Kara mused about her dream but was not interested in sharing her personal obsessions with a total stranger. Instead, she replied, "I just want to see the village and the farmlands first." The salmon was good, although there was no hazelnut puree, and she'd opted for wine instead of whiskey. He persisted in asking questions.

"I'm just doing some genealogical research," Kara offered.

"Oh?" He pulled up a chair without asking. "Is it for yourself? Are you for hire?" She didn't answer. He cleared his throat. "I hope you don't mind me asking. I dabble in family trees myself." Finally, he paused. "I'm James McKay, owner of all this," he said, indicating the inn with a broad gesture.

She offered a straight-forward fact. "My grandfather was born in Ballybeg." Kara wondered if this was the McKay in Mary's warning.

He grinned. "What family names are you researching?"

"My grandfather's name was McKinney. But I also have Sweeney, McKay, and Gillan."

"McKinney, Sweeney, McKay, and Gillan." He raised his head as if he were savouring the sensation of the names in his mouth. "Only half the village. Including me, probably." His delivery was casual and friendly. "Have another glass of the Chardonnay? It's on the house, cousin."

Since he might be a cousin, Kara started to tell McKay about the Sweeney dairy farm and Mary Anderson, and about the argument outside the Standing Stone pub. He listened carefully and enquired about the three men. Could she describe the person called Michael? To her reply, McKay nodded. "Yes, yes, that is Michael Garrett, head of Ballybeg Biodiversity."

"Ah. An organization for preserving the natural biodiversity of the area?"

"Aye. Michael arrived in Ballybeg about eight years ago after university in Belfast. He coordinates the local wildlife protection groups. Folks say he'll go far in politics." McKay's voice dropped slightly. "So, there are rumours of a new development scheme? Some big scheme to swallow up land with the promise of jobs and tax revenues. Likely tax exemptions too for the investors. That's always an interesting subject to people around here." Then he went to fetch another bottle of Chardonnay.

As the sky darkened to a violet-tinged blue, a set of doors swung open. Kara approached to close them but was instead drawn out into the courtyard. No one was there. There was no wind and few clouds, but it had turned dark very quickly. There was no reason for the doors to have opened by themselves. It was odd. She stepped further into the middle of the courtyard and heard a faint whirring sound.

Thousands of fireflies rushed around the corner, mobbing the courtyard and dancing in the trees. A formation encircled the courtyard and flew in tight circles round her. She had never seen so many fireflies. Perhaps she'd drunk too much wine, but Kara saw patterns in their synchronized movements. First a heart, followed by a house, a pentacle, and a shield. Finally, they formed three small circles, which grew bigger and intertwined, forming a triangular cluster. The linked circles rose higher and higher and then disappeared into the night.

A rustling of bushes from the riverbank announced the arrival of an odd couple. He was a very old, dishevelled man, and she was a pretty blonde in a shimmering green evening dress. She looked a little like Kylie Minogue. They clung to each other and lurched towards Kara, the man staring at Kara with glassy pale blue eyes. "The first daughter's true heart will unlock the treasure," he

17

slurred, "the secret loves, the happy pleasures, and above the rest, a spell that binds two worlds together to guard against the foe." The pretty woman giggled. And then they descended back down the riverbank to the water. Kara peeked over the embankment. No one was there.

She heard McKay return with a fresh bottle and call her name, so she re-entered and closed the doors. She may have drunk too much Chardonnay already, but she didn't want to be rude. Now she *knew* she was in Ireland, initiated by a drunken Irishman reciting poetry. Could it get any more special? She didn't want to share this with McKay. Anyway, he might call it trespassing. Instead, she talked abut her plan to travel through Europe. She had booked two nights in Ballybeg. Once she finished exploring the village, she would continue on to the continent.

"Oh, no. You must stay longer. Find out everything you can about the village. I will give you a car anytime you need it. Any day you want it, the hired car will be out front to chauffer you about and bring you back in time for dinner." He refilled her wine glass. "No, no, no argument. It's no bother."

Kara returned to her room with a light heart. She yearned for a hot bath and a long lie in. It was very nice of her probable cousin, McKay, to arrange transport so she could stay longer and explore Ballybeg. That meant she could have a few days' rest. Soaking into lavender vanilla bubbles, she wondered if Michael Garrett or Mary Anderson were relatives too, or maybe Frank? Dennis? Or the very old, very dishevelled man? She shuddered. He and the woman in green had materialized and then vanished like ghosts. But no ghost could smell so strongly of Ballybeg Whiskey. The feel of soft cool sheets cleared her head. She was asleep in a heartbeat, listening to her grandfather singing to her: *"... and when the fields are fresh and green, I will take you to your home again ..."*

Two

David McKinney fell against the door of Devinder Singh's O'Grady's Bar and Grill and pounded it like a drum. It was half past four in the morning. Until the board of directors meeting the previous evening, he'd thought he owned Madison, Wisconsin. Now, Dev's bar was his only refuge from a cruel world. He continue to pound the door with his fist.

He was dead sober but miserable. He'd wandered downtown all night until it occurred to him that sitting and drinking would be the better option. "You're stupid, David!" he heard his father's voice in his head. David had stumbled between the lakes, bemoaning the fact that the McKinneys had paid for most of this thankless city. Now he was tired and hungry. He had a pounding headache. He should have just gotten drunk.

His father's angry voice continued, "The McKinneys built this state!" When David was small, his father, Marcus, would tell him how their ancestor, also named David McKinney, had arrived from Ireland to start his carpentry business in the 1840s, making money off the backs of tradesmen without ever breaking a sweat himself. With each new generation, the family's fortunes had grown. David's grandfather had returned from the Pacific in 1946 to take control by starting the McKinney Corporation, sweeping up a jumble of inherited business investments through one type of persuasion or another. David's father joined the corporation in the late sixties and had never left the office until his death last year. Marcus' tight grip on the business had given little for David to do except promote the corporation through golf tournaments, regattas, and galas. When Marcus died, the corporation's Board of Directors expected the fifty-one-year-old David to take up his father's role. David found this expectation tedious.

Some people—the polite ones—would label the McKinney family ambitious. A few might prefer to say, "They're driven by an unhealthy compulsion to succeed." Do-gooders and hippies called the McKinneys "scoundrels with no social conscious." David grinned at that one. *Yeah, and we keep my mother locked in the attic too, with her beadwork and macramé.*

The McKinney Corporation operated across the United States and three countries internationally. From the largest commercial complex in Madison, Wisconsin, it managed an army of local and branch employees in Los Angeles, Boston, and Houston. David was his late father's only heir, and as the new CEO of the corporation, he controlled all the assets. At least he had.

The front door finally unlocked with a "click," and David collapsed into the darkened bar, grasping Dev by the shoulder. He admitted, "I'm a little early."

David and Devinder had studied Engineering together at the Massachusetts Institute of Technology and spent a lot of time in Irish pubs. Dev had picked up on David's love of all things Irish— or at least a Hollywood version of Irish—and David's mother had adopted Dev, found him a home, and introduced him to the original owner of the bar.

"I've been dumped." David slumped onto a stool. "It's bad, man."

Dev poured two large coffees. "Yes, I know. Your wife's divorcing you—"

"That bitch?" David spat. "Who cares about that bitch? I've got that particular shit show under control."

His friend stared at him. "Now, when you say, 'under control,' have you considered the fact that you've been living out of a 1979 Winnebago all winter? In Wisconsin!"

David looked around. No one else was in the room. "Only while my tax accountant makes me look as poor as possible."

"My apologies, my friend. You definitely have that 'under control.'" Dev reached for the pretzels. "So, what's wrong then?"

"It's the fucking Board of Directors! They're forcing me out!" He banged the counter. "It's *my* fucking company! My father's! My grandfather's! It's the fucking *McKinney* Corporation; not the Corporation of Weasel, Beancounter, and Shyster! I won't be able to face anyone in this town! And it's *my* town!"

"Oh dear." Dev added some Irish whiskey to the coffee and glanced through the windows to the street. "Anyway, where's Bugsy?" Bugsy was David's steadfast bodyguard.

David smiled grimly. "I managed to lose him downtown." David was confident that Bugsy would catch up soon.

After a few of those coffees, David's head felt clearer, and he saw an avenue of escape. "I need to get away from here. I need a new start. I need a strategy." With that, everything went black.

When he woke up, he was in the Winnebago. The clock on the microwave told him it was mid-afternoon. His phone rang. His hand was trapped in a pizza box and smelled of pepperoni, so he wiped it on a T-shirt, hit the button on the phone, and barked, "McKinney here."

The caller's voice was quiet and refined. "Yes? Mr. McKinney. It's Henry Cooper." When David didn't respond, Cooper continued. "I'm the genealogist that your daughter Kathleen hired to trace your family tree. I believe it was a Christmas present? In any case, I have your chart ready if you'd like to see it."

David rolled his eyes. *A waste of time*, but it had been Kathleen's Christmas present to him, and he wanted to please her. "Do you know O'Grady's Bar and Grill?" he growled. "Meet me there tomorrow at one o'clock." He would squeeze this genea-whatever in between meetings with his tax accountant and his divorce attorney.

Kathleen. His younger daughter. Like David, she was passionate about being Irish but knew nothing about it. Kathleen loved all her grandmother's folktales but especially the Irish ones. She knew them so well that, even at seven years of age, she would recite the stories to David at bedtime until she fell asleep. Instead of playing with dolls or computers, Kathleen had pretended to be an old Irish immigrant and had drawn David into this game. His older daughter, Diane, and his soon-to-be ex-wife had wanted nothing to do with this Irish roleplaying, as they preferred to keep themselves "productive."

David remembered the day Kathleen had gone missing. The family had panicked and rushed to search for her—except for David's father, who couldn't leave the office. Bugsy, normally unmoveable, had dashed out to scour the streets and alleyways downtown. David's wife had examined the gardens while Diane had searched the public park. David's mother, Margaret, had chased down the chief of police, who was an old friend from her anti-war protests.

The large house had become quiet. David stood frozen, his eyes welling with tears. Suddenly, tiny footfalls had crossed the attic, or as Kathleen called it, the "garret." He'd discovered his daughter perched on a pile of old green clothes that she had spilled out from various trunks. He'd greeted her pleasantly. "Top o' the mornin' ta ya, missus."

She'd rolled her eyes. "I'm no missus, sir. I'm an old maid! Can I do your washin', sir?"

He'd chosen a shirt, which Kathleen had pretended to wash and pin out to dry. Then they'd sat alone, singing old songs. At dinner, when neither of them had touched anything but the potatoes, his wife had called David a fool and fed the beef wellington to the dogs.

David shrugged. "Blame my mother"—who had not stayed to dine with them—"she's the one who spends her time collecting protest songs and folktales. I've never learned anything important from her."

For once, David's wife agreed with him. She sniffed. "I don't know why your father married her."

David didn't know either. He couldn't imagine two people more incompatible. His mother floated around the McKinney mansion, writing letters to Congress. His father lived at the office and expected young David, their only child, to do the same. As a child, he'd felt privileged that his father permitted him to tag along and knew he would inherit the corporation one day. When he'd started with the company officially, he'd been handed the simplest files. This allowed David plenty of time for golf, sailing, fishing, and Irish pubs while Marcus McKinney ran the business.

His mother had preferred her tie-dyed world, where she was still trying to Stop the Bomb. His wife had managed her own social circle and had packed off the girls to the best schools.

When David hung up on Henry Cooper, he called Bugsy. He heard the phone ring outside the Winnebago, and then the bodyguard answered.

"Boss?"

"Call the limo, Bugsy."

"Can't do that, Boss. The board cut all your benefits."

"What about the club membership?"

"That too. All of them, really."

David growled and punched through the pizza box. "Bugsy, load up your Lincoln. We're going to find a golf course where they don't know us." He remembered a third-rate course a few miles away.

The next day, David took over the biggest table in the back corner of O'Grady's. Since David was now *persona non grata* at the McKinney Corporation, the bar was his new office. Bugsy, a giant dressed in a plain blue suit, stood guard near the door, his gaze straight ahead, reacting to nothing.

David's tax accountant sat across the table with a stack of papers. When David motioned that he was done with him, the man arose from the table, awkwardly shovelling up the papers into a large black leather case, saying, "I'll connect with Geneva this afternoon about those accounts."

A timid little man entered the pub, cradling a large paper scroll. Bugsy stopped him with one outstretched finger. The little man squeaked, "I'm Mr. Cooper." Bugsy waved him through to the table.

The tax accountant exited. David's gaze fell abruptly on the genealogist with an almost reptilian movement of his head. "Your turn," he drawled.

Cooper gulped and glanced at Bugsy as he took the seat. David noticed the look. "My ... business associate, Bugsy Carter," he muttered by way of an introduction. The genealogist stretched the scroll out over the table and started to babble about sixteen branches of David's family.

"Did any of them own a castle?" David asked, interrupting.

Cooper offered a sympathetic grin. "No. Just a farm in Ballybeg." He then explained that some branches had been traced back to

England, the Netherlands, and Spain. *Boring.* David checked his watch. They were due on the green at three o'clock. He wanted to work on the alignment of his downswing. He gestured to Bugsy to call the golf instructor.

David's phone rang. It was his divorce attorney, running late. He hung up and noticed that Cooper had stopped talking. David looked down at the sprawling chart. He needed a minute to focus. His finger traced one branch—the paternal line, the McKinneys— up to a place called Ballybeg.

"Where is that?" he asked, checking his messages again.

Cooper squeaked, "Northern Ireland."

"Right." David nodded. "Ireland. Right. Where?" David resolved to pay attention to the details from now on. He badly needed a manicure.

"On the coast. In Northern Ireland."

"Northern coast. Right."

"And, oh dear, there's a lot more for me to show you. You see ..."

David was thinking and Cooper's voice faded into the background. There had to be some way to use this information to his advantage, but what? And how? His advisors normally fed him strategies and market indicators when he needed a sign, but now he would need to find one himself.

A young, blonde Kylie Minogue lookalike swished past the table, dropping a half-empty whiskey glass. The amber liquid trickled across the table, and the girl disappeared down the hallway. David regarded the glass, lying on its side, its logo facing up. "Ballybeg? Ballybeg? Wait! Is that where the whiskey comes from?"

Mr. Cooper feebly pointed to a mirrored pub sign on the wall. "Yes, indeed."

The spilled whiskey soaked into an open *Forbes Magazine*. The headline declared, "Leading French Firm Seeking Intro to Northern Ireland's Hospitality Market." The article highlighted the plans of the *Syndicat international de Tours* to secure a foothold on Antrim's north coast for a breathtaking new leisure complex. Mr. Marcel Laurel had been interviewed in his London office: "The Syndicat is searching for secure local partners for the venture. This is only the first phase. We plan expansive future growth."

David glanced at the *Forbes* article and the upended glass. A market indicator! He bashed the table. "That's it!" he said, swatting the small man roughly on the shoulder and lunging for the door. Bugsy Carter moved to open it, but David got there first. He yanked it open and knocked his just-arriving divorce attorney back onto the sidewalk. David didn't look back. He was going home. To Ballybeg. The Old Country.

Three

Kara awoke to find that the sun had conquered the threatening grey sky of yesterday. She knew that in Ireland, when the day is warm and sunny, one gets outside. There is no point dawdling inside if the weather is good, since the rain will return soon enough, leaving plenty of time for indoor activities. Therefore, if the sun is filling the sky with light and warmth, one drops everything else. Luckily, this aligned with Kara's plans.

Crossing the hotel foyer, she glimpsed McKay's back at the doorway to the bar. He was on his cell phone, speaking French in a high, officious manner. It sounded like he was setting up a later phone appointment for the afternoon with someone from Paris who was apparently staying in London that week. Kara was impressed with his level of French.

Two quiet, rainy days had passed in Ballybeg. Kara had used the time to confirm some research online and also familiarize herself with the streets of the village and the roads out to the countryside. Today she threw on her hiking shoes to prepare for a long day. She started at Dundurn Castle.

A steep hike up a winding stone path led to the ruins of Dundurn, clinging to a cliff edge overlooking the sea. Kara realised that this was the castle from her dreams. *How close were her dream images to reality?* In order to compare, she needed to stand right on the edge of the crumbling walls. She broke loose from the tour group, ignored the security barriers, and wandered towards the collapsing ledges and treacherous drops in order to get a better look. The water below was deep and the current strong. It would carry someone out quickly, assuming they survived the fall. Dangerous if you had enemies but beautiful in the spring morning light. A wind came out of nowhere and pushed her away from the precipice.

Satisfied with her self-guided tour, Kara waited in an alcove to mingle with the others. The guides, dressed in historical costume, explained that Dundurn had been referred to as "the old castle" when St. Patrick had visited in the fifth century. General Muircheartaigh had seized it in the eleventh century. There were great halls that had once been painted and decorated with tapestries and furniture, been lit by dozens of candles in golden brackets, and had hosted feasts and dances. Only the cold brown stone remained. She started down the worn staircase to head back to the village.

The hike to the village from the coastal road took her through the farmlands along Beeswax Road, where her grandfather had been born. Kara was surprised to see Mary Anderson appearing from a barn near the road.

"Beautiful morning, isn't it, Mary? A great day for a hike!" she called out with a wave.

"Hello, Kara. Yes, well, it was a beautiful morning." The farmer laughed and pointed out a fast-moving clump of dark grey clouds. Then she swept her arm toward the north side of Beeswax Road. "Knocknageragh here is my family's farm."

Kara pulled her large notebook from her satchel and scrawled across a clean page.

Mary continued. "All this land used to be part of the estate of the Duke of Inish-Rathcarrick, but over time, tenant farmers bought their land. This parcel of land next over is Lisnasidhe. Most of the land is pasture that we rent from the church for grazing sheep. But you can see Rosheen Wood—that forest grove further back on the right."

"It looks abandoned."

"It's overgrown. No one goes in there."

Lisnasidhe was the property on which her Sweeney ancestors had lived and grazed their cows over a hundred years earlier. She conjured an image of her grandfather as a boy, helping his own grandfather in the pasture. Her ancestors must have walked this old road for centuries. Kara wasn't paying attention to the weather anymore. Standing on the land where her ancestors had lived made the morning all the more beautiful.

"Lisnasidhe isn't owned by Sweeneys now?"

"No. The Sweeneys never bought it."

Kara scribbled. That made sense since the younger family members had settled in Scotland after her great-grandfather's employer had relocated him to the shipyards in Glasgow.

"Who bought it? The church?"

Mary shrugged. "No one knows. It's held in trust."

Lisnasidhe was surrounded by short drystone walls. A pond nestled in a corner near the road. A narrow path wrapped around the pond and Rosheen Wood, continuing back to a wooden gate in the stone wall beside the grove of trees. The property stretched back for perhaps a hundred acres. Along the road frontage, it looked like a well-maintained sheep pasture except for the uncared-for Rosheen Wood.

The two followed the narrow path closer to Rosheen Wood. Kara could not see an opening into the dense grove. She could see the tops of oak, pine, elm, and ash trees surrounded by brambles of blackthorn and hawthorn. A further outside ring of waist-high brush revealed that it hadn't been touched by a human hand for a very long time. Kara asked Mary, "What's wrong with the grove?"

"Wrong? Nothing. Nothing really—just that it belongs to the fairy folk. It's unlucky to disturb it. But I use the rest of the pasture. And my beehives are just beyond that stone wall there." Mary pointed to the tops of her beehives, just visible above the wooden gate. The movement of the bees around the apiary drew Kara's attention, but she quickly came back to Mary's previous statement.

"Fairies? Real fairies?"

Mary grimaced. "Well, better safe than sorry. You get used to it."

Kara wasn't sure how to continue with that, so she pivoted to the left. "And the next property is the church?"

"Yes. Your ancestors would have gone there."

Kara flipped a few pages about and tapped at a page with her pen. "Is that the Ballybeg Parish Church?"

"Yes."

"My great-grandparents were married there, and my grandfather baptised." Kara imagined her great-grandparents strolling together to the church.

Walking back to the road, Mary pointed past the church to a white-painted two-storey house built in the Edwardian style, sitting in a cultivated English garden. The stone walls surrounding the property were richly draped with fuchsia. "And that is Aghnagoogh. It means 'the cuckoo's field.' That's Imogen Currie. She's a heritage conservationist from London, but her mother's family came from here. She's a little stuck up, but she's alright when you know her."

"I'm not staying that long."

"We'll see."

The sudden downpour forced them to run to Mary's barn for coverage. Mary took a jar of honey from a shelf and said, "Let's hop into my truck. I'll run you into the village."

Mary dropped Kara off at a corner on Victoria Street, armed with a good umbrella. The smell of fresh French fries carried Kara along the pavement. It was a little after one o'clock. She tracked the smell to the Chippy—the fish and chip shop—and joined the queue that filled the bright, white-tiled interior, then waited her turn before requesting, "One order of chips, please."

The tall man in front of her, who had just received his food, peeked back over his shoulder at the sound of her voice. "Hello. You must be the Canadian that came up on the bus with Mary the other day."

"With Mary Anderson? Yes, guilty as charged, sir." She held up her jar of honey as if proof was required.

"I'm a friend of hers. I'm Keith." Keith stood well over six feet and wore a red bandana casually tied at his neck. He had a shock of unruly blond curls that repeatedly fell into his eyes. He tossed them back. "Are you alone?"

When she told him that she was, Keith invited Kara to join his friends. "They're just next door. I'm picking up the order."

Next door was the Yarn Barn. The name was self-explanatory. The walls displayed a riot of colours and textiles. They climbed a flight of stairs and found a lounge that seemed littered with abandoned knitting, in the centre of which sat a circle of ten or so people, chatting and laughing together. As Keith entered, a cheer arose.

He placed the wrapped food on the centre table and backed away from the melee. Kara settled into an empty chair with her chips.

Morag, the owner of the Yarn Barn, handed Kara a glass of white wine. "Welcome to the Ballybeg Yarnbombers for Heritage."

Kara's stunned reaction started everyone laughing.

Keith smiled at her. "Don't you drink wine?"

Kara laughed and studied her glass. "Oh, no. Love the wine! Just didn't quite catch the name."

Morag explained. "Yarnbombing. It's a type of graffiti using knitting."

"Or crochet!" added someone.

"It's street art. An installation in yarn," Keith offered. "Using the traditionally feminine, so-called 'craft pursuits' in expressive counterbalance to the cold sterile environments created by male-dominated society."

Morag told her that Keith was a painter and taught art theory at the local college. Kara smiled. "That all makes sense then."

A red-headed girl in the corner boasted, "Yarnbombing is a form of peaceful protest. We've blocked streets with our knitting."

Morag continued. "We are dedicated to preserving the natural heritage of Ballybeg through protests in wool. We meet once a week but more frequently if required." Then she introduced Sarah, who owned the tea shop across the street.

Sarah reached out to shake Kara's hand. "The Teaspot, it's called. Drop by tomorrow." Sarah lowered her voice as if to share a state secret. "The Yarnbombers are doing something big for the pride parade. The first annual Ballybeg Pride Parade. Keith is on the parade planning committee, and he's our liaison there."

Keith finished his fish. "We've been planning the parade for years. I never thought it would happen!" He stabbed an invisible enemy in the air with a chip. "This is the real dividing line. Not religion anymore. Now it's LGBT equality. The right-wing dingers have created no end of grief with their puritanical ideals. The Ballybeg Pride Parade celebrates our future. June eighteenth will be a change day."

The others finished their fish and chips and went back to their knitting. Morag, Keith, and Sarah invited Kara to join them on the back rooftop patio, as the rain had stopped as dramatically as it had begun.

Sarah sipped her wine. "Yarnbombing also has a practical social purpose. Mittens, scarves, etc., wrapped around posts and benches can provide warmth for the homeless or the *Sidhe*—" Morag shot a quick look at Sarah, who corrected herself. "Not *Sidhe*. I meant… for nests and such for wild creatures."

"What are the *Sidhe*?" asked Kara.

"Nothing." Morag glanced at Keith and Sarah. "It's a word for the fairy folk. Just old stories." Morag pointed out beyond the rooftop. "There's an advantage to my little patio. It looks out over the recreational courtyard of the fire hall."

Kara peered over to the next yard below. A group of firefighters were playing basketball.

Keith sighed. "Morag, what a lovely view you have! I could stand here all day."

Kara soon continued her touring, wandering over to the Ballybeg Whiskey distillery. The outward, old-fashioned appearance belied the clean and efficient industrial processing going on inside. One of the Master Blenders came out to chat. He was a Gillan, one of Kara's family names, and he was interested in genealogy. They traded notes, and he introduced Kara to several other key staff people. After the distillery, she stopped at the art gallery and the bookshop. Everyone was friendly and happy to share general knowledge about the village history.

When she arrived back at the inn, McKay was waiting to hear all about it. A bottle of wine sat opened on her dinner table. McKay requested a summary of what she'd discovered that day. Who had she met? What new facts had she learned? He took a keen interest in her answers. In exchange, he gossiped about how villagers were related, what they were like as children, their jobs, and their salaries.

The inn was quieter that evening. Only two families dined, and they said that they were leaving in the morning. No new guests had checked in all day. Kara chatted with others in the bar who were also leaving soon. Logically, it was the opposite of regular business for the end of May. She heard the staff discussing a new, large booking, arriving in a few days, that would fill all the rooms.

As the twilight darkened the sky to a deep blue, Kara lingered alone in the courtyard and gazed at the river. She took her tarot cards out of her bag and laid out a Celtic Cross on the table. Herself the Queen of Cups—a well-intentioned woman—crossed by the Fool. The Tower was a problem. Behind her, the Six of Cups: happy family memories. Above, the High Priestess—a woman of knowledge—and ahead, the Magician. *Who are these people?* She continued. Nine of Wands: caution. Around her, the Seven of Cups: strange chalices of vision. Hope. Justice. She hesitated to turn the last card. She held her breath as she flipped it over. It was the Ace of Cups, an auspicious card. Perhaps her decision to visit Ballybeg was a good one. She pondered all the sights she'd seen and the new people she'd met. There were no fireflies and no drunken poets this evening. There was nothing disagreeable, but even so, how could anything disagreeable ever vex her in Ballybeg? It was like heaven. Her contentment lasted through the night.

The next day, Kara returned to her seat in the courtyard and sipped her morning coffee. She listened to the river that was whooshing past her on its way to the sea. One could lose one's sense of time in Ballybeg, sitting in the courtyard near the riverbank, wandering through the village or out along the country roads in the warm spring air. Certainly, even here, modern life must march briskly in the law offices, or the council chambers, or the banks, or other spaces where important business occurred. But not in Kara's Ballybeg—here it was serene and friendly. With this new intoxicating freedom to live slowly, Kara truly felt at ease for the first time since she'd retired.

That day she wandered the village again, stopping to talk to anyone and everyone. The villagers did not ask direct questions about her and ventured even less about themselves. However, they would talk about each other. Kara had initially experimented by asking general questions and just letting people talk. Now this became her strategy. Do not ask targeted questions, or they will clam up. Mention other people. Hear what they say. Do not offer an opinion. Kara was quickly learning people's names, their relatives, and their occupations. Of course, there was another side to this. The more they gossiped *with* her, the more they knew and gossiped *about* her. She didn't care. The familiarity gave them comfort to speak to her without reserve.

A woman in the bookshop approached Kara. "You're the Canadian McKinney, aren't you?"

Kara blushed a little. "Yes. But my name is Kara Gordon."

"Oh. I know. From Canada. You took early retirement from a government post. In your mid-fifties, are you, and lost your husband? Your parents were Scottish, but your grandparents are from here."

"Yes. That's right; I'm fifty-five. Well, I have one grandparent from here. I was an analyst for the government before I retired. And I'm divorced, not widowed. All that's correct." Kara now took over the reins of the conversation. "I met Morag from the Yarn Barn yesterday. She has a nice shop."

"My word! Yes. Morag, poor soul. Run off her feet, she is! She has the shop, her knitting circle and those two wild sons—Owen and Liam—always mowing down folks on their bicycles. On top of that, she attends to her father, Seamus. He is nearly ninety-six. The Seanchaí and the oldest man in the village, mind you, but you would never know it. He's up and out every day, telling the old folktales to anyone who will listen and some that won't."

And that's how it works.

Stepping out of the bookshop, Kara saw Frank and Dennis bickering outside the Standing Stone. She began to pass them but then stopped to call each by name, just to see how they would react. "Frank! Dennis! How are you doing today?" They stared at her, stammering and exchanging fearful expressions. Then each flung an arm over the other's shoulders, and they darted back into the pub. Kara was satisfied, hoping that she'd been able to heal their friendship, at least momentarily, and thereby contribute to the community.

Like the evening before, McKay peppered her with questions as soon as she'd returned. The wine was on the table. There were no other guests. After her dinner, she lingered alone at her table to work on her family tree. Referring to details she'd written in her notebook, she compared them to a chart she'd created to sort out who was related to whom, more or less. Gradually, voices in the lobby drew her attention. They grew louder. One was clearly McKay, though the other voice was only vaguely familiar.

" ... so you think you can ..." This from the unidentified speaker.

36

"No, I KNOW I can," McKay interrupted him. "I've got proof."

"Show me your proof!"

"Okay. I'll be getting the proof—the confirmation of title—any day now. I'll have it in time."

"It wouldn't matter, McKay. Even if you can prove this connection, this claim, this isn't the fifties; we have laws."

"Nothing important."

"There's the District Land Use Policy Framework, 2012, for one—"

"That's a policy, not a law. Anyone with a good solicitor can work around that." McKay sounded sarcastic.

The penny dropped. Kara shifted her chair and peered a little more to the left of the half-closed door. *Yes.* It was Michael Garrett, whom she'd seen the first evening outside the pub with Frank and Dennis. *What had they been arguing about that first time she'd seen him?* Developers. And now he's arguing with McKay about land title. Kara strained to remember exactly what she'd revealed to McKay that first evening. *Too much chardonnay!*

Michael stepped back. "I am not engaging in this argument right now, McKay. But I am not dropping this either." His back remained turned to the dining room. He did not see Kara, and now he was reaching for the front door handle. "You can bring it to the committee. You can take it to court; it will do you no good at all."

McKay sneered. "We'll see who has the most influence. We'll see who I have in my camp."

Michael scoffed. "Careful, McKay. People who play with dragons catch fire."

The door opened and slammed shut. Michael was storming across the courtyard to the bridge. McKay wandered casually into the dining room. Kara was too polite to ask what was going on. It was his inn. He could fight with whomever he wanted. Still, with her head at a sneaky tilt, she did not take her eyes off him. He wandered from one end of the room to the other and back again. Twice. Finally, he stopped. He smiled, gesturing towards the door. "A minor business disagreement."

Kara cleared her throat. "Really? I didn't hear it." She drew a random green line in her chart.

"Oh yes, you did."

"Okay. Yes, I did." She gave him a direct stare. "Forgive me for saying so, but it sounded like it was related to what I told you the evening I first arrived."

"No, not at all…. How's your research going?" He tried to peek at her chart.

Kara snatched it up and rolled it tightly.

McKay smiled. "I thought you planned to finish your research quickly and start your travelling?" His eyes narrowed, and he glanced away before turning back to stare at her through his round, wire-rim spectacles.

Kara studied McKay. He was, she'd discovered, her fourth cousin from the marriage of Agnes McKay to John McKinney in 1855. Her analytical skills were buzzing at 99 percent, and McKay was easy to read. She responded with a drawl. "I dunno. I think I might settle down in Ballybeg for a longer stay. Get to know the natives better. Find out what makes them tick."

"Ah. Well, unfortunately, there is a major group arriving tomorrow. Every room is booked starting from the end of the week, I'm afraid."

"That's alright. I've been making friends. I'll figure something out."

"You do that." McKay headed back to the lobby. "But be careful with those friends. Don't pick the wrong side."

In the morning, McKay avoided Kara. She wasn't worried. The village was interesting enough. Over breakfast, she spread out her village map, taking note of more addresses where her ancestors had lived or worked, in the village and out to the farming townlands. Exploring the area and talking with real people provided more tangible information for her family history than sitting looking at the records online or in Belfast. She ventured out.

As she crossed Memorial Square, Kara heard steps close behind her. Was it McKay? Turning, she saw nothing. But as she moved, it started again. Click, click, click. She stopped. So did the footsteps. Her head turned slightly. She wouldn't be surprised to find the ghost woman in the green evening dress in her high heels. *Can't be ghosts. It's daylight!* She ducked into the chemist shop and turned to watch out the front window. A shadow stopped just to the left of the doorway. Possibly at the door of the stationary shop next door.

Kara felt all ninja-ish. She exited the chemist's quickly in the same direction she'd started and then pivoted 180 degrees on her heel. Nothing. She turned back to continue up the road. The footsteps started again. She wished she were the type of woman who kept a mirror in her bag. She ran across the road and then ran back immediately. She saw it! That is, she saw something. A flash of something small and white.

She was certain it was a dog, hiding under a bush at the side of the schoolyard. She bent down for a better look. She could see two small black eyes and a black nose in a clump of white fur—sort of white anyway. *Probably dirty.* She tried to coax out the animal. It wouldn't budge.

"Alright. You can follow me if you want, but it won't be very interesting." She continued her walk up the road. The dog trotted behind at a distance.

The Ballybeg Teaspot was located in an old two-storey house. A little bell rang as Kara entered. A number of tables were populated with people knitting and drinking tea. A small table by the window was free. Sarah waved from the kitchen.

Three very old women sat nearby, engrossed in their own gossip. Kara could not help listening when people spoke so loudly. She ordered a tea and a couple of scones.

A young woman with long chestnut-coloured hair passed by the window. The oldest of the women pointed a thin, gloved finger in her direction. "See her? She's up to no good. Works in the hospital, no less."

The youngest one gasped. "Really!"

The first one nodded. "Oh! She's no Roseann McKinney, that's for certain, but it's still quite the scandal."

The third old woman cackled. "Roseann! My word! My grandmother used to warn me not to be like Roseann McKinney. Once she fled Ballybeg, she could never come back again."

"When did she leave?" the younger one queried.

What a tasty scone! It's a good cup of tea too.

The cackling one lit up, happy to be a source of information. "Let me think. Roseann McKinney went to the church school with my great-grandmother. So that would be..." She started to count on her fingers.

The gloved one fondled the tabletop. "Her mother Peggy Ann was in service with my great-great-grandmother. Got herself pregnant! That's when it all started. Gave birth to Roseann, a disgrace to Ballybeg."

This interrupted the cackling one from her calculations. "Yes, that's right. To his shame, James McKinney, Peggy Ann's father, refused to turn his daughter out of the house, despite it all. They kept the bastard and raised her."

The younger one was eager to join in. "That would make it all the worse!"

The dog tucked itself under an outdoor table with an eye on the door.

Finger counting calculations done, the woman announced, "1876! That was it! The very day she turned fourteen, Roseann ran away to England and never came back. But then, years later, her daughter Molly came back, all proper full of herself to buy Aghnagoogh and build a grand house." She paused to draw breath. "And well, then there's Imogen, Molly's granddaughter—Who does she think she is?"

Kara sighed softly. *This is how everybody knows everything about everyone in Ballybeg. Poor Roseann!*

Sarah emerged from the kitchen and came over to sit with Kara, who confided that she'd decided to remain longer but would need to find another place to stay before the end of the week. The knitting needles fell silent. "I'll probably find a B and B." The needles resumed their rhythmic clicking.

Kara noted the on-and-off rhythm of the knitting needles. She leaned forward and lowered her voice to ask Sarah, "Do you know the best local expert on the history of the village?"

Sarah was quick. "Oh history! For that, you'll want to speak with Imogen Currie." The trio of old women went silent. "Imogen's the biggest expert that I've ever heard talking. She's English. She's a conservative."

Kara raised an eyebrow and repeated, "A Conservative?"

"No, I mean ... a *conservationist*. You'll probably find her halfway up a tower at the Ballybeg Parish Church. Just up Beeswax Road there." The knitting resumed.

"I know the place. I was near there with Mary Anderson." The knitting paused again.

Twenty minutes later, in a Torontonian rush, Kara walked briskly to the church. She was curious to see a woman floating halfway up a tower. The dog followed.

Today was another day that had started warm, sunny, and dry. It couldn't last. Three cars and two tourist buses passed, heading for the coastal road. The dog maintained a distant but steady pace. The noon bell rang out from the church across the beautiful green pastures.

Soon the churchyard was visible on her left. The graveyard stretched over more land than the church. It was well tended. The family names on the headstones were all familiar. Most were paired as neatly as the records office in Belfast. McKinney-Gillan, Gillan-McKay, McKay-Sweeney. A genealogical card index in stone.

Kara sat on a large stone bench under a willow tree. The dog crept closer. She tried to speak to it. "Have you eaten today? Who do you belong to?" She pulled half a scone from the pocket of her patchwork silk coat and held it out. The dog shifted closer and nibbled until it was gone. Then it settled into the grass under the bench.

Kara recognized not only the family names on the headstones, but by referring to the chart she kept in her notebook, she could match the headstones to specific couples. She stood to take photos of the headstones. Doing online research, she'd thought that people who did this were morbid. But since these were her own ancestors, she figured this was just record keeping in an ancient graveyard.

She returned to the bench and pulled her tabbed, colour-coded notebook from her bag to record observations. The dog touched her ankle with its wet nose.

A clergyman on a bicycle stopped at the gate. "Good morning!" He seemed a cheery sort, a little out of breath and red on the tip of his nose. "Can I help you?" The dog scampered under a hedge. The man took Kara's hand and shook it. "How do you do? I am Reverend Nesbitt, the rector, uh, minister, here. You're not familiar to me, but you don't quite seem like a tourist. I have not met you before, have I?"

Kara introduced herself and explained a little bit of the general reason she'd travelled to Ballybeg. "My great-grandparents were married here in 1888."

"So, you are returning home then. Welcome back."

Kara smiled. "You're very kind." Over the last few days, she'd sensed that she really belonged here, though she doubted the villagers saw her in the same light. "I came to speak with Imogen Currie. Sarah from the Teaspot thought she might be here today."

He responded easily. "Yes, she should be inside there now. I'm meeting her to discuss a bit of bother with the roof. Typical, really, for an old church, but it is a protected historical site, so Imogen's expertise is invaluable. Do you know Imogen?"

Kara suspected that the reason villagers naturally asked more questions than a city dweller from Toronto might expect was because everyone knew everyone else's business anyway. Still, it was better to be cautious about what she shared with whom—at least until she was as familiar with them as they were with each other. She did not repeat what she'd overheard in the Teaspot. "No, I've never met her, but I understand she's the best expert on the history of the village."

He considered that for a moment. "Likely. I can't think of anyone better."

"If she could spare me a few minutes, it could help." She produced a delicate embossed card with her name and contact information. Not a business card exactly—more like a Victorian calling card. "Is it alright if I wait here for her?"

"Sit as long as you'd like. And it's a lovely day, but you are welcome inside too, you know."

He seemed a genuinely nice guy, but then she had thought that about James McKay as well. Kara did not want to leave the dog alone here. "I would like to sit with the relatives a little longer. We have a lot to catch up on."

He gazed at Kara's card. "I will pass on the message." He headed to the church.

Kara bent down to check on the dog. She was starting to care about it.

A tour bus stopped on the roadside. A small group of tourists poured out from it and wandered into the churchyard. Morag descended and assisted an old man, who was shuffling along with the group. He was the same dishevelled drunk who'd climbed up from the riverbank and recited poetry to Kara on her first night. So, this was Morag's ninety-six-year-old father, Seamus. Clearly, Morag wasn't keeping track of him all the time. However, Seamus was much tidier and sober today.

The group moved together to a shady spot under a large oak. Morag opened a camp chair for her father. The tourists surrounded him as he started to speak in a remarkably loud voice for someone who appeared so frail. His arms and facial expressions were also very animated.

"The fairy folk, or the Sidhe, or the Fae, or fairies—whatever name you prefer—are not sparkly, happy little pixies. No, no, no. They can be kind and generous or wicked and mischievous. They are shape shifters and tricksters. For certain, they can look like that lovely young lass Kylie Minogue, if that is what you want to see. They can trick your gold away from you, make your cows disappear, or make the river flow blood. They can strike the birds silent. They can trap you in a field until the end of time.

"But once, long ago, the Fae were also strong and powerful fighters. Their armies won battles by changing the weather or stealing the wits of their opponents.

"Now, in this tale, which was given to me by my grandmother, who heard it from hers, and back before recorded time, Coinnigh was the head of an ancient family, only one of a number of families that preserved the old ways and beliefs."

His eyes flashed as he performed his story and glanced about at his audience. "This was a time with an even balance between the world of people and the world of fairies. A time when people understood the protection of the oak and the healing of the willow. When the sea had a voice to be heard, and the land sang with joy.

"But new chieftains rode over the land and brought change."

Seamus had pronounced the name "Coinnigh" as *Kinney*, which Kara thought was interesting, but she was soon distracted by a rustling under her feet. The dog crawled out of her hiding spot, attracted by Seamus's voice, to slip unnoticed through the tourists to his feet. Kara also drew nearer to the storyteller but stopped just short of the crowd.

"One such was Domhnaill MacDhuibhfinn. MacDhuibhfinn brought his armies to take control over the land and the people. All the other chieftains knelt and swore fealty to MacDhuibhfinn. Only Coinnigh stood against him.

"Coinnigh could not withstand the forces of MacDhuibhfinn alone. Coinnigh called on those people who had respect and affection for him for his courage and fairness. And he called on the Fae—the fairy folk who hid under the earth and in the trees. Coinnigh was the last true druid. Coinnigh's mother was one of the fairy folk, and she had taught him the magic needed to persuade the Fae to his cause. It was said Coinnigh could talk a Leprechaun out of his gold. When he called upon the fairy folk to join him in battle, many would come—after a good barter, of course."

"Kylie Minogue is his go-to 'lovely, young lass' nowadays," Morag said quietly to Kara after circling around the tourists and coming up behind her. With a laugh, she added, "It used to be Kate Bush. Anyway, whose dog is that?"

"I thought maybe you knew."

"No clue."

Morag pointed to Seamus. "My father is the Seanchaí." At Kara's blank expression, she explained. "He's like a bard. He remembers everything. He knows all the old tales." She paused. "He's really in demand."

"Does he know Imogen Currie?" Kara asked.

"Imogen Currie?" Morag's expression transformed from sunny to guarded. "Well, everybody knows everybody, of course. Imogen? Never married. She's smart. Went to Cambridge University. She has degrees and certificates in historical stuff and, uh, things. She's English. Well, her father's family is English. Her maternal line is from here. Her great-grandmother—I think it is—left to find work in England. Some sort of scandal. Never came back, but she married well, and sometime later, one of them built the house here at Aghnagoogh next door. Imogen lives there now."

Seamus still held his audience entranced with his easy chatty style: "Many generations passed. The fairy folk disappeared, hiding in the trees and under the earth, but they still watch. You may meet one on the road and not know it. Occasionally, the fairy folk will come along and try to steal your gold but you're safe with the ATMs." He laughed mischievously. "And some fairy folk *are* nice ... although others run for parliament. Stay near the rowan trees; that's the secret."

The crowd laughed. Seamus ended his story and motioned to his daughter. Morag responded and rushed back to the crowd. "Alright now, folks. The Seanchaí will tell you the legend of the King of the River on the bus, if you could all return to your seats." The group obeyed while Morag brought Seamus along after them.

As they crossed to the bus, Seamus stopped to stare at the dog. When he raised his eyes from the dog to Kara's face, he wore a dazed expression. Kara wondered if the sunlight was hitting him in the eyes. He recited, "The first daughter's true heart will unlock the treasure, the secret loves, the happy pleasures, and above the rest, a spell that binds two worlds together to guard against the foe." This was the same verse he had recited on Kara's first night when he climbed up from the riverbank. Could it mean something? Was it about his daughter Morag?

Morag smiled and helped her father up the steps of the bus. The doors closed, and a few moments later, the bus huffed off into the road toward the village.

The dog retook her not-very-secret position under the bush. Kara returned to the stone bench on the edge of the graveyard. She was trying to work out what Seamus had been talking about when she glanced in the direction of the church and saw a tall, thin, well-dressed woman in her late forties striding towards her. This must be Imogen Currie.

"Good afternoon," the well-dressed woman said, addressing her with a clipped, matter-of-fact English accent.

Four

Imogen Currie was familiar with the church bells. She used earplugs and kept a tight grasp on the ladder so that when the bell struck noon, she remained steadfast in her position thirty feet above the floor of the old Ballybeg Parish Church. From this advantaged position, she surveyed the village and the surrounding countryside through the chancel window. To the far west, the old asylum building (1844) sat abandoned. The Ballybeg Inn (former priory, 1265), not looking a day over two hundred, posed on its island across the river from the war memorial (1922) in the centre of the village square (1895). The substantial bulk of the distillery (1608) anchored the southeast of the village. She could even see the oldest tree in the village: a gigantic double oak tree on the eastern boundary that was more than eleven hundred years old. Its roots ran so deep and so far that no construction could occur on that side of the village without killing the tree. To the northeast, the ruins of Dundurn Castle (year unknown) clung to its rocky ledge above the ocean. But more locally, in fact directly below her, she saw that old charlatan Seamus in the churchyard, performing his usual malarky. His daughter, Morag, was chatting to a woman wearing a bright multicoloured jacket.

Imogen received high marks in her high ladder training. She won awards hanging from scaffolding. She would have made an excellent acrobat had she not pursued a career in architectural conservation. Of course, she would excel in any pursuit. She turned again to the wall directly in front of her. A small leak from the roof had been ignored for decades and had badly damaged the stonework. Imogen ran her fingers along a vertical crack and took some photos with her cell phone. "Let's see what they say about these at the Institute," she murmured in her clipped English accent to a resident pigeon. "And you, my friend, will need to relocate. But lucky for you, not today."

The Reverend Doctor Henry J. Nesbitt, Rector of Ballybeg Parish Church, had entered from the churchyard. He stared at the cracks on the wall. "And we thought that the roof replacement was the end of our troubles."

"Yes, well, the parish vestry took too long about it." Imogen pointed up, then waved her long fingers downward to the floor. "Rainwater ingress. Cycles of evaporation and condensation. The damage to the stonework is quite severe." She pulled a torch from her pocket and illuminated a dark corner. "See this efflorescence down here?" Imogen slid down the thirty feet to the floor, landing neatly beside Nesbitt. "Not an immediate health and safety issue, but it should be repaired before it gets worse."

He nodded. "Thank you, Imogen. I didn't understand it all, but I'm glad you are on our side. You should submit an invoice."

"All fees waived. I don't charge churches." Imogen removed her construction gloves and hardhat. She wiped her hands on a linen handkerchief that she folded up and popped into the pocket of her waxed-cotton jacket. "I'll follow-up on the cost estimate for the needed work. Then I can talk to the Institute and the Historic Trust about funding. In the meantime, please have the vestry set up a maintenance regime before something else goes awry. Oh, and we have a resident pigeon."

Nesbitt fell behind Imogen's broad strides as she moved to the main doors. "By the way, there's a Canadian woman wanting to talk with you." She stopped to face him. He indicated the side door. "In the churchyard." He took a large breath. "She seems pleasant. Her card."

Her card? How curiously Victorian, Imogen thought. The type was clear: Kara Gordon, Toronto, Ontario Canada. She'd heard there was a Canadian doing genealogy research. Imogen could not imagine any connection between her field of expertise and family trees. What could she want?

She spotted her perched on the stone bench, staring at the headstones. *That is one way of doing genealogy. I suppose everyone is in there.* A scruffy terrier was crouched under a nearby hedge. *Are they together?*

"Good afternoon," Imogen said, announcing her arrival.

The woman jumped to her feet. "Hello! I'm Kara Gordon!"

Imogen's mouth curled up slightly at the left corner, and she waved Kara's "calling card" coquettishly. "Yes, you are." Kara thrust forth her right hand, but instead of taking it, Imogen signalled for her to sit down. Kara dropped to the bench. Imogen insinuated herself into a sitting position on the bench. She was in no real hurry and curious about this visitor.

Imogen indicated the headstones. "Did you find who you were looking for?"

Kara revealed her own crooked smile. "I do most of my research on the internet and in the records office. But I do see some confirmations here."

Imogen studied Kara. "Gordon. Is that the family you are researching?"

"My father's surname," Kara clarified. "My mother's maiden name was McKinney." She pointed to the closest example of that name amongst the graves. "That's my great-great-grandfather, John."

Imogen leaned in to read the inscription: " ... and his wife, Agnes McKay."

Kara looked down at her tabbed, colour-coded notebook. "Are there McKinneys in your family? Do you think we're related?"

"Perhaps," mused Imogen. "My great-grandmother came from here. She was a McKinney. Beyond that, I know very little. I suppose, in a manner of speaking, anyone who can trace their ancestor back to Ballybeg in the eighteenth century is likely related somehow to everyone else. That's just science." She reached out her hand and shut Kara's book, asking, "Is that why you came to find me?"

Was that a look of impatience on Kara's face? There, no? Yes? No, it's gone again.

Kara stumbled over her words. "No, no, of course not. It is a question of—well, I have noticed some disagreement—Oh dear, that's not how I wanted to start. I heard that you have the most knowledge of local history."

Imogen nodded. "Apart from perhaps Michael Garrett. He has learned a lot since he moved here."

"Um, yes, really? I thought he was only concerned with biodiversity, not, you know, history. Uh. This is becoming awkward."

Imogen examined her manicure. "No problem. Collect your thoughts."

"Okay." Kara bent down to slip her notebook into her satchel. When she lifted her head, her expression was focused and thoughtful. "Is there some issue being debated about preserving land from foreign developers?"

Imogen sat quite straight-backed but suddenly felt her spine tingle. The hairs on the back of her neck stiffened. "In this district? All the time!" The conservation of historic properties was Imogen's livelihood. Her only love. Her work on the restoration of the 1855 Corn Mill had garnered several European heritage medals. Her specialty lay in built heritage, while Michael Garrett's concerns centred on nature conservation. Sometimes, both could be threatened by an ambitious developer.

She tried to explain to Kara by encircling the land in all directions with a wave of her fingers. "In Ballybeg, almost every bit of land is protected as either a legislated heritage property or an environmentally sensitive site. There's history all around you, and native plant and animal species. We need to preserve all of it. Land developers always talk about progress, but ironically, it is they who are backwards."

Kara nodded. "I have seen signs everywhere for sites of historical significance, and I know that none of the buildings in the village can be more than two stories. Then there are the monuments and the castle. The distillery is four hundred years old and still operating. Even the field where my ancestors grazed their animals is still the same. Perhaps, if something works, it doesn't need to be improved. It looks like heritage is valued here. I like the way I find it. It's tangible, a special energy, like a lifeforce from the earth that's in the trees, and the air, and the water too."

Imogen studied her new acquaintance closely, trying to read her like a new artefact. "Well, it's a long story, and I could bore you with the legislative text, but the shortcut is that, yes, the entire district is protected for conservation versus development."

Imogen could not see any specific indicator that Kara was particularly trustworthy, but somehow, she trusted her anyway. "Come to my house for tea. We can unpack this question a little."

It was a short walk to Aghnagoogh. "How long have you been in Ballybeg?"

"A few days," replied Kara.

Imogen looked back again. "Do you know there's a dog following you?"

"Oh yes."

"Have you adopted it?"

"I think she has adopted me."

Imogen rolled her eyes. Her own life was clean and uncomplicated. She focused on her work. She was careful not to attract things. She sensed Kara was a type of emotional magnet. Despite her advanced years, she was dressed like the synthesis of the Hippie and Goth periods. Her long greying hair was neither up nor down. Her satchel bulged with objects. She wore high-top American sneakers. And she'd attracted a grungy dog. She seemed friendly without boundaries, polite but impatient, smart but uninformed, and Canadian, or Scottish, or Irish. A representative example of the mid-twentieth century British immigrant experience in North America. Interesting. More importantly, there seemed to be new information about developers that Imogen needed to extract from her.

They arrived at Aghnagoogh. Imogen opened the gate for Kara to pass through the fuchsia-draped stone wall into her rose garden. The dog followed. They walked up the pebbled drive to her beautiful and well-positioned Edwardian house. Imogen started for the front door but paused and scrutinized the grungy dog. "Let's go around to the back garden. Perhaps tea on the terrace might be best. I will bring the dog some meat and water."

David McKinney looked down from the black private helicopter. Its shadow crawled across miles of land. Villages rushed past.

Green pastures rolled in sharp turns and inclines around lush woods or jagged crags. Farm animals. Buildings dotted the landscape: barns, stables, a variety of sheds, converted mills, and churches. The helicopter curved and plunged into the valley and over the village. The pilot announced that this was Ballybeg. David McKinney removed his Ray-Bans and peered closely at the scene below him before turning to Bugsy. "Ballybeg. How fucking quaint. This place needs our help."

"Sure, Boss."

The helicopter landed in a courtyard. "The Ballybeg Inn," reported the pilot coldly.

"It's pretty small, isn't it?" condemned David.

The pilot just shrugged.

David smirked. *Yeah. Small, like the rest of this place.* He stepped out into the courtyard of the inn and adjusted his sunglasses. He wandered onto the stone bridge over the river and stopped for a closer look at the surroundings. There was a strange uniformity to the buildings and the materials used to build them. The proportions were ridiculous. The river and the landscape dominated the view. It was boring.

The helicopter lifted off and rose higher and away. A moment later, an excited, thin man with round wire glasses burst out of the inn. "Mr. McKinney! Welcome! I am James McKay, the owner of the Ballybeg Inn!"

David hoped the man didn't expect a response. He pointed to Bugsy, who replied, "Hi. I'm Bugsy Carter. This is Mr. David McKinney."

The little man persisted in trying to draw David out. "Did you have a good journey?"—pause—"Is this your first time in Ballybeg?"—pause—"Ah ... or in Ireland?" To this, David nodded.

"Really? Fascinating! There will be a lot you want to see."

David silently shook his head.

James McKay continued his odd soliloquy: "No, not at the moment, of course. No, you will want to rest first. Did you fly directly from Wisconsin?—No? Ah! From London?" Nod. "Of course. Yes. I heard from Mr. Laurel."

Bugsy intervened. "Mr. McKinney has just completed five days of meetings at the Savoy. He is a little hungry. He will take dinner in his suite as he is very busy."

McKay persevered. "Five days at the Savoy! Lovely! London is certainly a great place for business! We will have you straight into your suite in a jiffy. We have everything ready exactly as requested. But dinner? Yes, well, no, the kitchen actually opens in a few hours, but the bar is always open."

David glared at the man, but it was Bugsy who replied: "Hamburgers and French fries. In the suite."

The man twitched. "Of course, we will make that especially and bring that right up to your suite, no problem, Mr. McKinney."

Mercifully, the innkeeper did not follow them upstairs. David needed the quiet. He checked the area from the windows of his suite. The north view was as monotonous as the village view: just a river lined with trees. His head was pounding after five days of drinking. He dropped onto the sofa and then noticed the silver tray with a bottle of Ballybeg Whiskey and a few glasses. The sight made him gag. He wandered into the bedroom to avoid it, fell onto the bed, and closed his eyes. But even then, his mind swirled around the events in England that had brought him here.

In London, David set his profit-churning charisma machine to full speed. He searched out the *Syndicat international de Tours*

and within hours, found himself dining in the Savoy Grill with Mr. Marcel Laurel and his partner, Mr. François Hardie. Bugsy was unable to stop laughing at their names. David tried kicking Bugsy beneath the table, despite knowing that the giant wouldn't feel anything short of a sledgehammer, then resorted to making the excuse that his friend had gone through dental surgery that afternoon.

A shady-looking character slid into the plush Savoy banquette beside them. He had a tough face, a heavy black moustache, and thick, black rimmed glasses. He said nothing but nodded and took another swig of whiskey whenever the phrases "economic development," "incentive schemes," or "tax exemptions" were mentioned.

Eventually, the new arrival spoke as Mr. Laurel nodded along. "The area is significantly under-populated, and previous governments have mollycoddled the locals' notions of preservation. It's time to stimulate the area with useful revenue-generating industries and force it to support its share of the GDP. This will bring thousands of new residents to the area. A greater need for infrastructure." The black moustache bobbed up and down again as the man neatly finished off a large glass of whiskey.

Mr. Hardie then revealed a schematic plan on his computer. The Syndicat was working on their first phase: Finn's Ultimate Ballybeg Amusements and Recreations plc; a signature amusement theme park with fun rides and games. This was to be their "toehold" in the area. They'd tried to buy land previously, but the Ballybeg farmers had resisted what Mr. Hardie described as their very generous offers.

Hardie's expression lightened. "This year, we are back. All we need to start development is one parcel, sixty or a hundred acres or so. If we can secure that one parcel, eventually the rest will follow. Your information, Mr. McKinney, suggests that you can play an important part. If—as you say—you are the inheritor of the McKinney parcel of land, and you sign on as a partner, we can secure that land and begin the development."

Mr. Laurel tapped his fingers together. "This is ... What is the English word?"

"Serendipity!" Mr. Hardie answered. "Yes." He plumped out his fat cheeks with a grin.

"Yes, it is." Laurel's smile stretched across his face.

The subsequent days of elevation drawings, pie charts, oysters, and whiskey were challenging for David. For example, once, he ordered a Heineken, and they still brought him whiskey. There was a constant huddle of attorneys who discussed the laws of the United Kingdom. David found this to be odd when the plan was for a project in Ireland, but he was happy to go along with the scheme. He thought it was brilliant and entirely suited to his talents.

Deployment started early this morning when a young bucktoothed law clerk dragged David out of bed when Bugsy was at the gym. The clerk filled him with overpriced orange juice while a crack team of estheticians steamed, pummelled, and trimmed him, and dressed him in a new grey suit. Bugsy materialized to accompany him to a private helicopter at Stansted Airport. *"Et voila!"* as Laurel would say, David arrived in Ballybeg as the head of Finn's Ultimate Ballybeg Amusements and Recreations plc, a major international retail and leisure development project, and with a personal development budget of £2.5 million.

David returned to the sitting room of his suite when he heard the burgers arrive. Bugsy was watching rugby on TV.

"Don't you have a TV in your room?" David asked as he stuffed the food into his mouth.

"Yes, Boss. But I need to keep an eye on you. I promised Kathleen." Bugsy cut his hamburger in half.

"Ah. Kathleen can make you do anything."

"Probably, Boss. But not because she's your daughter. I wouldn't do anything for Diane. It's just that Kathleen, even as a little girl, was always kind."

"She's just manipulating you. She's a chip off the old block."

"Does that mean you're manipulating me?"

"No. Forget it. Never mind."

"Okay, Boss."

The meal revived David. It was still only late afternoon. He had no desire for a walk, especially since it was raining, but he could at least start his reconnaissance of the area and the business community. The two men headed out to explore Ballybeg, starting with the Standing Stone pub. The space was underused, like most of the village. Inside, it was quiet. An old man sat on a stool at the side of the bar, a half-empty pint in front of him. He was reciting something in a loud voice to no one in particular:

"This is the story of the Lunatic. Long ago, he settled in a new land, where through cunning and tricks, he became very rich. He became very powerful, like a king in his own right. Although there were some that loved him, he was dissatisfied. He wanted nothing but gold and power but lacked the wisdom to use either well. Vain, selfish, and arrogant, he was blind..."

Clearly the village idiot, thought David, tuning the man out.

David and Bugsy approached the bar. The bartender, Archie, asked how their day was going. David boasted that he'd arrived by private helicopter from London.

"So, you're David McKinney then? Welcome home, son." The bartender placed two glasses of Ballybeg Whiskey in front of them. David said that he would prefer a Heineken instead. There was a conspicuous pause before the bartender responded, "No problem, son." A bottle appeared with a glass.

A few local businessmen wandered in. Archie introduced each one. Charlie the mechanic. Henry the banker. Mustapha the dentist. *So, all the little businesspeople,* David thought. Where was the mayor? The governor? But still, he turned on the charm and chatted easily. These small-time businessmen were always looking for an investment tip, so he placed the Finn's Ultimate investment prospectus on the bar as though it were an oversight. After a couple of Heinekens, he really felt like he was home with his own kind. This made him loquacious. He started asking questions:

"Say, I noticed that you fly the British flag. Why do you do that if you're in Ireland?"

"Ballybeg has a population of only a thousand people? Is that all? Why do you bother? Pack it in and live somewhere more interesting!"

As time passed, the responses he was getting seemed increasingly nonsensical, so David started his pitch session:

"So, here's what you want to know. Finn's Ultimate Ballybeg Amusements and Recreations plc, registered on the London Stock Exchange this week. It's easy for your broker to find; it's FUUK. A sixty-acre site for phase one. That's the theme park with rides and games, crazy golf, and a safari park."

Several residents shook their heads. One muttered, "Not another fecking safari park!"

David pushed on. "Thousands of jobs. Hundred-fold increase in local tourism. In phase two—that'll be in four years—we'll replace Dundurn Castle with a replica five-star hotel. Something new and useful, right? And for phase three, we are designing an oceanfront watersport park right on the causeway stones. By the time we're finished, the area will be unrecognizable. And you'll all be filthy rich."

Bugsy had retreated to the corner of the bar, where he was now chatting quietly with a tall man with a red bandana tied casually at his neck, whose shock of unruly blond curls repeatedly fell into his eyes. Occasionally, they paused to listen to the old drunk, who was still telling his story:

"… to summon from the otherworld a demon so reviled that the other demons are happy to be rid of him. But the witch transforms the demon into…"

David's presentation created quite the buzz in the room. He was certain that he had them onside with FU and had probably made a few new friends as well. He poked Archie in the ribs. "Britain would be toast if it wasn't for America. Just a bunch of wusses, right?" One by one, the enthusiastic Ballybeg business community made their excuses and ran home to their dinners.

David walked all the way back to the inn before realizing that Bugsy was still back in the Standing Stone, chatting to the large blond guy. Should he go back to get him? *No,* he thought, *even Bugsy's not so thick as to lose his way in this tiny village. Plus, if he's making friends, he can promote FU.* Not that he would give Bugsy a commission or anything.

Back in his room, David reviewed his first presentation while trying to find something other than rugby on the TV. He thought things had gone quite well so far and that Finn's Ultimate would soon be on the map of the coast. He would report to Laurel in the morning. It wasn't long before he was asleep.

Kara and the dog wandered the Aghnagoogh property while Imogen fetched the tea. Imogen's quintessential English country garden extended for an acre, with fuchsia and ivy marking its boundaries. Fruit trees clustered in corners near the stone walls. A miniature folly of an ancient Greek temple perched on a hillock to the northeast. To the south of the temple, a rose garden filled that corner of the garden and continued around to the front of the house. In the opposite back corner, in the northwest, a corrugated steel hut on wheels sat nestled in its own mini garden of local wildflowers, shaded by a large birch tree.

Imogen returned and set out tea and sandwiches on an elegant wrought-iron table on the back terrace, which was slightly elevated from the garden. They took their seats, and Imogen placed a Wedgewood cup and saucer before Kara's plate. Kara carefully lifted the cup with both hands and tried not to down the tea in one go. She envied the dog devouring a small plate of ham and potatoes, while she slowly helped herself to another cucumber sandwich.

"That dog has never had it so good," Imogen declared as she poured out another cup of tea. "That plate of ham disappeared in seconds."

"The dog must belong to someone. Have you no idea?"

"I've never seen it before. For a village of this size, that is rather odd, I admit." She offered Kara a faint smile. "Never mind, it's safe and comfortable enough. Now about this development —Tell me everything you know."

The dog was snoozing with her head planted firmly across Kara's foot. Kara felt more comfortable with Imogen's direct interrogation than McKay's sneaky conversations. Kara supposed that this was why she'd sought out Imogen Currie in the first place.

Where to start? Kara knew at least three key bits of the mystery. First, Michael Garrett had been arguing with two characters named Frank and Dennis outside the Standing Stone pub about possible plans of a foreign developer named Mr. Laurel. *Entertainment? Leisure? Where did I hear those words recently?* Then there was the remarkable interest of James McKay. It went beyond the gossip that was common in the village. He displayed a businessman's interest, keen to be in the loop before the rush. It dawned on Kara then that, in his French phone call, McKay had definitely referenced "your entertainment and leisure complex." And his contact had been from Paris but attending "planning sessions" in London. Finally, there had been the intense argument between McKay and Michael about a questionable land title, McKay's veiled threat to Kara about choosing sides, and his denying her a booking for the rest of the week as well as any of the assistance he had previously offered. Kara laid it all out in detail to Imogen, trying carefully not to add any guesses on her part.

Imogen looked up from her phone, where she was taking down notes. "My word! But you have no idea what site they are arguing about? Or the size of the project? Or who this Mr. Laurel might be?"

"No. And no. And no."

Imogen shook her head as she reviewed the notes. "I have no idea what is going on. It's quite clear that Michael and McKay know more than we do. We must get to the bottom of this. I'm going to call Michael and arrange a meeting."

Kara agreed, though she decided to take the dog for a brief walk along Beeswax Road first. Kara thought the dog looked happier after the serving of ham. Not only did she walk right beside her now, but the dog also allowed Kara to bend down and stroke her fur, even pushing her head into Kara's hand for the best of a good scratch. "Do you like that? Do you like that scratch? Maybe Scratch is a good name for you."

Kara passed the church and crossed onto the front pasture on Lisnasidhe. Scratch ran ahead along the path. Kara followed and walked closer to Rosheen Wood, at least as close as she could. The surrounding scrub grew very tight, heavy, and overgrown, full of weeds, long grasses, and fallen tree branches. Even worse, beyond the overgrowth, there was a barrier of thick brambles with intertwined blackthorn and hawthorn bushes.

This continued in all directions around Rosheen Wood. Kara circled it twice and still found no point of entry. However, behind the back of it and to the north, Kara discovered an apple orchard with a small clearing within it that was set apart. It was not overgrown. Kara found this strange. It was difficult to understand how everyone had allowed Rosheen Wood to close in on itself out of a fear of fairies. She wondered how dense it was. She could see the tops of trees, but all this was surrounded by the unbroken circle of tangled thicket. Kara tried to walk further into the overgrowth, but she was wearing the wrong shoes. If she wanted to see inside, she would need boots and tools.

She headed back to the road but stopped to admire the pond. It was about twenty feet long, barely six feet wide, and almost as deep. Its clear water revealed the multi-coloured stones on its bed. Small fish darted through the vegetation. Kara's reflection in the water seemed softer, somehow younger than how she felt. As she stared into the water, the sky above darkened. She lifted her head to study the sky. A black helicopter was flying overhead towards the village.

The wind was picking up. Clouds were rolling in from the coast, threatening rain. She started back down the road to Imogen's. In a moment, she realized that something was wrong. She turned on her heel, looking in all directions. Where did the dog go? *No! Where did Scratch go?*

There was no sign of her. Kara ran back up to the wooden gate and the apple orchard. Could the dog somehow have gone into the density of Rosheen Wood? Kara called her, but there was no movement, no sound. Carefully stepping around the overgrowth, she called again and again for the dog, retracing her steps around the perimeter of the grove. Nothing. Could Scratch have run back to Imogen's house? Kara didn't think that the dog could move that fast. It had tracked her in the village like a ninja; perhaps that was what it was doing now. But there were no footsteps, no shadows.

Scratch wasn't even her dog. Why should she care? Kara started back to Imogen's, but even as she did, she found herself walking slowly and calling out—just any old words and sometimes a bark, since Scratch wouldn't recognize her name.

Imogen looked up. "Did I hear you barking?" She studied Kara suspiciously.

"The dog is gone. Did she come back here?" Kara wandered the edge of the garden.

"No, I don't think so."

The two woman entered the house and sat down. It was quiet since each was wrapped up in their own concerns. Kara stared out at the gathering clouds. Imogen restlessly searched the internet for a hint regarding development plans for the area.

The wind brought the rain. Kara continued to peer out at the rain in case Scratch reappeared. Kara was concerned about the dog. She could have gone to her own home or taken shelter for the night. Or she could have found a new stranger to follow.

The landline rang. Imogen went into the hallway to answer it. Kara heard Imogen talking in a low voice for a while. Then she returned.

"That was Michael Garrett, returning my call. We can meet at the Standing Stone later. I hope you don't mind."

It took a few moments for Imogen's words to break into Kara's thoughts. *It makes no sense, waiting in a strange house for a strange dog to reappear.* She turned from the window then. "Whatever will help."

Imogen looked relieved. "Oh good. Our heritage legislation normally acts as an airtight barrier to thoughtless development. But the council has been known to be, umm, careless. If Michael Garrett has serious concerns, something must be going on. We can talk. We'll understand more if we put our heads together."

Kara felt engaged by this community issue. She hadn't felt that for a long time. "We might be able to help."

"Are you game?"

"Absolutely. The game's afoot."

"What did you say?"

"Nothing."

Imogen took Kara to the Standing Stone for the meeting with Michael. It was a few hours after dinner, and it bustled with villagers, whom Kara was beginning to recognize. Seamus sat at the front corner of the bar, a half-empty pint in front of him. He was speaking in a loud voice, and Kara assumed that he was in conversation until she noticed that, although some people were listening to him, no one spoke back. He was reciting again:

"On Midsummer Night, Coinnigh sought out the highest rampart of the castle in order to perform a special ritual to banish MacDhuibhfinn's army. As the sun set into the sea, Coinnigh unleashed his magic. The wind rushed in, the fairies gathered, and the fire leapt up to quicken the hearts of Coinnigh's soldiers and give them the strength to conquer their enemies." Same story. *That must become boring.*

"He's boring," Imogen announced. "I never listen to him."

Morag and Sarah whispered together in a way that suggested a good gossip session, then greeted Kara with a quick wave.

Michael must be very popular, thought Kara as she watched him command a large corner table by the window, with many people stopping to exchange words. Some took a seat for a longer chat. Michael stood as they approached the table. The others excused themselves. He heartily shook Kara's hand and welcomed her home to Ballybeg. He was, as she had noted the first time, tall, dark haired, attractive, and even younger looking than she remembered. A confident, intelligent man in his late twenties. The head of Ballybeg Biodiversity was professional, well spoken, and engaging, with a clear grasp of the important issues. He was familiar with Imogen's participation in any discussions regarding the historical assets and conservation policies and measures. Kara could see that he respected Imogen's opinions.

Kara volunteered to order a round of pints. Archie, the owner, served her. "So, you're the Canadian?" he acknowledged with a smile.

"Yes. Sorry."

He laughed. "I'll bring them over. No, don't apologize."

When Kara stood at the front, Seamus' voice could not be missed: "Coinnigh had three children, and each one different. Upon the news of their father's demise, they scattered to the ends of the earth with no possessions and no kin." He paused to drink his pint. "But the story foretells that they will return to fight a new battle."

Kara thought that was odd. Was this the same story? Was anyone else paying attention? She glanced at Morag, but she was nose to nose with Sarah. Kara looked to Imogen, whose long, thin fingers drew forms in the air as she spoke with Michael. She shook her head and reminded herself that Seamus just recited old folktales for the tourists.

She returned to the table. They discussed the questions and put all their facts together. Kara took notes. Mr. Marcel Laurel represented the *Syndicat international de Tours*. He was taking business meetings in London to push a development scheme for a combined retail-leisure complex worth £75 million in the area of the coastal road and requiring at least sixty acres.

A young couple sat at the next table. They were strikingly beautiful. Their skin glowed so warmly in the dim light of the pub that Kara assumed they were in love. The earthy natural colours and cut of their clothing suggested fashionable country but were made from a lightweight woven gossamer fabric that shimmered in the light of a nearby fireplace and could not have kept them warm on this rainy night. They held hands and stared silently into each others' eyes.

Michael expanded on what his office had discovered. "The local farmers told my assistant that two Frenchman had tried to buy their land several years ago, but no one had been interested in selling. Recently, they were seen in the area again. The rumour is that the French are looking for a workaround—an owner willing to supply the land in exchange for a corporate partnership. But they have hit a roadblock. The Syndicat won't give details to the media, but there have been a lot of searches at the Land Titles Office. Their solicitors keep going back there. It must be a question of property with an unclear land title, otherwise, they would already be moving forward with planning applications.

"Then, yesterday, McKay signed on with the Syndicat as an investor-slash-partner. He expects the Syndicat's development team to arrive in Ballybeg soon to set up their headquarters at his inn." Michael grimaced. "That's why I went to the inn to challenge him on it. He's always been an unscrupulous wee eejit! Oh, and some big cheese American partner is taking the project lead. Apparently, they met him at the Savoy and put him in charge."

The three of them had brought their heads so close together that they had not seen the small figure standing beside their table. Kara recognized her: a young girl named Fatima, who worked part time at the inn. She was holding Kara's large carpetbag with two hands. "I am very sorry, Ms. Gordon," she whispered as she let the bag drop with a thud to the wooden floor. "Mr. McKay told me to bring this to you and to tell you that he has cancelled your reservation for tonight."

Imogen admonished her. "Well, that's not very hospitable." The girl blushed.

Kara felt Fatima's discomfort and replied, "Don't you worry about that, dear. It's fine." The girl exited the pub. It wasn't fine. *Where am I going to sleep tonight?*

Imogen must have read Kara's expression. "Kara, it's not a problem. I have a shepherd's hut at the end of my garden. It's my guest house. You are welcome to stay in it as long as you want."

Kara remembered the small corrugated steel hut on wheels in the garden. It looked very cozy, but she said, "Oh no, Imogen, I can't impose on you!"

Imogen shook her head. "No, Kara, I insist. We can unravel this mystery together. You'll come home with me." She smiled at Kara. "And maybe the dog will reappear in the morning." Then she coldly returned to the matter at hand. She stressed every word, firmly tapping her index finger on the table as she spoke. "By every conservation policy developed at the national level, and supported by the local district council, this should be impossible, predominately due to the heritage status of the area. That alone should stop the concept dead."

Michael agreed. "Ballybeg Biodiversity needs to know what land is under consideration. That should have been part of the planning in order to evaluate the impact on the natural environment. But I can smell corruption already. Some political pressure at Westminster and Stormont is smoothing a path for the Syndicat. Someone is trying to peel away the red tape."

Imogen considered for a moment before speaking. "So, the impediment is a question of legal land ownership? Something like an unclear transfer of title?"

Michael nodded. "Yes. Because otherwise they would already be submitting applications to appeal the conservation laws, either the heritage or the environment, or both. They are not attempting an environmental survey because they know already it will fail. They won't even bother. But something has held them back. Something more mundane, like the question of ownership."

Michael pointed to a local property map on the table. "My assistant checked all the land records within the district. The only anomaly regarding the land title is Lisnasidhe. Its legal owner is only recorded as 'McKinnie.' No other identifying information. It's bizarre. But I think that's the land they want. It accesses both Beeswax Road on the south and the coastal road on the north."

Imogen shook her head. "It must be an error in the transcripts. That land belongs to the Andersons."

Kara jumped at the chance to correct Imogen: "Mary Anderson said they only rent that land."

Michael nodded again. "Correct, Kara. She owns Knocknageragh but pays rent to the church to graze their sheep on Lisnasidhe pasture. Her family has always leased it. They never knew who owned it."

Kara found all this exciting. "You think the land question is about Lisnasidhe? I was there today. It used to be the Sweeney farm." Her excitement shifted to sadness, thinking of the missing Scratch. As she went silent, she heard Seamus again, still reciting:

"Until the stars align and the separate become whole, the Mother and the sacred site are in danger from the Lunatic. He will approach with darkness in his heart."

Michael spoke up. "If the land ownership is the only thing that the Syndicat is waiting for, we need to find out first and start a full-on opposition to the plan. Which McKinnie, or McKinny, or McKinney is the real McKinnie?"

Kara ventured a thought. "I'm a McKinney. I mean, my grandfather was. If that helps."

Michael smiled. "And there are about a hundred other known living McKinneys in the area. The land title needs to be proven to be claimed."

Imogen leaned in. "Kara, there may be a need for a genealogist after all."

Kara opened her notebook and stared at the jumble of scribbles and post-it notes. She looked to her companions. "But like you said, everyone is related to everyone."

Imogen patted her hand. "I am confident you can untangle it."

Kara wasn't all that confident, but she insisted on picking up the bill.

They had started a campaign. Now, they strategized their next steps. Michael would review the land records and permit requests. Imogen would consult her governmental and non-governmental heritage-authority contacts for any relevant information. Kara's job would be to sort out her messy scrawled notes into a readable family tree and document the families with that name or similar.

The beautiful couple disappeared. On her way out, Kara waved goodbye to Morag and Sarah. They looked up and wished her well. As Imogen passed, the gossiping heads came together again as usual.

The last thing Kara heard was Seamus, whose recitation continued:

" ... while the village rejoices, the Lunatic will be held back by a magic spider's webs."

Five

Kara cracked open one eye. It was morning, grey and gloomy, but at least the rain had stopped. The crushing weight of guilt and disappointment kept her in bed a few more minutes. Her hope yesterday had been that the dog—that Scratch—would now be scrubbed clean and fed and curled up on the bed beside her. It was depressing to think that she was gone. Kara didn't know whether Scratch had returned to her home or wandered lost in the fields—or worse—in the dense and spooky Rosheen Wood. It was the last place that Kara had seen her. The previous night had been cold, windy, and wet—a horrible night to be left outside. She needed to find the dog. This determination forced her up. Wearing jeans and a baggy sweater, she crossed the garden, from the cozy shepherd's hut to the house, and wondered if Imogen was the kind of Englishwoman that would have coffee.

A vase of fresh-cut roses adorned the dining table. Imogen was quiet, floating about the kitchen effortlessly with minimal movement. *Do her feet actually touch the ground?* It was difficult to tell under the silk robe she wore. Kara was intimidated. She tried to pull her sweater straight. Imogen's fingers indicated the coffee machine and the pod collection, and the bread, fruit, and cheese on the table. Then she wandered off to find the newspapers and her phone.

She returned with a stack of newspapers and joined Kara at the table. Imogen nibbled at her toast and hid behind *The Guardian*. Kara finished her first cup of coffee and started her second. She wanted to know more about Rosheen Wood. "Have you ever tried to explore it?"

"No," declared *The Guardian*. "It's a fairy fort. An enchanted grove. Anyone who disturbs it will be cursed. You could be forced to dance to your death, or become invisible, or become trapped inside." Imogen peeked around the paper. "I could believe the last one. That is a very dense grove."

"I didn't think you would believe such things."

"I don't. But why risk it?"

"I think the dog may be there." Kara jumped up. "I'm going out to look for her."

Imogen surprised her. "I'll help you." She folded the newspaper neatly on the table. "I don't want you killed."

"By the fairies?"

"By the local farmers. I don't want you shot for trespassing."

Kara was not sure if Imogen was joking, but she was glad for her help.

Imogen changed and dug out an extra pair of wellingtons and a country jacket for Kara. A trip to the garden shed produced a loud whistle, binoculars, torches, gloves, two pair of large shears, and other garden tools. She also brought her rowan wood walking stick. In the garden, Imogen picked clumps of St. John's Wort and handed half to Kara. "Stuff that in all your pockets, just in case."

"In case I become nervous?"

"No. Fairies don't like St. John's Wort."

"The fairies you don't believe in."

Imogen did not reply but marched out onto Beeswax Road.

They began the search on the open fields and the road. Imogen stated that there was no point attempting Rosheen Wood if they didn't have to. Kara whistled and called. Imogen scanned the horizon with her field glasses for any animal that wasn't a cow or sheep. After an hour or so, they exchanged a look.

Kara started. "I guess we…"

"…look in Rosheen Wood," Imogen continued without enthusiasm.

Kara led the way now. She'd studied it yesterday from a variety of angles. They walked up the dirt road. The tangled overgrowth was as impenetrable as it was yesterday. Kara pointed to the tops of the trees, peeking up from inside, and the intricate circles within circles of overgrown scrub around the thorn bushes. Imogen examined them with a sigh and drew out the shears.

"At least now we have tools. We can cut all these plants, except this one with the berries. That's a protected species. We don't want Michael mad at us."

Each had their weapon and attacked the overgrowth to reach the thorn and bramble thicket. It took a while, but soon they cleared a path through the ground plants to the edge of the thicket. They were busy widening the cleared pastureland when Kara heard someone called out "Imogen!" from the road.

It was Reverend Nesbitt and his wife out for their morning cycle. As the women approached the pair, Kara heard a sort of squeal. She paused. It was likely a birdcall.

Nesbitt looked excited. "I have news! We have another McKinney! He arrived yesterday!"

"My word. It's a gathering of the clan," drawled Imogen. "Any chance that he is an American?"

Before he could reply, his wife asked what they were doing. Kara explained that they were looking for a dog. Mrs. Nesbitt insisted that she call her Esmée and then offered to help. She started with advice. "You need to be careful what you cut around here. For instance, that's an alder buckthorn. Definitely off limits! I am a senior member of the Friends of the Ballybeg Woodland Society." Esmée pulled work gloves from her small bag. "Give me those shears." She started to clear the scrub.

Nesbitt coughed and returned to his late-breaking news. "Yes, American. David McKinney from Wisconsin. He arrived by helicopter from London and is staying at the inn with an associate. He met a few local businessmen in the pub yesterday afternoon. He said that he's the front man for a new development called Finn's Ultimate Ballybeg Adventure and Recreation, funded by investors from France."

"FUBAR?" Kara's Canadian mind quickly skated over every nasty comment one could make about an American but decided to take the high road. After all, he might be a cousin, and ethical and, with any luck, smart.

"He was in the Standing Stone last night. Everyone seems to think he's a bit mad."

Kara bit her lip. "Mad? Like a lunatic?" She knew the moon was full now.

Nesbitt quoted, in fairly colourful language for a priest, the report he'd heard from Leo the Butcher—who'd heard it from Charlie the Mechanic, who had been at the pub the previous afternoon— all about the presentation made by David McKinney from Wisconsin, USA.

Imogen groaned. "Not another bloody safari park. And crazy golf? How tedious." She continued to hack away vigorously at the overgrown scrub.

Imogen imagined the weeds as David McKinney's head. He was the worst sort of invader. Foreign money trying to take over. It endangered the precious heritage that she had trained and worked all her career to preserve. She muttered, "It starts with the fairy forts; then it's the old church; then the older neighbourhoods are cleared away for what they call progress but is really just greed." The very thought of David McKinney angered her.

The sun cleared most of the clouds, and the weeds and the branches were soon not quite as wet, making them easier to cut through. Mrs. Nesbitt—Esmée—was clipping away as if she were saving someone's life. Imogen imagined that this was because of the missing dog. The two of them wasted little breath talking as they chopped their way into the weeds.

The late morning light was trickling down into the interior of Rosheen Wood, illuminating patches but revealing nothing solid. Suddenly, Kara screamed.

"What is it?" Nesbitt looked around.

"Something moved." Kara lifted her boots, alternating between left and right.

Just then, a pure white rabbit bolted from the overgrowth and flew over the corner of the pond, across the field, and was gone.

"A rabbit." Imogen sighed. "No rabbits in Canada?"

"Yeah, well—I'm a city girl."

The aggressive clearing of the ground vegetation was finally showing results. There was now an access path but the four still faced the impenetrable wall of interwoven brambles, blackthorn, and hawthorn. Esmée stopped cutting and requested an iron nail. Surprisingly, her husband pulled one straight out of his pocket and handed it to her.

Imogen explained to Kara that iron was another protection from the fairy folk. "The intertwined thorn bushes are a powerful enchanted barrier. As well as darn hard to cut through."

Imogen's phone bleeped, and she read aloud the message from Michael: "Heads up! McKay is on his way with David McKinney. I am following as fast as I can."

McKay's BMW approached. Imogen called out to Kara. "We have visitors!" The group turned to walk back to the road.

The BMW pulled up. McKay waved and got out of the car. Another man in an expensive but wrinkled grey suit, with his jacket open and no tie, dashed out and overtook the innkeeper. He bounded over the corner of the pond and onto the path. With a decidedly American accent, he cried, "Stop! Whoa! What do you think you're doing!" A third man, massive and solid-looking, stood silently beside the car.

A shot of electricity ran up Imogen's spine. David McKinney. She felt disdain at first glance. The epitome of the brash American, charging in where he did not belong. She replied to his question with a frozen stare. *Lisnasidhe must be the mystery property, after all.* She gripped her hedge cutters.

Michael arrived next, attempting a brisk authoritative walk, holding out a hand as if to do introductions. Then the arm came down again, and he waited.

Nesbitt spoke first. "We are searching for a missing dog. We think it may be in here, but we need to clear a path to enter."

McKay blurted out, "Lisnasidhe is not your land."

Kara replied, "It's not yours either."

David stepped closer to Kara. "You're American?"

"Canadian."

David pulled back. "Oh." Then with wide, sweeping movements, declared, "I have an interest in all this land."

"An interest?" scoffed Imogen. "What's that when it's at home?"

David's eyes narrowed at Imogen. Although his mouth moved, he was speechless.

McKay stepped in. "The land, um, Lisnasidhe—We have reason to think it's David McKinney's land, so—"

Michael interrupted. "There's no proof of that yet. So far, the owner of Lisnasidhe is unknown."

McKay shrugged. "No proof *yet*."

Michael continued. "Yet. Period. Therefore, Dr. Nesbitt and the women can cut through the overgrowth to look for the wee missing dog." Silence on all sides. "You *could* offer a hand."

McKay snorted and started back to the car. David drifted closer to Kara and Imogen. For several seconds, he stared at both women, and they stared back. In that moment, Imogen heard a strange sound nearby, like fingernails drawn across a blackboard. Was it the screech of a bird? She searched above her head.

McKay reached the car and called back to the American. "David? Mr. McKinney? Let's go back to the inn. You might want to ring your solicitors."

David's gaze pivoted to McKay. "My what?"

"Your attorneys."

David inched backwards slowly until he reached the car. The three men jostled into their seats, and they drove off as quickly as they had arrived.

Michael started to roll up his sleeves. "Do you have another pair of shears?" Kara smiled and handed the tool to Michael.

Now five strong, the group turned around to tackle the barrier of the thicket. They returned to the spot where they had been working.

What Imogen found confused her. In the place of an impenetrable barrier, there was now an opening of several metres through the thicket. "Do you see that?"

The rest confirmed that, as bizarre as it seemed, the thicket was now open.

Kara did not hesitate to walk through the opening, her hand outstretched. "Weird, eh?"

Esmée collapsed onto the nearby stone wall, clutching her iron nail. Michael paced back and forth along the edge, studying the brambles and the thorns. Nesbitt stood back and removed his hat to scratch his head.

Esmée shuddered. "This could be a fairy trick to lure us inside and trap us." She tried to peer inside but only from the safety of the wall.

The opening revealed a large sunny clearing within Rosheen Wood, in which Kara stood transfixed. The clearing was encircled with every possible tree—oak, pine, willow, rowan, and ash—and just as many plants and wildflowers. To Kara's right, nearest the opening, a massive ancient oak tree entwined with ivy seemed to be the oldest of them all, guarding the point of entry.

Michael passed Kara and examined the plants. Imogen was the third to walk into the clearing, which she calculated to be approximately a quarter acre of open space inside Rosheen Wood—a living, vibrant forest. The rustle of small animals and birdsong convinced her that there was nothing unnatural about Rosheen Wood, except how they'd accessed it.

The centre was completely clear except for a stone circle of a firepit, rising from the ground. On the north side were the ruins of a cottage: a traditional eighteenth-century building with whitewashed stone walls. The thatched roof had been blown away over time, the timber supports deteriorated, and the tops of the walls were crumbling. A faded and cracked red door hung diagonally by one hinge. The cottage looked very small in the clearing of the trees. Imogen needed to see this building, fairy trap or not. She pulled her phone out to record her findings.

It was about twenty feet long and eleven feet wide. A tall stone chimney remained intact. Some sections of the roof's wooden frame remained. Imogen stepped carefully across the threshold of the cottage. Inside, time and wind had blown dirt throughout. Kara followed her.

There was a movement at the base of the chimney. Kara cried out, "It's her! It's Scratch! She's fine."

"Oh bother," Imogen cursed as the dog started bounding happily around their feet. "Great." *The creature is back.* Kara rushed about after Scratch to lift her up. Imogen tried to ignore them both. She raised her eyes and was distracted by an ornate carving in a central stone on the chimney. *Now this is interesting!*

The next distraction was an excited cry from Michael, who had wandered into the trees to study the ecosystem. Imogen frowned. Michael's normal attitude was calm and professional. Only something quite awful could excite him. "Three separate dreys!" he called out.

Imogen wanted to focus on her cottage, in particular the chimney, but she stepped outside and strode after Michael. "I beg your pardon? What's a drey?"

He swept his arm to indicate a number of trees. He was like a child on Christmas morning. "Dreys! That's ... squirrel nests ... red squirrels." He tiptoed to where Mrs. Nesbitt waited outside, and in a hushed voice, said, "Esmée! Come quickly! Red squirrels!"

Imogen felt she was being observed. Fearing that fairies could be real, she looked about. On a branch of a hazel tree, a russet-red squirrel with tufts on the top of its ears watched her. It boasted an exceptionally fluffy tail. It was cute, of course, but why was it exciting?

Esmée took Michael's hand and followed him inside the grove. At the sight of the squirrels, she giggled and let go. She tried to explain to Imogen in breathless half sentences: "Endangered native species. Wildlife Order 1985 Schedule 5. European Squirrel Initiative? No?" She gave up and asked Michael. "Three dreys? Three?"

"Yes! Look! Here and on this tree, and this one too. At least eight kittens. No wonder! Look at the healthy food supply around here!"

"It's a natural red squirrel conservation centre."

"It's indisputably a Special Area of Conservation. It's not just the reds, although they are the stars. The plants, the birds, the butterflies." Michael's voice dropped. "Esmée, you have to be in charge of this. Call the other members of the Ballybeg Friends of the Red Squirrel. Organize the team."

Esmée saluted. "Save the reds!"

Imogen returned to the cottage to photograph the stonework and search for any objects that might be buried in the dirt floor. She ran her fingers across the ornate carving. It was unusual. After some time, Michael called out, "Imogen, we're done here!" Nesbitt was studying the round firepit at the centre of the clearing. Michael and Esmée joined him. Kara cradled Scratch in her arms.

Imogen stepped out of the cottage, wiping her hands. "For now, perhaps," she replied. There was much more to explore. "I will need to come back later." She hesitated. What if the thicket closed up again? *Is it worse if it closes when I'm inside or outside?* Probably better to go out and see if it stayed open. Definitely safer. Of course, she didn't believe in all that. She checked that she still had the St. John's Wort in her pockets.

The five made their way back to the road. Esmée rushed home to call a meeting of the Ballybeg Friends of the Red Squirrel. Nesbitt gathered up the bicycles that his wife had forgotten. Kara made ridiculous cooing sounds to her dog.

Michael stood beside his red 1940 Ford pickup. He was talking rapidly on the phone to his biodiversity officers, telling them to expect a workplan update. Then he offered Kara and Imogen a short hop in the truck. Kara lifted up Scratch and took her seat.

Imogen looked back. The grove was still open, and she opted to stay behind. She wanted some alone time with the old cottage. She could take more pictures and send them to the Ulster Museum. *There are no fairies.*

Six

Kara awoke at the first light. Scratch was snuggling with her foot. Two days had passed. Kara and the dog slept in the shepherd's hut and took long walks at Lisnasidhe. The thicket at Rosheen Wood remained open and no one had a sensible explanation for what they'd experienced. Michael returned with his crew every day for new tests. Esmée busied herself with notations on the habitat of the red squirrels. Imogen was pursuing architectural elements of the cottage that she believed could be archeologically interesting, burying herself in her study, either researching or making phone calls to colleagues.

Kara felt alone in trying to understand the phenomenon of the thicket, but even she was somewhat distracted by Scratch. A long bath and some grooming revealed that Scratch was at least part West Highland Terrier and not very young. Kara lay on her side, petting the dog. A great peace engulfed her. The various dramas— of McKay and David, Michael, Seamus, the Friends of the Red Squirrel, and the Yarnbombers—all floated away, and she could hardly remember why she'd come to Ballybeg in the first place.

As if to remind her, Scratch stretched a paw to touch Kara's locket. The carefully polished silver glinted in the sunlight. "Do you like that?" Kara murmured to the dog. "That locket belonged to my great-grandmother. It was a gift from her mother. It came from here, just like you." Kara always wore the locket. She had only two objects from her great-grandmother: the locket and a studio photograph of her in middle-age. In the picture, she wore the silver locket. The locket had a glass front, and on the back, an engraved five-point star. It was sealed shut, but the glass front revealed its contents: an elaborate mourning braid of hair and a small brass key with a star-shaped bow. The lock of hair was from Kara's great-great-grandmother. It was unclear what the key symbolized. As she'd heard it, her great-grandmother had left Ballybeg with her husband and children to start a new life in Glasgow in the 1890s, and her mother had given her the locket as a keepsake for fear they would never be together again.

The locket reminded Kara that she needed to do her genealogy research. She'd promised a more detailed McKinney family tree. She texted her genealogist contacts from the conference. They could access the Belfast and Dublin archives for documentation.

She turned to her laptop to search for family names, but her mind wandered back to Seamus' garbled folktales. She was drawn to his strange stories. So instead of research, she googled "Seamus McNamara Ballybeg." He'd never made any videos himself, but she found a BBC clip from a 1979 program called *Country Folk Tales*. The interviewer started simply:

"Tonight, we are in County Antrim in Northern Ireland. If you find yourself in the small village of Ballybeg, you might encounter one of its most colourful raconteurs, Mr. Seamus McNamara. Now, Mr. McNamara, you have lived in Ballybeg all your life?"

"Yes, sir. Born and bred and buttered."

"And you have made a lifetime of collecting all the old stories of the wee folk, the leprechauns and the pooka, the enchanted ring forts, and the water sprites?"

"Yes. I have done that."

Seamus didn't seem very colourful or chatty for a raconteur, although he was a great deal younger here in 1979.

The interviewer invited him to share one of his stories with the viewers at home. Seamus took a swig of his ale and a deep breath and began to speak with great gravity and resonance:

"In Ireland, there are many tales of fairy folks and their tricks. Many of you would use the word leprechaun, but a leprechaun is only one type of fairy—one who likes to hoard gold. There are other types of fairies who will swap your baby for one of their own, and those who will enchant you to dance to your death. There are some types, called brownies, who, for a bowl of milk, will do your housework. But watch out! For fairies seldom do anything that will benefit you, and an angry brownie will turn malicious very quickly. There is always a trick attached to the deal.

"Many nights, I sit out near the fairy forts, especially if it is a full moon. I listen to the stories the fairies tell each other. This is one of those stories. It is an old tale about the return of the children of Coinnigh, the unfortunate druid who fell into the sea during the battle of Dundurn Castle against Domhnaill MacDhuibhfinn. This is the story of one of the children. This is the story of the Lunatic. Long ago, he settled in a new land, where through cunning and tricks, he became very rich. He became very powerful, like a king in his own right. Although there were some that loved him, he was dissatisfied. He wanted nothing but gold and power but lacked the wisdom to use either of them well. Vain, selfish, and arrogant, he was blind to all understanding and reason. He could not foresee his enemies. Nor could he recognize his friends. He laughed at the people and mocked the fairies. Some said he was cursed by the fairies for this. His only hope was his daughter. She was joyful and loved him, but he cared little. Eventually, his queen and his court turned against him.

"He ran away and became a fugitive, seeking new wars and new fortunes in other countries. He had only one remaining servant: a Warrior who had fought with many wizards. The Lunatic treated the Warrior very badly. Despite the Lunatic's foul moods, this Warrior had sought redemption from his miserable youth by swearing an oath to stay beside the Lunatic out of loyalty to his master's daughter.

"The two still wander the earth. The fairy folk know that one day, the Lunatic will arrive in Ireland. They know that no one will trust him, and no one will want him.

"The fairy folk love to vex those who are vain or foolish. The Lunatic is both. If he wants gold, the fairy folk will give him gold. Of course, this will not satisfy him. He wants everything, and he will try to take it. The fairy folk dance for joy since it has been years since so perfect a target wandered onto the land, and they will have their fun.

"The Lunatic is angry that everyone blocks his path. He decides that he will destroy anything he cannot have for himself. The Warrior tries to distract him from destruction. The fairy folk will not help him. There is a Witch, who creates diversions and tricks to keep him from his goals. There is a High Priestess, who invokes the higher powers to stop him. Even the devils who first enticed him with stories of limitless fortune and power turn against him.

"One night, he uses his magic stone to summon from the otherworld a demon so reviled that the other demons are happy to be rid of him. But the Witch transforms the demon into—"

The broadcast cut to the BBC news desk. "And now we are going to an update on the transport workers' strike. It's over to Roger, reporting from Kingston upon Hull. Roger?" The clip ended.

Kara shook her computer as if more would fall out of it. "What did the Witch transform the demon *into*? And who's the Witch? For that matter, who's the High Priestess?"

She needed to talk to Seamus directly. More than a week had passed since she'd first seen him reciting his poem at her. She should have talked to him sooner. She called Morag.

Morag said that Seamus was away, walking the hills with his grandson, Liam, and wouldn't return for days.

"Can't he be reached?" Kara asked.

"No, no mobile phone, I'm afraid. He won't have anything to do with them. He is communing with nature, or with the fairies, if you believe him."

The problem was that Kara was starting to believe in fairies. She wandered across the garden.

Aghnagoogh buzzed. When they'd first met, Imogen had seemed rather reserved and quiet. Now, Imogen talked constantly and of little other than the Rosheen Wood cottage. It always began the same way: "In thirty years' work in local conservation, I have never seen—"

There were emails from Belfast, Dublin, and London and opened books and schematic drawings littering Imogen's lounge and dining room. Michael also dropped by frequently on his way to and from the grove, where his team were classifying the protected species. Books about biodiversity were piling up, and clippings in specimen bags were lined up in Imogen's refrigerator. Kara wiped up the kitchen and kept the kettle boiling. Breakfast was challenging. Kara needed to clear two spots at the table—three if Michael arrived, chattering about red squirrels.

One morning, Imogen reached out and took Kara's toast without looking as she thumbed through a book on Irish farm structures. "I must go back today for soil samples," she announced as she passed the butter dish to Kara, who caught it before it landed in her coffee mug.

Imogen sipped her morning tea from a Royal Albert mug. "This cottage has heritage significance. There's a section for the cow as well as the farmer and his family. You might think it odd, but they were all warm, dry, and secure together."

"Yes, I'm aware," Kara responded as she moved her plate further from Imogen. "I studied social history at the University of Toronto. The cow was the most valuable thing a farm family owned." Sheep could huddle in the pen. Hens were cheaper and stayed in the chicken coop. Cows were expensive but provided a new calf each year, daily milk for cooking, and eventually, meat and leather. To keep the cow inside at night deterred thieves and added another large body to warm the inside of the home in cold weather. As a child, Kara had imagined the family all curled up on top of the cow, but she later understood that the cow was at one end of the home and the family the other.

Imogen's books included images of a typical structure of arranged stone with a thatched roof on a wooden frame. On the residence side, there was a large fireplace and recessed beds in the walls. Wooden chairs sat close to the fire. Cabinets would hold the few possessions. They cooked over the fire. The cottage in Rosheen Wood seemed to conform to this layout.

Kara and Scratch returned to the cottage with Imogen. With the thatching blown away and the wood frame disintegrating, only the stone remained mostly intact. Kara felt a tingly premonition and instinctively clutched her locket. "I can feel the fairies here."

"Poppycock!" Imogen pointed out details in the stonework and dictated notes into her phone. The detailed stone carving on the chimney continued to capture her attention for a long time.

Kara imagined living there in the past. The recess in the stonework that would have held a bed seemed small. She supposed that cuddling up together was the best way to stay warm. She sat there and pulled Scratch up beside her. The dog gave a few small barks, looked up to catch Kara's attention, and then poked her nose into a corner of the stone wall. Kara bent down to peek in. Something metallic caught the sunlight. On an interior shelf, there was a small brass strongbox. She pulled it out and took it to Imogen.

Imogen turned it over. "Look at this metal worker's mark. A simple hand-manufactured brass strongbox circa mid-sixteenth century." A five-point star was engraved on the lid. It was locked. "Well made"—Imogen paused a moment—"and secure, I see."

They took the box back to the house to examine it. Imogen produced a paper bag of old keys. None worked. She tried to pick the lock without breaking it. The engraved star on the box matched the one on her locket and an obvious possibility struck Kara: the key within her locket. She turned the locket from side to side in the full sunlight, comparing the key to the lock. The locket's glass was old, thick, and rather smoky. The silver locket was her only cherished heirloom. It would be desecration to break it. *How badly did she want to open the brass box?*

Imogen held the two items together. "The key does *look* the right size."

Kara's tears welled up. "The locket is sealed shut. I would have to break it. What if it doesn't work?" Her keen curiosity and her reverence for the past were splitting her in half. Her intuition nagged her to do it, but her need to honour her family fought back.

She cradled the locket in her hand and heard her grandmother's voice crying out: "*Whit's fur ye'll no go by ye.*"

In one motion, she smashed the glass front flat onto the table, then slowly lifted the locket. The hair and the key spilled out. With a shaking hand, she tried the key in the lock. It opened.

She carefully lifted the lid of the strongbox. Inside were postcard-sized pictures and a small stack of letters tied with a pink ribbon. Also tied into the ribbon was a gold ring. When Kara tried it, the ring fit her finger nicely.

The letters were from Kara's great-grandmother, Greta Sweeney McKinney, living in Glasgow, and were addressed to "Mrs. Margaret Sweeney, Lisnasidhe, Ballybeg." The dates were between 1898 and 1911, and the salutation was always the same: "My dear mother." The contents revealed something of Greta and her family. "Glasgow is busy, crowded, and noisy, and I need to clean the soot from my windows every day, but Robert has good work, and the church and schools are helpful. The women you meet here come from all over. The *craic* is not as good, but I learn new things every day."

In 1900, she'd written, "I worry that my da works the farm himself. It's too bad about the McKays. My mother-in-law's family was always stuck up. If only our Davy had lived, Da would not be struggling alone. Every day, our William asks if he is big enough to come in the summer and help with the cows. It will not be too long now." The letters spoke of some things Kara didn't understand and some of which she knew. "Our William" was, of course, her grandfather. Through the letters, Kara read her history firsthand. There were hints of the homesickness and the frustration in choosing between earning a living or being with the family.

The photographs extended over a longer time period. Dating the images by the subject's clothes, the earliest were likely the 1860s. Kara later tried to lay them out in chronological order across the floor. A pleasant middle-aged couple in the Sunday best; a fair-haired young woman in the uniform of a house servant; a serious young couple on their wedding day, stiff and upright; and several more. There was a group photo of children, from the 1860s or 1870s, set in a summer meadow, all tousled hair, scrapped elbows, and grins. Another photo was of a later Edwardian group of children with a woman, scrubbed and proper in their best clothes. In a shaky hand, someone had carefully added their names and ages on the back: Roseann (14), William (12), Mary (9), and Margaretta (8 months). The woman in this photo, as in the portrait Kara already had, bore an undeniable likeness to Kara. In 1904, Greta had written, "I have enclosed a recent photograph of myself and the children. As you see, they are growing so big, and this is the first with the baby."

Kara sat quietly with the letters and the photographs arranged around her. This was a treasure trove that she valued more than the whole of Lisnasidhe. She could repair the locket, but the writing of her own great-grandmother had revealed her love for her family, her friends, and for Ballybeg. Although the letters were over a century old, they gave Kara a strong sense of belonging—a sense that she was finally where she ought to be.

She examined the gold ring. The engraving read, "Margaret Grainger Sweeney." Her great-great-grandmother's wedding ring? The engraving included the symbols for the moon and the sun, and the pentacle inside a circle. Kara slipped it back onto her finger and kissed it gently.

When Kara attempted to discuss her feelings with Imogen, she was ignored. The subject was quickly changed to a discussion about stonework and foundations. It wasn't fair that her cousin had been disconnected from the unknown, missing great-great-grandfather, and that the village had shamed her for it. But what concerned Kara most was that it made Imogen cold and unsympathetic, when her witchy intuition told her that Imogen was nothing of the kind.

Seven

*A*llow *me to interject: Hello Culture Vultures. Make a cup of tea; this might take a bit of concentration. Feel free to take notes. There will not be a test. Let us begin.*

The fragrant meadows of May are about to yield to the warmth of June. Kara and Scratch sit at the fireplace in the little guest hut. She marks her whiteboard with the family tree, but the best she can give you are dates connected by lines. Allow me to provide the fleshed-out version. You may have noticed that there are a lot of family names here, and many are repeated, but McKinney pops up a lot. Imogen doesn't want to talk about it. Kara can hardly speak of anything else. David doesn't care.

This story starts quite simply: In 1825, under the large birch tree where the shepherd's hut sits now, James McKinney proposed to the girl next door, a healthy, capable young woman named Catharine Anderson, and they called home his father's farm, Aghnagoogh. Catharine's family had Knocknageragh, just along the road. Both farms were successful. Catharine's brother ran Knocknageragh, and he had a great aptitude for raising sheep. James and Catharine inherited the tenancy of Aghnagoogh when James' father died. They had three children that survived infancy. Can you imagine the three children? Twin boys and then later a girl? Then picture, in your mind, three lines—one stemming from each of them.

John and David McKinney were twins. John was the older twin. He was responsible and hard working. From an age younger than you think appropriate, he was out in the fields with his father every day and was destined to take over the farm.

David, the younger twin, was impatient and ambitious. James knew he wasn't useful on the farm. He used his small savings to buy David an apprenticeship to a carpenter in Belfast. In 1844, when David was sixteen, Catharine was shocked to receive her son's letter from America. David had snuck aboard a ship as it sat in the Belfast harbour and ended up somewhere called Wisconsin. His parents never heard from him after that letter. You will not be surprised to learn that this line is the source of our present-day David.

After the twins came a baby girl, christened Margaret Ann but called Peggy Ann. She grew up attractive, good natured, and sharp as a tack. She helped in the kitchen and around the farm. When she was old enough, she took extra work as a domestic servant in the finer houses.

The decades were hard, for me and for the people. James and his son, John, took any work they could find. Catharine had two more children who did not survive. Little Peggy Ann was often sick. The McKinneys struggled to keep the family together, and they were lucky. They were unashamed to have nothing but their lives together.

By 1855, times were a little better. John married Agnes McKay. The McKays lived not too far away. They were upright and uptight. Nothing met their high standards, and they shared their opinions freely. Catharine McKinney held that the McKays sounded like chickens cackling in the yard, criticizing their neighbours behind their backs. In time, the neighbours responded in kind. Agnes McKay and John McKinney were married on a cold, sombre November day in the Ballybeg Parish Church. It was a while before they had their son, whom they named Robert McKay McKinney, after her father.

Typhus took John McKinney at thirty-six. As Agnes walked back from the funeral, the widow announced that she could not abide her parents-in-law and wanted a better life for her and her boy. She discovered her options to be limited. Her own parents thought it inappropriate for her to come back to them. In a panic, Agnes accepted an offer to stay with her childhood friend Margaret Grainger, who had married William Sweeney, a dairy farmer. The Sweeneys lived at Lisnasidhe in a strange old cottage nestled in a clearing of Rosheen Wood. They say that the fairies protected the Sweeney family because fairies like cream. They also say Margaret Grainger Sweeney was a witch. The widowed Agnes and baby Robert moved in. The fairies (if there were fairies) did not like Agnes, and soon she was off into the village to find work in a shop. Robert stayed back with the Sweeneys. Let us leave him there on Margaret Sweeney's lap for the moment.

James and Catharine McKinney's Peggy Ann secured a position as a domestic servant at the estate of a wealthy banker. Catharine paid for a photographic portrait of Peggy Ann in her new uniform, dressed head to toe in neatly pressed black and white linen, her long blonde hair pinned up, and her head held high. Catharine admired the portrait often. Friends said that she had a stately air about her. Folks were certain she would do well for herself and could marry a butler or a head groundskeeper.

Peggy Ann was twenty when she declared to her parents that she was going to have a child. She refused to name the father. It was the scandal of the village. She named her daughter Roseann McKinney. The otherwise stern James McKinney refused to turn away his daughter and granddaughter. He chose instead to keep them both close by. James and Catharine could not pretend the baby was theirs. The whole village and the townlands thought they knew the truth. The speculation as to the father's identity was rampant in the market and before and after church. Peggy Ann never divulged her secret. She never married. She kept her child.

We return to William and Margaret Sweeney, in the cottage with the fairies, with their son, Davy, and daughter, Greta, and Robert McKay McKinney, who grew up alongside them. Occasionally, Robert's mother Agnes would appear from town with a new toy. She would promise to take him soon, but she never did. Robert was happy as a member of the Sweeney clan, and William Sweeney allowed the boy to be a part of both his McKinney and McKay families.

Davy, Greta, Robert, and Roseann were frequently together. Four wonderful children. They hiked up the hills from Knocknageragh and lay on the grass on a summer day. They foraged for berries in Rosheen Wood. They climbed trees and picked apples. They helped the fishers bring in the salmon from the rivers. Davy and Robert stretched taller. They worked together on both the McKinney and Sweeney farms. Greta and Roseann were inseparable friends. Greta vowed to punish anyone who teased Roseann. Greta could protect Roseann from the other children, but as they approached womanhood, she soon discovered she could not defend her from the adults.

A few of the tenant farmers bought the land their families had worked for centuries. James McKinney gained new hope as the grandchildren grew up. He raised the funds to buy Aghnagoogh from the Sixth Duke of Inish-Rathcarrick as Catharine Anderson's brother bought Knocknageragh. But William Sweeney decided to wait.

Catharine McKinney watched her grandchildren as she grew old. Sometimes, she imagined that somewhere, perhaps Wisconsin, David had also had children, and if he brought them home, they would run in the fields and hills with their cousins. "One day, perhaps," she would murmur, and the wind would echo her wish to the trees. Catharine did not last much longer, but I hold her in my eternal embrace.

No one, in the village or on the townlands, allowed Roseann to forget her shame—a shame that wasn't even her own. On the day she turned fourteen, she escaped to England to restart her history. Unlike her uncle David, she wrote home to assure her grandfather, her mother, and her friend Greta that she was more cautious than her mother, and that she would be proper and industrious. Roseann held out until a promising Cambridgeshire greengrocer married her. From that day, she instilled lofty expectations in her own daughter and granddaughters. Her descendants ascended from grocery to accounting to the law—the girls, at first, only by marriage but eventually in their own right. And that, my dears, is how one rises from a scandal of the farming fields to the top of the church tower, overlooking the village.

Greta Sweeney judged Robert McKay McKinney to be the strongest, bravest, and kindest boy in all the world. When her brother Davy died in an accident in 1886, the two childhood friends were together in their common grief. They walked the hills side by side, then hand in hand. It was no surprise when they married in 1888.

The nineties brought a whole new world. Robert found work with Harland and Wolff in Belfast. The future would be shipbuilding. Greta was torn between staying with her parents or being with her husband. After a year or so apart, Greta took the children and joined her love. That family line travelled from Ballybeg to Belfast, then to Glasgow, and eventually to Toronto. From whence comes Kara.

Peggy Ann McKinney died a little too young, leaving her father, now ninety-two, alone. The year before, in Cambridge, Roseann had given birth to his English great-granddaughter Molly. James sold Aghnagoogh to a local farmer. Soon, he joined his wife and daughter.

The Andersons of Knocknageragh continued to raise a growing flock of sheep. Margaret and William Sweeney lived alone but happy in the cottage in the grove of Rosheen Wood on Lisnasidhe, with their cows. Greta Sweeney McKinney wrote letters frequently to her mother and sometimes included photographs. Each summer, as Kara was told, her grandfather came back to help his Sweeney grandfather tend the cows. That is, until William Sweeney died, and the land changed hands.

Now, that is a lot more specific detail than Kara will ever be able to confirm. If you study her family tree lines long enough, you can surmise the way it happened. But I give this to you happily as your time is valuable, while mine is … well … infinite.

Kara had spent the last twenty minutes studying Imogen and had come to the conclusion that the woman spent too much time studying. What's the point of sitting in the garden on such a lovely day if you waste it doing research? She was currently occupied with a pile of heavy, old books, an open notebook, and a poised pencil. Kara chased Scratch in wide circles around Imogen to distract her. It did not work. She shuffled over to Imogen. "More work on the church? What do you call it? Water ingress?"

"No. I am researching the Rosheen Wood cottage. It might be even older than I thought. At least the site, if not the building."

"Oh?" Did it matter how old it was? It was definitely old. Old enough not to be knocked down. That was clear.

Kara waved her hand in front of Imogen. "I want to show you how we are connected."

Imogen cleared her throat. Then in a flat tone, she recited by rote: "We do not speak of the past. It was horrible. We have risen above all that."

"Isn't it strange though that your grandmother Molly—the same woman who taught you that—also insisted on buying Aghnagoogh, the very property her own mother had wanted to escape?"

"She was a complicated woman. I suppose it was not enough to put the past behind her. She also wanted to show the village how successful we had been at doing it."

"She wanted to rub their collective nose in it."

"Yes," Imogen conceded.

Kara disappeared into her hut and dragged out her large, new whiteboard filled with names and dates. Imogen threw a quizzical look.

Kara responded. "Since I started researching family trees for others, I've found these useful." She held up a fistful of coloured markers.

Imogen sipped her tea and stared deeply into her book.

Kara began to draw connecting lines in different colours across the board. "Ta da!"

Imogen did not look up.

"Our three times great-grandparents: James McKinney and Catharine Anderson. That makes us related to Mary Anderson too, by the way. Anyway, they married in 1825." Kara underlined 1825. "You are descended from their daughter Peggy Ann." Kara circled Peggy Ann McKinney. "Your great-great grandmother."

"This Darjeeling is very good."

"I know you're listening. Her brother, my great-great grandfather, John, married a McKay and died. I wonder if that was a coincidence? Did she murder him?"

Imogen seemed to ponder the thought for a moment. Kara briefly hoped this had engaged her curiosity. No. When Imogen's eyes lowered to the book again, Kara hurriedly continued. "Her other brother, David—John's twin, by the way—left home for the U.S. That's our David's great-great-grandfather."

Imogen dropped the book on the grass. *"Our* David? Oh dear! Kara, you have been in the sun too long."

"Your great-great-grandmother stayed with her parents all her life and never married."

Imogen shrugged, picked up the book, and gave it a wipe. "I have never married either. It's overrated."

Kara stared at her fourth cousin. Imogen would not make eye contact.

The Englishwoman delivered her next speech, in her best Cambridge accent, directly into her book: "My grandmother's mother ran away from here as soon as possible. She spoke often about how the land was beautiful and enchanted. The green pastures, the clear streams, the mystic hills, and the fairies. The usual nostalgic nonsense." She made a familiar and dismissive hand motion. "My mother, Marjory, read Law at Cambridge. That's where she met my father. Both solicitors, both, unfortunately, have passed now. My brother and I also studied at Cambridge. He is a stockbroker, married with two children. My niece and nephew. That's all the family history that is important."

Kara made a mental note to add the brother, niece, and nephew to the family tree but refused to be distracted. "I cannot find any trace of Roseann's father in the records."

Imogen gave Kara a calm, lingering regard. "And you won't. We are a very respectable family. My grandmother taught me that her grandmother refused to expose whatever footman or valet she had been with, despite everyone in the village having an opinion." Imogen leaned closer. "And you know? To this day, the village somehow knows that I am descended from that illegitimate child, Roseann McKinney. They don't know anything else, but they know that!"

"Does it bother you?"

"Not a bit! I am a good deal better off than most of the gossips!" Imogen returned to her book. "And I have my work."

The gate creaked. Annie and Fatima, students who worked part time at the inn, asked if they could come in to see Scratch. Without lifting her head, Imogen replied, "Of course."

The two girls ran over to the dog. "She's so cute!" "Can I pet her?" Then there was nothing but squealing, cooing, and giggling. Scratch was eager for the extra attention and lay across Fatima's lap to catch a belly rub.

Kara watched them playing with tremendous joy. The immediate bond that she felt with Scratch had surprised her. She wondered where Scratch had come from and whose dog she had been before. Everyone in the village knew everything, but no one knew to whom Scratch belonged. Not even the vet could answer questions about the dog's history.

Kara laughed and glanced at Imogen. The conservationist sat perfectly still, reading and making notes, but there was a big smile on her face.

Fatima fussed over Scratch. "We can come by almost anytime to babysit. Mr. McKay has cut back our hours at the inn."

Annie continued. "There are only two guests now: that crazy American and his golfing buddy. They spend all their time at the Stonebridge Golf Club."

Fatima added, "Mr. McKay says that more guests will be arriving soon, but in the meantime, he doesn't need us."

Kara imagined David rambling about the inn all by himself, like Charles Foster Kane. It was nice to know he was getting some fresh air and exercise.

Within a few days, all the girls from the inn—and their friends from the village—were dropping by Aghnagoogh. They brought fresh biscuits and other house gifts. The *craic* was interesting, and Kara was quick to learn more about the villagers. Soon, the mothers started to drop by to chat. Kara described life in Canada, and everyone had travel stories of other countries to share. Fatima's mother talked of growing up in Norway. Imogen was engaging with the local women more and chatting easily about a range of topics, from the stores' closing hours to local politics. Kara observed how, without charts and certificates, they all knew how they were related to each other. She encouraged everyone to drop by her new family tree clinic at the Teaspot in the mornings to talk about genealogy.

Imogen knew that the "Teaspot's Family Tree Clinic with Kara Gordon, Genealogist" was very popular and that it meant a lot to Kara. A number of people went to discuss the gaps in their family trees. It was helping Kara settle into the community, and Imogen had become fond enough of this distant cousin to encourage that. Still, Kara reminded Imogen of an old woman who read tea leaves in the market. She also remembered that her mother would have crossed the road to avoid such a cousin.

Imogen arrived at the Teaspot with Kara to set up the display. There was time for a little second breakfast. Imogen watched as Kara carefully but copiously spooned sugar into her coffee. Of course, she was a cousin. Everyone was a cousin somehow. Kara was related from her great-great-grandmother's brother. Imogen briefly considered her own brother. How would he feel if she never again saw him or his children?

Since Kara had popped up that day in the graveyard, Imogen's life had been a little more interesting, albeit in a messy sort of way. She pondered the string of coincidences that had carried Kara into the heart of Rosheen Wood, into the cottage, and to that hidden brass box with the photographs and letters. Had Kara's ancestors deliberately hidden it for her to find one day? In Imogen's experience, ancestors were never beneficial. In contrast, old stone was a comfort, and the cottage was a treasure. About the dog, she was not sure.

Imogen's only concern now was Kara's continual pestering about the mystery of the father of Roseann McKinney. This morning was no exception. Kara poured a fresh cup of coffee. "If my colleagues in Belfast can access some of the parish records, or perhaps the estate records in Dublin, we might find a hint of Roseann's father. Churches are notoriously nosey, and that's putting it mildly."

Imogen raised an eyebrow. "Not *more* coffee?" She was anxious to change the subject.

Kara grinned. "It's only my second."

Imogen corrected her. "Second here. Fourth of the morning."

"What's your point?"

Imogen pointed. "These cups … What are they? Twelve ounces each? That is twenty-four ounces. Now, add to that, wait, listen … Two at breakfast, approximately twenty ounces there, plus—"

"Oh, stop. It doesn't affect me."

"At breakfast, you said you 'needed' a cup."

Kara picked at the edge of her mug.

"Then you said you needed a second one to get you started."

"Umm, yeah." Kara shifted in her seat and pushed aside the mug. "So?"

Imogen tapped the table in rhythm to her words. "So, how can you say that it does not affect you?"

Kara was silent at first, then attempted to pick up where she'd left off: "*Then* we could start to figure out the identity your great-great-grandfather."

Imogen picked a stray blonde hair from her green jacket and carefully rolled it into a tissue. She did not care to reveal what her great-great-grandmother had been so sensible to hide. She raised her chin. "I am descended from a long line of strong women. Women who have made something of their lives without assistance."

Kara began an apology, but Imogen raised her hand to stop her. Imogen's eyes were green and flecked at the centre with gold. When she was angry or excited, the gold flecks made them flash more brightly. "No! Whoever was the father of Roseann McKinney is not relevant to us." Kara stared at the table. "However, the old cottage and the more ancient foundation that it is built on, and the scientific methods we could use to properly date the building materials—*that* is *very* relevant! Historically, I mean."

Having made her point, Imogen was anxious to make the peace. She smiled. "And where would we be without good old Scratch?"

Kara raised up her grey eyes to meet Imogen's animated expression, and she smiled again. "As long as we watch out for the fairies, or we will be cursed!"

Imogen replied flatly, "I know. It's all terribly, *terribly* exciting." She checked the time on her phone. She was expected at a meeting at the Ballybeg Distillery café. She left Kara to her ancestor worship.

At the distillery, Michael, Dr. Nesbitt, and Lisle Christie from the planning permission office had snagged the best corner table at the café, which was partially hidden by large whiskey barrels. They did their best to be discreet and look like tourists, but it hardly mattered since the only other people there were actual tourists.

Imogen quipped, "No whiskey?"

Michael and Lisle hemmed and hawed. Nesbitt checked his watch. "It's not even noon yet. Would you like a coffee, Imogen?"

"No. Thank you."

Michael prattled about the endangered red squirrels. Imogen interrupted him.

"Michael! No one questions whether we should stop the FU project. Well, David McKinney does, of course, but never mind that. No one here disputes it. First order of business, the land ownership. Do we have more information?"

Lisle produced a survey map of the townlands, all the boundaries clearly marked. "It was all part of the Inish-Rathcarrick estate. The Andersons to the east. Knocknageragh had been farmed by the Andersons since the 1600s, as a tenancy, until Mary Anderson's great-grandfather purchased it. The other two townlands that face onto Beeswax Road and straddle the church lands to the right and the left are, respectively, Lisnasidhe and Aghnagoogh—"

Imogen interrupted. "Aghnagoogh is mine."

"Yes. The title on that one is clear. It was the McKinney farm. Like the Andersons, it was held in tenancy for hundreds of years, father to son, to James McKinney in 1829. He bought the land in the 1870s but later sold to another local farmer, Fitzgerald, in 1895. Then, in 1925, it was purchased from Fitzgerald by your grandmother Molly and transferred to you as an inheritance in 1980."

Imogen approved. "That sounds correct."

Lisle continued. "Right. So, that title is clear. It's the title on Lisnasidhe that's a mess. The records only show that it was transferred by the Sixth Duke of Inish-Rathcarrick, in 1912, directly from his estate and to a trust. The only name attached to the trust is McKinnie. Nothing else. It could be a misspelling of McKinney. On the original document, it looks like the name was smudged and written over, but there isn't anything that can be proven at this point. The property is managed by the Church."

Nesbitt explained that the Church acted as an administrator of the trust for an unknown but legal owner.

Michael shook his head. "How can the Church have a management agreement with an unknown party? Isn't there a document?"

Nesbitt shrugged. "It was a verbal agreement. The details of the agreement are recorded in the 1912 minute book of the parish but the note carefully shields the name of the third party, the presumed owner of the land at the time. The request was that, until further instruction was received from the rightful owner, the parish was to prepare a lease for the use of the pasture, except for, you know, that particular corner, the supposed fairy fort Rosheen Wood. The Andersons knew that too many odd things happened in Rosheen Wood, so they took the lease for the price of two hundred lambs a year, paid to the Church as administrator. The Church administers the property, paying taxes and maintenance from the proceeds of the lambs. But there's no document that indicates who was—or is—the title holder."

Lisle added, "And there's no one alive to remember. Even Mary Anderson doesn't know who owns the land. She just pays the rent and takes care of the pasture, using them for her sheep and the beehives."

Nesbitt checked his watch again. It was noon. He signalled the waiter for a tray of whiskey for the table. "The Church keeps an account book for the administration. The property taxes are up to date, there are no liens for maintenance, and there's a small reserve for emergencies."

Lisle was Ballybeg's chief planning officer. He reported that David McKinney had applied for the demolition of all structures and new construction. All the engineering and construction documents were under review in his office. "Their documents are all there except the proof of ownership. They claim both that the land is rightfully Mr. McKinney's title, and in any case, has been abandoned."

"Well, it can't be both!" Michael spat.

Imogen scoffed. "It's not abandoned if the Church continues to administer it."

"Well, it's a bureaucratic mess," replied Lisle. "Without documented proof of ownership, I will automatically recommend a decision of refusal to the council. But they've done some daft things lately when the influence is pressing. So, if it were me, what I would do is file all the heritage and environmental objections for when it comes up at the next planning committee meeting. It's harder to ignore three justifications for refusal than one."

Michael glanced at his phone again. "David McKinney's solicitors in Belfast and Dublin are looking for documentary evidence on the ownership of Lisnasidhe. When's the next meeting of the planning committee?"

Lisle replied, "Next Monday morning."

Michael groaned. "My officers have worked overtime to build the environmental objection. Our strongest point is the endangered status of the red squirrel. We'll file it tomorrow."

Imogen outlined her efforts to ensure a listed building status for the cottage. "In consultation with my colleagues, I can verify that the base of the cottage is earlier than thirteenth century, and not using local materials. I need time. Look at these photographs."

Michael added. "If we can file to have the site listed, then he will have to go to the Department of the Environment at Stormont for an exemption to the Conservation Act. That should give us more time." Then he grumbled, "But he's probably already buying some influence there."

Lisle spoke up again. "Mr. McKinney has hardly kept his ideas a secret. The councillors are already talking about it. A lot of the councillors are liking it too."

Michael was unfazed. He opened his portfolio. "We have one strategy: divide and conquer, as always. Let's look at the list of councillors on the planning committee first."

Imogen looked over at the list. "I will take anyone at the Stonebridge Golf Club. Councillor McMullen was talking to Kara last weekend about his family tree. Maybe we could put him on Kara's list?"

Lisle looked up from Imogen's photographs. "That Canadian doing family trees at the teashop? Councillor Shaw is livid with her. You know how Mrs. Shaw claims to be a descendent of the O'Neills? Well, apparently, she is not."

Michael grimaced. "I'll work on Councillor Shaw then."

"You are not taking notes, Michael," Imogen observed. "How do you keep track of everyone?"

He shrugged. "Some days, it seems that talking people around to our side of the issues is all I do. Politicians, pundits, plants, red squirrels; they're all the same once you classify them."

Nesbitt, Michael, and Imogen neatly divided the list of councillors between themselves as well as Esmée, Mary Anderson, and Kara. Then they attacked the tray of whiskies.

Eight

David's new solicitor had a reputation as an expert in land ownership. He faced David across the table in the dining room with a face designed for court. James McKay glared at David, who stared at the antique clock on the mantelpiece. The ticking annoyed him. He was missing a round of golf. It was sunny, and he had learned that weather doesn't last in Ballybeg.

In a few hours, the three men confirmed that David knew very little of the area, its history, its building codes, or its conservation regulations. In fact, David had also fallen short in terms of proving his own descent from the McKinney family, which formed the basis of his land claim. It fell to McKay to give the precise information connecting David McKinney, Irishman, born 1828, to David McKinney, American, born 1964. Then it would be up to the solicitor to deliver the goods: the proven ownership of Lisnasidhe on Beeswax Road. David was paying the firm large fees out of his development budget to chase down the documents.

McKay opened his portfolio of American certificates that linked David in a direct male line to his ancestors. The lawyer re-examined the evidence. "This is all fine as far as it goes. The real challenge is to prove your hypothesis that the first David McKinney inherited Lisnasidhe from his father in 1896. We have one half; now we need the second."

McKay poured another round of whiskey. "It's common knowledge that Lisnasidhe is McKinney land, purchased in 1875."

The solicitor concurred. "There's evidence of the Aghnagoogh and Knocknageragh purchases but not Lisnasidhe. But we still need the documents. Leave it with my firm. It might take a little time."

David was annoyed to see the sunlight disappearing behind thick grey clouds. "And what am I supposed to do?"

The solicitor stood up and gathered all the papers off the table. "Wander about. Learn something about the area. It is, as you keep saying"—he referred to his notes—"your ancestral home." He gave a little formal nod and went.

The rain battered the windows. The clock continued to scold. The chef entered and rummaged behind the bar for something. McKay broke the long silence. "Do you know when the other FU partners are expected?"

Why does McKay care? He murmured, "No. Not really." He raised his voice. "It's me that's out front anyway. I'm the FU lead. They gave FU phase one to me. I'm the expert on real estate development." He unrolled the engineering schematics and gently stroked them. "I don't need the rest of the FU investment group. It's going to be the best project in the whole of Northern Ireland."

McKay grumbled. "It's just that I cancelled all the other bookings for the month when I got the call from Monsieur Laurel that there would be dozens of your team staying here and that security and confidentiality was an issue." He waited for a replied. "So, we cleared the inn, even the dinner reservations."

David flushed with anger. "McKay! Don't be petty! So, you lose a few nights' bookings! You're going to be rich!" David stared at the schematics. "And besides, the inn is not exactly on par with The Savoy; is it?"

He looked up again from his drawings. McKay had left the room. The chef scowled from behind the bar.

The lawyer was right. Since he was the FU lead—the best development ever in the area—maybe he should get to know the village better. *Where has Bugsy gotten to?*

Benjamin Sorley Carter, also known as Bugsy, had grown up in Brooklyn. His early life was unknown, but rumours suggested juvenile incarceration. He'd worked as a bouncer at a Manhattan private gambling club. David had hired him on the spot as his personal security detail when a group of investors from Queens had disputed the profit split from a Maldives casino development. Ultimately, the McKinney Corporation had paid out the damages and removed the threat. Still, David kept Bugsy on the payroll. He was strong, scary looking, practically silent, and his golf game was a little worse than his own.

After a little trouble trying to understand how to open an umbrella, David stepped out and searched for Bugsy through the rainy village streets. He found him in O'Casey's Tailor and Clothier. Six feet, four inches of rock in a peat-coloured tweed jacket stood surrounded by mirrors and hand stitchers. The jacket had epaulettes, patched elbows, and leather-trimmed seams and buttons.

"That's some jacket, Bugsy." David tried to sound serious, but his crooked smile gave him away.

Bugsy warmed to the praise. "Check out the lining." He opened the jacket to reveal a tawny paisley patterned silk.

David flopped into a chair. "What's the deal, Bugsy? You want to dress like my grandfather?"

Bugsy smiled. He removed the jacket, revealing the matching vest. "It's colder here. I guess I just wanted to, you know, fit in." He acknowledged the clerk. "Thank you."

David doubted Bugsy would fit in anywhere. He was shocked to see a neatly stacked tower of folded items in linen and wool: cardigans, pullovers, shirts, and trousers. Bugsy was buying more than the jacket. "You know, Bugsy, this shop is expensive."

"I saw that," replied Bugsy. "Good thing I saved all my bonuses." The clerk filled several shopping bags with the items purchased and added boxes of leather shoes and wellie boots. Bugsy reached into the bag and pulled out a blue tweed flat cap. "This is for you, Boss. It matches your eyes."

"Thanks, Bugsy, but I don't need it."

"You might. I was talking to Kathleen, and she thinks that if you dress like a native, they would like you more."

David pulled it tight on his head. *Like me more? What does that mean?*

Bugsy reached into the pocket of his old jacket, retrieved a red multi-sided die with gold numbers, and thrust it into his new pocket.

Bugsy led David to the Standing Stone. Bugsy and Archie were now well acquainted. The pub was quiet. A pair of backpackers had tucked themselves away in the small window at the front. Archie silently dropped a Heineken in front of David and enquired politely how his business was going. David threw himself onto the barstool. "You won't believe it!"

Archie winked. "I've heard everything, son." When David didn't respond, he offered, "You're all ready to bring your French investors in to start the Finn's Ultimate leisure project at Lisnasidhe, and your Belfast solicitor is off trying to confirm that you are the legal inheritor of the land."

David pointed at Bugsy. "Is this you? Have you been blabbing our business?"

"C'mon, Boss, you know me."

David knew Bugsy was trustworthy. "Sorry, Bugsy." *I guess it's true,* he reflected. *Everyone in a small village knows everybody else's business.* He tried to use that to his advantage, turning back to Archie. "So, you know that Lisnasidhe is rightfully mine."

"It's said to be McKinney land, that's certain," was his guarded response.

Old Seamus shuffled in and settled into his preferred seat. Archie produced a whiskey and a pint in the same movement. After wetting his lips with whiskey, Seamus started to tell a story, David presumed, for the benefit of the backpackers: "Coinnigh's first child will be a Witch and a follower of the ancient tree worship. She has many tricks and incantations ..."

Archie offered advice. "Did you speak to Dr. Currie, or perhaps Michael Garrett about the heritage and environmental restrictions? Or to McKay about it, for that matter? It's about the heritage building on the site."

Archie's question startled David, but the storyteller's voice distracted his thoughts for a moment: "Coinnigh's second child will be a High Priestess who sits high in a tower overlooking the land. She protects the history of the village."

His phone rang. He wanted to tell Seamus to be quiet. He knew he couldn't, so he moved to the furthest corner of the pub and cupped his hand around the phone. It was François Hardie, informing him that the Syndicat was getting impatient. "You led us to believe you owned Lisnasidhe, and we would acquire construction permissions by next week. *Alors*—were you lying or were you—misinformed?"

David didn't like the man's tone. He would have blasted him good, but he was trying to build a certain reputation with the locals. He mumbled that he would call back shortly and hung up. David studied Archie, trying to make out what he was saying but getting confused between Archie, the Frenchman, and Seamus's ranting about wizards.

Seamus continued: "The Mother and the sacred site are in danger from the Lunatic. He will approach with darkness in his heart."

David shut out Seamus' voice again and focused on Archie. "What are you talking about? An old building?" David sneered. "What do you mean its heritage?" This business trip was just getting better and better.

The old man ranted on: "To defend the sacred site from the Lunatic, the High Priestess will gather the village to guard it day and night ..."

Archie motioned David closer. "That old cottage in the woods at Lisnasidhe is protected heritage." He handed David a second Heineken. "So, even if you do own the land, that would prevent you touching it."

David knew that with one word from him, Bugsy would silence Seamus permanently. But the old man continued: "Three enchantments thwart him, first blindness, then a shroud, and finally, endless pleasure."

Tick, tick, tick. It was as if the clock from the inn was in his head. The Syndicat was ready to take over the whole project from him unless he could guarantee an FU start date. He'd proved he was the descendent of James McKinney, who'd died in 1896. The solicitor was off researching the land transfer archives. But if an old cottage could delay the whole shebang? Tick, tick, tick.

David's brain raced forward. An old building was not going to stop the FU project—*Wait. Archie knows that McKay knows about it?* That was the last straw. "Where's the nearest building supply shop?" he snapped.

Archie provided the directions. David turned to his bodyguard. "Bugsy! We're gonna launch the Tompkins manoeuvre! Now!"

"In my new jacket?" The well-dressed giant groaned, then chugged his refreshment while sending a text message.

In the back of the hired black sedan, David muttered to Bugsy, "Get rid of the cottage, get rid of the problem."

"Like Tompkins in 2010?"

David turned his face up—way up—to look Bugsy straight in the eyes. "Exactly—serious damage to the cottage—flatten it to the ground."

Bugsy ran his hand over his new Irish tweed jacket.

"Then we'll corral McKay back at the inn and extract some answers."

"Okay, Boss."

Imogen had only a few more days to prepare the heritage site for a visit by a group of experts from Belfast and Dublin who would assess the historical providence of the cottage, and perhaps, its foundations. Her progress was somewhat dependent on the weather and today was no different than the last few days. The wind rose up from nowhere, bringing the rain at noon and then carrying it away again, leaving behind a quiet, warm, sunny afternoon. Clover, flowering buds on the trees, and wildflowers responded to the heat, presenting themselves with purpose while perfuming the air.

As she approached the wooden gate at the top of the path, the buzzing of Mary's beehives on the other side of the stone wall welcomed her. Mary herself was perched on the wall. She ran a school program in apiary management for thirteen-year-olds. Today's class included Owen, Morag's second son. Already a confident beekeeper, he was leading his classmates, all gloved and veiled, in an inspection of the hives.

Mary greeted Imogen. She wasn't wearing the beekeeper's protective gear that she insisted the kids wear. "The bees are used to me, and in any case, this old hide doesn't feel it." She was in a chatty mood, commenting on the weather and how her job was easier when she had Owen's class. "He does all the work."

Imogen pointed at the thicket. "Is the village talking about it?"

"Pretty much everybody. No one understands it so it's clearly the fairy folk."

Imogen did not want to encourage the notion that fairies were real. Still, the grove had been overgrown and closed up, and now it had a four-metre gap to access the interior. Eventually, everyone would forget that the transformation had occurred magically. Or maybe not. "I have no scientific explanation for this. I do have remarkable mental discipline though, and I choose not to think about it."

Mary laughed. "I suppose that works for you. Half the village have come up for a tour about, and the other half are too frightened."

"Pish posh!" Imogen retorted. *Still, if it keeps enough people away, so much the better.* "Everyone always thought Rosheen Wood was a fairy fort anyway; this just proves it."

The class was now moving away towards the apiary work shed. Mary jumped down from the wall. "Mind you, I'm not afraid. I've been keeping an eye on it. So has Esmée Nesbitt and Keith. We take turns on guard duty."

Imogen felt grateful that Mary was a strong ally. "I'm more worried about David McKinney than a nosy villager."

Imogen walked into the clearing. Mary stayed close to her. Inside, Mary looked back nervously at the thicket.

Imogen reassured her, "It won't close if it hasn't already."

A couple of red squirrels drew closer. They were usually timid. Imogen suspected that the years of claiming the territory only for themselves had made them bolder. "This is the area that interests Michael the most." Imogen laughed. "My refrigerator is full of his specimens. Just the plants. Not the squirrels."

Imogen indicated the round stone firepit.

"What's it for?" asked Mary.

"I have no idea," responded Imogen. "Human sacrifice?"

Imogen entered the cottage. On her last visit, Imogen had shifted and removed the piles of dirt that had accumulated in the corners. Surfaces were brushed. The principle architectural elements of note were marked. The hearth under the chimney had been cleaned out to expose the stone base and the interior shaft of the chimney.

Imogen sat on the bed alcove. It wasn't large. The Sweeneys would have padded this with a straw mattress and built up the wool and linen layers to make the bed. Enclosed with stone on three sides and close to the fireplace, it would have provided a warm, comfortable night's rest. Children slept in trundle beds: flat wooden boxes filled with padding that slid out from under the stone alcove bed.

Something shiny at the doorway caught Imogen's eye: a metal object buried under the threshold. Using gloves and a small brush, she gently coaxed it out from the ground. It was a piece of gold jewellery: a brooch. She held it out. "It's at least tenth-century construction. This supports my theory that the cottage, or at least the base of it, is very old. "And maybe—" She retrieved her magnifying glass and showed the design to Mary. "See this zoomorphic and geometric design? —even older—possibly ninth century. This could be the indication of a hoard further down. I should call the museum again before we go any further." Imogen carefully wrapped the brooch in a handkerchief and slipped it into her pocket.

She stepped briskly out of the cottage and crossed the clearing to the opening. Mary wasted no time getting in step with her. As they reached the wooden gate, they heard a car approach and stop. And then voices. American voices. "It's David McKinney!"

Mary glared. "What's he up to?"

Imogen cringed. "I don't know and I don't want to meet him!" The voices grew closer.

Mary opened the wooden gate. "Get through the gate and behind the wall." Both women crouched behind the stone wall.

A black sedan sat on the shoulder of the road. A figure sat in the driver's position. From the car, David and the big fellow were striding up the dirt path towards them. Each carried the sort of cloth bag that was often used for sporting equipment, which was incongruous with their clothing. David wore what Imogen supposed was his idea of casual wear: a blue business suit, rumpled and without a tie. The big fellow looked like an old-fashioned country squire right down to—or up to—the tweed flat cap.

Mary was peeking through a small hole in the wall. Imogen nudged her so they could both have an unobstructed view. The two men stopped directly in front of the opening in the thicket.

Imogen whispered, "Why are they here?"

David was angry. "I don't get it!" He threw down his bag, exposing some of the contents: a crowbar and a baseball bat. "How do they enter?"

The big fellow replied, "Well, they just walk in."

"Where?" asked David.

"Right there, Boss. Through the opening."

"What opening? I can't see an opening!"

The giant studied David's face, then the opening at which David glared. And back to David. "You can't see an opening in the thicket there, Boss? Between the brambles? The oak tree on the right?" For all his height, he looked frightened. He reached into his pocket and pulled out a red and gold twenty-sided object that he rolled between the fingers of one hand like a rosary bead.

David pointed directly at the opening. "You're talking about this prickly hedge here? Stop goofing around, Bugsy! I'll punch you."

"Some villagers say that Rosheen Wood is protected by the fairy folk, Boss."

"Get out!"

Bugsy fingered the red and gold object in his hand and studied his boss before muttering, "We could really use a Globe of Invulnerability right about now."

"What the fuck are you saying!?!" David raised his fist.

Imogen thought that was quite brave (or stupid) of David. This Bugsy fellow could flatten him in a second. She turned to Mary. "Who has been talking to the big American guy about the fairy lore?"

"Probably Keith."

"Keith?"

"They've been together quite a bit."

"Keith? … and that fellow?"

"Aye. His name is Benjamin, but he goes by Bugsy."

"Oh. Fancy that." Bugsy was more interesting than she had thought.

Bugsy lowered his head. "Well, Boss, I'm just thinking, if you need protection, gold might help, or an iron nail?"

David retrieved the crowbar from his bag. "We'll have to break through this thorny hedge first. Then we can knock down the old cottage."

On hearing this, Imogen started to jump up. Mary held her firmly in place, pressing down on her shoulder. "Trust the fairies."

"Trust the—"

"Watch."

David bashed at the opening with his crowbar. Nothing changed of course, as he was swinging at nothing, but David put his back into it. "C'mon Bugsy! This hedge is tough! We both need to do it."

Bugsy hesitated before reaching into his own bag and pulling out a heavy axe. He swung it about in rhythm with David's stokes of the crowbar. This farce lasted for fifteen minutes until both men were sweaty and breathless.

David collapsed and landed on the grass. Bugsy doubled over, gasping.

David rolled over to the bags of tools and rummaged in each. "No matches? Nothing to start a fire? Why don't you have matches?"

"I don't smoke, Boss."

"Arrrgh! Why do I have to do everything myself?" He turned onto his back and lay there.

Mary quietly applauded. "Fairies two, Yankees nil."

Imogen didn't believe in fairies but was grateful they were on the same side.

As if answering a call to arms, the gentle humming of the bees now increased to a loud buzzing. Above Imogen and Mary, the bees formed a military-like flanking position and targeted the men. Yelping, David and Bugsy scrambled down the dirt path into the waiting black sedan, the bees in hot pursuit. Their car sped off.

"Like General Hannibal at the Battle of Cannae," noted Imogen.

"No, just a swarm," corrected Mary. She stood up. "I'd better make sure they come home." She paused. "Kara thought we should set up a formal guard schedule. Given what we just witnessed, I think it's a good idea."

"Yes. A few more people will help."

"We'll meet at the market tomorrow. In the meantime, Owen and his friends are first-rate spies. When they're on their bicycles, they're silent and fast. I'll ask him to keep an eye on David's movements and report back."

Imogen recalled that she had a precious historical artefact in her pocket. She made her apologies to Mary and rushed to take it home. In her study, she stared at the brooch for an hour. She could not believe it. She was never excited. Intrigued, inquiring, involved, yes, but never excited. Why was she shaking? She carefully wrapped the brooch in a linen handkerchief, then placed it into a small steel box padded with rabbit fur. She shook her hands loose to calm down. She knew that, usually, where one such artefact was found, there would be more. The museums would be anxious to examine the area.

Nine

Kara loved the Saturday farmers' market. It brought the village to Memorial Square. Both local farmers and merchants lined the square with stalls. Kara could spend hours watching the locals. It was remarkable that there were many family resemblances to her relatives in the shape of their chin, or their hair or eyes, or sometimes even just an unusual laugh or a nod of the head.

Liam was doing bike stunts on the side street with his brother, Owen, and their friends. Kara was pleased to see him, since if Liam was back, then Seamus must be too.

Morag and the Ballybeg Yarnbombers for Heritage had covered several park benches with multicoloured knitting. Bench cozies, they called them. Kara hesitated to sit down on them. She opted to take pictures, capturing the reactions of tourists and residents alike to the covered benches.

"It's rare weather we're having," Morag noted to Kara. Kara asked her if Seamus was home from his country rambling. "He is indeed," Morag replied, "a bit tired but otherwise no better nor worse."

"Is he still reciting the same old story about the children of Coinnigh?"

"Yes. He talked himself to sleep last night with that story."

Sarah sold her last scone and closed her stall. "Do you think there's something important about Seamus' story? I thought he was just going senile."

Kara was biting her cuticles. "Yes. It might be a coincidence, but every time I see him, it's the same thing." She thrust her hands into her pockets and kept them there. "It haunts my dreams. I want to hear it all together and record it if I can."

Morag patted Kara on the shoulder. "Come round later then."

Mary Anderson's honey and beeswax candles were selling well, leaving no time for a break. Keith perched on a whiskey barrel beside her, writing a list onto his sketch board as they chatted. He was wearing an unpressed linen shirt with three buttons undone, short denim cut-offs, worker boots, and his red bandana kerchief. He stopped to ask Kara strange questions about Brooklyn.

Kara wanted to help, but she knew very little about Brooklyn. "I'm from Canada, remember? Not New York."

"Aye," he persevered, "but like, Brooklyn? Is it a good place to grow up? Is there a lot of crime?"

"I don't know," she replied. She started to ask why he was interested and then remembered hearing that Bugsy had grown up there. She paused. "But then it depends—"

Mary interrupted. "We're drawing up a schedule to guard Rosheen Wood from David."

"Sign me up," volunteered Sarah.

"Me too," added Morag, "and the boys."

"Of course," replied Mary. "I already have the boys. They've been monitoring him since yesterday."

Kara shook her head. "It's odd that David McKinney arrived the same week as me." *We're cousins, but so different.* "I want to keep everything just as it is, and David wants to pull it all apart."

"David has not made any friends in Ballybeg," Keith commented. "He has a brilliant knack for offending every time he opens his mouth."

Mary went on. "He's shown his hand as far as Rosheen Wood is concerned." She explained to the others what she and Imogen had witnessed the evening before. "And that big Bugsy fellow repeated to McKinney everything he's heard about the fairy folk." She turned to Keith. "He seemed really scared."

Keith shook his head. "Don't look at me. All he talks about are his games. When he talks."

"Well," Mary concluded, "McKinney didn't believe him anyway."

Imogen arrived with Lisle. "I've convinced Councillor McRoberts to vote against David's proposal when it appears at the planning committee." McRoberts was friendly to Imogen's position, having worked as a tour guide at Dundurn Castle in her youth. She still bragged that she knew her way around the castle in the dark.

Lisle repeated that and laughed. "No one wants to test her since the castle has many traps and drops throughout, and one might suffer the same fate as Coinnigh himself if they took the wrong step."

Imogen reviewed the guard duty rota with Kara. Esmée and Catherine Rooney, who was Father O'Connell's housekeeper, planned to take some of the weekday mornings on behalf of the Friends of the Red Squirrel. Keith was painting landscapes that required much time in the field with the sheep, the bees, and Rosheen Wood in all sorts of weather. Dr. Brownlie, the vet, declared himself to be very concerned with the health of the red squirrels. This would require him to drop by every few days to observe them.

But having watched Imogen's re-enactment of David's jousting with thin air, everyone concluded that the best defense had to be the mysterious thicket itself. However, since Imogen and Mary indicated that David's next move might be to set fire to the thicket, and that might do terrible damage, there was a consensus that they should keep him away from Rosheen Wood.

Kara mused, "We have to keep him occupied somehow."

Keith jumped to his feet. "Let's take Bugsy and David to see the touristy places of interest. The caves along the coast are interesting."

"Maybe I can reason with David," Kara added. *If I can keep him apart from Imogen.*

The group chatted across each other, their voices weaving about in alternation like a choir. Morag declared that David was bringing trouble to the village, and that Ballybeg "was not the right place for him."

In the midst of their conversation, McKay materialized from the market crowds, and the talk dropped dead, with a half-uttered preposition abandoned at the edge of Mary's mouth. He said nothing but scowled at the group as he passed. Lisle whispered that his mother had been a very nice woman. Mary concurred. They all watched his back until it was gone. When the market closed and the group split up, Kara and Keith decided to drop in at the inn.

David hunched over his unfinished lunch. *This food tastes odd.* He glanced at his bodyguard on the other side of the inn's bar.

Bugsy's muscular frame was stretched across a large wing-backed chair and ottoman. He caressed the side of his new linen trousers and the front of his new V-neck wool sweater. He was devouring a book called *Xanathar's Guide to Everything*. Occasionally, Bugsy paused to silently mouth the words. *Never thought Bugsy could read.* David coughed loudly and beat a rhythm on the table with his coffee spoon. Nothing distracted Bugsy.

David stared at his empty coffee cup. Given the hostility he had experienced in the village, he was now hiding in the inn. To force McKay to bring back Chef Phillippe, he'd promised that a gang of FU project consultants would descend on the inn any day now. Despite the incentive, the results were questionable. Phillippe's dishes had unpronounceable French names and unidentified cuts of meat. No one cleared the table. No one offered coffee. He checked his watch.

David glared at a white finch on the windowsill. He watched the anglers fishing for salmon. It seemed a stupid pursuit when you could just buy salmon in the grocery store. He checked his watch. He was experiencing what he would describe as a temporary low point. He could not shake the feeling that he was being watched. *Is it the finch on the windowsill?*

Going out would be worse. He'd noticed that most of the villagers talked rapidly to each other until he arrived, at which point, they'd fall silent. He sighed loudly. Such is the burden of power. He checked his watch again.

He picked at his plate, then pushed it aside. He snatched up his phone. As solace from the boredom, David messaged his daughter Kathleen who was studying Law at the University of California, Berkeley. He sent her a random text every three or four hours. *What's the time difference?* She would be angry if he woke her up again. "*Whassup?*" he typed. He'd seen that in a TV commercial. It was what all the kids were saying.

"Geez, Dad!" came the texted reply. "It's barely six a.m. here."

"Whoops. Again."

"Look at the phone, Dad. It will tell you the time in LA. Anyway, what's up with you? Are you coming home yet?"

"No. I've got the Finn's Ultimate project here. It's really big. We are lining up a consortium of international investors."

"Dad?"

"Yes?"

"Dad. When I hired Henry Cooper to trace our family tree, it was a Christmas present. To give you a hobby. To help you relax."

"I don't do hobbies."

"And Mom—"

"Don't you mention that woman to me!"

"My mother wants you to come home and see some doctors."

"I bet she does! She wants me committed!"

"I don't think they do that much anymore. Anyway, what's it like in Ireland? Is it fantastic?"

"It's"—his texting fingers paused—"pretty—backwards."

"You must have discovered some relatives, at least."

"Everyone is a relative. Well, not everyone. There are some others. But … a lot of relatives. I'm not clear on the connections."

"Okay, Dad. I'm going. Since I'm awake now, I may as well go for a run. Ciao!"

"Ciao, baby."

He lowered the phone. Kara Gordon was crossing the lobby. *What does she want?* That artist guy Keith was close behind.

Bugsy stood up, dropping his book on the floor.

Kara reached out her hand. "David? I can call you David, can't I? We are cousins after all."

"I suppose. I've never figured it out." *Really, what does she want?*

"Ah well. We share great-great-great-grandparents. James McKinney and Catharine Anderson. You are descended from their son David and me from their son John. They were twins."

"Fascinating."

"I'm your fourth cousin."

"Not kissing cousins."

"You're just being facetious now, aren't you?"

"You're so Canadian."

"I'll take that as a compliment."

"Whatever."

"You look really tense, David. You should let me read your cards."

"My cards?" David threw a desperate look to Bugsy. His bodyguard ignored him, focusing on a conversation with Keith.

"Tarot. You would probably pick the King of Pentacles."

David stared at her. *Tentacles? What is she talking about?* "Why are you here, Kara?"

"We have a car. We want to take you for a drive, out to the coastal road."

The woman was relentless. Where David came from, the expression "we want to take you for a drive" held a sinister meaning. He doubted that was her intention though, unless it was to bore him to death. "Okay. What's on the coast?"

"The sea. I think you should see it."

David scanned the room. Kara was balanced on her back foot, her other foot and arm outstretched to the door. Bugsy fidgeted. Keith was watching the verbal duel. David checked his phone again to see that there were no messages nor items in his agenda. He stood up. *I'll go, if only to get away from that annoying finch.* "Alright. Do your worst."

Keith drove along the road that followed the top of the ridge, in line with the rocky coast far below. The wind was strong and moving fast. Large clouds rolled overhead. Rain rushed in diagonally from the ocean. It rose and fell in spasms, washing the little car violently, then disappearing as quickly. The sea spray whipped over the coast. Instead of driving away from it, Keith drove down into it, closer to the beach, and there he parked the car.

Kara, Keith, and Bugsy rambled down a steep staircase to the large flat stones below. David reluctantly followed. The storm had driven away most of the tourists. The sea was choppy and made a thunderous noise as it struck the shore. The solid grey clouds pressed lower. David's feet slid on the stones.

The foursome staggered in the wind along the path to where the hexagonal stones stretched along the coastline. They hopped from one stone to the other to navigate across and then climbed a pyramid of stones on the edge of the water. Bugsy dragged David along. Once halfway up, David found it easier to climb up than step down. The little group arranged themselves on the stones at the top. The wet spray slapped their faces.

Kara pointed to the coastline of hexagon-shaped basalt stones all around them. "This is the proposed site for your FU Watersports Fun Park. Is that a joke?"

David was surprised. "How did you know our plans?"

Keith replied, "Damn, David. Everyone knows that. What's the idea? To use the stones as the base for a gigantic waterslide?"

It was the first time that David had seen the stones. They stretched for miles. They clustered together. Some towered above them. Others tapered down into the sea. They were an extraordinary sight. They didn't look man-made but not random either. *Pure fantasy. They were—*

"Beautiful!" Kara exclaimed, breaking into his thoughts.

"Dreadful!" He scowled.

"Lovely and wild!" She beamed as the wind whipped her long grey hair into her eyes.

"You're insane!" He swallowed salty water running down his face.

"Perhaps. But anyway, it's not boring!" his cousin replied. "It's nature. It's life, raw and uncontrollable!"

Keith and Bugsy jumped down and raced off together to the east.

I will not participate in this torture any longer. He attempted to climb down and almost fell. Angrily, he turned back to his captor, who maintained her footing against the wind. She frowned and pointed a finger at him.

"David, you can't be serious about destroying all of this!"

"All of what? Some stones?"

Kara flung out her arms as wide as her short body allowed. "All of this, David! It's *us!* It's what we are made from! The McKinneys! All this energy! All of this stone and wind and sea, challenging our ancestors to survive. They stood here and looked at this, and still they went out in boats to harvest the sea. Or cleared the fields to build homes and grow food and raise animals."

She was clearly irrational. David snapped back, "You sound like my mother. She's an old sixties hippie. She believes in communes and free love. But she took a lot of drugs. What's your excuse? I know what comes next: the old universal love lecture. Forget it!"

"You don't need to be a hippie to appreciate the land and the air and the water that give us life." She pointed to a nearby pool. "The water rained onto Lisnasidhe and Aghnagoogh and enriched them. It flowed into streams and rivers that carried it down to the sea here. It looks like such a small pool of water, but it feeds the land and gives itself to the enormity of the sea, then starts the cycle again."

"I'm not going to listen to this. I'm going back to Ballybeg."

"It's two miles back."

"I can walk." David lowered his foot to the stone below, slipped, and slid down three stones. Climbing back to his feet, he stormed off back to the staircase up to the coastal road. When he reached the top of the ridge, he looked back. Kara sat cross-legged with her arms extended as if embracing the weather. Bugsy and Keith had disappeared. *Fine.* He consulted the map on his phone to find his way back. It directed him straight down Beeswax Road. This would take him to Rosheen Wood. *How convenient is that?*

He felt for the large box of matches in his pocket. Last night, he and Bugsy had only been armed with axes and crowbars. Despite their best efforts, the branches of the thicket had refused to yield. *This time, I'll burn it all down.*

Beeswax Road was far from flat. It had been built over time from the natural landscape and wound side to side and up and down. David caught brief glimpses of kids on bikes at high points along the road. He strode briskly and soon arrived at Rosheen Wood. No nosey people in sight. No bees hovered in the air. Only sheep meandered about the fields. *Finally.* A flash, and it would be done. He approached the solid wall of the thicket, reached into his pocket, and found a hole instead of the matchbox. He looked back and saw it lying beside the pond.

As he bent down to grab the matchbox, a sudden beam of bright sunlight caused something in the water to glint, striking him in the eyes. A gold coin was nestled between two pebbles. He took the coin and the matchbox. The coin had a king's head on the obverse, and on the reverse, a knight on horseback trampling a conquered dragon. How could it be so polished? Why wasn't it dirty? He shrugged and pocketed it. Whatever. Perhaps the pond had washed it. *Lucky me! Finders keepers!*

He ran up the path to where he'd stood yesterday outside Rosheen Wood. The easiest way to destroy this obstacle was with a good fire. It would destroy everything outside and inside. He started to step forward, match in hand, when he sensed movement from the corner of his eye and felt a strong vibration in the ground. He glanced behind him.

A dense fluffy white mass coalesced and moved across the field toward him. *Sheep!* In what seemed like a single moment, he was up to his hips in sheep, pressing up against him from all sides. They swept him down the path, off Lisnasidhe, onto Beeswax Road, and toward the church. David strained to extract himself from the woolly riot. *Where is that damn Anderson woman?!* He struggled to keep his footing, and the unrelenting creatures forced him down the road away from his target.

At the church, the flock curiously broke formation and waddled back toward the pasture in twos and threes. David, breathless, limped to a bench in the churchyard. He couldn't feel his legs and collapsed onto the stone seat. *What the fuck!* He shook his head. Then he pulled the gold coin from his pocket and studied it. The text read, "GEORGIUS III D: G: BRITANNIARUM REX F: D: 1820." He watched the sheep wobbling away. Nothing made sense. He wasn't sure about his luck anymore. Maybe it was some old Irish curse. Was this leprechaun gold? Can leprechauns bewitch sheep?

He remained on the stone bench to catch his breath, hiding the coin in his pocket. Directly ahead, an inscription on a tombstone leapt out at him: "Robert McKinney 1711 – 1783 and his wife, Kathleen Gillan, 1717 – 1756." Were the ancestors laughing at him? The bench was cold. The graveyard gave him the creeps. He tried to call Bugsy, but it went to voicemail. *Well, I'm not going back to the inn.* He called a taxi to take him to a place of sanctuary—a place where all his problems would melt away: the Stonebridge Golf Club.

Imogen's study was the heart of Aghnagoogh. The room had once been the whole of the McKinney family cottage. But her grandmother Molly had surrounded it with renovations and extensions that hid it from the outside world. Its Victorian wallpaper, furniture, and tiled fireplace comforted Imogen. The room was further fortified by a lining of bookcases armed with classical literature. A first edition of *Cymbeline Refinished* lay open and unfinished on a fireside table. No one was permitted entry to Imogen's sanctuary. The windowless room also afforded museum-like climate controls that preserved any historical objects within it.

Imogen had rushed here when she'd arrived home from the market. She expected a phone call from her museum colleague in Belfast in response to her email about the ancient gold brooch. She retrieved the small metal box and brought out the artefact: a solid gold circle, two inches in diameter, with a long pin attached at the top by a rivet. The head of the pin was broad and decorated as much as the circle itself. The runic engraving translated as "To the Honourable Lady Imogen." *That's very odd.*

She nestled it gently in her left hand while she answered the telephone. It would be of significant interest to the Belfast museum. From the photos, the expert had identified it as an "Insular Penannular" brooch, dated earlier than 800 AD. "We will need to test it to narrow down its age," he said, but indicated that its elaborate metalwork in gold, with zoomorphic and geometric imagery and studded in small amber stones, suggested its origin.

"Pre-Viking?" Imogen said, echoing her colleague's revelation. She dropped into her carved walnut chair.

"Very rare," said the voice on the line. "Perhaps something captured as a trophy in war or a raid. Too valuable to have been dropped by a shepherd or lost in battle. I agree that there could be a larger treasure trove further down. Can you secure the area?"

Imogen took a deep breath. "We've formed a community group to guard the area. The land is not being used at this time, but there is a planning request for a leisure development there, and some very nasty people trying to do mischief to the site."

The voice replied harshly. "Terrible!" After a polite cough, it continued with a modified tone. "I mean, Imogen, *please* try to stop the development and preserve the site. This could be a major find, both the old foundation and the possible hoard. I'll come up early." Imogen discussed their arrangements and hung up the phone, then stretched out on the chair and stared at her coffered ceiling. She shook her head. She was surprised he'd tried to advise her. It was unimaginable that she would let anyone or anything ruin the historical site, even if she needed to sleep rough there. She wandered to the storage area to search out her old archaeological camping equipment.

The cuckoo clock struck seven, the mechanical birdcall reminding Imogen that she also needed to influence the councillors on the list Michael had given her. She knew exactly where to find one of them at this hour. She could skip supper. She slipped the ancient brooch into her pocket.

As she expected, Colonel Robert McNamara stood dominating the clubhouse bar at the exclusive Stonebridge Golf Club with tales of his adventures in the Falklands War. Imogen had heard all his stories—not surprising, as the retired colonel had attended

Cambridge University with her father. She also knew he was easily swayed by name-dropping.

When she entered the room, her confidence fell. David McKinney was comparing five-irons with McNamara. She needed a moment to think how to adapt her strategy. Instead of rushing over, she ordered a gin and tonic from the bar. The bartender, Sebastian, had been laid off from the Ballybeg Inn and was on Imogen's side. He slid Imogen's drink across to her with a wink. "Happy to do anything I can to help." He flashed a tiny vial of green liquid. "A few drops of this can temporarily remove any minor irritation. Just give me a signal." Imogen found this cloak and dagger world exciting, and her confidence returned.

Well-versed in working a room, the conservationist casually circled a few turns before sidling up to the pair and stopping. "Colonel McNamara! What a pleasant surprise to find you here!" She nodded coldly to David. "Mr. McKinney."

David returned the nod. "Miss Currie. Or is it Ms.?"

"Doctor Currie." She fixed her serious gaze on her distant cousin.

"Of course, it is." He glared back.

Robert McNamara, as ever ready to announce a notable connection, explained, "Dr. Currie is an alumnus of Cambridge University, as are her father and I. We were both half blue—"

David winced. "I see."

"In rowing," McNamara concluded grimly.

Imogen plunged in. "Colonel, I am sure Mr. McKinney is eager to hear your opinion on the FU planning application. I know I am." She sipped her gin and tonic.

McNamara pontificated as to his belief that cash was sacred, but grass is only grass. Once the colonel advanced to quoting Margaret

Thatcher, David grinned. "Exactly, McNamara, you are *so* right! You cannot stop progress because of a few red squirrels!"

"Precisely, McKinney! If the wee red squirrels are being dominated by the big grey squirrels, they bally well ought to buck up and learn to defend themselves!"

Imogen did not like her odds. "Colonel McNamara, don't you feel our local heritage ranks higher?"

"Perhaps, Imogen. But one can't eat history!"

She blinked. A serious maneuver was required to get this conversation out of the weeds. Imogen threw the signal to Sebastian and plowed in. "That is certainly a very popular approach, Colonel, and you show your earnest commitment to advancing the public's economic interest. But you know, I was discussing heritage with HRH last year at the Royal Gala, and he is very much on side with the preservation of local historical sites. He's written oodles on the subject. He confided to me, at the time, that he would always be available to inspect any such sites if I were to ask him. Possibly an official visit?"

Sebastian refreshed David's drink, which the American barely acknowledged, although he certainly knocked it back fast enough.

"The Prince of Wales," noted McNamara with interest. "That would be stupendous!"

David coughed. "The Prince of Wales?!"

Imogen smiled. Was the aggrieved surprise on David's face due to the threat of royalty or a sudden stabbing gut pain?

David glanced at the glass he had just drained. He excused himself rapidly. Imogen's eyes stalked him out of the room. She then swung back to McNamara with a sparkle.

Her hand lightly brushed the sleeve of his Harris Tweed. "Now don't say anything just yet, Colonel. You understand royal protocol better than anyone. Let's keep it our little secret. Old cottages sometimes have many hidden historical treasures." She flashed him the ancient brooch as if to say, "and there's more like this."

She slipped the brooch back into her pocket just as McNamara reached for it. "Tell Cousin David—oh, he's my cousin, yes, of course you didn't know—just tell Cousin David that I was joking about the prince. He's an American and royalty frightens him." She winked. "I must press on." She couldn't resist a little sashay step as she exited the clubhouse. Something was coming over her; she felt giddy. She was a different woman. A Machiavellian adventuress. She studied her reflection in her Jeep's rear-view mirror. Perhaps a fedora would suit her—like Indiana Jones.

The sun was setting. She was ravenous and wouldn't say no to a drink, so she started the engine and muttered to herself, "Home, James, and don't spare the horses." Imogen was confident now that she and Michael and their supporters would convince a majority of the councillors to vote against the FU proposal. She knew that Michael had been negotiating exchanges of support for other pet causes, including with the prickly Councillor Shaw. Kara had successfully used her genealogical research as a carrot. Nesbitt was working his way through the church choir, and Esmée was pulling together the many Friends of the Red Squirrel groups. No one knew how Mary was convincing people, but she was very effective.

However, all this would likely be only a stopgap since the council was always hungry for revenue-generating schemes. If David made a dynamic but false presentation to the planning committee, he could still convince them to approve the FU project. The best way to stop him permanently was to invoke the Conservation Act. For that, they would need to influence bigger fish. She had almost lost Colonel McNamara, and he might still slip away. After spontaneously conjuring up the Prince of Wales, Imogen realized that she needed some social heavyweights. She needed to call her old schoolmate Tommy.

An officious secretary answered the phone after two rings. Imogen stated that she would like to speak to the marquess as soon as possible. She was told that the Marquess MacGuffin was unavailable, but her message would be passed along. As Imogen hung up the phone, a wave of social inadequacy hit her. She was more used to hiding from the spotlight than seeking it due to the scandal of her great grandmother's birth.

She was relieved when, seconds later, her phone rang, and a friendly voice enquired, "What's going on, Moge? I'm just off the court and getting out of my kit." It was her childhood friend Tommy—the Marquess MacGuffin, and the son of the Duke of Inish-Rathcarrick.

Imogen gave the shortest possible version of the situation. "I won't sugar coat it, Tommy. It's a question of preserving heritage, and your father could be a great help."

"You've always avoided the old man, Moge, but if it's an audience you're after, I'll set something up and ring you back with a time. Bye for now." With that, the call ended with no hesitation and no waiting for confirmation. *Typical of an aristocrat,* she thought with amusement.

Kara felt Scratch licking her nose. This woke her from a trance, sitting cross-legged on the stones, facing the sea. She had left the dog at home and was surprised that she had tracked her down. Kara was soaked in sea spray and thoroughly happy. Scratch wagged her tail and licked the salt from Kara's face. Bugsy and Keith were gone. David had disappeared long ago. She stood and descended from the stones easily. She and Scratch strolled back home so she could change her clothes. From there, they headed out to pay a visit to Seamus.

The Seanchaí lived in an old cottage behind Morag's house. It boasted a lush garden with vibrant plants and colourful flowers. At Kara's knock, Morag answered her father's door and ushered Kara and Scratch inside. The room had a low ceiling and white plaster walls. Brass plates on the wall caught the light. Turf was burning in the fireplace and gave a pleasant scent to the room, blending as it did with Seamus's favourite tobacco and the lavender plants on the windowsill. The old storyteller was snoring in a plush chair by the fire.

"Father?" Morag poked him gently. "Father, Kara has come to listen to your story."

He murmured in his sleep, "Which one?"

"Which one?" Morag repeated. "The only one you've been reciting for weeks now. That's which one."

"I wandered up and down the country for someone to listen." Seamus opened his eyes and blinked a few times. Morag propped him up on his pillows, straightened his throw, and handed him a fresh cup of tea.

Seamus smiled. This close to him, and in the clear evening light, Kara could see that Seamus's eyes looked cloudy. Did he have cataracts?

Kara pointed to her cell phone. "Is it okay if I record this?"

Seamus smiled.

"Oh, aye, no bother!" Morag responded as she offered a chair next to Seamus and a cup of tea. "It's faster than shorthand, isn't it?" She gave the room a quick look round. "If you don't mind," she indicated the door to the kitchen, "I have already heard this one much too often."

Kara balanced the mug of tea on her right knee. "Seamus, do you want to have your tea first or …?"

His eyes stared at the ceiling as his voice rose in that clear and resonant delivery reserved for telling stories. "This is a tale called The Trials of the Children of Coinnigh."

Kara scrambled to hit record on the phone. "Okay. We're off."

"Coinnigh was the head of an ancient family, only one of a number of families that preserved the old ways and beliefs. This was a time with an even balance between the world of people and the world of fairies. A time when people understood the protection of the oak and the healing of the willow. When the sea had a voice to be heard, and the land sang with joy.

"But new chieftains rode over the land and brought change. One such was Domhnaill MacDhuibhfinn. MacDhuibhfinn brought his armies to take control over the land and the people. All the other chieftains knelt and swore fealty to MacDhuibhfinn. Only Coinnigh stood against him.

"Coinnigh could not withstand the forces of MacDhuibhfinn alone. Coinnigh called on those people who had respect and affection for him for his courage and fairness. And he called on the Fae—the fairy folk who hid under the earth and in the trees. Coinnigh was the last true druid. Coinnigh's mother was one of the fairy folk, and she had taught him the magic that would persuade the Fae to his cause. It was said Coinnigh could talk a Leprechaun out of his gold. When he called upon the fairy folk to join him in battle, many would come—after a good barter, of course.

"The Fae won their battles by changing the weather or stealing the wits of their opponents. Coinnigh used the Fae to deliver havoc on MacDhuibhfinn, his sworn enemy. The war lasted for years. The fairy tricks were numerous, but eventually, MacDhuibhfinn squeezed Coinnigh into a tighter and tighter corner. He put siege to Coinnigh and his Fae army at Dundurn Castle. The fairy folk were fierce, but MacDhuibhfinn consulted a group of druids to find new ways to trick them.

"On Midsummer Night, Coinnigh sought out the highest rampart of the castle in order to perform a special ritual to banish MacDhuibhfinn's army. As the sun set into the sea, Coinnigh unleased his magic. The wind rushed in, the fairies gathered, and the fire leapt up to quicken the hearts of Coinnigh's soldiers to give them the strength to conquer their enemies. But when Coinnigh tried to leave the rampart to lead his army into battle, he was trapped by MacDhuibhfinn himself. The raging waters of the sea crashed behind him. As the two foes fought, the clash of their swords and shields thundered throughout the land. The moon rose higher in the sky, and its brightness distracted Coinnigh. He stepped backwards on the parapet. His foot slipped. His body plunged from that highest point of the castle down into the sea below. The last true druid was gone in a heartbeat. His distraught soldiers were thrown into confusion. A few peeked carefully over the parapet and down into the water. Coinnigh was never seen again. Their opponents cheered. MacDhuibhfinn declared himself the most powerful.

"Coinnigh had three children and each one different. Upon the news of their father's demise, they scattered to the ends of the earth with no possessions and no kin. But the story foretells that they will return to fight a new battle.

"And thus, the legend lives and will be fulfilled. When Coinnigh's three children return, they will speak strange languages and follow strange customs. When that day comes, they will carry magic learned from new wizards. When the land draws them back, the fairy folk will rejoice, and secrets will be revealed. But the people will not know them. In truth, the three children will not know each other. Only when the three gather during the full moon and combine their magic will all be safe again.

"Coinnigh's first child will be a Witch and a follower of the ancient tree worship. She has many tricks and incantations. She seeks that which will make her family resilient in a world that is fair. Her familiar will lead her to the sacred site. The Fae will fulfill her wishes.

"Coinnigh's second child will be a High Priestess who sits high in a tower overlooking the land. She protects the history of the village. She retains all knowledge. She seeks that which will ward off destruction. Her understanding of the writings will safeguard the sacred site. Her blood will end old hostilities.

"Coinnigh's third child will be a Lunatic, searching for respect. He has many riches. He cannot mend the world because his mind is fogged with madness, and he is blind. He wants what he does not need. He cannot understand the treasures that he holds. Destruction will follow in his wake.

"Until the stars align and the separate become whole, the Mother and the sacred site are in danger from the Lunatic. He will approach with darkness in his heart. Each time, he must be repelled, and yet he will try again. To defend the sacred site from the Lunatic, the High Priestess will gather the village to guard it day and night. The Witch will throw spells and deceptions to impede his steps. Three enchantments thwart him, first blindness, then a shroud, and finally, endless pleasure.

"The first daughter's true heart will unlock the treasure, the secret loves, the happy pleasures, and above the rest, a spell that binds two worlds together, to guard against the foe. The fairy folk will summon her and will reveal to her their splendour, restoring ancient charms and joy. Then the village will awake to love and brotherhood flowing through the streets. The Fae will celebrate with humans. Rainbows will descend from the heavens. Lovers, young and old, will avow their affection. Music will abound to make the people dance, but not the ancient fairy music that enthralls to the death. It will be joyous human music that feeds the soul. Choirs of children will lead the adults into the future. While the village rejoices, the Lunatic will be held back by a magic spider's web. Neighbours will dance into the night. Enemies will mend their differences as Artemis waxes bright in the summer twilight.

"But the Lunatic's rage grows with the lunar Goddess. He fights to fulfill the prophecy of doom, but the end is not within his control. When he escapes the third enchantment, it is the sign that the battle will soon begin.

"The Mother demands protection. The destiny of hope must be fulfilled. The Witch must gather thirteen, seven within and six without; three of the blood, and four of rank, and six good souls. The three of the blood are the children of Coinnigh. The four of rank are a nobleman, a priest, a paladin, and a shepherd. The six good souls hold the circle. With bell, book, and candle, and the incantations that her power will attract, the Witch will invoke the strength the Mother needs. Coinnigh's legacy to his children is three circles of gold, preserved for them by the Fae. Each child must find and keep their gold circle, for only when the three circles join will the fairies unleash their power.

"Hark! For the battle looms. The Mother lies abandoned by those who swore to care for her. Swiftly fly from stone to stone the messages of doom and ruin. The dawn sees birds of black iron descend, carrying betrayal, greed, and destruction. Two sons return to their families, one for ill, and one for good. All chieftains will close their eyes and ears and leave the people to defend the land, and only one amongst them will hear the cries for help. If the curse is broken, a new hero will arise."

He stopped. Kara thought that Seamus was asleep again. As she leaned over to take away his cup, the old man's cloudy eyes snapped open. "Do you have the story in your heart to carry always?" he demanded.

"Yes, I do." She replied.

"Good." He closed his eyes, and this time his snoring indicated that he was fast asleep.

Ten

K**ara** suffered from nightmares for the rest of the weekend as the words of Seamus' story swirled in her head. Obviously, she was the Witch who must "throw spells and deceptions to impede the steps" of David, the Lunatic, while Imogen, the High Priestess, was already working on her task: gathering knowledge and the village to guard Lisnasidhe. Kara recognized that not actually being a witch could be a setback, so she arranged a number of possible deceptions to use in the place of genuine magic.

On Monday morning, she arrived early at the Council chambers, ready for a fight, and there were no shortages of fights to engage her. She soon found herself sprawled across a bench with her satchel, computer, and several open notebooks. A small but noisy crowd hovered around her. Two cousins in dispute as to whose grandparent was the eldest had dragged Kara into the argument. "Quiet!" she called out. "I need to concentrate."

A heavy silence. The parties and their solicitors exchanged dirty looks. After several minutes, Kara looked up. "Derwood was born twelve minutes before Darrin," she pronounced. One side howled and the other cheered.

The happy solicitor nodded smugly at her. "Email that document to me, please." The crowd stampeded into a conference room.

When the crowd cleared, it revealed Imogen standing on the other side of the corridor, straight-backed, legs properly spaced, with her briefcase grasped firmly with both hands at hip level. In response to Kara's big wave, she waggled her head from side to side, then moved across the corridor with deliberate steps. Kara swept up the notebooks and laptop and threw it all in the bag.

Imogen sat. "Is Michael inside the chamber?"

"Yes. The session should start shortly. Have you seen David or McKay?"

"No." Imogen looked surprised. "Aren't they here yet?"

"No." Kara finished her coffee and sent a quick text on her phone.

They entered the chamber together. Imogen, as a representative speaking against the application on the grounds of heritage preservation, took a reserved seat next to Michael, who would present the findings of Ballybeg Biodiversity. Kara opted for the back row, hoping for a better vantage point if it all kicked off. Kara admired Michael in his suit and tie. *Very nice! Maybe a haircut? Still, quite convincing.*

The development application was number four on the agenda of the planning committee. Lisle Christie sat with the planning office staff, who gave their presentations on each agenda item. Morag, Sarah, and the Ballybeg Yarnbombers for Heritage sat knitting in the front row. A shadowy figure in a hoodie and sweatpants sat motionless with a cell phone on his lap on the right side.

David and McKay were late. Even the knitters were searching the room as the committee moved quickly through the agenda. Soon the clerk announced the next item: "Finn's Ultimate Ballybeg Amusements and Recreations plc, being an application for planning permission for a one-hundred-acre leisure and commercial centre on the townland known as Lisnasidhe on

Beeswax Road. Submitted to the council's planning office by Mr. David McKinney."

Representing the planning office, Lisle now gave a summary of the application in his driest and most official voice. The recommendation from the planning office was to reject the application. "All the details are in the report that we have prepared." He summarized it nicely.

It was obvious that David was not in the room, but protocol necessitated that the clerk leave the chamber to search for Mr. McKinney. Everyone else stayed in their seats and exchanged looks. Colonel McNamara, chairing the meeting, extruded a few harrumphs and rapped his fingers against his open microphone. Imogen watched the chamber doors. Kara checked the texts on her phone.

When the clerk returned empty-handed, McNamara exerted his authority as far as it went. "Perhaps the representatives speaking against the application could save us from wasting our time. We will hear from Mr. McKinney afterwards, if he arrives."

Imogen rose to speak. She eloquently presented her arguments, citing her initial consultations with the Historic Buildings Authority and heritage and conservation specialists in London, Belfast, and Dublin. She focused on the cultural significance of the old cottage structure at the foundation level, unique in the local area. To conclude, she casually mentioned that Mr. McKinney had not yet irrefutably proved his claim of ownership of Lisnasidhe. Then she took her seat.

Michael stood. "Thank you, Dr. Currie." He went on to deliver his team's presentation regarding the protected red squirrel colony in Rosheen Wood.

When it was done, Colonel McNamara tapped his microphone. Kara bit her nails. "As the applicant appears to think it unnecessary to attend and to present further information regarding the application, I move that the committee consider the recommendation of the planning office with the information as presented to them today. Do I have a seconder for this motion?"

Councillor McMullen seconded the motion. The committee then quickly voted to uphold the planning office's recommendation for a refusal. Only two councillors voted against the recommendation; one was Councillor Shaw, who did so with a wicked smile.

The other business of the committee proceeded. Kara slipped out into the corridor, followed by Imogen.

Imogen touched Kara's arm. "What the devil was that?"

Michael joined them. "What the hell was that?"

Kara smiled mischievously. "Perhaps they couldn't decide what to wear?"

She received a text from Fatima at the inn: "Operation successful. The emperors have no trousers." Another. "And no kilts either."

Michael craned his neck to see. "What does it say?"

"Hold on." Kara typed, "I am too slow with texting. Call me." The phone rang almost immediately. Kara answered, saying, "It worked; didn't it?"

Fatima's voice was excited and breathless. "It worked! Early this morning, Annie and I stole all their trousers, just like you suggested, and took them all to the cleaner. The cleaner was nice enough to send them straight away to the plant in Coleraine."

Then Annie sang into the phone, "No trousers until tomorrow!" Then she added, "And they have no kilts either! Tell her that was *my* line!"

"Yes, I already texted that to Kara, Annie."

As she listened, Imogen's expression changed from astonishment to admiration. "I don't believe you, Kara! You are some sort of witch!" She leaned into Kara's phone. "Girls, run. Escape now before one of them finds something to cover himself."

"Okay." The rest was just giggling, stomping, and happy shrieking.

Michael shook his head. "Incredible! But it's only a delay. David can come back with a new application, and next time, he might have secured the proof of ownership."

"Then it's time to celebrate small victories." Kara chuckled. "Shall we go for a coffee?"

"No more coffee!" Imogen rolled her eyes.

David, in a standard-issue hospitality bathrobe, searched for wine behind the bar in the Ballybeg Inn. McKay, also in a bathrobe, put out a sign—"Closed for Repairs"—and locked the inn's front doors. Bugsy tightened the sash of his white cotton robe. He stared at the loudly ticking clock in the dining room as if it could answer the mystery of his lost trousers. There were no other guests. The housekeeping and kitchen staff were missing. There were no "pants!" as David called them. McKay had corrected him with the proper British word, "trousers," and called David rude. David had responded with a five-minute demonstration of what rude actually sounded like.

It had been a horrendous day. It was now two o'clock, hours after the council's planning committee meeting. David had refused to come out of his room, sitting on the floor in his underpants until half past one. McKay had yelled through the door that there was no staff to bring him room service, and he wasn't going to carry things upstairs for him. "I'll cook something to eat downstairs, but that's all!"

Hungry, David had flung on a bathrobe and trudged down the stairs.

Behind the bar now, David snagged the most expensive bottle he could see and carried it to the table, announcing to McKay, "I'd like a steak, rare, with roasted baby potatoes."

McKay froze halfway to the kitchen. Without turning, the innkeeper replied, "I'm making scrambled eggs and toast. Take it or leave it!" He paused. "If you behave, I'll also do some ham."

He remained frozen until he heard David say, "Okay." Only then did he continue to the kitchen.

Half the wine was gone by the time McKay returned with three plates of eggs, ham, and toast. They ate in silence.

Bugsy ate with one hand, the other gripping a large iron nail. "My beautiful new trousers!" he muttered. "Bad fairy magic! Abjuration fails."

David moaned. "*Abjuration?* What the fuck are you ranting about, Bugsy? Don't be an ass. It's a conspiracy!"

"Well, that's obvious, David," McKay said, pointing an eggy fork, "but the question you have to ask is why? How could one person alienate so many people so quickly?"

David snapped back, "I agree, McKay. You really need to ask yourself why the village hates you."

McKay closed his eyes. "Not me. You."

David could not believe this. "You're blaming me? It's *your* staff! I know you've got some shitty problems with unions in this country—Is it even a country? But really! If you don't know how to manage your employees or bring the customers in, you're a pretty crappy businessman."

David's phone rang. Before he could say, "Hello," Monsieur Laurel was screaming at him in a very Parisian manner. "*Insupportable!* have never witnessed such incompetence in my life! We put you there for two weeks to prepare the FU project for a very simple planning application. You take three weeks and then you do not even show up for the presentation to the planning committee! Do you think we are fools?"

David attempted to charm the Frenchman. "Well, hello to you too. I didn't know you were at the planning committee meeting. When did you arrive in town?"

"We were not at the planning committee meeting! And neither were you! *Vous êtes tellement*—an imbecile, David McKinney! Of course, we sent one of our people there. He recorded the whole thing on his phone. That little conservationist woman and her little cottage, she has set us back weeks! And that environmental radical? The one with the squirrels in his head? Squirrels?! Moreover, you were not there to defend it! Do you even know that you lost the request?"

"Well, I had supposed that the request would be remanded to another day—"

"Remanded? They do not remand these things! How did red squirrels become involved? What is going on about red squirrels? When did the rodents come into it?"

David didn't know what Laurel was talking about. He looked at Bugsy. "Red squirrels?"

Bugsy seemed happy for a question that he could answer. He nodded. "Red squirrels are an endangered species. They're protected," Bugsy offered.

"Apparently the red squirrels are endangered," David shrugged.

Laurel scoffed. "You are endangered, Mr. McKinney."

David slapped Bugsy.

McKay stared at David.

Laurel drawled, "Do you like rodents, McKinney?"

The question surprised David. "I haven't thought about them much—"

"Is Mr. McKay there? Put him on," the Frenchman ordered.

David handed the phone to McKay. He could only hear McKay's responses. "Yes. No. No. Yes." McKay gave him a shifty look then and turned away from him. "Yes. I understand completely. Yes, I will send that to you. Yes."

David hovered between anxiety and anger. "What did he want? What are you sending him?"

"The application package material and the objections report. They want to review them."

That can't be all. He grabbed his phone but heard only a dial tone. "Goddammit!" David spat at McKay. "You Europeans think you are all the best! Well, you aren't! I have powerful friends too! The Americans can take over FU. I'm going to call a friend of mine! He's super! The best real estate developer in the world. He's running for president! Very connected. He'll fly over here to push through FU."

McKay stood up, walked away from David, and peeked out between the curtains to the courtyard.

David continued to yell at the innkeeper's back. "All you stupid little Irish people won't know what hit you!" He speed-dialled a number in his phone, waited, and left a message, "Hey! It's David McKinney. Hey, I am over here in Ireland, and I have got a very sweet deal. It's all lined up at the tee. I just need the right guy to bash it out for a hole in one. It won't take too much of your time! I know you're busy with … you know. Ha-ha! Understatement, am I right? But call me back!"

Bugsy shifted uncomfortably. He looked up briefly at David, then returned to a text conversation on his phone. McKay disappeared into his office. David amused himself with thoughts of his friend flying to the rescue.

Eleven

Kara waited at her usual table upstairs at the Teaspot with Michael and Imogen. Scratch was asleep on the floor. McKay had called Michael to request a meeting in order to "start afresh" and "find common ground." After "yesterday's fiasco," he was taking control of the project, revising the FU planning application for a second run at the ball. The application still targeted Lisnasidhe but with McKay as the principal FU lead.

On the ground floor, the constant clacking of knitting needles formed a rhythmic soundscape. The Teaspot had become a hub for groups that shared a mandate to drive David McKinney out of Ballybeg. One of the largest groups was the Yarnbombers, who were busy creating an inventory of long scarves, squares and rectangles, pouches, and anything knitted, sometimes crocheted. The room was animated with moving elbows and flying needles. One woman was knitting super-strong purple acrylic into one long piece that was five inches wide. Her hands worked back and forth repeatedly while the yards of finished rows grew and spiralled down into a large basket. Kara couldn't imagine what was she making. Another woman crocheted long strips of recycled plastic bags with thin lines of leather.

The Teaspot benefited from the increased business and sold an enormous number of baked goods, washed down with strong tea or coffee. Annie and Fatima, in hiding from McKay, were hired by Sarah to meet the demand. She brought in a Gaggia, which Fatima handled with a deft touch for the cappuccinos.

Kara gazed out the upper-front window, watching the street below and nibbling at her cuticles. From here, she would be able to see them coming. The upper floor was more formal Georgian in decor, with tall paned windows and long linen-silk curtains. Annie stood at a table at the back wall, quietly folding freshly washed linen and sneaking peeks at Michael.

Kara wanted a reconciliation and had thought the upper floor of the Teaspot might be neutral territory. She hoped that the light pleasant atmosphere would convince David that they could all be friends. This could really be the beginning of a new partnership with equal considerations to all parties. If not, well, she kept adding to her list of witchy tricks.

Imogen interrupted Kara's thoughts. "McKay is smarter than David. He knows he can promote FU faster if he pretends to partner with the conservationists and the community. He'll promise anything to win his planning permission and then ignore us. I've seen it before."

Still at the window, Kara started to wave her left hand frantically. Michael correctly interpreted Kara's gesture. "They must be here."

An eerie silence fell below them, broken only by the jangling of the bell above the front door. Downstairs, the needles had stopped clicking, and voices were hushed. Two sets of footsteps sounded on the wooden floors, crossing the room to the front staircase, and then ascending. Alerted by the footfalls on the front stairs, Annie bounded backwards and scuttled down the back staircase.

McKay appeared first, businesslike, bright, and pleasant. Behind him lumbered David, rumpled and sulking. Bugsy was not with them. Seats were offered and taken. Kara poured tea from the pot on the table and passed around the scones. David insisted on coffee. Imogen texted Fatima for an Americano, black.

McKay thanked them for the meeting and complimented their appearance. He promised that he would quickly come to the point, and then didn't. He commented instead on the weather and the traffic in the village.

A shaking hand placed a cup of coffee upon the newel post at the top of the stairs, then frantic footfalls descended to safety. Kara rose to fetch the coffee for David, who forgot to thank her.

McKay began a preamble on the themes of historical buildings and protected species to show that he understood the positions of Michael and Imogen. He hesitated, looking at Kara, who said, "Oh, I'm just here for the ride."

David sneered. "On a broomstick?"

Imogen rolled her eyes. David ignored the look and continued, frowning at Kara. "Never mind, you old witch. I found this gold coin." He dropped his phone on the table and fished out the coin from a pocket. "Bugsy told me that gold wards off witchcraft. I'm keeping it as a talisman to protect me."

Imogen sighed disapprovingly. "An *amulet* then."

David's face reddened. "What?"

Imogen expanded her lesson. "An amulet is for protection against something. A talisman is to attract good luck. Which is it? A talisman or an amulet?"

David locked eyes with Imogen. "It is an amulet to protect me from you witches."

"Gold won't protect you from witches. Just from the Pooka. And a mysterious coin? That could be a trick of the fairy folk. You should be careful."

McKay laughed nervously.

"What type of coin is it?" Kara stretched forward across the table to see it. This would mean that each McKinney had found their own gold circle. David moved it out of Kara's view but held it out for Michael to examine.

Michael's eyes grew wide. "An 1820 George the Third Double Sovereign. In mint condition. Wow! That is lucky, fairies or no fairies."

Imogen was suspicious. "Where did you find it?"

"In the pond on Lisnasidhe. My land."

McKay seemed suspicious. "How could it be in such good condition if you scooped it out of the water?" Kara agreed with McKay on this point, but no one else was listening.

Imogen snorted. "Lisnasidhe is *not* your land."

"*My land!*" David insisted. He slipped the sovereign back into his pocket.

Michael scowled. "I suppose now you think there's a hoard of old coins on Lisnasidhe."

David motioned with a thumb. "If there is, it's mine, and you better leave it alone!"

McKay rested his eyes for a moment, waiting for a lull in the conversation, then returned to his point. "In any case, I am certain that we are all much closer in our positions than things have suggested up to now. Finn's Ultimate can combine the dynamism of commerce and the deference to our common heritage and ecosystem while providing a secure financial future for the community."

After thirty years in bureaucracy, Kara knew hogwash when she heard it. A politician uses gobbledygook when they are promising nothing. Kara had written a lot of twaddle herself and could easily create charts and statistics to back it up too. It was one talent of which she was not proud.

Surprisingly, the first objection to McKay's new approach did not come from Michael, Kara, or Imogen, but from David himself. He jumped to his feet and slammed the table, jostling the teacups, the plates of scones, and the various cell phones. "Bullshit! Why are you wasting time on these losers, McKay?! FU is the best thing that ever happened to Ballybeg! We don't need to have them on side!"

Scratch sprang awake and settled onto Kara's lap, guarding her.

Imogen stood up and approached David. "In all the projects, all the development projects I have worked on in Europe, in America, or here, I have *never* met anyone as asinine as you!"

David scoffed. "Really?"

"Yes, really. You're the most boorish, most incompetent, most selfish person—"

McKay stepped in, his hands in the air. "David, you're out of line. Let's sit down."

Michael joined the group. "David, you're out of control. Can you calm down?"

But David was on a roll. *"I don't need to calm down!* You—*all of you*—need to get out of my way! Because if you don't, you'll wish you did! Because I've called in the big guns! The big scary American guns!"

McKay tried to grab David's shoulders. "David! Don't, please don't—" David pushed him off.

Kara was the only one still seated. Scratch was pawing at something on the table. Kara's gaze fluctuated between the dog and the argument, voicing her opinion that David was looking somewhat ill, physically.

Finally, gasping for breath, David said, "Enough! I have already called my friends for help, the best real estate developers in America! They'll be on their way. So, look out!"

McKay took David's arm. "Kara might be right. He may be ill. Come along, David. You need to rest."

A scramble started as McKay tried to leave money for the bill, but David grabbed the banknotes. McKay returned the cash to the table, and David grabbed it again. Michael finally called out, "Just leave it McKay!"

McKay dragged David out of the room and back downstairs. Kara imagined the two negotiating a path through all those needles as she listened for the bell on the door to indicate their departure from the shop.

It rang, and peace resumed. The trio settled back down at the table and looked down into their teacups. Scratch returned to the floor to lie down. Imogen patted her brow with her linen handkerchief. Michael started to speak but stopped himself. Kara pulled a cell phone from her satchel and started to check its contact list and call history.

Imogen looked a little ill. "His friend? David mentioned his big-shot American friend. Do you think he meant …?" Her voice trailed off.

Kara found the contact's name in the phone. She held it up so the others could see the screen. "Apparently, yes. David meant him."

"Oh my god!" Michael moaned, cradling his head in his hands. "That's the last thing we need." Then his head snapped up. "Wait. Is that David's phone?"

"Yup," replied Kara, "but don't worry. I just texted David's big-shot friend to say that it was all a joke." She smiled. "And I wished him well in the election. There's no way he'll win."

Kara then explained that her chief motivation for "borrowing" David's phone was to find contact numbers for someone— anyone—who could help calm David. "But I'll have to work fast before he misses his phone." She didn't tell them it had been Scratch's idea.

The midsummer sun set briefly between ten p.m. and four a.m. The hours in between were barely twilight. If the evening was warm and dry, like tonight, Kara liked to sit outside her little hut in the gloaming with Scratch. A few fireflies lingered around them.

Kara wasn't surprised that David kept his phone unlocked. She considered all the things she might still do with David's phone, but now that the threat of big-shot help from America had been handled, she decided it was enough to contact someone who might have a beneficial calming effect on him. She had listened to Keith, who listened to Bugsy, so she knew that neither David's wife nor his elder daughter would be the right person to help. No one from the corporation, and not his lawyer or his accountant either. His father was dead. Apparently, David hated his mother. There was a bar owner named Dev, but Bugsy thought Dev was intimidated by David. *I know who it should be.* There was one person who could help to calm David's temper. Kara made a note of the phone number and turned off David's phone.

Kara dialled the number from her own cell phone. After she politely introduced herself, she explained her purpose. "I'm concerned for your father's well-being. He's not coping well, you see, despite what he's told you, Kathleen." She repeated some of the interactions between David and the locals. She omitted that David's trousers had disappeared one day or that bees had swarmed him. She also happened to forget that Mary's sheep had stampeded him, and that Sebastian and Imogen had poisoned him once in a trivial way. Oh, and that his phone had been hijacked. But she talked about all the rest.

Kathleen was very friendly. It was a pleasant conversation, although it drifted into a small disagreement as to whether the Pittsburgh Penguins would be as good a team without Sidney Crosby. However, that matter was deferred. In the end, Kara persuaded Kathleen McKinney to fly over and help her father. *I'm certain that David needs Kathleen in order to calm down and rethink his plans for world domination.*

Things were looking up, at last. With that task done, Kara listened again to her recording of Seamus's story. She had almost memorized it, but the challenge was understanding it. Clearly, she was the Witch, Imogen the High Priestess, and David the Lunatic, the three children of Coinnigh, pronounced Kinney, therefore MacCoinnigh, which would be an early form of McKinney. The three gold circles had been delivered in the form of a ring, a brooch, and a coin, but how were they to use them? Her theory was that in order to save Lisnasidhe or at least Rosheen Wood, the McKinneys would need to find and fight MacDhuibhfinn. *I hope it won't be a violent fight.* But how could the three of them work together if David continued to work against them? It was for this reason that Kara had invested so much hope in Kathleen's ability to win him over. But then, what about all the other things?

Am I supposed to find the fairies? How do I summon fairies? Would they do my bidding? What are the magic spiders and the birds of black iron? How do messages "fly from stone to stone?"

It was true that if David continued as he was, he would cause destruction. But Imogen had created her army of villagers to defend the sacred site. *Which is, of course, Rosheen Wood.*

But if Kara was the Witch, how was she supposed to unlock "the treasure, the secret loves, the happy pleasures, and above the rest, a spell that binds two worlds together to guard against the foe?"

Who are the thirteen? We three McKinneys, the children of Coinnigh. And the rest? A nobleman and a priest; a paladin and a shepherd? Mary is a shepherd. Nesbitt is a priest. Imogen said she knew a marquess, and that's a nobleman.

She googled: "What's a paladin?" Apparently, some kind of holy knight. That just sounded like a combination of a priest and a noble.

She snuggled into bed. *And the six good souls? Could that be just anyone?* She yawned. If she figured out who they were, what was she supposed to do with them? Her hand clutched the repaired silver locket. Scratch climbed onto the bed to bury her nose under Kara's side.

> *Life-sized, living chess pieces glided across a giant board, and Kara knew she was asleep and dreaming. This chess board had more than just the two normal colours of squares. They were gold, green, red, or blue. The chess pieces wore the faces of local people she knew. They wore the faces like masks, and as each piece took its move, diagonally or ahead, or in a knight's sweep, the masks changed. Each time she tried to speak to someone, their face morphed into someone else. Sometimes two would exchange faces, and sometimes the faces circulated like a game of Ring Around the Rosey, with only the faces moving while the bodies did not. Finally, Kara tried to curl up to sleep in a basket of twigs with Scratch. McKay shook the basket and announced that it was check-out time. She grabbed hold of Scratch's collar, and the dog led her to Rosheen Wood to hide in the trees with the red squirrels. Scratch dug deep into the ground and found a rolled-up parchment which read:*

"Bring the people together at the sacred site
when Sister Moon, in her fullness,
meets Brother Sun on his longest path.
Summon the fairies with the Priestess's candles,
the Witch's spell book,
and the Lunatic's bells.
At the appointed hour, gather the gold circles to
the fire.
When the fairy folk are content,
the power of the moon will course through
the people
and prepare them for the fight."

Kathleen emerged from the old cottage. She looked like the photo in David's phone: an attractive young woman with bright red hair. She held in her outstretched hands Kara's family ring, Imogen's ancient brooch, and David's mad king coin. Kathleen turned about, and as she did, she saw Michael standing back-to-back with the red-haired girl. The three gold objects disappeared from Kathleen's hands and reappeared in Michael's. Or had the two just switched faces? She reached for the objects, but the more she reached, the further away the two-faced Kathleen/Michael retreated.

Twelve

Kara awoke in a sweat. It was late. She grabbed her dream book and wrote out the dream as best she could, focusing on the poem. She would analyze the symbolism later. This morning, her mission was to return David's phone without him noticing. Magic was hard work. She'd planned to do it while he was at breakfast in the dining room, and now she was almost late for that.

Imogen offered her a ride into the village. Kara threw herself into the passenger side. "You're up later than usual," Imogen observed. Kara tried to describe her dream, but Imogen dismissed it. "Don't eat so late."

As she approached the inn, Sebastian motioned her away from the building and toward the bridge. "You're late. Anyway, McKinney ordered breakfast in his suite."

"Drat!" She pondered for a moment. "So then, option two, I guess. Sebastian, it's Operation Single Malt. I was hoping to save that one for later."

The bartender nodded. "Operation Single Malt it is." He saluted. "Captain."

She returned the salute. "Make it so." She sat on the bridge and waited until David's car started for the distillery, then she entered quietly. David and Bugsy might be gone, but she also wanted to avoid McKay. Luckily, he was busy with new staff.

Chef Phillippe greeted her in the lobby and slipped her the key to David's suite.

It was a spacious suite. She could not resist having a look around. The closet was full of business suits, shirts, and ties. Nothing casual or cozy. Not a jumper nor cardigan. No slippers. Not even a sports shirt of some team or other. It wasn't normal.

No family pictures. No souvenirs of home. No souvenirs of here. No newspapers or magazines. The computer and business papers were presumably locked in the suite's safe. David had lived here for weeks, and yet the entire place was devoid of life.

She wiped David's phone and dropped it on the floor between the bed and the nightstand, close to the charging cord. Then she scurried back downstairs. A quick pass of the key to Phillippe and she was out of the inn. Her heart was racing. She needed a cup of tea. She headed for the Teaspot.

David draped himself across his sofa like a Victorian damsel-in-distress. One arm shielded his eyes from the glare of sunlight. His half-eaten breakfast sat precariously on the hassock beside him. He called out, "Bugsy! Did you look under my bed?"

"Yes, Boss."

"Did you check my suit pockets?"

"Yes, Boss, and I checked at the front desk, and I asked the cleaners to keep an eye out for it too."

It's damn inconvenient not knowing where your phone is. Like losing an arm. David sat up. He pushed away the hassock and a croissant skited off. He was certain he'd left the cell phone in the Teaspot or maybe in the car coming back. But no one had seen it. His demands to McKay to find it were ignored. Apparently, McKay was training new staff and didn't want to speak to David. The feeling was mutual, but David objected to his invisibility. *Might as well get dressed.* As he opened the closet in his room, he took a quick inventory to ensure that all his pants were still there.

He heard a quiet knock on the suite's door and Bugsy opening it. It was the bartender. Striding into the bedroom, Sebastian brashly handed David an invitation from the distillery.

"What's this?"

"I believe it's an invitation for a personal tour. It's from Sean O'Brien. He's the boss."

David quickly read the note. "What? Today?"

"Mr. O'Brien says he has a business proposal to discuss. They have arranged a tasting session and a lunch." Sebastian politely nodded toward Bugsy. "Mr. Carter too, of course."

"Why? What does he have in mind?"

"I wouldn't know, sir. Shall I accept it for you? The distillery is sending a car at noon."

Someone was treating him with the attention he deserved. "Yeah, yeah. Why not? Nothing else to do in this village but drink. Drinking tea, drinking whiskey, drinking seawater, drinking rain. Drink, drink, drink." He bent down to find his shoes. "Look at the river, look at the ocean, look in the pond, get drowned in the rain, get soaked in the mist. It's very liquid here." When he looked up, the bartender was gone. Bugsy laughed softly.

The hired car took David and Bugsy on a short drive to the Ballybeg Whiskey distillery. Its predominance within the village was unmissable. At the street, through the black-iron gates, it presented as an historic and well-preserved factory. Within the enclosure, wooden sheds and stacked barrels filled the cobblestones of the courtyard.

Small outdoor tables and chairs of black ironwork dotted a neat grass lawn. A tall, red-haired man stood at the entrance as the car pulled up. He introduced himself as Sean O'Brien, head of the distillery, and welcomed the two visitors inside.

The impressive Victorian structure proved to be more like a centre foyer, through which one could access more modern areas. The lobby had old wood panelling and painted plaster walls surrounding a grey slate floor. A café and tourist shop sat to either side. Behind a heavy door on the back wall, the building extended into a modern industrial facility.

Bugsy thanked the man for inviting them. David said nothing. His eyes took in the complex around him. Normally, an old building like this should have been knocked down to make room for something bigger and better, but the distillery seemed to have adapted the existing structure efficiently enough. David saw nothing there he could change. *A waste of my time.* A side room in the café was set for a private lunch.

As the salad was served, Sean O'Brien cleared his throat. "Call me Sean. Certain you're a busy man, Mr. McKinney. Mr. McKinney? David. Can I call you David? We at Ballybeg Whiskey are honoured to give you the opportunity to see what we are all about and how we can help you secure the expansion of your"—he coughed—"FU project."

David threw O'Brien a death-ray stare.

O'Brien studied Bugsy's passive expression for a moment, then returned to David. "I'll come to the point. Let us help you make money."

David thought that O'Brien was improving. He might hear him out. He opted for the burger instead of the salmon and coffee instead of water. "Go on."

"We considered your plans for the new FU leisure facility on Beeswax Road. If—"

David shot him a look.

"*When* it goes forward, we at Ballybeg Whiskey are certain that the food and beverage services would be best placed in our experienced hands. We are the oldest distillery in Ireland. *Legal* distillery of course." O'Brien and Bugsy chuckled. David did not.

"So, let us show you why the Ballybeg brand and our facility management are your best choice for consumer satisfaction. Shall we?" O'Brien gestured towards a media presentation on the screen. David filtered out the standard marketing language: "… an internationally recognized brand label … blah, blah, blah … an exemplary range of quality whiskies."

O'Brien spouted last year's sales statistics, both domestic and international, then stood up. "But talking only conveys the bones of our strength. The best demonstration is the product itself." He led them to the mash house to see the start of the whiskey production.

There was a nice girl with a tray of whiskeys. *I like this.*

"Try this. This is our twenty-one-year-old, aged in madeira casks."

"Nice," David pronounced.

"Can you taste the nuttiness? The dried fruit?"

"Yes, of course." It was whiskey, plain and simple. He drank it back.

O'Brien smiled. "Let's move on." The girl with the tray followed.

Whitewashed stone walls confined tall slender-necked copper stills in a tight space. It was hot here. The stills connected to a system of pipes. Bugsy listened intently to O'Brien's description of the distillation process.

O'Brien replaced David's glass. "This one is only ten years, lighter, nice in the summer over ice, with honey, coriander, and vanilla notes." After that glass, the girl handed him another.

Very nice girl, he thought. *Nice smile*. O'Brien was talking about "vapour" now. David was bored. It wasn't as if he wanted to learn how to make the whiskey.

These buildings formed a tiny village within the village, connected by narrow lanes with sharp turns, metal bridges, and steep ramps. David was surrounded by vents and pipes and equipment, and he had no idea where he was going. He felt Bugsy's hand on his shoulder.

O'Brien warned him, "Oh! Watch your step there, David! We don't want you banging your head."

A different glass. O'Brien clearly liked his work. "Ah! So now, that glass you have is our original blended whiskey. An old friend on a cold day. Tastes a little like porridge with caramel." Everyone giggled except David.

"Porridge?" Was this the third or the fourth glass?

How big is this place? Some rooms smelled sour, some sweet. The Master Blender magically appeared to talk about the blending process. He was fed spoonfuls of whiskey. It was crowded. Bugsy, O'Brien, the girl with the tray, the Master Blender, and a blonde woman in a green sequined suit—*no wait*— What? He tried to focus his eyes and surveyed the room. *I'm imagining things.*

Now it was cooler. They were in a large dark room full of wooden barrels. "Casks," O'Brien called them as he banged on one with a mallet until the cork popped out. Then he used a tool to dig into and draw out the whiskey into glasses. O'Brien offered a glass. *"Slainte."*

"Slainche," David repeated.

More whiskey. Some sort of band played. Bugsy was humming along to the music. It sounded like "Children of the Revolution." David heard his mother's voice join in. He tried to open his eyes to see her. The lights blinded him. He could see better with his eyes closed.

There she is: on a crate in the back of the Mifflin Street Co-op, all soft, colourful, tie-dyed Indian cotton and patchouli. She is telling him a story. He climbs into her lap, rests his head on her breast, and plays with the glass beads in her hair. She is saying, "The maiden tried to run from the dragon, but the dragon spoke and explained that he was a magic dragon, and he would protect her."

There's Daddy. Daddy has a beard and faded jeans. He's sad. He looks beaten. A letter hangs from his fingers. He says to Mummy, "We aren't going to Canada. I promised to stay. My father says he'll make this go away, but in exchange, I have to—"

"You have to what, Marc?" Mummy says. "What do you have to do?"

"I—we—all of us—have to go back to the family. I have to work in the corporation. You have to, I dunno, play Bridge or something."

"I won't do it, Marc. I love you, but I won't do it."

"Please, Magpie? Maggie? It's what's best for David."

David awoke from a bad dream. He was in his bedroom at the Ballybeg Inn. His cell phone was charging on the nightstand.

Kara rushed back to her favourite table in the Teaspot. Sneaking David's phone back into his suite had overexcited her. She needed to lower her blood pressure. A strong cup of tea and the constant clicking of the Yarnbombers below lulled her into a state of calm. The radio played on the overhead speakers. It only added to the ambience; there was news and weather, folk music, and poetry.

Kara drank up the view of Victoria Street below. Like a beehive, on the surface, the village had seemed quiet, but Kara could now read the signs of activity everywhere. Despite the quiet streets, cronies were meeting at the Teaspot, the golf club, the markets, the rugby pitch, or at the pub. Or outside the schools dropping off or picking up children, or in the seniors' recreation centre. They ran into each other in the art gallery, the chamber of commerce meetings, or the small local museum. The opportunities to meet were numerous. The most popular topic had almost always been each other, but now it was the threat of David McKinney and Finn's Ultimate Ballybeg Adventures and Recreations.

Ironically, with the village occupied against David, he roamed freely. Bugsy tagged along unless he was sitting as a model for Keith. Spies like Sebastian and Phillippe watched him in the inn and the golf club. Owen and Liam and the bike gang surveilled his movements elsewhere. Today, they'd reported that David had returned from the distillery sodden drunk and singing an old Fleetwood Mac song. Bugsy had dragged David back into his suite to sleep it off.

However, things were calm today in the Teaspot. Kara anticipated Kathleen's arrival later. She felt confident that the good guys were winning. Sarah joined Kara for afternoon tea. They chatted about the upcoming first annual Ballybeg Pride Parade—another hot topic of village conversation. Their tête-à-tête was enough to push the voice on the radio deeper into the background. Fatima interrupted them with a fresh pot of tea. As they paused to enjoy the freshened cups, Kara actually heard the voice coming from the radio.

Kara poked Sarah. "That sounds like Seamus! On the radio?"

Sarah glanced at the ceiling. "Yes. But with a new story."

"Oh no! A new story?" Kara listened to the storyteller:

"It was at this time that there was, in the village, a King of the River and the Forests. He was young, but he learned much from his mother and his grandmother, who taught him to be wise and kind. The land blessed him and watched over him. The people favoured him to lead them. He had but one problem. He was without a Queen. He lived in hope of a great alliance, for he would show her the wild heather and make her Queen of his heart. A soothsayer foretold that, if he could rid the land of trouble for seven years, he would attract the fairest of maidens. He would find her on the old stone bridge in the centre of the village. Therefore, each day, the young King worked tirelessly to ensure that the land would be the most desirable to attract the fairest maidens. Each night, he prayed that tomorrow, he would meet her. Each morning, he awoke anew, searching for the foretold maiden at the old stone bridge.

"As it came to be, a Lunatic, who wanted to destroy the young King's land, raged alone in a cursed mansion. He used a magic stone to invoke from hell a demon to rage with him. But a Witch, hearing of the Lunatic's invocations, blocked him with a spell of transmogrification."

Kara had been studying the recordings of Seamus in order to understand the symbolism of the language he used. Before, it had been a mishmash of old legends. Now, images formed in her mind as she listened. For instance, the Lunatic was clearly David. But who was the King of the River and the Forests?

A flight of hurried footsteps announced Morag's sudden appearance. She was out of breath. "Is it three o'clock yet?"

Kara looked at the phone. "About twenty minutes past."

"My da's on the radio." She was pointing at the ceiling.

Sarah looked at her. "He's not been on the radio before. Is this new?"

Morag fell into a chair. "It was quite the surprise. The DJ never showed up for his shift. The producer called me about an hour ago. He dragged in Frank and Dennis to play their fiddles, and he invited Da to tell one of his stories. So, I dropped him off at the station and came over here."

Three faces turned up towards heaven as the transmitted voice continued:

"The Lunatic knew nothing of the Witch's spell. He expected the demon as summoned. Midnight approached. The wind howled. He heard the creak of the door. The expected guest arrived! The clock struck midnight. But where there should have been noise and commotion, there were soft steps crossing the room to the rhythm of the clock's ticking. A gentle voice called out to him. In the darkened room, he reached out and discovered the hand of his daughter. Transmogrification!

"This maiden was young and lovely, and much wiser than was her father. But the touch of her hand and the sound of her pleasing voice, which should have quelled the rage in his heart, instead drove him deeper into his lunacy. The maiden listened as her mad father devised a scheme even more evil than before. The Lunatic ordered his lovely daughter to seduce the young King and win him over to his own destructive plans.

"The next morning, as every morning, the young King stepped outside. He looked to the old stone bridge. The bright sun caught his eyes for a moment, but when they cleared, he saw the fairest maiden he had ever imagined, crossing the bridge towards him. Little did he know—"

The fire alarm rang out. Annie had burnt the scones in the kitchen. Billowing black smoke filled the shop. Everyone emptied out to the street. Standing on the pavement, Kara turned to Morag. "Do you know how that story ends?"

Morag shrugged. "No idea."

Kara didn't need yet another mysteriously familiar legend from Seamus. She was still analysing the "Children of Coinnigh." How did the "Lunatic" and the "River King" connect? Did they *all* connect?

Kathleen McKinney was due to arrive just before midnight tonight. Was it a coincidence that Kara had invited her in the place of David's dubious real estate developer? Kara was betting that David's favourite daughter would have a positive effect on him. Was this the Witch's spell of transmogrification? Her mind was in turmoil. What would tomorrow bring? Kara wished she'd heard the end of the story. She needed to clarify the truth. Her rational side was reassuring: *It's only Old Seamus telling one of his stories.* But her intuitive side was afraid the battle was being led by a mystical hand, and the pieces on the chessboard were still exchanging faces.

Imogen, after leaving Kara at the inn in the morning, continued on to meet Tommy at his father's estate. True to his word, Tommy had carefully approached his father regarding a meeting with Dr. Imogen Currie on a vital matter of local heritage preservation. He said it was like a diplomat brokering a peace negotiation.

Imogen's audience was at the duke's hereditary home, Castle Rathcarrick. Despite her long friendship with Tommy, she'd always avoided the castle. It was unclear whether the duke cared about her family reputation, but she knew for certain that the servants would gossip. This grey morning, she paused under the arched portico. It was only for the sake of preserving the cottage at Rosheen Wood that she would risk this horrific situation. She examined her reflection in a window to the side of the door. Her suit was perfect and her hair correct. The portfolio under her arm was detailed and complete. She rang the bell, and the butler ushered her into the main reception salon.

The vast, high-vaulted chamber seemed like a feudal airplane hanger, if such a thing could exist. Thomas Brightman MacGuffin, the Marquess MacGuffin, smiled and busied himself with tunes on the grand piano. Imogen knew that he was a little afraid of his father. Archibald Clarence Burford MacGuffin, the Eighth Duke of Inish-Rathcarrick, held the centre of the room with a military stance. The familial resemblance was subtle. The hierarchy was obvious.

The castle displayed no pretense of modernity. The architecture ranged loosely from Restoration to Edwardian, decorated in a weight of oil paintings, ancient weapons, and faded tapestries. A few animal heads were thrown in for effect. It appealed to Imogen academically, but she was glad not to live there.

Under the disguise of a friendly greeting, Tommy whispered, "No politics."

As if I need that advice. She whispered back, "But what about your plan to run for—"

Tommy hushed her and patted her hand. The duke smiled warmly at the condescending gesture as if this was a good sign of something or other.

"Father. Dr. Imogen Currie. We were at Cambridge together. Her maternal line originated from here."

"The marquess tells me that you are an archeologist."

"A conservationist, Your Grace."

"Ah, what is the distinction then?"

"An archeologist finds things. I help preserve them afterwards."

"Ha-ha! Yes. Like a banker!"

"Just so, Your Grace. I save people's things."

Tommy added, "Especially things in the national interest. Preserving the past. Honouring our history."

The duke threw a cold glance at his son. "Yes, boy. I get it. I'm not an eejit yet."

They sat. At a signal, a tea tray materialized. The duke stared at Imogen. After a pause, she enquired, "Shall I pour?"

He murmured, "Please do." Very old school.

"Sugar?" she offered.

They settled quickly with their refreshments, and Imogen wasted no time in recounting the historical findings in Rosheen Wood on Lisnasidhe. The interest of the local museums. The possibility of a previous settlement site hidden under the surface. She shared the photos of the cottage's architectural details. Then she hinted at the indicators of a new treasure trove and pulled out her feature attraction: the brooch. *Shiny old things always stimulate the imagination.*

The father's reaction to the brooch was as Imogen hoped. The afternoon that followed was exhausted with timelines and schematic drawings, a publicity campaign, and a letter-writing operation, in the old-school tradition, to a large number of the duke's contacts, who would be expected to support the archeological project. And more tea. The Duke of Inish-Rathcarrick talked about a large fundraising ball in the autumn in support of what would clearly be a heritage project of national and possibly international significance.

As Tommy walked Imogen to her Jeep, he bounced, kicking pebbles out of his path and whistling some unrecognizable tune. Finally, he spun on his heel and pointed to Castle Rathcarrick. "Right then, Moge—in there—you were *glorious!* Triumphant!" A cloud flitted out of the way of the sun, which caught the little gold flecks in the green of his eyes. They sparkled. "No one has *ever* won him over as quickly as you just did!"

Imogen giggled. He was still the same as the boy she'd met when they were seven years old. "Yes, Tommy. You always said your father was a monster. I think he's darling."

"Because he is much nicer to you than he is to me. But then, you preserve old things. He is an old thing. Maybe he thinks you'll preserve him someday."

The marquess presented his friend with a deep, regal bow, complete with hand flourishes. "Queen Moge, I marvel at your higher power!" Imogen nudged him with her elbow. He tried to nudge her back, but she sidestepped out of the way. They laughed.

As Imogen drove home with the events of the day replaying in her mind, her confidence grew, and as it had at the Stonebridge Golf Club, her inner Machiavellian adventuress reappeared. She was both elated and frightened by this bold avatar. Imogen had been raised to hide flaws, but this adventuress wanted to blow everything open, to take chances, to be close to the elements and to the fairies. But that risked exposing the family secrets. In conservation terminology, Roseann McKinney was a fissure in Imogen's foundation, and the truth must remain covered up.

Imogen remembered the Japanese art known as *Kintsugi*, meaning "golden joinery," mending broken pottery with gold or silver. The purpose is to celebrate the history of the object by gilding the crack rather than hiding or covering it up. This was not a methodology that Imogen had ever considered. Her conservation work strove to provide the illusion that nothing was broken. But this inner adventuress nudged her, demanding that she celebrate the imperfections.

When Roseann McKinney had fled Ballybeg in 1876, she had done so as the illegitimate daughter of a domestic servant and an unknown father. Tongues wagged; her shame could never be erased. The old women repeated that story, generation to generation. The line of Peggy Ann McKinney and her illegitimate child was still a significant part of the village history.

But Imogen's grandmother Molly had refused to surrender to the gossip. Instead, she'd returned to rebuild the old house and flaunt her family success. Imogen had taken a higher road and focused on the social history of the community instead of her own family. Eventually, this had established itself as the preservation of artefacts and historical architecture. A first-class student and renowned in her career, she'd believed that, if she retained the local history for the community, she could rise above it all. Although she would never have children of her own, she'd imagined every schoolchild of Ballybeg as her own progeny. But only now that she had acquired the support of the Duke of Inish-Rathcarrick could she admit how good it felt.

With so much career success, the fissure in the foundation still taunted Imogen. *Who was my great-great-grandfather?* She angered herself. Would this new desire to expose the flaws ruin her newly gained advancement? The pedal hit the floor. Imogen raced home, leaving a spray of gravel in her wake.

She arrived at Kara's door with a bottle of wine. Kara never refused wine. Imogen recounted her meeting with the duke, then dropped her head. "How's the genealogy research going?"

Kara leaned forward and grabbed her notes. "Here's an interesting tidbit: John McKinney and David Sweeney married two McNish sisters in the 1720s, so my McKinney and Sweeney lines are also descended from a common link to the McNish family—"

Imogen interrupted, "Did you find Roseann McKinney's father?"

"Ah!" Kara paused. Her attitude became serious. "All the public records read, 'father unknown.'"

Imogen whispered, "It would be nice to know." The fissure widened. The inner adventuress was poking about inside.

Kara replied, "We have genealogists in Belfast and Dublin looking into written archives. Rent books, letters, and such."

"Never mind. Forget I mentioned it." Imogen lifted her wine glass. "Here's to us!"

Kara reciprocated. "*Wha's like us? Gey few, and they're a' deid!*"

Imogen wasn't sure what Kara was saying, but it sounded like a Scottish curse.

Thirteen

K**ara** arose out of bed at sunrise with a purpose: she had to ensure that the meeting between Kathleen and Michael did not occur as in Seamus' legend. Her sleep had been disrupted by the recurring image of Kathleen and Michael together as the old storyteller recited the line, "He saw the fairest maiden he had ever imagined, crossing the bridge towards him."

She needed to stop that ill-fated appointment from happening because the fragment she had heard had ended with, "Little did he know—" Still, Imogen had offered her a different purpose: "to prove that these fears are all hooey."

She washed, dressed, and soon found herself in Memorial Square long before the traffic started or the shops opened. She had left Scratch at home. She circled the square several times to find the spot that provided the best view in all directions. Exhausted, she dropped onto a bench from which she could see the inn on her left, the bottom of Michael's street on her right, and the bridge in between. She slugged strong coffee from a thermos to calm her nerves. For a second, the notion of finding peace in Ballybeg hovered over the flooded landscape of her thoughts, but without a place to roost, it flew away. The belief that Seamus' legends foretold real-life situations—or that her increasingly vivid dreams dictated the necessity of performing magic—overwhelmed her. "It's only a coincidence," she muttered. "Seamus has been telling the same folk tales for decades."

Pedestrians and cars began to pass by. Shop doors opened. Kara checked her watch. It wasn't that she was turning into a snoop or any suchlike, but since she'd started her daily David-watch, the opportunities had increased for her to see the villagers going about their business. Kara knew everyone's schedules by now. David would snooze for hours yet. In comparison, Michael would pick up his daily newspaper from the tobacco shop, then arrive at the corner near Memorial Square in nine—no, *seven*—minutes. The fishmonger unfurling the shop's awning would greet Michael as he passed. After the fishmonger, Michael would turn the corner onto Mill Street and continue on to his office.

Equally, Kara was certain that Kathleen would not be up this early after flying from Los Angeles the day before, and when she did get up, she would probably wait in the inn to have breakfast with her father. And like most young people, Kathleen would likely text her friends in the States before she even started her day.

So, while Kathleen would still be at the inn, Michael would soon turn the corner to Mill Street, find a coffee, arrive in his office, and check the newspaper headlines. Everyone would be where Kara expected them to be. This would prove to her that Seamus's story and the images that had plagued her sleep all night meant nothing.

A series of sights and sounds occurred on schedule. A noisy seagull followed the fishmonger to his shop. A nun on her bicycle charged by. A car engine started. Michael appeared near the fishmonger's as the awning descended. Kara waved at him. He waved back, and instead of turning the corner onto Mill Street in the direction of his office, he crossed the road and approached her. "Good morning, Kara. You're early up."

Kara stood to stretch and to greet him. "Good morning. I couldn't sleep. Too much on my mind."

"Ah, you picked a grand day for it."

"It is indeed. The air's fresh. I've got my coffee. I've got my Birks on. I'm all ready for another busy day."

Michael was smiling, squinting in the sunlight. Then his hand came up to shade his eyes, and his smile brightened. Kara realized then that his attention had shifted to something he was seeing over her shoulder. Her throat tightened as she started to turn around. Before she'd even completed her turn, she heard the voice of a young American woman:

"Excuse me, I'm visiting. Do you know if there's a Starbucks?"

Kara also shaded her eyes now. The visitor had red hair, blue eyes, and a pleasant, confident air. Kara approved of her appearance. Clearing her throat, she forced out, "Kathleen?"

"Oh my god!" Kathleen's eyes darted back and forth from Michael to Kara. She reached out gently to touch Kara's shoulder. "Are you Kara? I don't believe it!" She looked Kara up and down. "You've not been waiting all night for me? I should have texted you when I arrived last night." Kathleen's attention moved back to Michael then, who returned her gaze with his persistent smile.

Is the world spinning? In a vague and formal manner, Kara introduced them. Then, apparently invisible, she watched their exchange.

Kathleen laughed easily at her own gauche American desire for Starbucks. "Typical American! What a fool!" She blushed. "What must you think of me?"

"No, you're grand," Michael responded, not taking his eyes from her. He didn't appear bothered that she was David's daughter. His

Irish accent deepened as he went on. "Perfectly normal. I'd be the same myself."

"Really?"

"Aye. Very fussy about my coffee, me. So, don't worry about it at all. There's a wee Italian café around the corner. Would you like to try it out?"

Kathleen placed her hand on Kara's shoulder as she replied to Michael. "I don't want to be a bother."

Michael grazed Kathleen's elbow. "It's no bother. It's on the way to my office. Let's all go."

Around the corner. On the way to his office? Kara's fragmented thoughts reconfigured like a video of a shattered vase played backwards and coming back together. She retraced the last half hour. In horror, she realized that if she had not drawn Michael's attention by waving at him, he would now have been alone in that Italian café. Like Oedipus, Kara had manifested the fate she'd sought to avoid. She followed behind the pair. *Is that the sound of fairy laughter that I hear?*

The trio strolled to the Cafe Due Gazze. Kathleen linked her arm into Kara's as if they were old friends or close relatives chatting easily. "Thank you for asking me to come. My father has never looked worse. He needs a lot of TLC. He hasn't been himself since Mother started the divorce proceedings. Then the market crashed, and his investments tanked. That really brought him down." She paused, and then added, as though it were an afterthought, "Oh! And *then* the board of directors kicked him out of the management of our family's corporation. That might have been the last straw."

Over coffee, Kathleen expressed how much she had always wanted to visit Ireland. Michael made sure that his own love for Ireland, and Ballybeg in particular, was obvious. Kathleen displayed great interest in the village, and Michael displayed great interest in helping her to explore it.

Kara was not sure whether Michael was trying to increase diplomatic relations or boast of his own interests when he launched into a babbling story about his 1940 Ford pickup and how he was trying to convert it to a biofuel engine, perhaps using local dairy by-products. Mechanics was not his area of expertise, but he knew it was better for the planet if people converted old cars instead of replacing them. "After all, in Cuba ..."

Kara rolled her eyes. Kathleen just listened with her chin balanced on the back of one hand.

"A Ford pickup, how interesting," she murmured.

Kara sipped her coffee quietly.

Michael was the first to leave, but not before offering to take Kathleen out to the distillery for a tour and dinner later. She accepted without hesitation.

After Michael went to his office, Kara and Kathleen strolled through the village. Kathleen seemed at ease, openly confiding in Kara. "Dad doesn't have a head for business. He likes the networking and the socializing but not the work. My grandfather understood that about him. He let him study Engineering at M.I.T. It's not clear what he learned there, but—" She stopped mid-sentence to scrutinise a post box covered in a pink and blue knitted cozy.

"Yarnbombers," explained Kara, raising a fist of protest.

"Here?" Kathleen mused. "I never imagined."

Kara wanted to know more about the McKinney Corporation. Kathleen described the elaborate corporate structure, then said, "As long as my grandfather was in charge, it hummed along. He was a shark." She stole a glance back at the yarnbombing. "Now they are likely to name my older sister, Diane, as the new CEO. She is the MBA in the family."

"What about you?"

"Me? No. I'm studying Law. I think I'm more like my grandmother McKinney. She was part of the hippie commune in Madison—you know, stop the war, ban the bomb, save the dolphins, share the wealth. That kind of thing. She's still out protesting. She might need a good lawyer one day."

Kara liked this young McKinney cousin. She seemed sincere, intelligent, and thoughtful, just as she had on the phone. She reassured Kathleen that she was exactly the support David needed right now and encouraged her to help him.

Kara felt a little dizzy. The world was still spinning. The ground was shifting. The little grey cogs in Kara's brain needed a gyroscope to steady them. *Was she wrong about David?* Kathleen's account humanized him. Why had Kara conjured all the tricks and traps to block his way? She reminded herself that it had all been well-intended.

The complications resulting from her tricks were too hard to unravel. Perhaps the real message of Seamus's story was that all things happen for a reason. In her grandmother's words, "What's for you will not go by you." She would stop all the games. Let Kathleen take care of David. Let Michael run his Biodiversity organization. Tell the village to stand down. They should all accept David McKinney as a son of the village and not as an evil American clown.

When they arrived back at the inn, David was torturing the server over breakfast. Kathleen intervened to the girl's relief. David wore a smug smile. "My daughter Kathleen!" he crowed.

Kara smiled. "We've met. We've done a coffee and a walk about the village."

"She's very special. She's my favourite."

"Father! That's not fair to Diane!"

Kathleen settled beside her father at the table. Kara excused herself to find her co-conspirators. She needed to tell them that all the games against David were at an end. But everyone she tried to contact was busy. On her return through the lobby, McKay stopped her. "Did you get Kathleen to come over?"

Kara drew a deep breath. Her resolve for total honesty started now. "Yes. I did." She waited for the argument to come.

McKay hugged her. "THANK YOU. I couldn't take much more of him."

Amazing. When she'd first arrived, McKay had been friendly but in a cold, phoney manner. Perhaps no one was who they first seemed. She peeled him off. McKay blushed and sidestepped off to the kitchen to see if the chef was preparing the stew.

Kara approached the dining room unnoticed. Was David talking about Michael? "So, you met him already? Good girl! Now, what did I say last night?" *He must be referring to Michael. Who else can he be talking about?*

David continued. "Wasn't I right? He'll be a pushover; won't he?" Kathleen stared directly ahead. "Once we have him on side with FU, he'll convince the others. He'll forget about the red squirrels. We'll be back on track in no time at all."

Kathleen raised her head. "Are you sure—"

"Of course," her father interrupted. "With you on my side, I'll conquer this village."

Kara shrank back from the doorway. *What had Robbie Burns written?* "The best laid schemes o' mice and men gang aft agley."

So, her new plan to change the old plan was off the table. It was the third period; the team was down by two, and the goalie was in the penalty box. *Time for some fancy skating.*

She knew she must return to Michael and warn him to stay away from Kathleen. *No, even better*—persuade him to turn it around and persuade Kathleen to side with them. Simple. But Michael didn't reply to her texts. He had gone to Slemish and wouldn't be back until later.

It was no accident that, in the evening, Kara wandered past the distillery. Michael and Kathleen sat close at a small table in the dining courtyard. Both leaned forward. Their faces were inches apart. Their expressions were animated, but their words were soft and indistinguishable. Kara stole quickly down the street.

She waited until the next morning to catch Michael in his office. She knew he would be working, but this meant it was unlikely that Kathleen would be with him. Kara was right. He threw her a stern look when she charged into his private office. "I'm busy writing petitions to save Rosheen Wood," he scolded.

"I never imagined that you and Kathleen McKinney would hit it off so quickly," she blurted out.

Michael flew out of his chair. "Please, don't waste time getting to the point."

"You claim you're busy. I don't want to waste your time."

He picked up the desk telephone, stared at Kara, and slammed it down again. "Anyway. Kathleen's a fine girl. Nothing like her father." He waited for a reaction. "Nothing," he repeated. When she still gave no reply, he continued. "What's your point? Do you not want me to see her?"

Kara raised her hands. "Oh no! I want you to spend a lot of time with her."

"Well." He threw her a quizzical look. "That's good then. I was worried you wouldn't approve."

"You're being sarcastic."

"*Of course,* I'm being sarcastic!"

Kara stared at him. Something was too familiar. She realized then that she saw Michael as a son. She mustered up a patient smile and an understanding nod of the head. "I just hope you will use your time together to teach her about Lisnasidhe and Rosheen Wood, the old cottage, and the red squirrels. Show her the heritage of the area and the culture. After all, it's her heritage too."

Michael spoke with his best political tone. "Of course. I doubt I could do anything else. If she entertained the same crazy ideas as her father, I wouldn't like …. I mean I wouldn't find her …. Ah damn! You know what I'm saying."

"Yes. I do." Kara turned to leave. "Just—as they say in Glasgow—'keep the head,' eh?"

"Yes, Mother."

Fourteen

Imogen stood in the clearing beside the massive oak tree. Sunday may be a day of rest in Ballybeg, but Lisnasidhe was open for business. *Not David's type of business, but mine.* Researchers and curators from Belfast and Dublin had arrived to examine the ruins of an older building below the cottage. The instruments were set up, and the preliminary work was in progress. One team prepared sample testing of the ground. Another examined the base structure of the old cottage. Two archeologists focused on the spot near the cottage door where Imogen had found the ancient penannular brooch. Despite their anticipation of uncovering a hoard of long-ago buried objects, they meticulously brushed and sifted the dirt one shallow layer at a time.

Tommy, self-appointed overseer, watched the cataloguing of soil samples, stopping to ask polite questions and offer free advice. A BBC crew arrived to capture a few seconds of tape for the weekend news. They were conflicted as to whether to cover the old cottage or the red squirrels. In the end, they interrogated Tommy on his possible political plans. Mary also courted the BBC, taking on the role of an expert, pointing out that her family had farmed there as long as anyone could remember.

Imogen considered that the one possible glitch in her perfectly arranged agenda would be a mention of the charmed elements of Rosheen Wood to the journalists or the heritage personnel. She was afraid of the uproar a whiff of enchantment could cause. The villagers welcomed a little fairy magic as long as it didn't hit Twitter or the six o'clock news. Luckily, the journalists completed their assignment quickly and headed for the Standing Stone.

Imogen was relieved when the BBC left and delighted to see McKay at the opening to Rosheen Wood, his mouth agape. Imogen perceived no clear indicators to ascertain what caused his astonishment. Was it the mysterious opening of the thicket and the exposure of the clearing? Was it the number of people buzzing about inside? *At least he's alone.* Then his face turned scarlet. *Was this apoplexy?* Perhaps he needed help. But when he stormed into Rosheen Wood, pushing others aside and charging towards her, Imogen overturned that concern.

"What do you call this?" he shrieked. He whipped out his phone and captured pictures with a rapid clicking sound.

Imogen folded her arms. "I call it heritage conservation." She murmured. "Lower your voice. You're frightening people."

"I call it trespassing! That's what I call it." He waved his phone in her face. "Now I have the proof."

"Don't make a scene, McKay. It's an embarrassment." She smiled and nudged him. "David is having a very bad influence on you. You're not usually this awful."

McKay lowered his head. He looked exhausted. Imogen imagined that having to work with David all day for weeks would be tiring. She reached out to touch the back of the innkeeper's hand.

McKay snatched away his hand. "You can blame David if you want. He is, I will not deny it, a handful. But the fact is that this land that you are marching all over with your friends is not your land, and you haven't got legal permission."

Imogen ignored his outburst. She led him through the site and introduced him to each individual in the field. Finally, Imogen introduced him to Thomas Brightman MacGuffin, the Marquess MacGuffin.

McKay stood mortified. He bowed his head and sputtered, "M-My Lord."

Tommy chuckled. "Pshaw! I'm not my father. Call me Tommy." He offered his hand.

McKay took the proffered handshake. "Tommy. If you insist, My Lord." With that, McKay was neutralized.

Tommy dragged McKay along to mingle and discuss evidence and what it might signify. The marquess exercised his well-honed manners, shaking hands and making casual banter and producing serious expressions and head nodding when listening to the scientists discuss soil samples and carbon dating. Tommy confided that he was determined to run as a candidate in the next elections, despite his father's disapproval. This was a bit of an uphill battle. He would need to bury most of his privilege to hook the party's acceptance and convince enough voters that he was the progressive choice. He confided to Imogen and McKay, "Archeology isn't really my thing. But fascinating."

McKay's face lit up. "No? What a pity."

Tommy turned to McKay. "But it *is* a passion of the Duke of Inish-Rathcarrick. Like all good sons, I want to please my father."

Tommy invited everyone for supper at his home. Imogen imagined that McKay felt trapped. His face was white. The worse he looked, the happier she felt. She linked arms with McKay and teased him. "Lighten up!" She realized the irony as she herself seldom "lightened up."

The Marquess MacGuffin resided in a striking coastal villa. It overlooked the sea not far from Dundurn Castle. The gorgeous summer evening permitted a cold banquet and drinks on the terrace. The atmosphere was convivial and gracious. Unlike Castle Rathcarrick, Imogen was familiar with Tommy's home. She encircled the terrace, checking in with the other guests.

Kara and Mary were deep in conversation as they draped over the Italian marble terrace wall.

Imogen chatted to the visiting archeologists. She enquired if they were comfortable at the Ballybeg Inn. The inn had been her recommendation despite McKay's staffing issues. To her surprise, they told her they'd needed to book at another hotel an hour away from the village.

"Whatever for?" Imogen responded. "The inn is a lovely place."

The project lead shrugged. "It may be. But when we tried to make reservations, we were informed it was fully booked."

Imogen was confused as she knew the only guests were the McKinneys. Three rooms maximum.

His assistant stepped in to correct him. "No, Neil. We made reservations for everyone, but they were cancelled without explanation."

Imogen blushed. "I don't understand—" Her voice trailed off. *That little cheat!* Where was he? She scanned the terrace for her target. McKay was perched between Tommy and Nesbitt like a tennis spectator listening to a discussion about rugby.

"James McKay!"

The innkeeper's guilty expression suggested that he knew what was coming. He stood.

"Tell me it's not possible that you cancelled all these visitors' reservations?"

His eyes searched about for something to rest upon. "Um, ah—that doesn't make sense; does it?"

The visitors were closing in on all sides.

"And yet, it seems to have occurred." She raised her voice again. "What was it then? Fairy mischief?"

McKay staggered backwards to the door. "My apologies, My Lord. I have just remembered, uh, something." He moved quickly to escape.

Imogen ran after him. "See you, James McKay! Don't think for one moment that you can slink off …."

He darted through the crowd like a ferret on acid. Tommy caught up behind Imogen and stopped her. "Let me handle this." He patted her shoulder. "It is my house, after all." McKay was taking advantage of the moment to put more distance between them. Imogen reached forward over Tommy's arm as though to catch the miscreant.

Tommy gently pushed her back. "No really. I've got this. Simply turn around, very slowly, and be courteous. I'll be back." He dashed inside his villa in pursuit of McKay.

Imogen spun on her heel and forced the corners of her mouth up. She picked up two wine bottles and started her second turn around the terrace. "Right, who needs a top up?"

Over in the far corner, Kara, Keith, and Mary were engrossed in some discussion or other, oblivious. *Do I really care what it's about?* She returned to the archeologists.

Eventually, Tommy returned, beaming. "Sorted. I have finagled James' assurance that they can stay at the inn tonight and for as long as necessary. Furthermore, he won't interfere with the preliminary testing of the site, until (as he puts it) the FU application is approved."

"You will make a good politician, Tommy." Imogen returned to her conversation with the museum curators.

Kara hung over the terrace wall, sipping a very nice white. The last rays of the sun peeked from behind the horizon, reflecting dazzling colours across the ocean surface. The bright half-moon mirrored the light further, illuminating the shadowy corners beneath her in rosy shades, making objects more visible in the gloaming. Lamps sputtered into life. The walking path from Dundurn Castle to the coastal road passed directly below.

Kara mused that, although Imogen could be pretty uptight, she excelled in having good friends who were not. Tommy, for example, was warm and amiable. And he called Imogen "Moge." Kara thought that was brave. She had liked him immediately, and this surprised her since she wasn't accustomed to socializing with the aristocracy. Mary Anderson muttered, "You get used to having them about," as if she were referring to mice or midges.

Two figures on the walking path below caught her eye. They were clinging tightly to each other, a man and a woman for certain, as they walked slowly from the castle. As they passed under a lamp, Kara saw that it was Michael and Kathleen. She drew Mary's attention to them.

"Ah yes, those two have been inseparable since they met. They've been seen in every café, pub, and tearoom. Mrs. Clancy observed them along the riverbank. Yesterday, Michael bought Kathleen a wee figure in the art gallery. The day before, Kathleen dragged him into O'Casey's to buy a jacket. A tweed jacket, you know, like Bugsy Carter's. I think Michael has shown her the area from Rathlin to Stranocum, perhaps further. 'Mickleen' the villagers call them."

"Oh dear," said Kara.

Mary laughed. "The village is very excited."

"Why excited?" *Why do they care?*

"She's a very beautiful girl."

"Yes, so?"

Mary sighed. "Well, its two-fold, really. On one hand, everyone's been wanting Michael to find a girl, and you know, be happy. But also, they want him to occupy himself with something else. I mean, the wildlife is important and all, but you know, he's a bit tiring sometimes."

Kara was aghast. "But not Kathleen! She's David McKinney's daughter!"

"What does that matter? Clearly, Kathleen is nothing like her father." Mary swigged her wine. "It would give me no greater pleasure than to see the American with his nose put out of joint when his daughter runs to the other camp."

As "Mickleen" paused in the rose-coloured shadows for a long embrace, Kara hoped Mary was right. The couple lingered for some time. Kara realized that she was in an isolated position. She alone had witnessed David telling Kathleen to be a secret agent. Everyone else took the couple at face value.

Kara turned to Mary, who was equally transfixed on Mickleen. "What if she's a Mata Hari? If he's taken her everywhere, have they been to Rosheen Wood?"

"Of course. They spent hours with the red squirrels. She is helping him build feeding boxes."

Further back down the walkway, a third figure strolled but stopped moving whenever Mickleen did. At first, Kara assumed the silhouette was David, but it was too bulky. She drew Keith's attention to the figure. "Is that Bugsy?" she asked, pointing.

"How would I know?!" he grumbled in a huff.

Mary gave him a look. "Keith. You're in Ballybeg, remember?"

"Alright, then." He conceded. "Yes. That's our dear Bugsy, right enough."

"What is he doing?" Kara asked. "Is he following her out of jealousy? I thought he had other interests."

Keith frowned. "He does, as you put it, have other interests. Me, for instance. But since Kathleen arrived, he's had no time for his own interests. Too busy guarding Kathleen. He thinks she's a little girl that needs protection."

"Guarding Kathleen from what? From Michael? Is he going to hurt Michael?"

"Well, no. Not Michael exactly. Bugsy's a sweetheart. He would never hurt Michael." Keith glanced down again at the path below. "I don't think Bugsy would hurt anyone. He's like one of those big, hardened warriors that scare the opposition just enough to stop them. But he's trying to protect Kathleen from—anything else, like— Well, it's like this. Bugsy was pretty spooked by the visit to Lisnasidhe. He returned to the inn and looked up some of the fairy stories online. I warned him not to do that." He sighed. "Now he's loaded up with iron, gorse and cowslip, bits of gold, and all sorts of crap to ward off the evil."

Kara winced. What a mess. Bugsy protecting Kathleen from fairies, Kara protecting Michael from Kathleen, Michael protecting his red squirrels. And Rosheen Wood and the fairies? Were the fairy folk protecting Rosheen Wood from David? Most likely. Kara caught herself. *When did fairy protection become the most normal explanation?*

David, she thought, then repeated it out loud. "David. He's the most dangerous part of all this. Let's not lose sight of the bigger picture. David convinced Kathleen to pull Michael onto their side. She's playing him."

Mary and Keith laughed at this. *Well, they can laugh, but they haven't heard Seamus' stories.* They would not understand how the stories were coming true.

Keith shook his head. "I bet David believes that. He thinks he's in control. He's happy that Bugsy is playing bodyguard for Kathleen. But I don't believe David controls Kathleen that much."

The sun disappeared. The lovers continued their stroll. Bugsy paced his distant surveillance. A few minutes later, all three were out of sight.

Kara frowned, deep in thought. "If David thinks Kathleen is off doing his nasty work, what's he up to in the meantime?"

"David?" Keith shrugged. "David just hangs about the inn, antagonizing the staff. He drives them to quit. McKay interviews new applicants every day. He's posted advertisements everywhere from here to Cork."

Keith and Mary left Kara and her thoughts. She checked her email. There was a progress report from green_fairy_kylie, her genealogist contact in the archives office:

"We have started into the estate records for Inish-Rathcarrick. Letters regarding tenancies and notes on agricultural practices, but you never know what's buried in here. BTW, I've attached an interesting entry in the estate book from June 1872 about Lisnasidhe. Will send update soon."

A photograph of a note was attached. It read:

> *I am obligated to record a strange incident on Lisnasidhe. As noted, the intention of the Duke of Inish-Rathcarrick is to clear this land of its woods. This improvement would increase the grazing land and provide a sizable profit from the resulting lumber. On the morning of the 21st, the duke's brigade accompanied the woodsmen to begin the clearing of*

the woods. However, there arose such local opposition that the work could not commence.

The duke's men, soldiers and woodsmen, likewise, are tough, cynical men who have survived the worst of conditions. I regret to state that their accounts as to the obstacles they encountered are not consistent, nor I declare, credible. All the men have suffered injuries or hysteria, characteristic of battle. To a man, they are fearful and vow to never set foot on Lisnasidhe again.

It was also reported that on the prior evening, being the longest day of the year, a group that numbered more than a dozen, led by Margaret Sweeney, the wife of the tenant of the land, gathered within Rosheen Woods. They encircled a bonfire and chanted under the full moon in a manner reminiscent of a coven of witches.

In my judgement, there can be no relation between this pagan ritual, which the Church has publicly denounced, and the difficulties faced by the duke's men. Various testimonials as to sightings of the fairy folk at the witches' coven and during the subsequent skirmish must also be disregarded.

Kara studied the message all the way home. She opened her notebook to compare this story to the words on the parchment in her dream:

"*Bring the people together at the sacred site*
when Sister Moon, in her fullness,
meets Brother Sun on his longest path.
Summon the fairies with the Priestess's candles,
the Witch's spell book,
and the Lunatic's bells.

At the appointed hour, gather the gold circles to the fire.
When the fairy folk are content,
the power of the moon will course through the people
and prepare them for the fight."

It was very similar. *Did my great-great grandmother lead a similar ritual in 1872?* The full moon and the summer solstice both fell on June twentieth this year, which was uncommon, though such had been the case in 1872 as well. Kara felt butterflies in her stomach. She was clearly the inheritor of her ancestor's role in leading the ritual.

Kara revisited the words of the legend of the Children of Coinnigh. "But the Lunatic's rage grows with the lunar goddess." *So, David will become more erratic as the moon waxes towards the twentieth.* Then followed instructions for the Witch to prepare. "The Mother demands protection. The destiny of hope must be fulfilled. The Witch must gather thirteen … Hark! For the battle looms." But it was still not clear what the battle would actually be.

Fifteen

David stumbled from the bedroom, shielding his eyes from the morning light. The clock struck nine. He caught himself in the mirror. His hair was longer and out of control. A half-hearted beard sullied his chin. A pungent smell lingered with him from room to room.

In the sitting room, Kathleen paced the carpet. Her jacket, scarf, gloves, and bag were draped over a chair near the door. Bugsy dwarfed the sofa beneath him, but at least he was showered, shaved, and neatly dressed. His skin glowed from his morning workout. The breakfast for three on the table smelled delicious.

David was pleased to see his daughter. She had captured Michael's attention so decisively that David had hardly seen her for four days. Sure, he'd instructed her to go after Michael, but still, he'd expected progress reports. Bugsy was accompanying Kathleen everywhere, and David was tired of being alone. *But now the three of us can spend some quality time together.*

He opened the French doors to the balcony to breathe the warm fresh air. The sky was clear. A perfect day for golf. *We can do a round before lunch.* "That smells great. What's for breakfast?"

Kathleen exchanged glances with Bugsy. She offered her father a chair at the table. "Eggs benedict, but I think you should sit down."

David got comfortable and poured a coffee. He was invigorated and ready for anything. His phone beeped repeatedly. He muted it. He considered telling the Syndicat that he was out. He didn't need their harassment. Laurel and Hardie abused him hourly via voice and text messages. Ever since the botched council hearing, after which they'd shifted their confidence to McKay, their messages had been, at best, snide if not actually threatening. It hadn't been his idea to take a cash advance of half a million euro. They'd forced him. That's what he remembered. Those first days in London were still a bit vague.

Kathleen sat down. She held a number of envelopes in her hand. "Dad." She signalled Bugsy to take a seat. "Dad, I picked up some important letters that you haven't opened yet."

He didn't like her attitude. "What letters?" He looked closely at what she was holding. "Have you opened them already?"

Kathleen removed the letters from their envelopes one by one. "Well, I thought it was a good idea. This one is from the McKinney Corporation. It says that the board has frozen your shares, pending the divorce action."

David had considered giving back the advance money to the Syndicat and calling it a day. Now he was determined not to give up a penny.

"That can't be permanent."

"Well, I'm not sure. There is also something about the expense accounts and a condo in Nevada? But anyways," Kathleen moved to the second envelope, "Mum's divorce attorney has written to advise you that a number of Swiss accounts have been discovered that will impact the calculation of the proceeds of the divorce. It might take a few months. He wanted you to be prepared for that."

"How very sweet of him." He didn't really feel like golf anymore. "Is there a letter from my attorney? Or my tax accountant?"

Kathleen and Bugsy exchanged concerned looks. "Ah! No. So, this third letter is from the IRS. The discovery of the Swiss accounts—oh, and the condo in Nevada—has caused them to reopen your tax files for the past six years. They indicate that you should keep them informed of your address, and that they will be in touch."

David was glum. "Anything else?"

Kathleen reached over to take his hand. "The next letter is from Mom. She hopes you're doing well and enjoying your vacation in Ireland. She says your mother is doing well and keeping busy doing fundraising for the Democrats. Devinder says hello. And she wants you not to worry about the corporation, as the board has appointed Diane as the new CEO and Chair."

"Great." So that was it then. He poked holes in his Eggs Benedict. The yolk oozed over the plate.

The trio sat together in mournful silence.

Eventually, David said, "Aren't you supposed to be somewhere, Kathleen? I believe you have an Irish fish to reel in."

Bugsy blushed and kicked the carpet.

Kathleen shook her head. "Oh, Dad." She stood and gathered her things. "Dad, if you call me, I will come right back."

"I won't call you."

"Okay, but if you do … "

As she headed for the door, Bugsy stood up. "So, Boss, I have to go—uh—see someone."

Kathleen laughed. "Bugsy! I know you follow me. Just come along. You can sit in the back seat."

David glared at his bodyguard. *Some spy. More of a deterrent than a stealth weapon.*

Bugsy trotted across the room to join Kathleen.

"Remember, Dad. Just call me."

"Right."

They left.

A few moments later, a handwritten message was slipped under the door. The handwriting was shaky. McKay was requesting a meeting in his office. *Clearly McKay is failing, despite getting the nod to take the project lead from me.* This was David's opportunity to gain back control. He rolled off the sofa and headed for the bathroom.

Who was that loser in the mirror? He showered. He took extra care to shave and to style his hair. Did he need a haircut? He definitely needed a manicure. Opening his closet, he chose a new grey suit. The old one looked rumpled; he would have to throw it out.

He took the stairs. He needed to pump up the international businessman inside him. *Get ready to take the FU reins back.* He loved the smell of unfettered capitalism in the morning. He swaggered into McKay's office and slammed the door behind him. McKay startled at the sound.

First shot over the bow. "So, McKay, I'm guessing you've fucked up."

"No. Not really, but I wanted to discuss our options with you."

"Options? We don't do options, buddy. We just go in, review the pitch, and take control."

McKay was splaying out his hands again the way he always did. "I think we can compromise. Find a way for all parties to cooperate. Bring in local and cultural partners. Maybe drop the Wildlife Safari."

"No. That's not what I want. That's not what the Syndicat wants. You're a pussy, McKay. I knew it from the beginning."

McKay began to protest, but David dismissed him with a gesture and went to find a coffee. The inn was busier than usual. The dining room was full. He moved to the bar instead and ordered his coffee. It came on a tray with a smallish parcel. The postmark was Paris, France. *Suspicious.* Laurel and Hardie had been very unpleasant. Perhaps they regretted how they'd been treating him?

He shook the parcel. It weighed less than a pound. The contents shifted, but there was no rattling, clattering, or ticking. It could be anthrax powder or poisonous gas. *This is where Bugsy was useful.* To be safe, David carried it into the back garden to open it. The fresh air was safer if the parcel gave off a poison. He placed it on a table and sat down, taking a sip of his coffee.

I can handle this without a bodyguard. It was better that Bugsy guarded Kathleen. He was proud of Kathleen. He had raised her well. She had a head for business, just like him, and a charming manner. Under her influence, Michael Garrett would make the council revisit and approve his original FU planning application. Then Kathleen could dump Michael and go back to Los Angeles.

He would revive FU under his name rather than McKay's. David would force him to sell the inn on the cheap. McKay would lose a lot of money. With the FU approval in his back pocket, he would recruit new investors in Belfast and Dublin to achieve two ends: one, to buy out the French interest; and two, to persuade their governments to oppose the whole archeological and wildlife conservation malarky. He would schedule the construction for August. All these plans cheered David's heart.

A curious squirrel, small and red with tufts on the top of her ears, landed on the table and studied David. *So cute.* "I'm sure we can find you a new home somewhere." He smiled at the squirrel. The squirrel cocked her head with a quizzical squirrel expression.

He chuckled as he took his Swiss Army knife to the parcel. He was back in control and impervious to threats. The adhesive was barely cut through when a sudden movement flew at his face. Teeth sank into his left cheek. He instinctively grabbed hold of the creature to pull it off. The extraction was more painful than the bite. He was staring eye-to-eye with a weasel, thrashing and snarling. It bit his hand. He let go. The animal flew onto the table and went after the squirrel, who in turn, scampered up the nearest tree. The weasel gave chase, and the pursuit continued from branch to branch and to another tree until the two were out of sight.

His cheek felt warm, and he raised his left hand to touch it. There was so much blood he didn't know if it was coming from his cheek or his hand.

He staggered back into the building. The room churned. Then he was on the cold floor.

When he came to, he was on the sofa in the bar. Mr. Dougherty, the local GP, was cleaning David's hand in a basin of water. David's face was already bandaged. As Dougherty was stitching the wound on his hand, David noticed McKay lingering against the wall. His expression teetered between unease and disgust, giving him a look of seasickness.

Dougherty was matter-of-fact. "I've already given you a tetanus shot and two shots for rabies to be safe. You will need more shots over the next fortnight. I've taken blood for other testing." He sat back. "So, those are some shocking wounds. Did you see what attacked you?"

"A devil."

"Yes. No. But really … Can you identify it?"

"A weasel. A big weasel."

"How big?"

David demonstrated the length.

Dougherty wrote in a notebook and said, "A small weasel."

McKay hugged the wall. "A weasel? Where did it *come* from?" His eyes moved nervously around the floor. "More importantly, where did it *go?*"

David groaned. "It was in the mail."

"The post?" Dougherty asked, for clarification. "It was in the post? Who would have sent you that?"

"Friends."

The doctor whistled. "Nice friends you have got there, sir." He turned to McKay. "A wee bit of whiskey will probably help." Sebastian had anticipated the medicinal requirement.

David grunted. "The local elixir. The cure all. *Slainte.*"

"Weasels!" McKay cried. "Nasty creatures, and they're bad luck." He moaned. "Where did it go?"

David waved his good hand, making circles. "I don't remember. It ran away."

"To where did it run away?"

"I don't know."

McKay turned his back and walked out to the front courtyard.

Sebastian dumped David on the bed in his suite. David never noticed before the exposed wooden beams on the ceiling. The painkillers that the doctor prescribed were pretty sweet. Maybe he'd caught rabies. How would he know? He stared at the glass of water on his bedside table for ten minutes to see how he felt about it. As hard as he stared, the water did not frighten him. He gave up and texted Kathleen until she was standing over him.

She put her hand on his forehead. "What happened to you! Oh, Dad! Does it hurt?"

He sank back into his pillows. The painkillers had slowed his responses, but eventually he described the parcel with the weasel and its subsequent attack. "The doctors here are very efficient. They have nice pills."

Kathleen sat beside him on the bed and stroked his hair. "You poor thing. I'll order some soup."

David was exhausted and a little fuzzy in the head. Everything moved in slow motion. He heard a knock on the door. It was his "cousin" Imogen. She shuffled in like a hospital visitor and introduced herself to Kathleen before enquiring after the patient. Kathleen provided an update as Imogen listened and nodded.

"Oh, that's good. Yes, he should rest." Imogen smiled. "Brilliant that you're here then, Kathleen. Just what he needs."

"I am sure it is all lovely," David said. "Now if you don't mind, the American McKinneys have secrets, I mean plans, to discuss."

Imogen gave him a cold stare. "I only stopped by since Kara will ask me if you are alright." Imogen patted the back of Kathleen's hand. "Kathleen, we will chat later. David, get well soon." Halfway to the door, she turned back. "Oh, David, do you remember where the weasel went after it attacked you?"

David replied that it chased after a squirrel through the trees.

"So outside then."

"Yes. Outside."

"McKay will be relieved."

That was funny. David could not control his laughter and blurted out, "Poor fucking McKay!"

Kathleen held him onto the bed. The drugs were kicking in, and his eyes were heavy. His mother was tucking him into bed.

"Mom?"

"Yes, Davie?"

"What's a glockenspiel?"

"It's just one of the musical instruments."

"It sounds funny when he says it."

"I know, dear. Go to sleep now."

"Okay. G'night, Mom."

Imogen walked out of David's suite and down to the lobby. She wondered where Bugsy Carter was, if not at David's bedside. Then she saw him in the bar, chatting to Keith. Keith unwrapped a miniature medieval knight in blue and purple armour, carrying a sword and shield. He gave it to Bugsy. The bodyguard examined it, a small tear rolling down his cheek.

She continued outside to where McKay sat upright in the courtyard. Despite his posture, his state was comatose. An empty bottle of whiskey and one glass gave some explanation for his lack of movement. She held her hand to his face to check, but he was breathing.

"McKay?" Imogen grabbed his hand. "Are you alright?"

"It's around here!"

"What? Where?"

"Somewhere! Somewhere outside, I think, but maybe not. It is probably crawling through the ventilation system as we speak!"

Imogen observed his wild-eyed scrutiny of the building. "McKay, if you refer to the weasel, it's gone off into the trees and away."

"It's inside. I know it is. The place is cursed."

"It's not. Don't believe all that."

"It is cursed! It wasn't really a coaching inn, you know. It was an abattoir."

Imogen glanced again at the fake façade. "Well, you've made it over very nice."

McKay rocked back and forth. His eyes were closed. He was muttering. "It was in the post this morning. I wasn't there." His eyes flipped back and forth from Imogen to the inn. "Really. I wasn't there."

She took his hand. "Tell me what happened McKay."

"I really can't take anymore." He explained that he hadn't seen the weasel. "The creature could be hiding in the building, waiting to pounce again."

"No, James. It has gone. Really." Imogen felt real sympathy for McKay. "Perhaps we should go inside?"

"*No!*" he recoiled, leaping to his feet. His shirt was loose on one side. His fingers clawed his scalp and disordered his hair. "I, I'm, I am going to Paris—or London! Yes. That's what I have to do. I will go to Paris and fix all this!"

"McKay! Come inside with me!"

"No! Send out one of the staff!"

"But there are so few of them." She paused. "No problem, McKay. No problem." She signalled the groundskeeper to watch his boss while she rang the doctor to return to the inn.

She drove home. After she parked the car, she walked over to sit in the graveyard of the church. Imogen loved the old church. Her mother had allowed her to wander on the grass and among the headstones as soon as she could walk. The feel of old cut stone on the cheek was cool, but she found warmth in it too. The energy of the stone, and of those that had touched it in the past, breathed in and out of her skin, trading old memories for new ones, whispering, *"I have always been here, and I always will."*

She entered the empty church. The interior gave off another energy: an airy musical vibration. Imogen's sensitive ear could hear the echoing of voices, bells, and shuffling feet blend, swirl, and rise into the rafters, resulting in fine high-pitched ringing. This was not discernable to many others. Imogen believed that the echoes of past congregations still resonated in tiny remnants, welcoming the newer sounds into their everlasting song.

To care for the stone, for its energy and acoustics, was her personal joy. It was her contribution to the church, and she hoped it made up for her lack of interest in scripture. She searched up to the roof. The resident pigeon was still nesting near the chancel window. Since she'd first identified the small roof leak that had caused so much damage, she had submitted her documentation to the institute in order to begin the restoration work that the church so badly needed. The institute had responded positively that funding support would be possible. She would soon assemble a team for the work.

At the same time, archaeologists were preparing their paperwork for a dig around the old cottage in Rosheen Wood. Michael, in his official role for Ballybeg Biodiversity, helped them develop a plan that wouldn't disturb the wildlife within the site. But the local council was divided as much on this proposal as on David's FU project, since the ownership of the land itself was still in question.

Nesbitt was closing up after the afternoon study group. "I'm glad you're here, Imogen. I discovered something interesting in the old church record books."

"Oh?"

He led her to his office and opened a large and musty leather-bound book on his desk. Each page was a heavy weight of paper, requiring two hands to turn. The entries were in a curvy formal writing, in a thick but faded ink, neatly arranged within the printed lines. He pointed to the text.

"It's the minutes of a meeting from 1912. Most of the words have been inked over. It's impossible to read. But a word or two are visible still. 'Lisnasidhe' and 'McKinney.' And 'inherit' too. Not sure if that is a verb or the beginning of 'inheritance.' But this added note is very clear. 'The marquess requests a review of the duke's instructions.'"

He closed the book. "I don't think it's proof, but it looks to me that the duke—that would be George, the Sixth Duke of Inish-Rathcarrick—bequeathed Lisnasidhe to a McKinney. We don't know who, but it wouldn't be James McKinney, who died in 1896, and not likely David, who emigrated in 1844.

"The duke's son, Clarence, the Marquess McGuffin, opposed that decision and advised the parish. Now, the duke would have been eighty-two in 1912, and the Marquess McGuffin was managing the estate for his father. The marquess predeceased his father seven years later in 1919. The sixth duke died in 1924, and his grandson, the viscount, inherited the title. This suggests to me that, in 1912, the marquess tried to have this record erased while he controlled the estate. Of course, then he died, and when the duke died, no one could reconcile the transfer."

Imogen found it all confusing. She only wanted to know the legal owner of the property so that the archeology project and the preservation of those damn red squirrels could proceed. Whatever was going on with the duke and the marquess in 1912, and how McKinneys were involved didn't matter. She wandered back home in the twilight. She wanted her projects to move forward, but maybe she also wanted to be free. Free from the mystery and free from the scandal of her great-grandmother's birth. Imogen realized that she wanted to be herself, and not an artefact of her ancestor's decisions. She'd hoped Kara's light would still be on, but all was dark and quiet in the garden. She retreated to the safety of her study to think.

Sixteen

Kara *left her bed and walked across Lisnasidhe to Rosheen Wood at twilight. Scratch trotted beside her. "Stay close to the rowan tree," Seamus had said. Kara wished now that her knowledge of botany was better. She could identify the oak and the willow, but which one was the rowan tree? She decided to look it up on her phone, but when she took the phone from her pocket, it was nothing but a flat grey stone. She heard a girl's laugh. Kathleen was enticing Michael into the old cottage with an apple. Behind her back, hidden from Michael, Kathleen held a lit torch. Kara called out a warning, but her voice was silenced. All of Rosheen Wood, the cottage, and the trees, were now aflame. The red squirrels leapt from tree to tree in a panic. The fairy folk called to each other with bell-like squeals as they tried to rescue their hidden gold before escaping by jumping into the stone-circle pit. Scratch tried to pull Kara into the pit to follow the fairies, but Kara's feet were cemented into place. She was trapped.*

She awoke in a sweat. *These dreams are increasingly intense!* Scratch was stretched out at her side, and Kara drew the dog up onto her lap for comfort. Then she opened her notebook to write it all down: rowan tree, stone phone, Eve's apple, fire, fairies' gold, stone-circle pit, and Kathleen's betrayal.

Now that she was awake, she picked up the gossip in her text messages. David was recuperating in bed from a very nasty weasel attack. McKay had disappeared. Bugsy had not followed Kathleen last night, and now, it seemed she had not slept at the inn. *Everyone knows what that means.* Kara paused. She couldn't believe she was taking for granted that David had been attacked by a weasel in a parcel. But then, nothing was normal anymore.

Kara understood now that she had five days until the full moon kissed the moment of the summer solstice on Monday evening. They would meet in Rosheen Wood, the thirteen essential participants. First, the three children of Coinnigh: herself, Imogen, and David. *How can I persuade David to cooperate?*

Then there were the four: Mary the shepherd, Nesbitt the priest, and Tommy the nobleman. And the paladin? A warrior knight. She had no idea. If she could figure that out, she still needed to find six "good" people to assist. How could she define good? Definitely not McKay. She wouldn't include Kathleen either, Kara supposed. And not Michael, if Kathleen got her way.

She wrote out a shopping list of arcane tools. Google told her there was an enchantment shop in Coleraine. Candles, bells, and ribbons to bind things. And a spell book? Was she supposed to have a book of spells that included one that would "bind two worlds together to guard against the foe?"

She wasn't forgetting the need for the three gold circles either: the ring, the brooch, and the coin. *Perhaps this is payment for the fairies' help?*

All this to make the fairies happy? It didn't sound like the fairies would be happy anyway since it would all end in a fight. So, if everybody just skipped it all and went to bed early that night, they could avoid the fight? Maybe. But then "the Mother demands protection, and the destiny of hope must be fulfilled." Kara's thoughts returned full circle. Scratch licked her arm. It made Kara's eyelids heavy, and she fell back asleep.

Later that day, Kara called again on Seamus. He was tending the garden and handed her a clump of freshly picked gorse. "This is good for coughs and colds, and well, just about anything really."

"Thank you." Kara stuffed it into a pocket in her satchel. "But I came to ask you to explain some of your stories."

He offered a seat at the garden table. "Of course you'll have a cup of tea first."

Kara smiled and dropped impatiently onto the small chair. Scratch wandered further amongst the flowers, where she engaged with some white moths.

Seamus poured. Kara sniffed the tea. *Earl Grey.* Kara explained that she wanted to know more about the children of Coinnigh and the tales of the Lunatic and the King of the River.

"What about them? They're legends passed down from parent to child. My grandmother taught me as a child." Seamus was sober, calm, tidy, and very ordinary, in direct contrast to the Seamus she had experienced up until now. She remembered the milkiness of his eyes when he'd recited the Children of Coinnigh for her to memorize. Now his eyes were completely clear.

Kara persisted. "Well, for example, I never heard the end of the King of the River. When he meets the beautiful maiden on the old stone bridge, what happens next?"

Seamus shrugged. "They live happily ever after."

Not helpful. "What about the end of the tale of the Lunatic. What did the Witch change the demon into?"

"Into a beautiful maiden."

"Into the beautiful maiden that the King of the River meets?"

"Oh, I never thought of that. Do you think the stories are connected?"

"Well, yes. The Lunatic is David."

"Oh, I see. Tell me more of how you think David is like the Lunatic."

He reminded Kara of Dr. Greenberg, a therapist she used to see in Toronto. She tried to turn the conversation back. "Don't you think David is like the Lunatic, Seamus?"

"The old legends are powerful symbolic retellings of actions familiar to most humans around the world. To some people, they mean nothing, to others everything. It sounds like you are in the second group. I am glad that they engage you. If you're really interested in exploring them in depth, you are welcome to come to my classes on Monday afternoons at Holy Cross."

"Okay, thanks." Kara pressed on. "But what about the birds of black iron or the magic spider's web? What are those?"

"No idea."

"Do you have a girlfriend in a green sequined dress? She looks a little like Kylie Minogue."

"No, no, no. I'm ninety-six! No. That's a nice idea, thank you, but I have always fancied Kate Bush, myself, if I had the energy and the looks."

"Thanks, Seamus. You've been very helpful." *As helpful as a chocolate teapot!*

"You are very welcome, my dear. Mind the Monday afternoon class."

Scratch finished with the moths. Kara wished Seamus well and exited the garden with the dog at her heel.

Morag, Sarah, Keith, Mary, and Imogen awaited Kara at the Teaspot to plan the Moon Ritual. She sold it as an event to celebrate the reopening of Rosheen Wood. "We need to ensure that we have enough people to take all the roles. For instance, we need a shepherd, and that would be you, Mary."

"Are we doing a Christmas pageant?"

"No," replied Kara, "just one real shepherd. And we need a priest. How about Dr. Nesbitt?"

Imogen replied, "If I find the right excuse that doesn't scare him."

"And I need a nobleman. I thought Tommy might do."

"He would be very happy to do that," agreed Imogen.

Wonderful, thought Kara. *One shepherd, check. One priest, check. One nobleman, check.* "Okay, so the only problem is that I need a paladin."

Keith looked startled.

Sarah asked, "What's a paladin? Something Middle Eastern?"

"I guess. I still have no idea."

Morag read the results of a quick search on her phone: "'Paladins are twelve fictional knights of legend, the foremost members of Charlemagne's court in the eighth century. A holy knight. A warrior monk.'"

"Yes. Thanks, Morag. That's what I had."

Keith coughed. He flipped open his sketchbook and displayed a full-length image of a medieval knight in blue and purple armour, carrying a sword and shield. Despite the outfit, the subject was clearly Bugsy.

"Bugsy?"

"Dungeons and Dragons. He's a paladin. I mean, he plays a paladin. A paladin with a redemption oath." He blushed, then added, "And as far as I can tell, he's very good at it."

Kara pondered the image of Bugsy as a medieval knight, standing guard over David in his crumpled wool suit, fighting demon fairies to protect Kathleen, and then slipping off home with Keith for a quiet evening. *People. You just never know.*

With the four positions determined, they still needed the six good souls. Keith, Morag, and Sarah volunteered. It was likely that Esmée Nesbitt would participate. The others thought that Michael and Kathleen could help. Kara couldn't convince them that Mickleen wasn't trustworthy. But then, she needed to draw David to the Moon Ritual too, so perhaps it was a package deal.

Morag said that she would bring Seamus. Until that morning, Seamus would have provided confidence, but now, Kara wasn't certain he could be any help. But she didn't dissuade Morag.

Seventeen

David was back on his feet after two days of legally prescribed bliss. It was the vacation of a lifetime, playing old songs from the library in his phone and tripping out.

Bugsy arrived late in the morning, wearing the clothes from the night before. Never a talkative soul, he was silent, but he brought David's breakfast. Bugsy stood at the large window, scanning the village and the square with a telescope. David wondered what he was looking for.

David examined the healing wound on his cheek. He approved. *It's a serious "don't mess with me" look.* Laurel and Hardie had surely mailed the weasel to him as a threat, but it had strengthened his resolve to refocus and realign his energy. This little FU project was nothing compared to projects his family corporation managed at home. He should have flown in with a team, set everything up in a week, and been outta here by now. But from the day he'd arrived in Ballybeg, random things kept arising to block him. Small as it was, this project could be his new life as he had been planning just before the weasel had attacked.

James McKay had disappeared. Rumour was that he had fled to London or Paris. McKay was a spineless, untrustworthy dog. David knew McKay was trying to push him out of the FU agreement and take over. It all made sense now. How convenient for McKay to have been missing right when David had opened the parcel with the weasel. The inn was a failing business. He never saw any other guests, except the group of scientists that had stayed a few days ago. *Anyway, good luck, McKay!* David's FU contract was airtight.

David considered the villagers. They hated him. No idea why. He had done nothing but try to fit in. Obviously, they just hated Americans. They hated "the American capitalist machine." They would rather live in a backwater than be hardworking middle-class winners. *Mother would love it here.*

But what about the missing pants and the missing phone? That day at the distillery? Bushes tougher than steel? And what was it with the animals around here?! Red squirrels? Bees? Those sheep? That weasel? *Well, that was imported, but still ...* Conspiracy or coincidence?

And his so-called cousins! He knew that Imogen was the dangerous one, with her hoity-toity connections to that international heritage cabal that closes down projects all over the world, UNESCO, society of shit disturbers. And getting the local aristocracy on her side? That's just immoral. *No aristocrats in America. No, sir!*

But Kara? That one was strange. Shape shifter of some sort. Typical Canadian. Always trying to pretend they're different. Either lying or confused. She dresses like an old hippie. Meditates on the edge of the ocean, reads tarot cards, traces people's ancestors, takes in stray dogs. But why did she pop up at the same time he had? *Can't be a coincidence!* What did she know? And what was she trying to do?

Suddenly, it dawned on him. Kara was a spy for his ex-wife! His eyes widened. *No wait! For my mother!* Of course. That old Mifflin Street radical! His mother had never liked the McKinney family's corporate world. She creeps around the McKinney mansion like a ninja flowerchild, raising havoc wherever she goes, protesting, petitioning, fundraising for Democrats. His mother must have met Kara at a craft fair or folk festival.

Then there was Michael Garrett, the so-called protector of red squirrels. *Lightweight. What's wrong with grey squirrels? Sounds racist! Kathleen will eat him for breakfast. She'll turn him inside out. He'll be begging for FU to start asap. Once that's done, she'll be back in California in a heartbeat and leave him abandoned, betrayed, and crying into his porridge. Poor baby!*

David's left hand itched, and he rubbed both hands together. He admired his scar in the mirror once more and wandered to the desk, carefully laying out paper and pens. He would write up the strategy. Strengths, weaknesses, opportunities, and threats:

> Strengths: Savvy business sense. Signed FU development contract. Historical claim on Lisnasidhe. Business contacts in the States.

Should have been enough on its own to succeed.

> Weaknesses: lack of local knowledge, and the natives don't like visitors.

> Opportunities: Smart, beautiful daughter distracting Michael, getting access to Rosheen Wood to destroy it.

> Threats: Laurel and Hardie, bees, bushes, sheep, weasels, archeologists, red squirrels, Friends of the Red Squirrel, distant cousins, housekeeping staff.

He made a new plan. "Bugsy, go out and rent us a car, a local map, and a flamethrower. Two flamethrowers."

Bugsy didn't blink at flamethrower. "A hired car, Boss?"

"No, just a rental car." David was taking direct action. He could drive.

In the car, David handed the local map, marked with the route to Lisnasidhe, to Bugsy. He pointed to a large "X" on the map. "We are here." He pointed then to another marker. "And we are going to here. All you have to do right now is give me the directions."

"Not to Rosheen Wood, Boss. I don't think you should—"

"Do what you're told, Bugsy."

"Okay," Bugsy agreed though his expression suggested doubt.

David was mindful that he needed to drive on the left and do everything backwards. He started well. In the village, David just stayed behind other cars until he needed to turn. But his left turns were wide, and he needed to find the left side quickly. His right turns were worse. Brakes screeched; horns blared. He got back to the left and trailed behind a car up to Beeswax Road.

More rain and fog. *Big surprise.* "It's just up this road." David fiddled to find the wiper controls.

"Boss, I think Kathleen would prefer you stay at the inn to wait for her."

"Who's your boss, Bugsy? Kathleen or me?"

"You, Boss." Bugsy stared down at his feet. "But she's always been nice to me, Kathleen."

Bugsy had said "Kathleen" as though it were a magic word or a dreamy memory. David hoped he hadn't made a mistake with Bugsy. *Look at him,* David thought as he stared at the man beside him, *some tough guy. Just a giant baby staring at his big feet.*

He looked forward and saw a blonde child with a green sequined baseball cap riding her bike toward him at an impossibly aggressive speed. He swerved. A large hay truck approached out of nowhere, horn blasting.

David's forehead was flat against a warm, wet surface. White sheep moved across a blackboard. Strange music played. What was he doing? He raised his head. Bugsy was pulling him into something . . . or out of something. He wasn't sure which.

He sat on grass on the side of a road. His head cleared a little. The crash was real. The damage to the car was irrefutable, its front bumper crunched back, almost even with the windshield. Bugsy paced on the grass. A farmer bent over him. An Anglican priest wiped his face. "David? Do you remember me? Dr. Nesbitt? There's an ambulance coming. Won't be too long. You're looking better. The gash isn't too deep."

Then there was singing. " *... tis the gift to come down where we ought to be ...* "

Was that his mother? He forced his eyes open and winced in the harsh light. He was in a hospital gown, in a hospital bed, in a hospital room. Kathleen was brushing her fingers over his forehead. It was her singing, " *... till by turning, turning, we come round right.*"

Despite his insistence that she 'get him out,' Kathleen promised to take him back to the inn only once Dougherty gave him the all-clear. Dougherty suggested he might keep David in over a few days for more tests.

"A CT scan, Doctor?" asked Kathleen.

Dougherty snapped back, "No, a psychiatric evaluation."

Eighteen

Imogen checked her phone as she entered the Ballybeg Inn. It was the day of the Pride Parade, and everyone was coordinating their schedules. Kara followed along. She had invited herself to strategically check up on Kathleen. "And on David, of course, now that he is out of the hospital."

The place buzzed with guests preparing to go out to see the parade. Bugsy sat at the bar, where Imogen imagined he had a clear view of the door.

Alone in the dining room, Kathleen picked at her food. Imogen and Kara sat down at her table without asking. The young woman hardly looked up. It was difficult to engage her. Kara drew out of Kathleen that David was quietly asleep in his bed, and McKay was still away somewhere. This was sufficient information for Imogen, and she steered the conversation towards chitchat. She succeeded only so far as getting Kathleen to raise her head from her plate to the ceiling and ask without any real interest, "What do you suppose was the decor inspiration of this room?"

Imogen chuckled. "It's a sort of Nouveau Georgian Rustic French Empire."

Kathleen looked lost. Kara interjected. "So, you might call it eclectic."

"Oh, eclectic. I see," replied Kathleen flatly.

Kathleen was hard work today. Imogen tried diversion, pointing to Kara's cup. "How many cups has that been?"

Kara glared at her. "Two."

"So that means—"

"Oh, don't start that again!" snapped Kara.

"Grumpy?"

"Right. I haven't drunk enough coffee yet." Kara turned to Kathleen. "So, you must have seen a lot of the area, at least when David's not getting himself hurt. What do you enjoy the most about Ballybeg?"

Kathleen was distant. "What do you mean?"

"Well, what do you find more desirable? The landscape or the people?"

"I'm not sure." Kathleen's lip quivered.

"What have you been looking at lately?"

"Well, I—we toured the castle yesterday."

Kara persisted. "The castle? In the daytime? But it's so romantic in the moonlight, don't you think?"

Kathleen focused on her phone. "It's really nice," she murmured.

Imogen tried to rescue Kathleen from this interrogation. "You saw the castle interior then. That's good. It's an excellent example of its period." She turned her head. "Kara! Stop giving Kathleen the third degree."

Kara shot her a dirty look, but she stopped.

The sky was clear, and the sun was warm. Groups of young people were running excitedly, intermingling, chatting, and laughing. Kathleen's eyes were drawn to the window. So, it was no surprise when the young woman leapt up. "I have to go. See you both later." She paused on the way to talk to Bugsy. Then she scurried out of the inn. Bugsy, in turn, had a brief exchange with the front desk and then sprinted out of the inn to catch up to Kathleen.

Kara also watched Kathleen and Bugsy. "I wonder what that was about."

"Probably nothing but young love. What's your verdict on Kathleen?" asked Imogen. "Help or hindrance?"

Kara bit her lip. "Not certain yet. I hadn't really imagined that Kathleen and Michael would even be a possibility. I only thought that she could help temper her father's mood. But I have a lot of faith in Michael to keep control of the situation."

Imogen snorted. "You have confidence that a man can keep control of a romance? No wonder you're divorced."

Kara flipped her scarf back. "At least I have *had* romances."

Ouch. "That's a low blow, Kara. A low blow. And as for Michael, I am hedging my bets."

Kara threw the money for the coffee on the table. "That leaves me to keep an eye on the contestants, so please excuse me." She dashed off in pursuit of Kathleen.

Imogen stood and sauntered into the lobby to check how the staff was doing. The Yarn Barn van pulled up into the courtyard. A red van followed in behind. They parked, but no one got out. Imogen stepped into the courtyard to see what was going on. The police were placing "road closed" barriers and alternate route signs in strategic places on the other side of the bridge entrance to the inn.

When the last police officer disappeared, the doors of the vans opened wide. Two dozen members of the Ballybeg Yarnbombers for Heritage spilled out. Sarah instructed them to wait in the parking lot, then accompanied Imogen inside. At Imogen's signal, two servers carried trays of refreshments outside.

Sarah did a cautious sweep of the territory. "McKay is still away?"

"Check."

"The inn staff is all on board."

"Check."

"David still in his suite?"

"Asleep, at last report."

"Were there a lot of other guests last night?"

"Twenty rooms. Sebastian is just double checking that they are all on their way out now."

A steady stream of strangers in bright party clothes exited the inn. Each cluster paused, pointed, checked their maps, and bustled off across the bridge.

Sarah returned to her troops. At her signal, they dragged huge bags from the vans and into the inn. As they entered, the inn staff exited, following in the same direction as the guests.

Imogen checked the names off her list. When the last staff person was accounted for, Imogen saluted Sarah. "Time for me to go."

Sarah returned the gesture.

Hundreds of people filled the village centre. The crowd's excitement fueled Imogen's growing fondness for the villagers. People were already playing dance music. Spectators staked out their spots along the parade route.

Imogen didn't need to go far to find Nesbitt and Father O'Connell. They'd settled into folding chairs on Memorial Square and were bickering about whether the parade route went down Mill Street and up Bridge Street or vice versa. Esmée and Catherine Rooney sat in front and ignored them. Imogen pulled a folded map from her pocket to clarify the question.

"Hey, Moge!" Tommy approached, crossing the square with his father.

"Your Grace." She nodded her head. Then she turned a little to Tommy. "My Lord."

Tommy waived off the formality. The duke, however, responded to his son with a tsk-tsk sound. "Dr. Currie is a well-brought-up young lady. Don't be so disrespectful, boy!" They were both in their late forties, and the duke's perception of their age amused Imogen. At Tommy's protest, his father continued. "She's a damn sight more respectful than you, sir, and not interested in playing about in politics either!" The old man addressed Imogen. "Am I correct, Dr. Currie?"

Imogen glanced from one to the other. "As to the politics, certainly. I am very happy with my old buildings."

Tommy drew her aside. "Since you two are getting on so well, it makes it easier for me to ask if you could watch him for a bit. I ran into my party's nominating officer, and I need to review a few things with her."

Imogen was happy to sit with His Grace. It was odd that she had always been afraid to meet him, although she and Tommy had been friends since childhood. The duke was quite pleasant and showed great interest in her work. He made some blindingly funny remarks about the villagers that revealed that he knew more about them than she would have imagined. As she laughed, her face turned up into the light. She felt the duke's hand on her arm. "Isn't it odd," the old man remarked, "but your eyes are the exact same green colour as my son's. And with gold flecks." He stared at her closely. "Very unusual, indeed."

A dozen white Swan Princesses from the Ballet and Jazz School floated by, preceding the local rugby team, each one dressed as the Queen.

Kara was running to the firehall. With a loud horn, Mary stopped her scooter directly in front of Kara. She was dressed head to toe in black leather. "Any sign of David?"

"Still asleep last we heard." Kara responded. "Who's on guard duty today?"

"Don't worry," replied Mary. "We've got the David problem covered." At Mary's offer, Kara jumped on the back of the scooter. They passed the distillery, where a large reproduction delivery cart with six horses was being decorated as a float for their staff.

At the school, children gathered into their class groups, with songbooks in hand and multicoloured hats, wigs, and big mustaches. Teachers counted heads, and with pointed fingers, assigned the parent volunteers to their groups.

The municipal workers union was out in force, with matching T-shirts, beads, and temporary tattoos. They were planning out their positions on the big-rig rescue truck covered in the rainbow flag.

At the firehall, a team of firefighters flipped pancakes and sausages. Bugsy supervised. The firemen wore their normal firefighting gear but no shirts. They were feeding staff from the local hospital, wearing 1960 nurses' uniforms in striped lilac and white aprons and beehive wigs.

Michael served coffee. Kathleen cleared the tables, stopping to chat with people. Villagers responded well to Kathleen. She seemed so different from her father. *So how could she be helping him?*

A trio of upright, wigged, and gowned judges with bare legs passed; each carried a pair of red stilettos. Mary called to them, "If you can't wear them, how are you going to march in them?"

"We just need to find our float, but we don't want to bust a heel on these cobbles, darling!"

Kara and Mary found Keith in a stunning black moiré silk ballgown and hot-pink feather boa. He kissed them both and grasped their hands. "I never thought this would ever happen!" He led a large party of friends, both locals and visitors. They had partied all night and were still animated.

Despite minor delays in moving out so many separate units, each waiting their turn to start out onto Market Street, the parade got started up with clapping and whistles. Then music filled the air. The crowds cheered. *Glorious!* thought Kara.

After an hour of watching the parade at the starting point, Kara arrived back in Memorial Square to look for Imogen. The dense throng of spectators blocked her view across the square, but she pushed on. As she circumnavigated the base of the memorial statue, the Ballybeg Inn became visible. At least, Kara thought it was the inn.

The building had been replaced by a humongous tea cozy; the entire structure swathed in multicoloured wool, acrylic, and other fibres. As Kara studied it, she saw an intricate pattern of overlapping wool chains, forming spider webs, over large panels. Some central panels recreated the colour order of the pride flag, but along the sides and the edges of the roof, the colours ran out in sunburst or spiral patterns to custom wrap around the sections of the building that extended from the main block. The front doors were sealed shut by yellow, red, and blue block-stitched granny squares, the front-door handles fastened together with yards of thick knitted rope. Flower, Sunburst, or Celtic Knot granny squares secured the windows tight.

At the top left, a banner declared this to be "A Pride Day Art Installation by the Ballybeg Yarnbombers for Heritage." The flagpole wore a knitted rainbow-coloured sheath, and the flag itself was replaced by a knitted Pride Flag. From inside, the faint outline of a man was visible. He pushed in vain at a dining room window. The sound was stifled by a gigantic muffler that tied the building together at the waist. Perched above the dining room windows, and above the man's head, sat a giant, knitted spider.

Kara's body melted into a crumpled heap of amazement. Overwhelmed by spasms of laughter at David's predicament, she fell sideways to a fetal position on the granite base of the war memorial.

I must say that the Ballybeg Yarnbombers for Heritage are a real credit to me. In fact, the whole day delighted me in a way I haven't felt in centuries. It is not as if I have never witnessed a parade. Parades happen all the time in the village. But this parade was superior to the others. First of all, it was not one colour; it was all of them. Ergo, anyone could march in it since it represented all the colours. A thousand or so humans agreed with me since the streets were filled with residents, visitors, and fairies.

Oh. Fairies? I refer to the supernatural kind. The Fae that have been with me since the beginning of—well—me. The fairy folk hide in my forests and my rocks and under my soil. Or sometimes, they stay in the sea, close beside me. They freely intermingle with humans all the time, but you would not recognize them. For example, that parade float supposedly from the bank, with the great big teddy bears, had emerged out of a hawthorn bush in Carrickfergus that morning.

Being fairies, they have lots of gold, though it is impossible to secure a loan from them.

Everything gaily decorated in multicoloured flags, banners, balloons, and ribbons. All the beautiful ladies! The ladies with their bouffant hair, lavish eyelashes, and impossible nails. So lovely! And so many materials: leather, silk, vinyl, velvet, fur, lace, taffeta, feathers, and my favourite, corduroy. The rainbow scarves, the fans, the parasols, and the necklaces. Sequins and cat-eyed sunglasses! All the happy music!

It brought me such joyful remembrances of times long past that it roused me from my languor. The people danced. They sang. They drank. They recited verse. They fell in love. It was great craic! So much positive energy for me to quaff—I had been so parched from the lack of it—that I was revived.

Clap if you believe in fairies. Do you believe in fairies? Because they do need the applause. It is true. And humans need them. It is true. There are humans, and there are fairies. It looks like two worlds, but is it? I love humans, but they can become a little repetitive, and after a few dozen generations or so, they become boring. But the fairies bring the sparkle, the variations, and the imagination that give me sustenance. The humans that believe in fairies learn that anything is possible.

Once in a blue moon, humans demonstrate how the fairies have inspired them. That day was just such a day. I say that because the most remarkable memory of the day was not the work of the fairies. It was the sight of the Ballybeg Inn enfolded in the multicoloured splendour of knitted, crocheted, or sometimes woven textiles that embraced the old building as it had never been before. For once, the old building, which had suffered through being both worshipped and abused for generations, was swaddled like a baby and held close against my bosom. It was cozy. It was warm. It had never felt so much love.

In return for this love, the building held onto its prisoner as long as it could, until the parade had travelled across the village and north up the Beeswax Road to end the day in Mr. Kelly's cow pasture, where the gathering became a celebration.

David, trapped in the inn by knitting of all things, could think of nothing better than to fill his pockets with bottles of beer. He blamed McKay for sneaking off, leaving the nut cases in charge. He rummaged about in the kitchen for something to eat. He had never learned to cook. He snagged some already cooked chicken and dropped down to eat cross-legged on the floor, chucking first the bones into a corner, then the plate, and finally the empty beer bottles.

Resting against the dishwasher, David heard the distant laughter of the staff returning to see the work of the Yarnbombers. After some commotion, they cleared some of the knitting out of the way and filed in to take up their posts.

David hid in a supply cupboard between the kitchen and the front desk until he could sneak out. He would deny anyone the chance to lock him up. His one goal was to destroy Rosheen Wood. Outside the inn, the streets were quiet. At least it wasn't raining.

David had imagined that the walk to Lisnasidhe would calm him, but instead, he found that the journey only increased his anger. As he passed people celebrating, he saw that the pride parade party had relocated from the village to the farmlands. Everything was centred on Mr. Kelly's pasture across the road from (and with a good view of) Rosheen Wood. That would make destroying the grove a little trickier.

A large festival banner suspended over the gate to Kelly's field celebrated "Ballybeg's First Annual Pride Parade." A local band were warming up on the makeshift stage. Communal wooden tables had been lined up end to end.

David saw that Archie had set up a Standing Stone Caravan. "Excellent." *I need another drink.* Barbeques lined the fence. Mr. Kelly enclosed his cows in the farther field to spare their feelings and to keep the grass clean.

The barbeque smelled appetizing, but all David really wanted was an excuse to throttle anyone who tried to stop him from his mission. Unfortunately, that opportunity didn't arise. The sight of him parted the partygoers like the Red Sea. He half-heartedly swatted at the crowd, but it was already moving away from him. Wherever he walked, there was a sort of hush in the conversation.

He found Kara. His primary objective might be to destroy Rosheen Wood in any way he could, but there was still room for emotional appetizers. "Hey, yo! Witch! Yeah, you!"

Despite his threatening tone, Kara smiled at him. "Hello, David. Everything good?"

"You know it fucking isn't. When I get hold of that coven of knitting harpies—"

"It was just a bit of fun, David. To dress up the inn. No one knew you were still inside."

"I doubt that." David caught sight of Imogen several yards away. She smirked and toasted him with a glass of wine. "Somehow, I really doubt that." Partygoers populated the fields on both sides of the road. He pointed at Lisnasidhe while staring at Kara. "You won't be able to keep your grubby army of weak-minded hippies guarding the property indefinitely. Hippies become bored and wander away. I should know."

Kara stared back at David. "Don't be rash, David. Let's be adults and take a little time to examine all the facts."

"Your facts might burn to the ground."

"I can't believe that you are so desperate about this one little project. A big-shot developer like you? You must have other projects on the go somewhere. I could give you some government contacts in Toronto."

"Nice try."

A roar went up from the crowd as the musicians began to play. David stared at the bunch of ignorant chumps around him. He hated them. He realized that he hadn't seen Kathleen nor Michael all day and began to search for his daughter in the crowd. A trad music band performed an old folk song. Father O'Connell interrupted his discussion with Mr. Kelly to join in the singing with a notable tenor voice. The festivities moved along, and no one was paying any attention to David or Kara.

Kara cried out to David then, with a sweeping arm gesture, "These people are your family! Why don't you meet them? Talk to them?"

David's eyes hit the ground briefly; then he glared back. "I'm *trying* to help them. You're the one standing in their way. FU will bring millions of visitors to Ballybeg. Jobs and money. Think of what's good for them. For the village." With a dismissive gesture, he walked away from her.

The village was singing, eating, and talking. He was invisible. It would be easy to gradually wander over and just light a match. It was a dry evening after a warm day, and a well-placed fire would likely do a lot of damage before it was noticed. What had been, up to now, his biggest problem, could easily become the greatest bonfire in Ballybeg's history, and a brilliant addition to the festival.

The Ballybeg Yarnbombers had decorated the fields with crocheted chains. He ran his fingers along a very long piece. How ironic it would be if he used these as the wick for his surprise. Even better, it would allow him to start the fire from some distance and escape the blame. The perfect crime. And the perfect revenge for having been yarn-bound in the inn. He grabbed the end of a crocheted line strung along the fence, pulled it all together, and stuffed it in his pocket.

He ambled across the road then and circled slowly around the east side of Rosheen Wood to the back. There was a dense apple orchard back there. This would give him cover. At the edge of the orchard, he paused. Kathleen's voice came from amongst the apple trees. He hid and carefully peered in. Kathleen and Michael were spread out on a blanket in a tiny clearing amongst the apple trees. Kathleen lay on her side with her back towards David. She was facing Michael, who lay flat on his back staring at the sky.

Michael's voice sounded stressed. "I can't stand it anymore, Kath. All these days together—"

"And nights." She laughed.

Michael's eyes turned to meet hers. "And nights. You know what I told you the other night up on the castle?"

"It was a beautiful night. The full moon shining on the ocean."

"Not quite full. Not yet. And it was only beautiful until the storm rushed in."

"You look gorgeous when you're soaking wet."

"Kath. You're trying to distract me, I know, but I have to say this: What I shared with you that night is absolutely true. You might not want to know. You might want to fly back to California and leave me here. I can understand that. But you need to accept that what I said is the absolutely truth about my feelings, and I won't change my mind. Because I don't change my mind—not about—well— that. If you go away and never come back, I will feel exactly the same about you five years, ten years, forty-five years from now."

Kathleen sighed. Both were silent for several minutes, then she reached out and took his right hand. Their fingers intertwined in a slow dance. Finally, she spoke, "I just can't see a way around the problem."

"The problem?" Michael scoffed. "The problem isn't a problem. It is just your father wanting everything to go his way. He's a bully, Kathleen."

David felt the heat on the back of his neck. But he clamped his mouth shut.

Kathleen played with Michael's hair. "But I really do love my father, and he needs my help right now. Dad's not a bully. You don't know the real man. He needs our help."

David was enjoying this. He calmed down a little. *Good girl, Kathleen, good girl. Reel him in.*

Silence again. Kathleen let go of Michael's hair, and leaning closer, draped her body over Michael, burying her face into the small of his neck.

Michael lightly touched her shoulders. "Hey, there, Kath. Don't cry. You'll smear mascara all over my shirt."

This made Kathleen raise her head and giggle. She sat up. Michael did too and wrapped her in his arms.

"I thought you wanted a clean shirt."

"Hang the shirt. I love you. You love your father, and that's natural, but what about me?"

"Do I love you? Well, maybe just a little tiny bit more."

"Alright then. That's grand. What do you want me to do?"

David stuffed the lighter and the yarn back into his pockets. He needed to keep his hands over his mouth to stop himself from making gleeful noises. *Mission accomplished.* Kathleen had proved herself a star. She'd won over Michael Garrett. He would do whatever she told him from now on, so David now had control over him.

He quietly snuck back and came out near the wooden gate where the bees had attacked him. As he examined again the impenetrable thicket surrounding Rosheen Wood, he spied Bugsy sitting in the sheep pasture. David was horrified that he was sitting right beside Mary's beehives. And he was sitting with that artist. Keith. *That's just wrong,* David thought. *Those bees could kill him.*

Bugsy didn't see David. His eyes were riveted on an apple in Keith's hand as he listened to Keith explain something about art theory, for which the apple was apparently a prop. David listened to the lecture. *Gobbledygook.* Bugsy probably didn't even understand the words.

Bugsy took his eyes from the apple. "Hey, Boss! Where've you been? Did you watch the parade?"

David opened the gate and signalled for Bugsy to come away from the beehives. To his dismay, Keith came along with Bugsy. The three settled on a spot at the centre of the Lisnasidhe open pasture, roughly halfway between the church and the grove.

Keith ignored David's nasty looks and broad hints to go away. Instead, he yanked a large bottle of whiskey from his satchel and offered David a swig. David, triumphant about the victory over Michael, accepted the drink and offered a toast: "Here's to Kathleen and Michael! To Mickleen!"

Bugsy smiled. "You approve of Kathleen's relationship with Michael?"

David smirked. "Of course!" He wouldn't tell Bugsy that it would be a short-lived affair. He continued to drink to their health for the rest of the evening. The two young men engaged in banter that David didn't understand as the whiskey disappeared.

236

David awoke face down in the grass. He rolled onto his back and looked around. He was alone in the middle of the open Lisnasidhe pasture between the church and Rosheen Wood.

The field was bathed in a greenish-blue light. He yawned. He checked the time: 2:34 a.m. Sunday. In the strange light, the surroundings were vaguely visible. He stood. A small group were clustered on Kelly's field. A few sat to the north, beside Mary Anderson's sheep pens. Both parties were distant, and the conversations and music were muted.

No one moved, except one figure who approached from the church across the field. Her energetic motions indicated a quick stride, but this was out of sync with her progression, which was slow. David thought that was a trick of the light. She was in costume and carried only a basket. Perhaps it was the heavy skirt that slowed her down. As she came closer, David recognized her. *Kathleen.* Her breath was belaboured. She passed him with hurried gestures but no faster than a sloth.

"Keep up!" she ordered in a thick Irish accent. Her voice sounded like it had risen up from the bottom of a well. "We need to take these chicks to Mrs. Sweeney before they feel the cold."

What game was Kathleen playing? Was it some festival pageant? That would explain the accent. David turned slowly to follow her in the direction of Rosheen Wood.

As he rushed through the field and across the dirt path to catch Kathleen, he was shocked to find that the thicket, which had always blocked him from entering Rosheen Wood, was now open. *Wide open.* The vast interior was visible to him in the greenish-blue moonlight. He hastened his steps and passed Kathleen, entering the clearing first and coming to a stop beside a massive oak tree enclosed in ivy. In seconds, he took in the ancient remnant of the cottage on the north side and the taped off trees at the other end.

Between the two was an open area of ground with only a stone-circle pit in the middle. The trees of Rosheen Wood guarded it all. A girl with long blonde hair slept curled up on a blanket just in front of the cottage.

All this he saw in a few seconds. Then he was distracted by the hard *bump* he felt as Kathleen brushed against him on her way to the cottage. Her lethargic movements were gone. She moved in real time now, disappearing into the cottage with the basket. She reappeared just as quickly. The basket was gone. She pulled back her shawl from her head and reached out her arms. "David, you've come back." Her voice was clear and not distant at all. David stepped back. *This isn't Kathleen.* Despite the familiar features, this was an older woman. One who knew his name.

"Oh, David, my boy. You've finally come home. You'll never know how happy you've made your old mother!" She ran to him, and before he could recoil, wrapped her arms around him. He felt the pressure of her touch and a warmth radiated through him.

She stepped back a little, without releasing her grip on his arm, and studied him from head to toe. "You look healthy enough. You must have done well in America." She shook her finger at him. "But you could have written a line or two. Your father and I have worried about you." David was held captive by her gaze. Her eyes glinted with moonlight. She smiled, and he smiled back.

From behind the massive vine-wrapped oak, a small fiddler materialized, playing a merry tune. The woman grabbed David by both arms and pushed him into a dance. "Come on, David, remember as I taught you. One, two. One, two." She forced him to lead. The two twirled faster and faster around the stone-circle pit.

She stopped dancing as quickly as she started. "Oh Lord!" She beamed and brushed his cheek. David was silent, but he could not look away. A strange feeling washed over him. He wanted to say something nice, but the words failed him.

"I must go tell your father. He will be so happy that you have come home." She ran for the opening. Before she stepped out, she glanced back at him. "You stay here." Then her retreating figure vanished into the twilight.

Everything twisted around. He stepped out of the clearing, straining to find her figure crossing the field back to the church, but he saw nothing. He heard nothing. David muttered, "It must be a dream." Then the landscape pitched about like a raft in an Atlantic storm. He dropped to the muddy grass at the edge of the pond.

Nineteen

Kara yawned. She had returned to Lisnasidhe from a comfortable night in her bed only to find abandoned clothes and hats decorating the bushes. Scattered stragglers slumbered in the bushes and amongst the long grasses. Scratch bustled along at her side. Archie reopened the Standing Stone van to make tea and coffee. Cheerful voices arose here and there as little groups came to life with only a few signs of hangover.

Imogen had entrenched herself inside Rosheen Wood all night, in a sleeping bag near the door of the cottage. It was her inner line of protection to defend the grove from the friendly supporters partying all around it. Kara approached with a large flask of tea and a bag of scones. She almost tripped over a body near the pond. It was David lying face down, his hair dipping into the pond. Dead. Or so she thought at first. But no, he was breathing. She was relieved. She didn't want him dead. They didn't need a murder investigation on top of everything else. Besides, David was an essential part of tomorrow's Moon Ritual. Scratch licked his face. Kara stepped over him to awaken Imogen.

"I had the strangest dream," Imogen muttered as she poured them both a cup of tea. "I dreamt I saw our great-great-great-grandmother visiting with your Sweeney ancestors in the cottage. And they talked about raising chickens."

"Chickens?" Kara checked her dream-interpretation app for 'chickens' and remembered David. She called out to the lifeless body. "David? Do you want a cup of tea?"

Imogen frowned. "David? Is he here?"

There was no immediate reply, but then heavy feet shuffled to the entrance, and David appeared. Scratch was at his heel. David leaned on the ancient oak. Kara offered him a cup of tea, but he waved it away.

"Poor cousin David looks confused," Kara said.

Imogen smirked. "I am familiar with that look."

David studied the clearing. His voice was raspy. "How long has the thicket been open like this?"

"For almost a month." Kara paused to think. "Since the day after you arrived."

He shook his head. "That can't be. It's always been closed when I saw it. Until now. Or was it last night?" His eyes moved from the cottage to the stone-circle pit. "No, that was a dream. There was a woman that forced me to dance. And there was a young blonde girl sleeping on the ground—"

Imogen interrupted. "I was sleeping there last night."

David shook his head. "You're blonde, but you're not young."

"Charming. You're not so boyish yourself."

David seemed too distracted to respond in kind to Imogen. "The opening to the clearing wasn't here until—but then—now it's open? Or *still* open. I don't understand."

Imogen continued to dig. "I would think not understanding things is a state of mind to which you are accustomed."

"Ha ha. Thanks, Lady Cambridge."

"What can I say? Some of us were educated at the best schools. Where did you study?"

The verbal tussle shook David out of his stupor. He stood up straight and even took a few steps further inside. "M.I.T., thank you. Engineering. Class of '87." He smiled. "You haven't lived until you've put a Ford pickup on the roof of the central library."

Kara laughed. Imogen looked shocked.

"Winner, winner, chicken dinner!" David crowed. He glanced about the clearing. "So, this is where you're holding your Witchiepoo party tomorrow?"

Kara stopped laughing. "It's an important—"

"Yeah, sure. It won't help you save—" He went quiet, his eyes examining the cottage, and then the trees. "I'm going to find me some coffee." He disappeared. Scratch stayed and stretched out on the ground.

Kara smiled. "That went rather well for a change. I think he's warming to us."

Imogen rolled her eyes. "You wish."

It was another clear sunny day. Slowly, the festival started up again. A solo guitar played an old folk song, and soon, several voices were singing, though not too loudly out of respect for their hungover compatriots. Mary's bees buzzed. Her sheep ambled across the north pasture. Several locals arrived, motivated by either curiosity or fraternity. Lisle drove up with a heritage inspector. Imogen greeted them and led them to the cottage. Mary and Keith patrolled the protected red squirrels' territory. Kara headed down to the road.

Morning gave way to afternoon as music floated across the farmlands, then storytellers took over the stage. Seamus had just started with, "Now, you are all familiar with the legends of Finn McCool." when David approached Kara at the side of the road.

"I want to know how you make the thickets disappear and reappear. Is it 3D? A hologram?"

"It's not me, David. It just happened. Poof. There it was. An opening."

"Things don't just happen."

"Really, David? Have you noticed the lack of electricity back there? Maybe it's the fairies."

"Don't be stupid, Kara."

Kara shrugged. "I don't know, David. It's Ballybeg. Things happen."

A bell tringed repeatedly.

David guffawed, and he continued to glare at Kara.

"Look David, if you couldn't see the opening, it was because you weren't ready to see it!"

David and Kara faced off in the middle of the road, nose to nose.

David started. "That's absolutely impossible! You've done something."

The tringing bell grew louder. Bugsy rushed up on a bicycle behind David. "Boss! Boss! I need to talk to you!"

"Later, Bugsy." David held his position without turning his head. Kara refused to be the first to break the staring match.

"It's really important, Boss."

"Sure it can't wait? I'm busy trying to harass my cousin."

David's eyes shifted to something over Kara's shoulder; then he called out, "There you are!"

Kathleen climbed down from Michael's pickup. As she approached, her father scurried towards her. Kara tried to beat him there. She felt some sense of entitlement; after all, if David was her fourth cousin, then Kathleen was her fourth cousin once removed. Michael followed Kathleen. The four reached ground zero simultaneously. There was something momentous in the encounter that attracted several others, including Imogen. A small circle surrounded them.

"Morning, Dad!" Kathleen hugged her father. "What a great day!" She smiled and waved to the others, then turned slightly to Michael. "Is it always busy like this on a Sunday?"

Michael smirked. "Only on the day after Pride Day."

David had focused on Kathleen, but this comment drew David's gaze to Michael. Their eyes locked. Kara searched each face for a clue as to what was happening. There it was! She saw it in Kathleen's glowing expression.

David drew Kathleen slightly apart from Michael. "Are you okay?" he asked her. "How are things? Is he ... you know?" He whispered something in her ear. Kara knew what he was asking her. David wasn't subtle. Kathleen pulled away, but she smiled at her father.

Kara noticed something remarkable about Michael and Kathleen. They hardly looked away from each other. They mirrored each other's facial responses. Their eyes shone like candlelight reflected in glass. They breathed in rhythm. They had indeed transformed into *Mickleen*. So, what did Mickleen think about David's FU project? Kara was frightened. She knew that David saw the same signs. Was he enjoying it? If he was, it meant trouble.

Kathleen rubbed her father's shoulder. "Dad, don't you worry about anything. We—" She reached out and dragged Michael closer to her. "Michael and I were up all night." Michael smiled sheepishly. Kathleen continued. "We talked about FU and the history of Rosheen Wood and what's beneficial for the village, and I think"—she nodded to Michael—"we are completely on the same page here."

David grinned. Kathleen hugged her father. She smiled at him and smiled at Kara. Then she turned back to smile at Michael. Altogether too much smiling, even for an American.

That's it then. My worst fear. She had really made a mess of things when she'd invited Kathleen to come over from the States. She started to ask a question, but the only word that came out was "Michael?"

Michael had caught the smiling bug. "David, Kara, I think you will find that Kathleen is in complete agreement with me."

Kathleen laughed too hard at that, then blushed, then shuffled her foot. "Of course. Don't worry, Dad. And let me reveal to you all Exhibit A." She pulled her left hand from her pocket, showing off her engagement ring, perhaps more modest than what one might expect but official nonetheless. Kathleen moved her hand so that the diamond flashed in the sunlight.

The "oohs," "aahs," "congratulations," and "best wishes" filled the air. Kara was crestfallen, but it surprised her that David seemed upset too. She tried to catch his eye, but he looked away and seemed to fix his gaze on Rosheen Wood.

A mini party within the bigger party began. Ballybeg liked Michael Garrett. Even if Kathleen had turned out to be unpleasant, they would still accept her if she made Michael happy. But in the last few days, they had discovered that she was quite agreeable. Their engagement was a cause for celebration. The music and drinking expanded across the fields and blocked the road.

David stood alone. He was unwilling to engage with anyone. Bugsy was pacing in a triangle as he attempted to console his boss, cheer Kathleen's happiness, and revel with Keith all at the same time. Kara guessed that it was more than the man could endure.

He and Keith soon drifted into the throng of well-wishers, leaving David behind.

Imogen and Mary, concerned that the party could spin out of control, retreated onto Lisnasidhe to guard Rosheen Wood. Kara watched the celebration. How would the villagers feel if they knew the truth about Kathleen's motives? Scratch followed Kathleen and Michael, tail wagging, looking from one to the other with a happy face. Kara watched her go and muttered, "Traitor."

A new blip on her phone drew Scratch back to Kara's side. It was an email from green_fairy_kylie. The subject was, "News at last." It read:

"We have uncovered evidence of the assumed owner of Lisnasidhe. Entries from 1912, in the estate books of the Duke of Inish-Rathcarrick, refer to the duke's intention to gift the land to his natural daughter, Roseann McKinney, daughter of Peggy Ann McKinney, and to the females of her line. I attach images of several documents, including the 1912 letter of instruction to his solicitors. We have confirmed with the legal firm that the duke's instructions were initiated. However, later circumstances appear to have contradicted and obscured the conveyance of the title, leaving it in limbo. A recent review of the file by the solicitor's firm concluded that a claim of the land title by Dr. Currie would most definitely stand up in court, as it would fulfill the intention of the sixth duke and the actions he took in support of those intentions."

Kara shrieked aloud. Scratch barked excitedly. It was as if the dog understood the news that Kara had just received and could give to Imogen. Together, they ran to the clearing to find her.

Imogen read Kara's email standing near the stone firepit in the middle of the clearing, in the middle of Rosheen Wood, in the middle of Lisnasidhe, which was (as it turned out) her land. She was of two minds about this news, or was it three minds? She appreciated that Kara had shared it with her privately, with only the dog as a witness. She questioned what she was supposed to make of it though. Did she care? But then, how could she not care? It seemed bizarre, and at the same time, perfectly logical. She tried to classify the new information but was perplexed as to how to establish the criteria.

Kara dragged over a couple of garden chairs. "Why don't you sit?"

Good idea, Imogen thought. She fell back into the chair with a thud. She needed to focus. Until Kara had arrived in Ballybeg, she'd never thought about the vacant land next door or the supposedly enchanted Rosheen Wood. The Andersons grazed their sheep there, and that was all. Then Kara, or more precisely, Kara's adopted dog, had led them to find the interior of Rosheen Wood and the secret ruin of an old cottage. A trove of letters and photos hidden for Kara to find. The secret forest that sheltered the red squirrels. The ancient brooch, hidden ancient treasure, and the interest of the heritage community. The recognition and the support of her work from the Duke of Inish-Rathcarrick. How long had that been? A month? One cycle of the moon? *No, no, no. That sounds like Kara.*

And now this? Lisnasidhe and everything on it belonged to her, and her long-unidentified great-great-grandfather had turned out to be the current duke's ancestor! *What would Grandmother Molly have thought of that? And wait—*

"That makes Tommy my ... ?"

"Your third cousin." Kara giggled. "Your third cousin is the Marquess MacGuffin. Isn't that wonderful?" And you've been friends since childhood!" Imogen noticed a bewildered expression cross Kara's face as she dove into her bottomless bag to retrieve her notebook.

She is such a Canadian. "What's wrong now?" Imogen asked. "I thought you were happy about this."

"I am. I'm still very happy," came a muffled reply. Kara arose, book open, mouthing words as she read. "Look. It's here, in the tale of the Children of Coinnigh."

"What's this now?"

Kara's finger traced the text. "Here: 'Coinnigh's second child will be a High Priestess who sits high in a tower … and … Her blood will end old hostilities.' Coinnigh's enemy was Domhnaill MacDhuibhfinn. The MacGuffins. Your blood is both McKinney and MacGuffin. Bringing the families together and ending old hostilities! And I was afraid you might need to shed blood! Phew!"

"Oh, that's nothing."

"Maybe. Except that it *is* the legend. And if it is true, so must be the rest of it."

"I always knew you were a Witch. And David is a Lunatic—no doubt of that."

Dr. Imogen Currie analyzed the new evidence and determined that it did not force her to reclassify herself. She could continue as she was despite being a relative of Inish-Rathcarrick. It would hardly stop the village gossip, but it would certainly change the story for the first time in 154 years. Perhaps it would now be easier to snag a last-minute reservation in the best restaurants. Beyond that? *Well, whatever.* The fissure was truly open now.

"We don't need to keep this a secret."

In the clearing, Imogen called together the Nesbitts, Mary, Keith, Morag, and Sarah. Michael arrived too, with Kathleen and Bugsy in tow.

Kara asked, "Where's David?"

Bugsy shrugged. "He's wandered off again."

Imogen gave them the news and read from some of the documents. She read aloud the 1912 letter to the solicitors from the duke, or as Kara repeated ad nauseum, her great-great-grandfather:

> " … declare truthfully, that Roseann McKinney, born at Aghnagoogh in March 1862, is my natural daughter … that I freely gift to aforesaid natural daughter, Roseann McKinney, daughter of Peggy Ann McKinney, and to the females of her line …

> " … the property known as Lisnasidhe, being ten collops of land on the townland of Derrycoinnigh, bounded on the west by the lands of Ballybeg Parish Church, to the east by Knocknageragh, to the south by the Bothar Céirbheach, and to the north by the Coastal Road."

Dr. Nesbitt led the group in a round of cheers.

Imogen bowed. "This should stop David and his partners. It proves the land was never his, and he has no advantage to try to use it for FU. I will never sell it to him or the Syndicat or anyone else for that purpose. Even David should be able to understand that."

Scratch sat beside Imogen and placed her paw on her lap. For once, Imogen did not brush it away but took hold of it gently and reached out to stroke the dog's ear. Her hand felt the softness of Scratch's fur. Imogen's thoughts wandered to David. It was dark now, and he was alone. Where had he hidden himself? How was he feeling? How could she help him to appreciate Ballybeg?

Twenty

David hid in the apple orchard that extended out to the north of Rosheen Wood. He glared at the stars above. His head reeled. *Another boring midsummer night in a nowhere village on the edge of the world.* He slumped across a fallen tree. His limbs ached. He was sick of everything. The darkness of the orchard seemed safe. A quiet rustling heralded the arrival of a ghostly white owl onto a nearby branch. It pivoted its head as its eyes scanned David from end to end.

"What do you want?" He tried to stare down the owl but failed. *That figures.* He felt like he was really striking out this year. Why was Kathleen acting strange? He no longer trusted her. Whose side was she on? Flashing that tiny engagement diamond to the crowd as if it were something valuable? He hoped that it was part of their plan to deceive Michael. Yet the glow in her cheeks and the fire in her eyes told him that Kathleen was not lying. He couldn't dismiss the powerful stirring in his heart as he realized that his little girl was now a woman in love.

Maybe he wasn't a good parent, but Kathleen, more than anyone, understood him. Kathleen was always willing to follow him into all sorts of mischief, like when they skipped work and school to go to the dairy for mammoth ice cream sundaes. Neither snitched. "Thick as thieves," as his mother had once accused. His girl Kathleen was more like himself than her sister was. Kathleen was Teflon. She loved to play games. When had it gone sour? This love thing seemed genuine. If so, FU might be doomed. She had jumped ship. He beat the ground with a branch.

It was also clear that Bugsy went wherever Kathleen led. If she deserted the USS *David*, then he would be gone too. *I could have guessed that.* Four-year-old Kathleen had adopted Bugsy the day David had brought home the eighteen-year-old bodyguard from Brooklyn. Bugsy had entered the McKinney home without family, education, or etiquette. David's wife had given him good cause to fear her. Yet, within hours, the six-foot-four-inch bodyguard was sitting happily on the floor beside Kathleen as she introduced all her dolls, their backgrounds, their connections, and their dreams. David always suspected that Bugsy was the child and Kathleen the mother. Other children teased her, talking about "Kathleen's giant."

If it's about loyalty, Bugsy will go with Kathleen. The owl winked at him.

Arrrgh! Slumped on a log in the dark, David felt like a captain without a crew, abandoned mid-ocean, beleaguered by the family corporation, the IRS, and his ex-wife. He needed to set a new tack alone.

He had missed the opportunity to set fire to Rosheen Wood because of his misguided faith in Kathleen. David reached for his box of matches. He appealed to the owl. "It's never too late to— whatever, something, something. You know what I mean." The owl became animated, letting out a series of shrieks and flapping its wings. David snorted.

At that moment, out of the dark, Kara's voice called out, "Over here!"

David jumped, as her voice was so close. A number of voices answered her, including the turncoats Kathleen and Bugsy. David stood up to trace the direction and realized that they were in the clearing of Rosheen Wood, through the trees. He slipped the box of matches back into his pocket and strained to listen. Were they talking about Kathleen and Michael?

He heard Imogen's dry, clipped voice announcing her proof that she was the legal owner of Lisnasidhe. *Fuck!* Only fragments of what followed stuck in his brain: " letter of instruction dated 1912 … proves the land was never his … I will never sell it to him or the Syndicat or anyone else for that purpose."

Nothing had worked. Did it matter if he lost Kathleen? He had lost her help anyway. If Lisnasidhe was not even his, if Lisnasidhe was Dr. Currie's, and if she would rather die than work with the Syndicat, then so be it. "It's war." The owl rotated his head and continued its stare.

I have to focus on my position with the foreign investors. He had to be indispensable. McKay was missing. David was their most valuable local informer. He recalled the brainstorming sessions in London. There had been one killer strategy, a full-on offensive action, complicated and expensive, and had been intended to be used only as a last resort. *Does anything else matter except winning?* This clearly was the last resort.

The owl shifted from foot to foot. It flapped its wings. Otherwise, it remained on its branch, staring at David. A mouse ran close to David's foot, but the owl did not pursue it. *Frigging Ireland. Even the owls are lazy.*

He was certain that once the new strategy had succeeded, poor Kathleen would discover that she had degraded herself with Michael for nothing. She would have to slink back to the family in the States. David didn't have that luxury. The McKinney Corporation and his ex-wife had made it crystal clear that there was nothing for him at home. If he wasn't successful with FU, his monthly income would drop to the level of "scraping by." His mother would disown him. He imagined her celebrating, with her Mifflin Street hippie friends, the takedown of another rotten capitalist.

"Right, that's it, so it is." He typed a text to Monsieur Laurel, informing him of the turn of events regarding the ownership of Lisnasidhe. He concluded with, "Swift action is highly advised. Our preferred plan now is as we discussed last month. Launch Operation Goliath. I will prepare the ground on this end."

The owl blinked. David felt uneasy. What other animals came to the orchard in the night? Or what strange people, like that woman last night? There was no way he was spending another night on Lisnasidhe. Lisnasidhe was a dangerous place, physically and metaphysically. It would be better to walk the country road alone.

He passed the churchyard and felt a thousand eyes on him. *Were there footsteps behind him?* "Who's there?" he called. He turned but saw no one. In the last brace of trees before the road descended into the village, he saw the white owl again. *Is it the same one?* Was he going to be dinner?

He turned Operation Goliath over in his head. It required careful timing and no witnesses. He needed to get everyone away from Lisnasidhe. He could use Kara's Moon Ritual. Apparently, they couldn't do it without him. He would use that to draw them away from the target area. If he ran away, they would all have to leave Ballybeg in order to find him. He hadn't played hide and seek in years. A golf course was the perfect place to hide, but not at the Stonebridge Club. He needed somewhere farther away and harder to find. He had heard of a first-rate golf club in Belfast.

He found a number in his phone for the Emerald Helicopter Service. He didn't remember adding them, but still, he called. A cheery voice answered. "Emerald Helicopters. We bring you to the magic!"

David gave them the name of the golf club in Belfast but admitted he didn't have the address. "I hope that won't be a problem."

"No, you're grand, sir," the voice replied. "We'll get you there. No problem. Shall we pick you up at your current location, sir?"

His current location? *Where am I exactly?* The midsummer sun had begun to reappear. It revealed the sleeping village in the valley and the empty field to David's left. "I'm not exactly sure where—"

"No bother, sir. We know where you are. We'll swing by shortly. Just watch the skies."

The owl flew close over David's head, its feathers brushing against his ear; then it circled back into the country, screeching into the early light.

David stood alone. He noticed a rosy tint to the morning light as he pondered his FU failure to date. Although none of it had been his fault, he did admit to himself that he was too soft-hearted. He had brought Bugsy along as security, but the giant puffball had succumbed to a belief in fairies, and now any change of wind sent him running. He'd been too friendly with Kara and Imogen at the beginning, and so they had learned to take advantage of him. He'd relied on McKay to move the project forward, but the guy didn't have the chops to do the job and had been frightened off by a weasel. And Kathleen? He couldn't find the words for how much she had betrayed him. He realized that he should have come in fast and cruel, alone, and crushed the opposition before they knew what was happening. That had been his mistake. No more.

It was almost five a.m. Clouds were rolling in. David sat under a grouping of large elder trees. A herd of cows meandered out across a neighbouring field. No cars or farm vehicles were nearby, but David heard a faint humming sound. It grew louder.

A bright green helicopter appeared from the south, hovered overhead, and then descended onto the field. The sight of it gave David an unexpected feeling of elation. He ran forward and grabbed hold of the door as it touched down.

He gave only a nod to the pilot before climbing in and slamming the door shut behind him. Within seconds, the helicopter ascended into the sky. "To Belfast, right?"

"Yes, sir," the pilot replied, looking ahead as they flew south of the village.

David rubbed his hands together. He'd go to this famous golf club in Belfast, do a round, and a have a bit of lunch. Midday, he would send a message to Kathleen to find him there. That would draw her away from Ballybeg. If the others wanted him to do Kara's moon thingy, they would have to come with Kathleen. Then he could force them to stay in Belfast, leaving Lisnasidhe vacant tonight.

The helicopter sputtered, and the whooshing of the blades slowed down. Then they descended into an empty farm field. David wasn't clear about geography, but they couldn't be in Belfast yet. "What's going on?"

"Engine trouble, sir," the pilot responded, before cutting the engine and opening the door. David climbed out. He glared at the pilot, who said, "Sir, we'll call out our maintenance crew, and you'll be on your way in no time. Meanwhile, I don't know if you saw it, but there's a first-class golf club just over the hedge there."

David looked over the hedge. The field bordered onto a manicured lawn with a walkway that led to a three-storey, grey-stone clubhouse. The green-tinted glass flashed in the sunlight, beckoning David closer. "Go ahead, sir," the pilot said. "I will fetch you when we are ready."

David stepped onto the walkway, which glittered like emeralds. The fairways stretched green, smooth, and calm as far as he could see. The thick morning mist smelled like patchouli, vanilla, and leather with a top note of lavender. The grey stone of the clubhouse flickered with pink and silver. The green glass of the windows reflected rhythmic wavy lines of light. David felt mesmerized and calm. There was a sign above the doors: "Tir na Nóg. Exclusive. Members Only." *Of course, it's exclusive, but they'll admit me.*

The tall, blonde, and beautiful staff wore elegant uniforms, emerald with gold threads. Their manners were exquisite. *They must offer highly competitive salaries.* It was all very elegant. As per David's expectations, at the desk, they accepted him without a word. There was no paperwork to complete, no request for payment. The manager appeared and offered David a tour of the club.

If David were to design a golf club himself, Tir na Nóg couldn't have been more to his taste. Each room was more impressive than the last. The three-storey lounge bathed in a soft green light from the windows and featured a young female singer at a grand piano, warbling a song in three-part harmony. This led into a cozier members' bar with framed Heineken posters on every wall. Every beer tap handle along the bar sported the Heineken logo. Oversized leather lounge chairs matched the brand's green. A spiral staircase led up to the formal dining room, overlooking the fairways. The manager enquired if David liked the club.

"Very much. I've never seen such a perfect golf club. I could spend eternity here."

The manager smiled. "The course was designed by Mr. James Braid and Mr. John Henry Taylor."

"They worked on it together?"

"Well, not exactly," the manager responded. "They alternate from week to week." This did not exactly make sense to David, but the course was so perfect that he ignored it.

They passed through a hall of conference rooms. Raucous laughter escaped from within. The manager said, "Upstairs, the third floor has overnight suites for members and a recreation room with a pool. You Americans like a pool, do you not?" He handed David a room key, in case "you choose to stay over." From here, they descended to the ground level where the tour continued. "This is the pro shop, and over here, the men's locker room." As they entered the pro shop, he asked David if he was interested in a round of golf.

"Just try to stop me," David gushed. Staff brought the gear and equipment to kit him out properly. In minutes, he was at the first tee box. A trio of gentlemen in tweed approached him. Each one sported an ostentatious moustache and flat cap. They invited David to make up their foursome, introducing themselves as Harry Vardon, J.H. Taylor, and Jimmy Braid.

An attractive woman zipped up in a golfcart. David offered seats to the other players, but they declined. "We prefer to walk the course," said J.H.

They teed off, and the foursome started out onto the fairway. The round was somewhat delayed when Jimmy and J.H. began to bicker about the placement of the first dogleg. "Never mind them," Harry said to David. "Let me look at your grip there." Harry gave David tips on his downswing until the other two moved on, and the round continued. To his surprise, David won the round. The three gentlemen soundly bashed David in the back and congratulated him. Then they vanished into the rough.

David headed to the dining room. The food was delicious to the point of intoxication. He ordered more. And lots of Heineken. The strange thing was, no matter how many servings he devoured, he still had room for more. No matter how much he drank, he didn't feel drunk. He eventually stopped, not because he was satiated but because he had tried everything on the menu, and he couldn't resist another go around the course.

He ran back to the first tee box, ready for more. Some flirty women joined him for his second round. On the ninth tee, David's ball landed in the sand trap. As he walked into the sand trap, the ball jumped out on its own and waited at the edge of the fairway for him to take his swing. On the green of the twelfth, the hole arose out of the ground to catch and swallow David's ball. He was sure that the ball would have curved to the left otherwise. A small bar cart, carrying only cold Heinekens, caught up at the fifteenth. On the eighteenth, the ball flew in a flawless curved arc from the tee straight into the hole.

No sooner had David returned to the members' bar than he was ready for a third go around. It was such a perfect day that he never wanted it to end. The manager popped up at David's side. "Are you enjoying your stay at Tir na Nóg, sir?"

"Immensely! I have never known a place like this!" David declared.

The manager winked at him. "You're welcome to stay as long as you like." He drifted away up the spiral staircase.

David was eager for his next round of golf. All other thoughts vanished.

Twenty-One

Kara followed Scratch over the field towards home. Both she and Imogen were exhausted from the excitement of Imogen's news, and Scratch could find a route in the dark that did not step onto the fairies' path. *Stepping onto the fairies' path might invoke their anger.* Imogen, following in line directly behind Kara, declared that it wasn't magic, and that any dog had the knowledge. Kara thought that even if Imogen owned half the neighbourhood, the fairies were clearly more powerful.

Imogen said that she anticipated a long and strange phone conversation with Tommy. Kara asked her how the duke would take the news. "I don't know," mused Imogen. "He seems to like me now, but this might change his mind."

Kara's dreams that night circled and recircled back to the Moon Ritual.

A voice giggled, saying, "Although you needn't be a witch to practice witchcraft, there are some witchy things you must do," and "You will need a white candle, a gold candle, a sprig of heather, the ashes of a burnt thorn branch, and a small jug of cream. No, wait. That's for warts. Let me see . . ."

Seamus appeared, declaring in a feminine voice, "We call upon the Goddess of the Moon for the strength to fight the invaders, to protect your children, to protect Mother Earth."

Coloured rockets flew out of a bonfire. Her adrenaline surged. There were floating images of tea and biscuits, and a magpie calling from a distant tree. A single magpie. Seamus recited, "One for sorrow, two for joy."

Morning arrived suddenly. Kara barely clung to the edge of her bed. Scratch had been on a territorial offensive all night. As she sat up, Kara blurted out, "One for sorrow, two for joy."

In the dream, the magpie had been helpful, but she knew magpies were bad luck. *Are the fairies trying to confuse me?* She searched the treetops as she crossed the garden to Imogen's kitchen. Entering the house, Kara found Imogen staring into the refrigerator. "Do you see a lot of magpies?"

Imogen's head turned. "In the refrigerator? Has Michael been leaving more specimens?"

Kara sighed. "No, just, around." She waved her arms in circles. Imogen did not respond. The arms dropped to her side. "Did you talk to Tommy?"

Imogen's eyes were back on the fridge. "Oh, yes," Imogen answered in a flat and distracted voice. "He's fine with it."

Kara rolled her eyes. *So bloody English! Pardon me, I had to tell my aristocrat best friend that I'm his cousin from the bastard line, but it's all good and no more to say about it.* "Well, cool then."

"Yeaah," Imogen said, mimicking Kara's Canadian accent.

Kathleen arrived, looking tired and dishevelled. Her father was still missing, and she was worried for his mental health. He didn't answer his phone. Bugsy had wandered the fields while Michael had checked around the village. Her main concern was that, in his weakened state, he would sink even lower when he heard Imogen's news. This might be his breaking point.

The inn staff were overheard whispering that they wouldn't mind if the fairies had carried him away. Michael was trying to convince the villagers to join a search party. Kathleen begged Imogen's help.

Imogen grabbed her keys, phone, and field boots. She promised, "Don't worry. We'll find the lying scoundrel." Imogen advised Kara to go to Rosheen Wood to practice her ritual. "He can't go far so he'll probably reappear at Rosheen Wood soon. When he does, just call me." Imogen and Kathleen rushed out.

Kara's Moon Ritual notebook—much smaller than her tabbed, colour-coded genealogy notebook—taunted her from the dining table. Only twelve hours remained, and many details were not decided. For example, she needed her Witch's spell, so she had filled the notebook with all the spells and rituals she'd found on the internet, but which to use? None were an exact fit. *Perhaps Imogen was right. Better to be in Rosheen Wood.* She could rehearse the ritual on site.

She called Scratch, and soon they entered the clearing. David was not there. She relaxed under a hazel tree and reviewed the witchcraft incantations in her messy scrawl. "Spells invoke the powers to add their energy to the circle." She recited a few lines aloud. "Unleash my power! Let the moon maiden illuminate our path to the understanding of the universe and send her sycophants to deliver the signs." She rolled her eyes. As she called out the next incantation, an avalanche of hazelnuts fell onto her head. When she looked up, she was sure she heard little squirrelly chuckles. "Give me a break. I'm not a real witch," she called up to the squirrels. "If I was, I could materialize David here on the spot." She rubbed her head.

She read further. "A spell can ricochet on the witch that casts it, so caution should always be taken to recite it correctly." Kara supposed that anyone who read *Harry Potter* would know that. The text continued: "Music is a vital part of the ritual. To set the mood, find the perfect music as your soundtrack. I always use the theme from Sherlock. It creates a mystical ambience. Stretch the energy from the music, catching the end of the musical threads and wrapping them around your circle."

Kara pondered this advice. Perhaps the theme from *Dark Shadows?* Or *Dracula?* (1979 version, of course). Or something more specific? Van Morrison's "Moondance," for example? She shook her head. *No. No one will stay put in their places if I play that.* She opened the music library on her phone.

Scratch was digging in the earth around the firepit. At first, Kara thought that the dog was just playing and rolling about in the dirt, but Scratch's movements were too focused, sweeping aside the displaced dirt and revealing coloured stones embedded all around the firepit. Kara dropped her books and wandered over to the dog. She knelt down and carefully brushed away more of the earth. As she cleared an increasingly wider area, a pattern emerged, arranged in different colours of flattened stones. Each colour formed a separate pattern around the centre of the firepit, first gold, then green, then red, and finally the blue—the largest shape and the furthest away from the centre of the firepit all the way around.

Kara remembered her chessboard dream with its squares of gold, green, red, and blue. The figures had moved from square to square in a particular order. Was there an order to these stones? And if there was, what did it mean? Perhaps indicating the correct positioning of the participants? For a better view, she stood on the seat of a garden chair and looked down. Three gold stones formed an equilateral triangle around the stone-circle firepit. If the firepit was the centre, then the next shape outside of the triangle were four green stones set at ninety-degree angles, forming a square. Outside of the square, the five red stones formed a pentagon. The last shape on the outside perimeter was a circle formed by six large, blue stones connected by smaller blue ones to make a continuous chain.

Kara couldn't determine the meaning of these shapes, but the purpose seemed clear enough, since each one was centred perfectly around the circular firepit. A triangle, then square, then pentagon, then circle. She considered this for some time until the meaning became clear. "Thirteen will gather, seven within and six without; three of the blood, four of rank, and six good souls. The six good souls hold the circle."

This meant that the six good souls would stand on the six blue stones for the outer circle. The four of rank would be positioned on the four green stones. *Imogen, David, and I belong on the three gold stones*, forming the triangle closest to the fire itself. That made the thirteen. *So, who or what are the red stones for?* She descended the chair to examine them. The red stones were not flat and broad like the others. They were a little smaller, but each had a round dent in the middle. *They're candle holders!*

She returned to the chair. The red stones didn't represent a pentagon, but a pentacle—a five-point star, like the one engraved on the back of her silver locket, and the brass strongbox, and on her gold ring as well. Scratch sat up at attention and listened as Kara began to speak.

"My great-great-grandmother, Margaret Grainger Sweeney .... " Scratch barked three times. "Well, she could have left me clearer instructions in her brass box." She pointed down at the stones. "Sometimes, humans find it difficult to see a pattern at first. But once we see it, it's impossible to ignore. It all makes sense." *The red pentacle of fire. The blue circle of water. Then the green is earth.*

"So, what is the gold?" The dog did not respond. "Well, it must be air—the breath of life. The elements together. The geometric shapes together." Scratch again barked three times.

This just might work. But only if David cooperates.

Imogen drove Kathleen back to the village in her Jeep. Yesterday, she wouldn't have cared less if David disappeared off the face of the earth, never to be seen again. But this was a new day, and she was truly sympathetic, not just for Kathleen but also for David. She feared that he was ill. Kathleen updated her on the steps they had taken so far. Most of the village had been alerted to watch for David. Sebastian watched the Stonebridge Golf Club, and Keith was on duty at the distillery. Nesbitt and Esmée kept vigil at the church. Mary rode her ATV, searching the other farms along the coastline. Bugsy held down the fort at the Ballybeg Inn while making phone calls to contacts in the States just in case his boss was flying home. No one had seen him. David had simply vanished into thin air.

Imogen entered the Standing Stone with Michael and Kathleen. Seamus and Father O'Connell were sharing a pot of tea. While the young couple talked to Archie, Imogen joined the two older men.

Seamus listened as Imogen described David's misdeeds. "Yes, he has been a bit of trouble, hasn't he? But so was his ancestor, David McKinney," he smiled and leaned back, "according to the family histories."

Imogen snorted. "Are you trying to tell me, Seamus McNamara, that you memorized all the local families' histories as well?"

The ninety-six-year-old exchanged a glance with the priest and gave Imogen a steady look. "That is just what I am saying. The histories were passed down to me by my grandmother, and she had learned them from her own. The family stories are the first things they teach us to train our memories." He tapped his forehead. "It's all in here. No one needs the public registrar's office. Just ask me."

She scoffed. "You couldn't have told me that my third great-grandfather was the Duke of Inish-Rathcarrick?"

"I could have indeed. Anytime." He poured Imogen a cup of tea. "It was June 1861—the night of the Midsummer Ball. The duke was so enchanted by the look of Peggy Ann in the moonlight that he was sure she was the Fairy Queen herself. She was equally charmed by his green eyes, although she was only there to serve the smoked salmon, poor girl!"

"So why didn't you tell me?"

"You never asked. I'm no gossip, me."

Imogen stood and pointed her bony index finger at the Seanchaí. She lacked the words, at least words that wouldn't offend the priest. Her hand dropped to her side.

Seamus grinned. "Please tell Kara that Morag and I will come tonight to her Moon Rit"—Father O'Connell threw him a suspicious look—"to her Solstice Celebration. In the spirit of our heritage."

Imogen promised to pass on the message. Clearly, she'd underestimated the Seanchaí. *I suppose there is more to history than stones,* she thought.

Michael and Kathleen were waiting at the door. Imogen had not forgotten the task at hand and rushed away with them to beat the bushes for David.

Checking back in with Bugsy at the inn, they found the bodyguard hunched over a long hand-written list with many names crossed out. "Not only did I call everyone stateside, the airlines, and the hotels where he usually stays, I called the transportation companies we hire as well—you know, limousine drivers, private jets, etc. For instance, I realized that if he were going to fly back to the States, he would hire a helicopter service to take him to the international airport. So, I called all the ones we use, and nothing. He didn't call them.

"And he wouldn't take the bus?" Imogen asked.

Kathleen's sombre demeanour broke momentarily into a faint smile. "No."

They wolfed down some sandwiches, washing them down with strong black tea. Even Kathleen finished her tea, for which she had already developed a taste. Michael called around to the teams for updates but without results. They'd covered the entire village and known points of interest. "Except," remembered Michael with a start, "the castle."

Kathleen gasped. "Dad might throw himself into the sea, just like our ancestor did!"

Imogen thought, *we can't be that lucky,* but she reassured Kathleen. "No, no, I am sure he won't have thought of that. Anyway, he was forced over the edge. He didn't jump."

Kathleen looked puzzled. "Who was?"

"Coinnigh. Our ancestor."

They took both Imogen's Jeep and Michael's pickup since they might need to split up. At the castle, a small group of tourists wandered the ruins until a passing shower descended, driving them all back to the tour bus. No one else was there.

Michael had considered his next idea. "Alright, the country roads." On the tailgate of Michael's truck, they strategized the routes from a local map. Michael would take the outer roads, travelling counter-clockwise, and Imogen would search the inner roads, driving clockwise. When they finished their circles, they would stop and check in.

Imogen watched Michael drive off, then turned her Jeep in the opposite direction. The farmlands to the south of the village stretched out with large properties. The fields were filled with sheep and cows, punctuated with some horse farms and crops. There was no sign of David. Imogen slowed down to get a better look into the ditches on either side. Whenever she saw a person that she knew, she would stop to ask if they'd noticed anything unusual.

All afternoon, the rain stopped and started, the sun repeatedly peeking out from the clouds only to hide again.

In the late afternoon, they reconnected. Kathleen was slumped down in her seat and she wore a frantic look, with pale skin, drawn features, and swollen eyes. Michael instructed her to wait in the truck. Liam, Morag's older son, was doing bike stunts at the side of the road. He approached them.

Michael furtively checked his fiancée in the truck before offering a suggestion: "We need to go further. At least twenty miles out."

Imogen shook her head. "How far could he walk?"

Again, Michael's eyes shifted to Kathleen. He lowered his voice. "What if he wasn't walking? What if he hitched a ride? What if the mafia showed up to settle a score?"

I hope Kathleen isn't hearing this. "I was checking the ditches. Did you?" Michael nodded. Liam was leaning closer over the handlebars of his bike.

Imogen checked her watch. It was almost half past four. "Okay. Let's go further. I'll sweep from Ballymena to Kilrea and west. You go east to Carnlough. Lucky that it's light despite the rain—"

Liam interrupted. "I can bring my drone and come with you, Dr. Currie. That's a faster way to check the ditches."

The ingenuity of youth is reassuring. "Thanks. If your mother lets you—"

"She'll be grand." Liam was off on his bike and returned just as quickly with his laptop and camera drone. He climbed into the passenger side and patted Imogen's arm. "Don't worry, Dr. Currie. We'll find him." *God give me courage,* she thought.

The two vehicles started off together, keeping to the side roads. Liam's drone followed along but periodically swayed off to the left or right to hover over the fields.

Somewhere between Dunminning and Ballymena, Liam called out, "Stop! I think I found something!" Imogen pulled to the side of the road. Michael stopped behind her. Everyone strained to see anything in the fields around them. Kathleen crossed the road and back, stretching to find something other than green pastures or cows. Liam manoeuvred the drone, and it sailed back over the fields to the left. Imogen studied the image on the laptop.

"There! There! Look!"

They hunched over Imogen. On the grainy screen, a distant movement had been captured. The drone moved closer, and Liam zoomed the camera in tighter. A lone figure marched confidently through the empty field. It was a man in a blue suit. He gestured and chatted to himself. He stopped walking. He posed like a golfer taking a driver swing. The camera focused. It was David. He was not holding a golf club.

Kathleen was first over the fence and bounding across the pasture. Imogen was close behind. David called out a friendly greeting to his daughter. "Kathleen! My dear girl! I'd like you to meet some wonderful people." He gestured to the vacant air to make introductions.

Kathleen flung her arms around him. "Dad! What are you doing all alone in the field?"

David chided her. "Don't be silly, Kathleen. Come and check out this fantastic golf club!" He tried to wriggle out of his daughter's grasp. "And don't cling so much!"

Kathleen refused to let go as David shivered in the rain. Imogen called to Michael to bring a blanket.

Michael and Liam caught up. Michael threw the blanket over David's shoulders. David ignored them and addressed Kathleen. "Your friends are acting extremely rude. This is an exclusive club. They can't just run—"

Kathleen covered her face with her hands and sobbed.

Now David was reaching out to his daughter. "Kathleen, what has frightened you? Don't let them scare you. You're safe with me." He persisted in his attempt to make introductions. "Look, these are my new friends—"

Michael touched David's arm. "Just come with us, David. Kathleen has been frightened enough today."

David's behaviour turned nasty. "Take your frigging hand off me!" He started to pull away, but Imogen wrapped her arms around him. This proved to be awkward when David dragged her off her feet as he tried to run away across the bare grass. "Help, help!" he called out to the air around him. "I'm being kidnapped!"

Michael grabbed the blanket and threw it over David's head as if he were a wild animal. This stilled the older man momentarily, and Michael picked him up by the shoulders while Imogen and Kathleen took a leg each. Liam filmed the fracas with his drone camera. They threw David in the backseat of Imogen's Jeep and strapped him down.

When they carried his thrashing body into the Ballybeg Inn, Bugsy fussed over him as much as Kathleen had, forcing him into a hot shower and then wrapping him up. Kathleen fed him hot broth with milk and soda bread with butter. After an hour or so, David was quiet, almost his normal self albeit still confused and angry. "I have never been so humiliated. That is a very exclusive golf club. I was in the middle of an excellent round of golf with a good group of new friends. Very fine people. Good quality. Why did you kidnap me like that? It's so embarrassing! What were you so worried about?"

Kathleen started. "Dad, it was all an illusion. You were alone in an empty field. There was no golf club, exclusive or otherwise. You were cold and wet."

"Don't be ridiculous! Your mother put you up to this, didn't she? Or was it your fiancé?" He spat out the last word.

Michael shook his head. Imogen tried to assist. "Just calm down, David."

"Oh, calm down, huh? Is that a command, Lady Imogen of Lisnasidhe?"

The rest exchanged concerned looks.

David snickered. "Yes, I know all about your inheritance. Isn't that the way it works around here? Everybody knows everything! But here's the joke. It isn't going to help you."

Imogen asked, "What do you mean?"

David leaned back, and looking at the ceiling, said only, "Boom, boom, boom."

Kathleen felt his forehead. "He's feverish."

David grabbed her wrist. "Kathleen, we have to go hide at the golf course!"

Michael took a deep breath. "The imaginary golf course?"

David screamed, *"It's real!"*

Michael glanced at Kathleen and tried to sound patient. "David, where do you think you were today? What were you doing all day?"

David sounded exasperated with the questioning. "Look. I simply discovered the most exquisite golf course in Ireland. I played a few rounds on the course, I ate lunch in the dining room, sang in the bar with the others, drank beer, played some cards. I was planning to stay the night."

Kathleen interrupted. "Sang in the bar, Dad? You haven't sung in years."

Imogen sat facing him. "Well, what were the names of your new friends?"

David paused. "Let's see. There was Harry Vardon and Jimmy Braid. Oh, and J.H. Taylor."

Imogen rolled her eyes. "Three long-dead golf experts?"

David huffed. "What?"

Imogen looked directly into David's eyes. "Those three golfers were famous. They died decades ago."

David covered his eyes with his hand.

Kathleen hugged her father as Imogen persisted. "What's its name? This exquisite golf club?"

"I can't remember." He stopped. "No, wait. It's Tir na—something."

Bugsy shuddered. "Was it *Tir na Nóg*, Boss?"

David nodded. "Yes. Right. That's it."

Kathleen looked around. "What does that mean?"

Imogen sighed. "It means I can't believe anything anymore, or I believe everything, or I'm not sure—"

Bugsy cried, "We were lucky to get him back!"

Michael explained to Katheen that Tir na Nóg is the name of the mystical fairy world. "The legends say that the fairies entice humans there, and then they are trapped forever."

Bugsy murmured, "If the fairies wanted to keep David, he would have been lost forever. If they let him go, it's because they want him to do something for them."

David exclaimed, "That's just bullsh—" He stopped himself, looking at Kathleen. "Nonsense. It's just nonsense."

Michael retrieved the recording from Liam's camera drone on his phone and played it for David, so he could see his actions, all alone in an empty field, pretending to play golf. While Kathleen and Bugsy looked away, Imogen and Michael watched David's reaction to the images. His expression slowly morphed from disbelief, to surprise, and finally to dread. When the footage finished, he stared at his companions one by one. Finally, he whispered, "But it seemed so real." Then he passed out on the sofa.

Imogen sent an update to Kara, assuring her that David would be fine. "Just fine."

A couple of hours later, David awoke almost as suddenly as he had passed out. He was attentive and clear-headed. Everyone rushed back to his side.

David recalled what Bugsy had said. "*If* it was the fairies—and I am not saying that it was—and *if* they want me to do something, then what would that be? How much wiggle room do you think we have to bargain with?"

Imogen crossed her arms. Even in his current state, David was trying to negotiate a deal. *But alright, I can use this.* She shot back, "Perhaps it's about you taking your part in Kara's Moon Ritual."

David looked uncomfortable. "What's in it for me?" His voice couldn't quite carry the energy of his words. He sounded weak. He stared at the carpet.

Bugsy brought over warm clothes for David. "Boss, you shouldn't trifle with the Irish fairies. They're worse than the mafia. I think Kara's a druid, and she knows what to do. We should just follow her lead."

David was dressed and ready in a few minutes. The clock struck half past nine.

Imogen said, "It's time to go to the party."

Twenty-Two

Kara sat on the grass outside the clearing. The farmers had finished their day's work but the sun, strong and bright, dawdled in its descent. Golden light played across the land and made the stone walls shimmer. The shadow of the church began to stretch across the field towards her. The moon, full and ghostlike in the bright sun, had started its journey upwards. A few wispy clouds crossed between the sun and the moon.

Her afternoon had been spent preparing the circle. She had collected twigs and branches from the nine sacred trees for the ritual fire. She'd fastened little bundles from various types of wood—birch, rowan, ash, alder, willow, hawthorn, oak, holly, and hazel—while sitting on the forest floor, cross-legged, reciting an old rhyme: "Nine woods in the cauldron go, burn them quick a' burn them slow, Elder be ye Lady's tree; burn it not or cursed ye'll be." Scratch had sat quietly, watching. As fond as the dog was of a good stick, she had not interfered with Kara's bundling. They'd swept clear the ground and stone hearth of loose dirt, then wiped clean the coloured stones until they sparkled in the dappled light.

Now, in the clearing behind her, Sarah and Keith bickered as they prepared the refreshment tables. The horizontal rays of the sun infiltrated the trees and lingered on papier-mâché suns and moons hung from branches. Lights were threaded through the trees to add to the festivity once the sun had set.

Sarah motioned to Kara, then handed her a Lidl shopping bag. Kara looked at it quizzically. *Groceries? Maybe Lidl sold books of incantations? Bells, books, and candles?*

Sarah giggled at Kara's expression. "The Ballybeg Yarnbombers for Heritage made you something for tonight. Open it." Kara peeked inside and pulled out a knitted cardigan in a riot of colours. She slipped it on. It was long, falling below her knees. The words "Chief Witch of Ballybeg" had been embroidered, in gold, on a patch on the upper back. Reaching into the shopping bag again, she then produced a matching dog coat for Scratch, embroidered with the title: "Chief Familiar." Kara dressed the dog, then smiled at her friends. "Thank you! They both fit perfectly!"

Mary arrived, flaunting an old-fashioned shepherd's crook and a sheepskin vest. She examined the scene as if it were a tableau in a museum, pausing at Kara in her multicoloured dream coat. "Am I late?"

Keith handed her a basket of biscuits for the table. "No, right on time. Take this." Curious, he grabbed the crook from her as she placed the basket on the table. "What's this for?"

"I'm the shepherd, aren't I?" She snatched it back.

Others arrived gradually. Kara welcomed them into the clearing. Scratch sat proudly beside her.

Nesbitt lagged behind his wife when they arrived. He grimaced at the surroundings but shook hands politely. Esmée, with a firm grip on her husband's arm, delivered him to Kara. "I bring you your required priest."

To which Nesbitt lifted his arms in the air and declared, "I have to say that I am somewhat uncomfortable with this pagan ritual. The forces of good and evil are things with which not to trifle. I believe that God—"

Esmée nudged him. "Henry, shush! It's not real magic. It's just a cultural experiment."

This threw him off his prepared lecture. "Cultural?"

"Yes, dear. Just a bit of cultural heritage."

"Like a re-enactment?"

"Exactly so, dear. Just a cultural re-enactment."

A new body burst in. "A re-enactment? And here's me without my musket. Drat!" It was Tommy, the marquess. "One nobleman as ordered, your exceptional wizardness."

Mrs. Nesbitt curtsied. Mary rolled her eyes.

Kara left them to mingle and stood on her gold-coloured stone. *Just one minor detail—what to say for the incantation?* She sought inspiration by facing the west and waving her arms about. Her own great-great-grandmother had probably stood on this very spot on June 20, 1872. Now it was her turn to lead the village to "stand against the foe." Still, couldn't her ancestor have left instructions in the brass box? Something like *A Beginner's Guide to Defending against a Foe with Simple Magic.*

She pulled her Moon Ritual notebook out of her satchel, opened it, and leafed through it for the hundredth time, going over the various spells and rituals she had found online. "Stand naked in the clear moonlight." She glanced at the Nesbitts. *Nope. Not that one.* "Dance in a counter-clockwise direction, drumming and chanting." *There was none of that in her dreams.* One more page: "Sacrifice a freshly washed virgin over the sacred flame." She slammed shut the notebook and threw it back into her satchel. She would have to wing it. She began to fill the hearth with her sacred wood bundles and prayed for divine intervention.

Dr. Nesbitt stepped over to her side. "It's a beautiful full moon. I don't know if I have ever seen it as big as this one. They call the June full moon the Strawberry Moon. That's Canadian, isn't it?"

Kara nodded distractedly. "Algonquin, signifying the start of the strawberry season. See, it's starting to turn pink." *Bells, Books, Candles—*

The Seanchaí appeared on her other side. Scratch approached the old man but suddenly backed away and watched him. The dog surprised Kara, but she turned to the storyteller with a smile. "Seamus, thank you for joining us. I hope you will speak up if you think I am forgetting something or doing it incorrectly. Maybe you can help me find the right verse for the spell."

"I wouldn't know. Just a bit of fun, isn't it?" His laugh started very high, but a cough brought his pitch down two octaves. "I mean, witches, elves, and fairies, and such. They don't really exist."

Then he shuffled away, unsteady on his feet. Morag helped him to a chair. Kara couldn't figure out where Seamus was coming from. So inconsistent. But then, he was ninety-six years old. *Poor thing!* Scratch didn't move and kept her eyes on the old man. Even the appearance of Fatima and Annie did not shift the dog from her surveillance.

Kara pointed out the green stones to Tommy, Mary, and Nesbitt. "You will each be on a green stone." They each looked to see if there was any difference between the green stones.

Next, she wandered up to Keith, who was reorganizing the sandwiches organized by Sarah. "You can arrange the others on the blue stones?"

"No bother," He replied.

"Any word about David?"

"Nothing." He separated the meat-filled refreshments from the vegetarian.

She checked her phone again. "Imogen said he was better. So, what could have happened to him?"

Keith's unruly blond curls shook from side to side. "I always thought he was away with the fairies. Maybe this time he really is."

Kara glanced back at Seamus. "Perhaps. If you believe in fairies."

More villagers were now pouring in, eager to see a druid Moon Ritual. Morag and Sarah busied themselves with the refreshments. Seamus slept on his chair in the far corner.

The moon was a light rose colour, and it was growing larger. It was close to ten o'clock, and the solstice would occur exactly at 11:34 p.m.

Kara stood, staring up at the sky and murmuring the verse from her dream:

> "Bring the people together at the sacred site
> when Sister Moon, in her fullness,
> meets Brother Sun on his longest path.
> Summon the fairies with the Priestess's candles,
> the Witch's spell book,
> and the Lunatic's bells.
> At the appointed hour, gather the gold circles to the fire.
> When the fairy folk are content,
> the power of the moon will course through the people
> and prepare them for the fight."

She dug deep into her satchel to retrieve her Moon Ritual notebook. Her hand fished about on the bottom of the bag and grabbed hold of something unexpected: a small, thin paperback, about half the size of a normal book. *This is not my Moon Ritual notebook.* She pulled it out and studied it. The cover image was a white cat with a black candle and red beads. The text on the cover read, "*Everyday Witchcraft* by Delphine C. Lyons. Sorcery in the '70s! Modern witchcraft for today's woman."

She had bought this small book at the Dominion grocery store checkout when she was twelve years old and had lost it decades ago. *How can it be here?* She leafed through the pages. The little book was so familiar. Love spells and wealth spells. Spells to make you hair curl. To train your dog.

She stopped at a strange page. An extra page. A page that wasn't in the original book. Under the title "For When the Full Moon Falls Upon the Summer Solstice," was the explanatory text:

"Align your participants in their positions. Start the sacred fire. Play the music selected. Speak the incantation. When the colours rise and merge, the gold circles must be raised and touching above the flames. Then the power will come to the people and the message will be delivered to the magpie."

Below that was printed an incantation that began with the words "Circles and squares." Kara quickly memorized it.

So, they had a spell book, but their paladin, David, and Imogen had yet to arrive. *And David's bells? Imogen's candles?* "One step forward and three steps back." Kara sighed as the sun dropped below the horizon. Still not dark, just a darker shade of twilight. Stars were revealing themselves when she finally received a message from Imogen. "We're coming. All of us. Finally."

Finally. She peered out to the fields, bathed in twilight.

There was a commotion in the field. Crossing over Lisnasidhe in the gloaming was: *McKinney party of five.* In front, Imogen strode swiftly on her long legs. Then came Bugsy and Michael supporting David, who looked too weak to walk on his own. Kathleen rushed along behind. Scratch ran out to lead them safely into the clearing.

Michael spread a blanket on the ground. Kathleen sat down on it and held up her arms to help Bugsy carefully lower David down. The man stretched out, his head resting on Kathleen's lap. Michael squatted beside his fiancée with his hand on her shoulder. Bugsy stepped back, leaning on the massive oak tree, breathing heavily and rolling a red and gold twenty-sided die between his fingers.

Imogen stood triumphant near the firepit. She motioned Kara over and whispered in her ear. "You will never believe it—"

She recounted to Kara how David had been found after twelve hours, alone in a farm field, pretending to play golf. "He thought he was with a group of"—she curled her fingers into air quotes—"'friends.' He talked about a beautiful golf club, with only beautiful people. He gushed about the grilled steak unlike anything he'd ever tasted, how the Heineken was chilled to exactly the right temperature, the softness of the leather chairs, and the immaculate course where the holes seemed to reach up to catch the golf ball. But Kara, worse than all that, look at him. He's so weak; he can barely stand."

Kara exchanged a few kind words with Kathleen and looked directly at David. He smiled back at her. That in itself was odd, but his vagueness suggested that he was either drugged, or very drunk, or suffering the effects of some physical trauma. Considering what David had experienced over the last few weeks, perhaps any further small injury would be enough to caused irreparable damage. "David? Are you alright?"

"Hi, cousin! I'm just fine." He grinned weakly.

Kara patted his arm. "David, do you have any bells? The bells are supposed to be yours."

He shook his head. "No, cousin. I don't think so."

Kathleen wiped back some tears. "I'm just glad we found him."

Seamus sprang out of his seat, bounded over, and pulled out a silver flask. "Give him a dash of this," the old man offered, "and he'll be better in a tick." Kathleen checked with Michael, who agreed. She administered the dosage.

Kara sighed. "Ballybeg Whiskey. The local cure-all."

Seamus grinned. "No. Something a wee bit stronger."

As the Seanchaí predicted, within minutes, David was back on his feet. He still looked a little vague, but he seemed to have regained his physical strength. Kara asked to see his gold sovereign. Kathleen retrieved it from his jacket's inner pocket and held it up before putting it back.

The moon hovered so large that it filled its corner of the sky. Kara resumed her position on her gold-coloured stone facing the west.

Imogen had brought five large white candles which she now placed on the red stones. Then she bent over to light the first candle. As the wick caught fire, a gust of wind blew its flame onto the next, spontaneously lighting each in turn. Imogen, followed the direction of the flames, moving to her position on Kara's right and closed her eyes very tight.

Kara motioned to Mary, Tommy, Bugsy, and Nesbitt to each find a green stone.

She then beckoned to David, who trundled to the gold stone on Kara's left. She signalled Keith to position Kathleen, Michael, Morag, Sarah, and Esmée on the circle of blue stones. The observers gathered in clusters outside the circle.

Everyone, except David, stared at Kara while she considered what to do next. It was moving closer to 11:34, the exact time of the solstice. If she understood the story, it was all up to Imogen, David, and herself to carry out the ritual correctly.

Kara addressed the crowd. "We must fulfill the legend. The three of us are together here on the sacred site. And in a way, it was David who brought us all here."

David beamed at that remark. "You're welcome."

"Listen, everyone, we need to follow the legend. Tonight, at the moment of the solstice, which is ... " She tried to find her phone.

Michael declared, "In about twenty minutes."

"Thanks, Michael," Kara nodded. "David, we need you to help us."

David smiled. "Are we fighting a dragon?"

"Yes. Some sort of dragon, David. An unknown dragon. We have to stop it."

David called to his daughter as she took her position on a blue stone. "Kathleen, we are going to fight an evil dragon."

"A very good idea, Father." She gazed at Michael across the circle.

Tommy stood on his green stone to Kara's right. The aristocrat smirked. "Odd. It all looks like a witches' coven."

Imogen made a gasping sound and wiggled her shoulders to loosen her neck muscles. "Tommy, I am shocked that you could even suggest it! The good Reverend Dr. Nesbitt and Mrs. Nesbitt could not possibly be involved with witchcraft!"

From his own green stone on Kara's left, Nesbitt added, "The bishop simply wouldn't have it."

"Exactly!" Imogen winked.

Tommy shrugged. "I'm up for anything. Kara's your cousin. You're my cousin. She's my cousin's cousin. I think that might make her my cousin too. I always help my cousins. I am certain if we dig around, we will discover that Esmée is our cousin too."

Mrs. Nesbitt giggled from a blue stone behind Tommy.

It was 11:20. Kara stared up at the treetops. *Maybe the bells will ring out from there.*

Seamus stepped deftly through the circle, weaving in between the participants. There was colour in his cheeks, and his eyes were focused. He stopped directly in front of David. "Do you have your phone?"

David seemed intimidated. "Yes, sir." He produced his Samsung.

Seamus took the attitude of a traffic cop asking to see David's license. His feet balanced firmly on the dirt ground; he crossed his arms behind his back.

"Can you open it?"

"Sure."

"Well, then do it."

"Yes, sir."

"I bet you've got a lot of songs in that phone."

"Yes, sir."

"Do you have your mother's favourite song?"

David paused. "Is this some strange security question?"

Seamus frowned. "Are you being flippant, sir?!"

David shook his head. "No, sir." He opened his music library and scanned the list.

Seamus peered over David's shoulder as David nodded. "Yes. It's here."

"Then play it, man!"

"Yes, sir." David ran his thumb down the list and pressed the track. The music filled the clearing with bright ringing notes in a repetitive rhythm that gradually layered in additional instruments, building complexity while retaining the rhythmic base.

Nesbitt shivered, "Isn't this music about demonic possession?"

Keith replied, "Only in Hollywood."

Kara lit the fire in the hearth. Steady flames rose immediately.

Seamus left David and placed himself not at the back with the crowd, but at Kara's left shoulder.

The wind rushed through the trees, preceding a procession of bright lights above their heads—fireflies—thousands of them, dancing within the clearing, further illuminating the circle.

David stared at the lights above his head. Then his eyes shifted to Seamus. When had the crazy old man become so pushy? Everyone seemed, well, not afraid of him exactly, but in awe.

David couldn't remember ever seeing so many fireflies together. They danced to his mother's favourite song: "Tubular Bells."

She's an odd old hippie, my mother.

The twilight deepened to a darker blue. The stars were clearer now, and the moon was higher and all the more dramatic.

He observed Michael and Kathleen standing on opposite sides of the circle, and despite the distance, still managing to gaze into each other's eyes. Why had he been blind to the fact that they were both madly in love with each other? This wasn't a competition of who could dominate the other. They were in partnership, ready to help the other. He recognized the signs, but he couldn't remember the last time he'd seen that in a couple. *Where could Kathleen have learned that?* Certainly not from her parents or his own.

Kara instructed the group to hold hands to close the blue circle. David glanced quickly at Kathleen and saw that she was smiling. She was always smiling!

It was now 11:34 p.m. The exact moment of the solstice. Kara looked up to the moon and recited the incantation from her little book:

> "Circles and squares, triangles and pentacles,
> And the number of stars in the sky.
> Until we are one, we are nothing."

The fireflies flew in formations and patterns, weaving in amongst the participants, encircling each head as they passed. Some people winced or closed their eyes, others watched the lights flit past them.

Sarah stepped off her stone, and Seamus barked at her. "Sarah! Back on your spot, or it won't work!"

Sarah quickly stood on her blue stone. No one else moved.

Seamus snapped his fingers vigorously. "Green corners! Attention! You are holding the foundations!" They stretched up. David wondered if Seamus had ever directed theatre.

After a glance at Seamus, Kara continued the incantation:

> "Fire and earth, water and breath, in the blood
> That ties us all together. In gaudium.
> In pace. United. In vita."

Kara finished and looked around. Nothing happened.

"What is supposed to happen next?" Imogen asked.

Kara answered: "'When the signal is raised' ... but there *is* no signal." Everyone in the blue circle stayed in position, grasping hands tight. They all searched around with their eyes for some sort of signal. The fireflies continued their lively dance.

Seamus leaned forward to Kara. "The three of you must also hold hands."

Kara closed her eyes. She was holding Imogen's hand but now held out her other hand to David to join her. David took it, and then reached out to Imogen. The three held hands and stood around the hearth fire. *That's it,* David thought. *Now I'm trapped.*

Seamus clapped his hands together and called out, "Alright folks, let's try it again! From the top!"

Kara opened her eyes. For a second time, she raised her face to the sky.

> "Circles and squares, triangles and pentacles,
> And the number of stars in the sky.
> Until we are one, we are nothing.
> Fire and earth, water and breath, in the blood
> That ties us all together. In gaudium.
> In pace. United. In vita."

In response, the fire jumped higher in flames of every colour imaginable: yellows, greens, blues, reds, purples, pinks, turquoises, mauves, tangerines, and apricots. The flames wove patterns like braiding hair. They reached up ten feet above the firepit. Then the coloured flames settled down once more into a vigorous fullness.

"The colours have risen and merged. Quick!" called Kara. "Raise your gold circle!" David fished his lucky gold sovereign from his pocket and thrust it as high as he could over the flames. Imogen raised her brooch and Kara her ring similarly. The three gold objects touched, causing the cousins' palms to form the shape of a three-handed prayer.

The bells in the music rang loud and clear. The fireflies multiplied again another hundredfold. Millions of sparks of light danced and swirled around everyone. They soared up to the blue twilight sky and dipped back in a murmuration, broke into separate swarms, and repeated the actions. David heard high-pitched laughter each time they flew close to his ear. The fireflies synchronized into patterns around the circle.

"Keep holding hands everyone!" Kara called out as coloured vines of light arose again from the fire, drawn up through the combined gold objects, and from there, shot out to touch every human.

David felt a warm shock of playful energy, starting at his centre, radiating through his whole body to shoot out along his fingers and toes. It invigorated and excited him. *Is this what happiness feels like?* He felt vital. He felt strong.

Seamus roared, "This is the Quickening!" The energy grew to a vibrant force that caused the clasped hands to separate. In response, everyone stretched or leapt, or pivoted on their toes. Some grasped their chests while others held out their arms. The air was full of giggles and hoots, gasps and cheers. Faces glowed. The temperature within the clearing increased. Some people later reported that their feet left the ground, but no one could say for certain that they'd witnessed this or that, since at that moment, each was enraptured within themselves. The Quickening gave them extraordinary energy. The circle broke up, and everyone mingled. There was laughing and hugging. Friends and enemies reached out to each other with smiles or hugs, grasping their arms or patting their backs.

The fire had left the firepit to circulate as energy throughout the crowd. The fireflies danced high above the humans and became a rapidly spinning circle, which drew tighter and tighter. Finally, the fireflies descended into one last convergence in the centre above the circle. They merged into a single ball of light and disappeared down into the empty firepit. The music ended. The fire returned to the firepit and shrunk to ordinary flames.

Chattering and exclamations filled the clearing. "That felt amazing!" "I wouldn't have believed that!" "I feel ten years younger!" Kathleen looked beautiful and happy. *But then, doesn't she always?* David wondered if he looked as good as he felt. He examined his gold sovereign. It was intact. His feeling of euphoria remained.

David held out his hand to Michael. The young man beamed and took it. It was the first time that David had truly seen Michael. A tall, handsome young man with black wavy hair and eyes both intelligent and kind. His complexion blazed. This was likely due to his daughter Kathleen, but David could see that Michael's good qualities had been there from the beginning. It was just that David had never bothered to look.

"Michael," Even now, the words were hard to say. "Michael, I hope you can forgive me. I can see how much Kathleen loves you. And she is never wrong."

Michael shook David's hand vigorously.

"Oh, Dad, shush!" Kathleen turned away for a moment. "This isn't like you." Then she looked back. "Thanks, Dad." She put her arms around him.

"All I can say is, Michael, welcome to the family!" Here he paused and added, "You aren't already related to me, are you?"

Michael laughed. "Not so much, sir." He glanced at Kathleen. "No. I'm certain."

Bugsy was back against the massive oak tree with Keith at his side. The two were engrossed in a quiet conversation. David understood many things better now. *I've been an idiot—and for a very long time.* He left them alone.

He circled back to Kara and Imogen, holding out the gold sovereign to show them it was still in good condition. "Are *your* lucky charms still intact?" he joked.

Imogen corrected him. "They are not lucky charms; they are amulets. In my case, a ninth-century penannular brooch. And yes, thank you. It is in tip-top condition still."

Kara's dog approached David and pressed against his leg. He patted its head.

His peace was disturbed by a commotion near the entrance to the clearing. Morag was in a panic. "My father is missing!" She ran out of the clearing in search of Seamus.

Kara was just heading out to help Morag find her father when Officer McNulty entered the clearing. Behind him followed a confused-looking Morag and an equally confused Seamus. Officer Fergus shepherded them back to the party and fetched a seat for the old man. McNulty lectured Morag. "You need to be more careful with old people like Seamus. He was wandering in the village about an hour ago. We were going to take him home, Morag, but someone said you were here." He uttered 'here' as if he found it all suspicious. He surveyed the gathering.

Morag stared at her father but responded to McNulty. "Thank you. But an hour ago? That can't be. He was sitting over in that corner an hour ago, and he's been here all along."

Officer Fergus was fussing over Seamus. "Would you be calling us liars, Morag? Your da there was all on his own on Victoria Street." Seamus swatted at the police officer.

"No, no." She emitted a forced laugh. "You know my father. Always away with the fairies! I never know what he's up to."

Sarah distracted the officers with a large plate of sandwiches. "Corned beef or chicken? You'll find the tea over there." McNulty and Fergus left Seamus and continued their investigation of the party.

Morag leaned over her father and felt for his temperature. He grumbled, "I'm alright! I'm just hungry! You shouldn't have left me all alone!"

A look of horror crossed the daughter's face. "But, but I didn't! You've been right here all along."

"How could I be here if I was there?"

"But we all saw you, Dad, and talked to you. Kara talked to you. Didn't you, Kara?"

Kara nodded, handing him a cup of tea and a plate of sandwiches as she tried to square the many versions of Seamus she had experienced since arriving in Ballybeg. "Well, anyway," she said, shrugging, "he's safe now."

The "Quickening" had revitalized the crowd. Despite the late hour, Frank and Dennis had started up the music, and rosy-cheeked villagers danced. Archie from the Standing Stone had nipped out to fetch a large box, which he promptly hid when he saw the police. The crowd was warming up for an all-nighter.

David stole Kathleen's cup of tea and took a sip. "Nope," he declared. "Some things don't change."

Sarah pulled a small flask from her apron pocket and handed it to him. "Coffee. Extra strong. No milk."

He beamed at her. "You really are a doll, Sarah. Thanks."

Whether it was the energy of the Quickening or relief that it was over, everyone mingled and chatted. The Reverend Doctor Henry J. Nesbitt, however, remained transfixed on the hearth. He devoured four sandwiches, two cups of tea, and engaged in conversation with several people without ever taking his eyes off the flames. His wife ignored him, lecturing the old gossips about the campaign to save the red squirrels.

Kara felt the Quickening and the relief as much as the rest, but hers was mixed with a dread of something yet to come. As the hours passed, she retreated to a corner. Eventually, Imogen joined her. While observing the crowd, Imogen admitted that she was shocked at the change in David. "I like the new David, but mind you don't tell him I said that."

Kara agreed, pointing to where he stood talking to Michael and Kathleen. "What I enjoy the most is that he's really talking *with* them for the first time."

Kara and Imogen watched them laugh. David was telling some long story, his hands illustrating it as he went on. Imogen smirked. "He's probably telling Michael how to put his Ford pickup on a roof."

Kara chuckled, but immediately, her pleasure was pushed aside by concern. "Imogen, all my witchy senses are telling me that whatever this all is, it's not finished yet."

Imogen closed her eyes. "There *is* something more to come. I can feel it in the air."

"When did you develop second sight?"

"Perhaps the Quickening has improved the connections between my sensory receptors and my conscious perception," she mused.

So, she's not changed too much then, Kara thought.

Kara found her Moon Ritual notebook in her satchel and read the text of the dream parchment for the hundredth time, her finger passing over that which related to what had already occurred, even as she murmured the rhythm of the words. She stopped then, her finger indicating to Imogen as she read, "Look here. 'The power of the moon will course through the people and prepare them for the fight.'"

"What fight?"

"No idea. That's the problem." She thrust the notebook into the pocket of her cardigan.

Scratch had been sprawling at their feet. Suddenly, she jumped up, and with three strong barks, ran out of the clearing into the fields of Lisnasidhe. Kara and Imogen ran to the opening of the clearing in pursuit of the dog.

Simultaneously, David and Michael each received a message on their phone that caused them to react with shocked expressions. They exchanged looks, surprised that the other was also surprised. They also leapt to their feet and rushed out to the moonlit fields. So quickly did they move that they almost collided.

Scratch had jumped the stone wall to Mary's bee yard, then continued on to the middle of the next field. David stood near the apple orchard and calmly texted something to someone, then watched his phone for a reply. But Michael, further away in the middle of the field, scanned the sky in all directions, searching for something.

Kara pointed to David. "Imogen, do you remember the line in Seamus' story: 'Swiftly fly from *stone* to *stone* the messages of doom and ruin.'"

"Yes?" Imogen replied, "What are you getting at?"

"Well, in one of my dreams, my cell phone became a stone."

The sky lightened from violet-blue to pale blue. The stars faded. The moon, her leading role now passed, sat small and high over the western horizon. David was still checking his messages with a concerned look. Finally, he moved across to the centre of the field to join Michael, searching the sky.

Kara ran to them. "What are you looking for?"

David exchanged a guarded look with Michael. "Nothing at all." He smiled. "You know, Kara, I might need somewhere to stay other than the inn. Do you think Imogen has any more of those shepherd's huts going spare?"

Kara didn't reply. She knew David well enough to see this was a diversion. He knew something. Her eyes followed the gaze of the two men. Imogen caught up, and the four of them stared northward into the pre-dawn sky. Kathleen, Bugsy, and Tommy joined them. At the opening of the clearing at Rosheen Wood, some of the villagers gathered to see what was going on. Kara whispered, "What are we looking for?"

Then there was a strange whirring sound in the air, distant, like thunder, but not natural. More mechanical. Kara muttered, "The next line in the story: 'The dawn sees birds of black iron descend, carrying betrayal, greed, and destruction.'"

David coughed violently.

Officers McNulty and Fergus approached them. "Hey! Can you hear that?"

Kara replied with a nod. David mumbled, "Yes," and looked at his shoes. Michael was trying to call someone. More of the villagers ran to the field. Inside the clearing, the music stopped.

In the faint light, a swarm of black hornets approached. Kara knew that they were not hornets. The objects were so far in the distance as to appear small, still crossing the sea from the north and growing in size as they advanced. The sound they made also grew from a distant whirring to a repetitive clanging and whooshing sound that gradually became deafening. The tiny forms solidified into helicopters, dozens of them, looming over the pastures from the sea to Lisnasidhe. The helicopters' lights flooded the pasture, revealing Scratch chasing them. Some of the helicopters were hauling huge, strange cargo beneath them.

David inhaled and exhaled dramatically. Finally, he explained what they were seeing with the flat delivery of a newscaster. "It is Operation Goliath. They're really coming."

Kara thought that she had fully comprehended every nasty thing that David was capable of, but no. She studied his impassive face for a moment, then turned to Imogen.

Imogen's expression was shocked and anxious as she said quietly, "Let the power of the moon course through the people and prepare them for the fight."

Twenty-Three

Imogen watched the invasion of "iron birds" coming in from the north with their rhythmic, choppy whirring. Real birds scattered, their breakfasts rudely interrupted.

The rising sun revealed the details of the menacing black helicopters as they approached. Some were construction helicopters, carrying suspended loads, including large crates, bulldozers, and excavators. A few small, sleek helicopters danced in the air, buzzing ahead of the slower-moving mammoths. She tried to tell herself that this was a coincidence and that they were passing on their way to another site further south. Then she glanced again at David, and she knew that they were coming for Lisnasidhe.

The people of Ballybeg instinctively lined up in a bowling pin formation across the field. Imogen took the lead. Kara and David flanked immediately behind her, followed by the members of the circle, while the villagers filled in the rear. They watched from the field at the side of Rosheen Wood as the helicopters landed in the fields surrounding them in the growing morning light.

A dozen cargo craft flew over their heads and landed across Beeswax Road. Other helicopters landed in the north pasture beyond the stone wall. Workers in construction gear disembarked and started unloading the heavy equipment into the surrounding farmland.

Imogen cried out, "David! What is this?"

David said nothing at first, looking around helplessly as everyone glared at him. "It's, well, it's, look, I clearly wasn't in my right mind."

Kara touched his shoulder. "David, Imogen didn't ask *who* was responsible. She asked *what* is happening."

David took a deep breath and explained Operation Goliath: a black-ops manoeuvre to destroy the land by stealth. This would allow the Syndicat to later respond to government requests to "rehabilitate" the ruined land.

David shook his head helplessly. "Obviously, they didn't expect to find a party in progress in the wee hours of the morning."

Imogen scanned the crowd. "At least we surprised their surprise attack. Where are McNulty and Fergus?"

Officer McNulty ran over. "Fergus is contacting HQ for back up."

Fergus approached, still on the phone and in mid-conversation with HQ. The voice at the other end of his call was laughing. No, three people were laughing. "That's some *quare craic*, Fergus!" More laughter. "Pull the other one!"

In a pleading voice, Fergus said, "I'm serious! We're being invaded."

"Ah, Fergus, you're lit. Take yourself off home." The call was abruptly ended.

McNulty tried to call in. "Situation at Lisnasidhe, above Ballybeg. Potential military intervention needed."

"Shutting you down, McNulty. Take the hint." Click.

Kara shifted from one foot to the other. "So, what next?"

Imogen knew Kara had directed the question to her, but David responded: "We wait, of course. Calmly."

"Calmly?" Imogen thought. "I don't think so!"

Three of the small, sleek, black helicopters, with no identifying markings, had landed on the field about twenty metres in front of them. The blades had ceased their rotation. Still, the doors remained closed. No one came out. In the fields, the equipment workers scattered to return to their helicopters.

"Look," David said. "There's clearly been some change in their agenda. Someone has redirected the demolition workers. They're awaiting further instructions. We have disrupted the plan. They're recalculating."

A complete silence dominated the fields. In response to an apparent standoff, a few villagers began to sing, "Why are we waiting?"

Imogen rolled her eyes. "Quiet!" she snapped. "This is not a football game."

The villagers mumbled protests, then continued their football chants, but in whispers now. Groups of the villagers backed toward Rosheen Wood and formed a human barricade around it, arranging and rearranging itself as people changed their minds about who wanted to sit beside whom. Finally, the human shield tightened up. Several took photos or videos, as did Keith, Kathleen, and Esmée from their different positions on the fields.

Without warning, the door of the centre helicopter slid open. James McKay stepped out, looking freshly groomed and smart in a new suit and black shades. Two other well-dressed men, one thin and one chubby, descended next and accompanied McKay as he approached.

"Who are they?" Kara asked David.

"That would be Monsieur Marcel Laurel and Monsieur François Hardie of *le Syndicat international de Tours*. Shit!"

"*Merde*," Kara said, correcting him.

Imogen was furious with David, though she repressed her desire to hurl abuse at him, determined to follow his lead. He seemed to know what was going on, and despite it all, she trusted him. *Oh my god! I do trust him!*

There were dozens of construction vehicles sitting in the surrounding fields, the faces of workers inside them watching the trio of black helicopters at the centre, two of which still sat with closed doors. No one else got out. This would be a complicated game of chess. Imogen placed her closed fists on her hips and waited, trying to be calm.

McKay strode forward. Imogen had never seen this air of assurance that he carried now. He ignored Imogen and Kara and went straight for David. The two men stared at each other for a moment, then McKay leaned forward to David, "What's this, McKinney? How does this fit into Operation Goliath?"

David raised his head and grinned. "It's a little change of plan, I suppose."

McKay stepped back. His face accused David of betrayal, but he spoke loudly in a friendly manner. "Mr. McKinney! This is such a surprise! We never imagined such a welcoming party! You know Monsieurs Laurel and Hardie, of course." McKay performed proper introductions to Imogen and Kara with too much flourishing. He did not acknowledge anyone else, although he was well familiar with everyone. The Frenchmen were notably civil, being French.

Imogen responded with a couple of proper handshakes and nods, then turned to McKay and dismissed him with a gesture. "Don't try to out-protocol me, McKay. Your and your friends are on my land now. Why are you here?"

McKay scoffed. "So, I hear you settled the land ownership issue. Well, it doesn't really matter which McKinney owns it."

David took Kara's hand and moved back slightly.

Imogen continued, "McKay, you didn't answer my question. We both know that this is now a matter of conservation. Heritage conservation for the cottage. Archaeological studies. Biosphere conservation. The land is too valuable to be used for development. You're breaking several laws. I can call Stormont!"

He shot back, "Hardly. Right now, it's trespassing at worse. But the bigger picture? That's about economic development, which is more important. So, yes! Stormont will talk to me!"

As the exchange continued, the witnesses looked like spectators at a tennis match, their heads moving from side to side.

Imogen switched to French, "*Celui-là est insupportable!* I can call UNESCO!"

"I can call the Prime Minister!"

Imogen felt her throat tighten. Desperate to respond, she spat out, "*Je peux téléphoner ... le pape!*" There was a stir in the crowd amongst those that cared about such things. She exhaled hard. Although she spoke to McKay, her target had actually been the Frenchmen, who recoiled at her words. Perhaps it had worked. Hardie motioned to McKay and the three huddled in a furious discussion before retreating into their helicopter. The door closed.

Kathleen, Michael, and Nesbitt drew closer.

Kara ventured, "Do you think we just won?"

David laughed. "Do you think the threat of excommunication would do it? No, they know their plan has been exposed. Now, they're consulting their masters."

Imogen frowned. "I saw this once in Siena. Just as you said, David, they expected to find the field empty to do their damage in secret, then work through legal channels to 'fix' the problem."

David agreed. "They don't have legal permission from Stormont or from Westminster to go ahead with their plan. They just have …. " He hesitated.

Michael finished the thought. "Silent agreements to turn a blind eye until the damage has already been done."

Kara looked shocked. "My god! That's corruption!"

The others stared at Kara, looking baffled.

"She's Canadian," David reminded them.

"Oh yeah."

"Of course."

"Right."

David sent them all off to make calls to anyone and everyone.

Michael was already looking through his contact list on his phone. "I'll contact the Office of the Minister for Investment in Belfast."

Nesbitt offered to help him. "They cannot ignore the local church. I can also call the bishop if that helps."

Michael chuckled. "Just don't tell the bishop about last night."

Nesbitt turned red. "Ha! But I spent a perfectly quiet night with my wife last night."

Imogen spoke up again. "The Minister for Investment can't pretend she knew nothing when we have put it straight in front of her. Tommy and I can do the same with the Secretary of State for Business in Westminster. Can't we, Tommy?"

Tommy saluted. "Absolutely. I'm eager for some direct political action."

David gestured to his daughter. "Kathleen, call the media and get the journalists out here."

Kathleen nodded, her fingers already on the buttons. "Of course, but first I'm calling Grandma."

My mother? He thought. "What's the point of that?"

Kathleen shrugged. She put the phone to her ear. "Hi, Grandma. Sorry to wake you. Oh! What? Something already woke you? Well, that's lucky then." She nudged David. "Dad, say hello to your mother."

Cringing, he took the phone. "Hi, Mom. Yeah, look, I'm a little busy here with a situation. I'll put Kathleen back on the line."

Kathleen took the phone and continued the conversation as she wandered off.

A magpie landed on the grass and hopped along behind Kathleen. The bird's call was harsh and raspy—a warning sound.

David felt the elation of the Quickening surging again through his brain. He turned to address his team.

"This is all a little déjà vu for me." He pointed to the helicopters. "So now, the enemy has played its cards and retreated to assess the risks. The terms of engagement have been determined. This is our chance to be aggressive and possibly dissuade them while they're still strategizing." It felt good to stretch his muscles for a bit. "First, we call their bluff."

Imogen snorted. "That's still only a delay."

David nodded. "Yes, you're right, Imogen." *It feels weird to agree with her.* "But we use the time we gain to call for reinforcements. It's still only five in the morning. We need to stall." Now David pointed to the field across the road. "Bugsy, keep an eye on those bulldozers and excavators. If they move at all, give us a signal and scare the heck out of them."

"Right, Boss."

David mustered a number of the villagers for a quick fact-finding consultation. *What a great village! Great people!* He was proud that it was the home of his ancestors. He could only wish that he had recognized that from the beginning.

The door of the centre helicopter opened. McKay crossed the field alone with his arms up. He was smiling. David rolled his eyes. It was the same smarmy act he'd put on that day in the Teaspot. *Bring it on, McKay.*

Showtime. David stepped forward. "Let me stop you right there, you trumped-up innkeeper!" He didn't want McKay close enough to the others to overhear their conversations. "Don't come too close to my people. You want to negotiate? It's just you and me."

"*Your* people?" McKay chuckled. "It's a little late for that, surely. It would probably be better to discuss things with the *legal* property owner." McKay tried to see over David's shoulder to find Imogen. David body-blocked him.

"Consider me her agent. I am the experienced property developer here."

"Have you gone native, David?"

David smiled. *Well, it's about time.*

He needed to get McKay to look at him and no one else. He remembered a trick used on cobras. Inch by inch, he pivoted to the right. McKay unwittingly turned away from the others to maintain eye contact.

"Something I observed, McKay, is that when you 'go native,' as you put it, people start trusting you. They start talking. They start telling you everything they think about other people." He snorted. "You don't even have to ask them."

"So what?"

"They've been telling me all about you. People who have known you since you were in diapers." David scanned McKay from head to toe. "And you were in diapers a long time."

"Don't be ridiculous."

"What was that thing about a Styrofoam wig head you carried everywhere in junior school? What was that?"

McKay blushed. "That was a science project."

Meanwhile, Imogen, Michael, Tommy, and Nesbitt were signalling David to keep stalling.

"I see. Was it a science project about sex?"

"No."

"Oh. That's what I'd heard."

"Well, they're lying."

"Didn't she have a name?"

"Who?"

"The Styrofoam wig head."

"No! She didn't have a name!"

"Oh. But it was definitely a female wig head then?"

"Forget about my wig head!"

"But she did have a name, I heard."

"Let's change the subject."

"Something like Phoebe? I think it was. Oh, and McKay?"

McKay scurried to the helicopter.

Michael returned to David to report that none of the phone targets were picking up their calls. They continued to leave messages and move down their lists to the next names. David gave Michael an encouraging pat on the shoulder. Imogen and Tommy had also left messages with both the Minister for Investment in Belfast and the Secretary of State for Business in Westminster. No one was taking the phone. No one was calling back.

David rubbed his hair. "Someone is muzzling them."

Tommy added. "Or paying them off. A little justification and a lot of bribery."

Imogen agreed. "Some financial reward or trade advantage to turn a blind eye. But all of that assumed Laurel and Hardie would be arriving to an empty field before dawn. Now they have been seen. They know that we all know. It's politically dangerous. Who's covering up for them?"

David stared at the two other mysterious helicopters. "Or who are *they* covering up for? Who's in those helicopters?"

Kara wondered. "What would be the cost of that kind of a bribe?"

David shrugged. "Perhaps less than you imagine."

An engine powered up. One of the bulldozers approached from the field across the road. A second front was opening up. Bugsy yelled, "I've got this!" He and his team threw themselves into the path of the bulldozer. Bugsy stood facing the machine. It stopped with its engine rumbling.

Hardie appeared as the helicopter door slid open again. David knew that Hardie was difficult to read. Hardie's main weapon was identifying the weaknesses of others, and then using every bit against them. Unfortunately, David had revealed many weaknesses. Now he needed to defuse them.

Hardie's opening shot was no surprise. "I see your daughter there. A natural redhead? She seems a very nice young woman. Intelligent too, I think."

David bunted his response. "Do you think so? I find her grades disappointing."

Hardie hissed. "Well, for a woman, brains are not as important. She is stunning."

"I wouldn't say so, really. Too many freckles. Too many teeth. She takes after her mother more than me. My other daughter, now she is a true beauty."

Hardie lobbed it forward. "What I mean to say is—you don't want anything to happen to her."

David aimed to make Hardie stretch for this one. "See, that's where I think you're wrong, Hardie. She has been too spoiled up to now. Impossible to handle. She expects too much." David kicked a stone out of his way and took a small step forward. "Is there something you could do to—How could we put it?—to *reset* her expectations?"

David was slowly advancing forward. Hardie took one step back. It was unintentional, and only one, but that was all it took to negate the force of his threats.

David pounced. "So, why don't you jump back into your little flying rat and think of another strategy."

With amazing elegance and poise, the Frenchman turned an exact 180 degrees and marched back to safety.

"Hey, batter, batter. Swing, batter, batter," David mumbled.

David was ready to congratulate himself when, all across the field, voices started calling out:

"Wait a second!"

"There's no signal!"

"The telephone networks have been cut off?"

"All of them!"

Everyone was checking their phones. David checked his, and sure enough, all connections had been lost. There would be no communication with media, with government, or with anyone else. *David knew that it takes a high level of authority to cut off all telecommunications.*

David surveyed the field and sighed. He knew that next up would be Laurel, the brains of the outfit. Laurel was a walking adding machine, a born bean counter, and equally as good with statistics as with finances.

David called Kara over. "So, you're a bureaucrat?"

"Former. Retired. And I prefer the term public servant. It tends to convey more confidence, you know?"

"Beautifully justified response. And you're experienced with project budget proposals, taxes, government regulations? All that crap?"

"Of course. Essential qualifications."

David took a pencil from his jacket and thrust it behind Kara's ear. "Good. Just follow my lead. Improvise."

The chopper released the next adversary. Laurel sauntered towards David.

"It's too bad you will not be able to join us, David," he drawled. "We have revisited the profit margins for the first twelve quarters."

David nodded. "My team and I have come up with a better plan than FU. Yes. Far more lucrative. I think you'd find it interesting. Maybe you would like to join us instead."

Laurel countered. "Our reforecasting is 25 percent higher based on sales increases of 15 percent year over year for the first two years."

David feigned surprise. "Oh really, is that all? We got something much higher than that. Didn't we, Kara?"

Kara improvised. "Absolutely! But then we were able to include the Cooley derivatives in the revenue forecasting."

Laurel's eyes narrowed. "What is that?"

Kara scoffed. "I'm surprised you missed it. It's a common financial partnership scheme here based on bovine acquisitions."

Laurel studied Kara's blank expression. He looked longingly at his dead phone, then back at the helicopter.

To tease Laurel further, David pretended to use the calculator on his phone as he spoke. "I bet, Monsieur Laurel, that you probably haven't even taken the time to consider the impact of the new … " He clicked his fingers at Kara.

"The new *Dinnseanchas* tax incentive," she chipped in.

Laurel leaned forward. "What?"

Kara explained in her most bureaucratic voice, "The government announced it in the house yesterday afternoon. The department is currently working on the criteria, but we are certain to qualify."

Laurel's eyes narrowed.

David continued. "Those incentives represent a 35 percent increased profit but only for certain types of projects. Have I got that right, Kara?"

Kara pulled her Moon Ritual notebook from her pocket and pretended to scan the contents. She adjusted her glasses. "With the new projections, I think it's, oh, hang on." She flipped a few more pages, and then nodded. "Yes. First quarter, 457 million."

"Euros, Kara?"

"No. Pounds, David."

"Oh yes, that's right. And the second quarter?"

"About the same. No wait, that's the mirror equation for the first quarter of the second year."

"What's the first quarter of the second year?"

"That would be the one after the fourth quarter of the first year."

"I mean, what's the numbers for the third quarter of the first year?"

"A bit of a dip. About half of the fourth quarter. Partly due to the Lia Fail tax, but that's only due every hundred years—in the North."

Laurel took a step back and waggled his finger. "I think the two of you are playing tricks with me."

David threw Laurel a stone-cold look. "You mean James McKay hasn't briefed you on all this? I would keep an eye on that one. That's what started this … "

"Kerfuffle?"

"Yes, indeed. Thank you, Kara. The kerfuffle. The council won't approve the permits until the kerfuffle issue is cleared up."

Laurel sniffed. "I need to consult my partners." He ran back to the helicopter.

David called after him, "Make sure McKay shows you the legal work regarding the kerfuffle!" He turned to Kara. "That won't last long, and I'm out of ideas."

Keith continued to wander the field, taking photos. Just as McKay disappeared into his helicopter, Keith approached the helicopter on the right and tried the door handle. In response, the door opened with a snap. Armed soldiers in unmarked uniforms poured out. The sounds of screaming and shouting rang across the fields. Rifles were pointed at Keith.

Bugsy called out then and began to run forward to Keith, but as soon as he stepped way from the bulldozer, the machine rumbled forward. He stopped and turned to address the driver. It stopped.

"Alright!" Keith called, backing carefully away from the rifles. The soldiers advanced toward him.

Imogen screamed at the soldiers, "What do you think you are *doing?!* Back down! Get off this land!" The rifles pivoted then to Imogen.

The apparent captain of the mercenaries ran to report to the helicopter on the left. After a quick knock on its window, the door slid open a crack. A faded denim jacket sleeve appeared briefly, a large gold ring flashing in the sunlight. After a short exchange, the captain jogged back to his troop. The rifles held their position on Imogen.

David said in a low voice, "I think you girls should move back slowly."

Imogen refused. "Firstly, I am not a 'girl.' Secondly, it's my bloody land."

Kara nodded. "I'm with her." Scratch barked.

David called out to the soldiers. "Hey! You want to be careful with those weapons?! Someone could get hurt!"

No reaction.

The grumble of the bulldozer's idling engine was the only sound on the fields. McKay, Hardie, and Laurel hid in their helicopter, as did the denim jacket in the other. The front line—David, Imogen, Kara, Michael, Keith, Nesbitt, and Tommy—stood facing the gunmen.

The Reverend Doctor Henry J. Nesbitt, Rector of Ballybeg Parish Church, stepped out of the line and shuffled in front of the soldiers as if handing out communion. Some of the rifles turned to Nesbitt, then back to Imogen. Nesbitt's eyes glowed an eerie shade of green.

"Release the Kraken!" he cried before charging into the dead centre of the troops. The soldiers scattered to the left and right, their rifles waving about in all directions. Then a shot rang out, the massive oak tree taking the bullet. Dozens of villagers followed Nesbitt into battle, engaging the enemies' left flank.

All hell broke loose. Scratch ran in circles under the enemies' feet. Sarah stopped a bullet with a heavy baking sheet, then whacked the soldier with it. Keith, in a notable bit of military strategy, circled behind David and reappeared from the right of the soldiers, flailing his camera and knocking out a pair of combatants who were descending on Kara. Kara and David confiscated the rifles.

A soldier moved forward to grab Michael, but Mary tripped him with her shepherd's crook, and he landed on his face. His rifle rolled off to his left, under the feet of the villagers.

Tommy made some strange sign to his opponent with his fingers, and the man handed Tommy the rifle and sat down near the trees.

Another shot went loose and high and hit one of Mary's beehives, with predictable results. The soldiers struggled to gain control while fighting off the bees. Mary pulled a whistle from her pocket, and with a low frequency sound, encouraged the bees to swarm in circles around the soldiers.

David saw his phone light up. He shouted, "The signal is back up!" With the battle raging, no one heard him. He shot a rifle into the air, and when the field went silent again, he repeated the news.

Mary blew into her whistle again and the bees swarmed up and away. The soldiers regrouped and took stock. Three of their numbers were unconscious on the field. One hid in the trees. Most of the rifles were now on the other side.

Nesbitt stood meekly behind Imogen, checking his watch as though he might be late for a christening.

Texts and messages dinged and popped all across the field. Everyone, including one of the soldiers, checked their beeping phones. Some sent their photos out to contacts. Two magpies alighted on a branch with a song that was high and sweet and loud.

Kathleen checked her messages. Obviously overjoyed by what she read, she called out, "Everyone! It's alright! We're safe!"

Michael raised an eyebrow. "How do you know that?" He strained to see her messages.

She smiled. "Just watch what happens."

The armed soldiers started helping each other to their feet and limping to their helicopter. The door slammed shut behind them. The helicopter's engine started up, and the blades started turning, but the helicopter remained on the ground.

Hardie climbed out of his helicopter then and banged on the closed door of the mysterious helicopter on the left. A thin sliver of the door opened again, allowing Hardie a brief exchange with the faded denim jacket inside. Then the door slammed shut again, and the mystery helicopter took off. Hardie stood and watched it go. The soldiers' helicopter followed after it.

Out in the south field, the heavy equipment helicopters reconnected to their heavy loads, and one by one, slowly lifted off and flew away. Finally, only one construction helicopter remained in the field, blades spinning, ready to go. Bugsy's nemesis, the bulldozer driver, turned off his engine and scrambled down. "No hard feelings, eh mate?" he called out to Bugsy. Leaving the bulldozer where it was, he ran across the field to his waiting helicopter, which quickly followed the others, rising into the air and disappearing to the north.

Only the central black helicopter remained. Hardie opened the door and rushed inside. A moment later, two pairs of hands shoved McKay out. Moments later, the last helicopter was gone, leaving McKay standing alone, facing the villagers.

Twenty-Four

Everyone collapsed onto the soft, warm summer grass and gathered closely to each other, tired but thrilled by their victory. Lisnasidhe was full of quiet chatting and rounds of laughter. Someone suggested that they all go to the Standing Stone, and there was much support for that notion until they realized it was only seven o'clock. The last plate of the sandwiches was passed around, until Mary Anderson handed it to Kara.

Kara took a small chicken piece from it to feed to Scratch, who was spread across her lap. She still couldn't believe that it had actually worked. But how? *Was it the fairies, or Seamus' mythic predictions*, or was it really just everyone working together? Regardless, it had worked. The invaders had retreated. Lisnasidhe was safe. The villagers were happy and congratulating each other. The McKinneys were a family again.

James McKay sat alone and ignored in a corner of the field. To him, it felt like school all over again but without Phoebe.

Kara glanced at McKay, but then turned to David. "Where are you going to stay now?"

David looked at the countryside around him. *Beautiful.* He thought of the strange old woman with whom he'd danced in the clearing two nights earlier. She had told him to stay. "I'm in no hurry to go anywhere. Maybe I can find an old Winnebago and plant it in Imogen's garden."

"Over my dead body!" Imogen screeched. "You can come for dinner, David, but that's all." *Even the thought of him practising his golf swings in my rose garden is distressing.*

Kathleen intervened. "Michael and I will help you find a place, Dad. But please, no more Winnebagos."

Michael drew her close up against him. "Now tell me the truth, Kathleen McKinney, how did you get the helicopters to leave? And how did you know it was happening? Are you a witch?"

"No." she grinned impishly. "Kara's the witch in the family."

Kara smiled. *It was a good thing that Kathleen came to Ballybeg.* "Well, you may not be a witch, Kathleen, but you just pulled some crazy type of magic. Tell us what it was."

Kathleen rolled onto her stomach to make a dandelion chain as she spoke. "My theory is that someone at Westminster got a call from the White House. Or someone got that call and called someone else. Or maybe someone got that call and called a lot of other people." She intensified her American accent. "We may never know. But it was definitely the White House."

Imogen thought about the rapid retreat of Operation Goliath. "A timely call from the right office would certainly have that result. We never discovered who was the faded denim jacket hiding in the helicopter."

David shrugged. "That might always be a mystery."

Kara looked confused. "But wait. The White House? The American President? First of all, how would that happen so quickly?"

Kathleen hugged Michael. "Because someone woke up the Obamas to tell them that American citizens were being held at gunpoint in a country field in Ballybeg."

That would do it, David thought. "Nevertheless, who would have called them? Who has direct contact to the Obamas? And in the middle of the night?"

Kathleen studied her father. "Can't you guess, Dad? Really?"

David shook his head. "I can't imagine anyone with that much influence. No."

Kathleen poked her father. "Grandma."

David buried his face in the grass. "Mom!? Oh, that old hippie! Of *course*, she has the president's phone number!" He turned onto his back, stretched out, and closed his eyes. "Tubular Bells" kept repeating in his head. Kathleen crowned him with the dandelion chain. *The women in my family are phenomenal.* He could learn a thing or two from them.

The villagers were leaving. Officers McNulty and Fergus had confiscated all the rifles strewn across the fields. Now they were taking them back to their colleagues at HQ. Archie realized that it might be a good idea to open the Standing Stone, after all. O'Brien from the distillery remembered that the whiskey wouldn't make itself. Sarah sent Annie and Fatima ahead to warm the ovens in the Teaspot.

Bugsy pointed out that the invaders had abandoned "a perfectly good bulldozer" in Mr. Kelly's field. Keith proposed a few good art installations to make use of it, but Mary noted that it probably belonged to Mr. Kelly now.

Esmée Nesbitt led her heroic husband back to the church for "a wee bit of peace and a cup of tea."

Bugsy and Keith were deep in conversation as they wandered in circles around Lisnasidhe. David watched them. "I never knew Bugsy was a paladin." Kathleen agreed that there was a lot about Bugsy that David had never noticed.

James McKay leaned against a willow like a discarded rag doll. Sarah called out, "James! James McKay!" He looked across the field at her. She stood with Morag and the other Ballybeg Yarnbombers. "Come on! We'll drop you home." Although he blushed with humiliation, he dragged himself along quietly.

Bugsy and Keith returned from their stroll. "Boss, I need a vacation."

David smiled at his bodyguard. "Good idea. Take as long as you want. Do you have plans?"

"Keith started a cooperative art project down in his Belfast studio. I'm gonna hang about. Give him a hand."

"That's a great idea, Benjamin."

The two men started back to the village together.

Michael Garrett leaned over David a bit, blocking the sun with his shadow, as Kathleen stood and wrapped her arms around Michael's waist.

Michael coughed. "There's just one thing."

David raised an eyebrow. "Yes?"

"Well, I haven't asked for your blessing yet."

"Damn! Go on then! You have my blessing." David grinned and closed his eyes again, feeling the land cradling him as he pondered how easy it really was to get along with people and find a sense of belonging.

Kathleen smiled and waved at everybody as she and Michael walked backwards towards the road. Then they climbed into Michael's old Ford pickup, which sputtered and backfired as it took off down the road.

David watched the Ford rumble off. "Why biofuel? We should try electric."

Only David, Kara, Imogen, Mary, and Tommy remained on the grass of Lisnasidhe, Kara's grandfather's birthplace and Imogen's inheritance from her great-great-grandfather. Kara felt a warm energy rising from the earth of Ballybeg. She wondered what other stories it could share with her.

Mary asked Imogen if the Andersons could continue to rent the Lisnasidhe pasture for their sheep.

"Of course. Nothing has to change," Imogen declared. "Now that all the hullaballoo is over, we'll secure Rosheen Wood while we do a full archeological investigation on the cottage. When that's done, we'll work on preserving the old building."

"Don't forget the red squirrels!" Kara reminded.

David guffawed. "You can't forget the red squirrels."

Imogen concurred. "We'll be very careful to balance the environmental protection with the heritage work, David."

"You know, Imogen," David drawled, "if you want any help with that, I'm a qualified Engineer. M.I.T., remember? Just saying."

Imogen stood and stretched. "Okay then, let's get started. Tommy, let's take David to the Ballybeg Church. I would like to hear his expert opinion of the rainwater ingress and the damage to the stonework. David, you'll love it! The efflorescence is quite remarkable."

David sat up. "It would be a pleasure. I'm quite the authority on rainwater ingress."

Kara continued to lie in the grass, basking in Ballybeg's lifeforce. She felt it running along her sinews and muscles and settling in her heart.

Mary Anderson looked down at her. "I told you that you'd be around for a while. Remember? On the bus from Belfast?"

Kara stared up at the blue sky. *The bus from Belfast. How long ago that seemed now.* "I guess I'm here to stay."

Her satchel was still in the clearing. She nudged at Scratch and stood up. The three wandered back to Rosheen Wood. Here, Mary left them to search for her swarmed bees.

Kara hesitated at the opening to Rosheen Wood. Now that the battle was won, the McKinneys were united, and Michael had found his queen, would the fairies keep the enchanted thicket open? She might need to keep the fairies happy. There were certainly enough descendants about to take good care of Rosheen Wood. Perhaps, as long as the fairies were content with that, the thicket would stay open. She stepped inside with the dog at her heel.

She found that the clearing had been restored to its normal, natural state. No obvious indications of human activity were evident. Except one. Seamus sat in a chair in the corner, a small box of sandwiches on his lap. He drank swigs from his silver flask. When Kara entered, he waved to her. Scratch bounded over and cozied up to his foot.

"Seamus!?! You're still here? Did you not go home with Morag?"

"No one told me that they'd gone. Typical," he muttered. "Forgetting the old man again."

Kara sat down on the grass beside him. "Well, I'll make sure you get home." She studied him. "If you are really you, that is."

"I am myself. Seamus McNamara, local Seanchaí, historian, and storyteller. No one else."

"How do I know you're not a fairy?"

"Goodness, woman! It's the middle of the morning!"

Kara leaned forward. "Does that guarantee it?" A couple of red squirrels crept down to lower branches of a nearby pine, wondering why the humans were still here. "Does the daylight guarantee that there's no fairy mischief going on?"

The Seanchaí lowered his eyes. "No, not really." He met her gaze. "But you have to learn to trust your instincts. And find the clues. Look at the dog. She wouldn't come near me if I were fairy folk."

"Is a human born with that kind of instinct?"

"Of course not. You develop it, like everything else in life."

"Seamus, how did you learn everything you keep in your head?"

"Well now, I started when I was four. I was taught by my grandmother, and she was very talented in that regard. And I had time to learn."

Kara didn't respond. She looked down and started to pull at the satchel.

Seamus continued. "You have enough time too. If you want it."

Kara settled back. "Do you really think I could learn? All the stories? All the history?"

"You must have some talent for it. I mean, you got this far."

"I'd like to do that."

"Good. Come to my classes Monday afternoons at Holy Cross."

Kara agreed, then called for a taxi. "Let's get you home, Seamus, before you drop."

Seamus took another swig from his flask and leaned back. "There's only the one taxi in the village. It could take a while. Tell me about those insane dreams you've been having. Maybe we can start with that."

"Okay." She nodded. "But first, what do you know about the Moon Ritual of 1872?"

"Ah, 1872. Well, it came to pass that the Sixth Duke of Inish-Rathcarrick wanted to drive all the tenant farmers off the land. That would have been on a Wednesday."

Epilogue

*T*he sea is always within sight, either blue and green, glinting in the light, or grey and cream with fermenting waves. She's moody that way. The vastness of the sea complements the miles of green pasture rolling in sharp turns and inclines around lush woods or jagged crags. There are many animals, both known and unknown. Buildings dot the landscape: barns, stables, a variety of sheds, converted mills, and churches. Then there's my village, the heart of Ballybeg. The word "quaint" could be used, but I think that word carries an unpleasant, condescending connotation—perhaps picturesque? Charming? Mystical?

Kara Gordon raises her head from her notebook and clips the pen onto the cover. The August sunshine has won out this afternoon, and she has stopped listening to me—for now. She turns her face up to the warmth. Scratch stretches lazily across her lap.

"Old" Seamus McNamara's weather forecast was correct as usual. The Seanchai and Kara walk together often, master and pupil. He recounts both the village's legends and its family trees. He teaches the flora, the fauna, and how to see the signs of fairy activity. Kara is learning how to remember without writing everything into her notebooks.

The Saturday market bustles, peddling the best of the county. There are many visitors today. From the corner of an improvised café, Frank and Dennis belt out some old tunes. The young boys practice death-defying bicycle tricks in the side street. A couple of old *women chatter, nose to nose, with the occasional finger pointing at a passing innocent.*

Kathleen McKinney, formerly of Madison, Wisconsin, holds a handwoven skirt against her small frame and poses for her fiancé. "I think I will buy three of these skirts," she calls out to Michael. He is multitasking as usual, giving her a thumbs-up with one hand while continuing to shake hands with potential constituents. Tommy, the reformed marquess and now fledgling politician, is close nearby, grabbing hold of conversations where he can.

Mary Anderson's market stall is much too busy for one person to handle. James McKay grabs an apron from the inn to lend her a hand. He wants to encourage her sales. Her Beeswax Apiary is the sole supplier to the inn, and the number of new beehives on the inn's roof is increasing. The duke sends his housekeeper to the market every month, in the Bentley, to purchase a case of Mary's honey. People say that the Lisnasidhe fairies are what makes the honey so exceptional.

The Ballybeg Yarnbombers for Heritage (meeting every Tuesday at seven at the Yarn Barn) enjoy the Ballybeg Inn's ice cream on the patio. Today, their maps are out on the table to plan a bus outing to Stormont for Friday next.

Closer to the street, a queue waits for a portrait in charcoal by Benjamin Carter. David McKinney is the current sitter, getting the star treatment. He sits proudly, slightly sunburnt, unshaven, and sporting a linen shirt undone at the neck. He crosses his arms and releases a great breath. The left corner of his mouth turns up into a crooked smile.

If you follow David's gaze, you will see that he is laughing at Dr. Imogen Currie, deep in discussion with the Reverend Dr. Nesbitt and Father O'Connell. Imogen is never happier than when she is embroiled in a good argument.

Annie and Fatima watch the boys do tricks on their bicycles, then come to sit with Kara and Scratch. They tell Kara everything they know about the boys and all their new schoolmates. Kara listens.

It is true that there are no tall buildings in the village, for to maintain the heritage on a human scale celebrates everyone as a part of my history. Times change. People evolve. A community strives forward, remembering its past.

I remember it all, and my memory cannot be altered, not by Pagans, Romans, Vikings, Normans, or come-what-may. Pirates, merchants, reformers, and grifters all try to use me, but I can withstand them. I am perfect. I am constant and unconquerable, loving and loved.

End

About the Author

Author C. A. Logan's previous writing consists of articles, plays, short stories, and ministerial memoranda. The Irish Within Us is her first novel and inspired by her genealogical research in Antrim, Northern Ireland (an area she loves to explore).

Logan retired in 2022 from Canadian Heritage's Arts Branch. Her academic studies include journalism, history, and French cultural studies, and interests include genealogy, occultism, and theatre. She is also a card-carrying Sherlockian through New York's Adventuresses of Sherlock Holmes and the Bootmakers of Toronto.

Although Logan lives in Ottawa, Ontario, she is equally at home in Toronto and in Glasgow, Scotland.

CPSIA information can be obtained
at www.ICGtesting.com
Printed in the USA
BVHW031209150323
660239BV00001B/3

9 781039 169005